THE FUTURE IS NOW

Present technologies rely on metal machine systems; future technologies will rely on molecular machine systems. Bulky metal machines squat in our factories and make almost everything we own. Cars and many other products are themselves metal machines, or similarly crude devices of plastic, ceramic, and silicon. These technologies will vanish, probably in the early decades of the next century. What does this mean for SF? Many tales of the future have filled whole galaxies and eons with people using similar machines, much as Greek mythology filled the cosmos with gods riding chariots rather than jets, and wielding arrows rather than guns. Like stone tools, then bronze, then iron, our present technology is on its way to being a historical curiosity. Like stone-age, bronze-age, and iron-age visions of the future, today's SF ... well, some of SF's classics have already survived futurological obsolescence ...

Stay alert. We are plunging into a future that wasn't on the schedule, and the pictures we share—good and bad myths, true and false understandings—will in large measure determine the shape of things to come.

—from the introduction by
K. Eric Drexler

NANODREAMS

EDITED BY
ELTON ELLIOTT

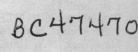

NANODREAMS

"Blood Music" is copyright © 1983 by Greg Bear and was first published in *Analog,* June 1983. "Statesmen" is copyright © 1989 by Poul Anderson and was first published in *New Destinies,* Fall 1989. "Deep Safari" is copyright © 1992 by Charles Sheffield and was first published in *Asimov's,* March 1992. "Dogged Persistence" is copyright © 1992 by Kevin J. Anderson and was first published in *The Magazine of Fantasy & Science Fiction,* September 1992. "The Gentle Seduction" is copyright © 1989 by Marc Stiegler and was first published in *Analog,* April 1989. All other material is original to this volume and is copyright © 1995 by the individual authors.

A Baen Books Original

Baen Publishing Enterprises
P.O. Box 1403
Riverdale, N.Y. 10471

ISBN: 0-671-87680-5

Cover art by Stephen Hickman

First printing, August 1995

Distributed by
SIMON & SCHUSTER
1230 Avenue of the Americas
New York, N.Y. 10020

Printed in the United States of America

DEDICATION

To my mother, LoVina—who has always believed that the future would be better than the present, or the past—thanks for a lifetime of optimism, faith, support, and love. I hope that the future she foresees comes to pass.

Editor's Acknowledgements

First and foremost, to Jim Baen, for his support and insightful ideas, in particular the inclusion of non-fiction, which enhanced the scope and impact of this book. From the editorship of the late, lamented *Worlds of IF* in 1974 (which was my introduction to magazine science fiction), to his own company, SF—like this book—has benefited from his presence. Thanks also to Toni Weisskopf, and all the other kind people at Baen.

For their inspiration and help, I also thank all of the writers in this book. Many supported it in its earliest stages, and my thanks to them. I also want to thank Norm Hartman, Bryan Hilterbrand, Alan Newcomer, Jerry Oltion, Pamela Sargent, Ed Stiner, Bryan Struve, Steve Watkins, Chris York, Steve York, and George Zebrowski for technical, logistical, and research help and to thank Doug Odell and Gene Semar for all their help.

And finally to my brother Dan, and mother, LoVina, for everything over the decades, I have indeed been blessed.

There are many others who have helped me over the years, and I thank you all, in particular Dr. K. Eric Drexler, for inventing such a cool word, and to Stanley Schmidt for a great editorial in *Analog*.

Any mistakes in the following book are mine, at least those on a macroscopic scale.

Contents

PREFACE

ELTON ELLIOTT

If science fiction is about anything, it is about change.

The sudden, stunning end of the Cold War brought the notion of vast, lightning-quick change home to a generation already experiencing the rapid appearance and evolution of many consumer goods, such as computers, VCRs, and CDs. Goods that had already had a profound impact on their lives. If molecular nanotechnology, as defined by the inventor of the term, Dr. K. Eric Drexler (see his Introduction), is about anything at the moment, it is as a metaphor for our changing view of the future. Therefore an anthology of SF stories dealing with nanotechnology is a good way to explore how SF views the future as we near the 21st century.

We used to view the future as something that would bring wondrous inventions, air cars, space travel, and as futuristic as that consensus future seemed, it had changed little in the margins since the beginning of science fiction as a genre in the 1920s. By the early 1980s it had become apparent to some that the future was going to be radically different from the science fictional views of earlier generations, so different in fact that it had become increasingly difficult to portray the future on its own terms in any convincing fashion. At some point ahead—say the middle of the next century—the future would become so different, so strange from today (if the writer took into account the impact of all the newly emerging technologies), that, in the view of SF writer and scientist Vernor Vinge, it would be too complex to understand—or at least depict. He called this

1

time the "singularity"—a black hole in the mind of those fargazers from the end of the 20th century. Those in the future would understand their own time well enough, but we in the past lacked the knowledge to properly depict the future, which was cut off from us by what Vinge termed the "event horizon of incomprehensibility."

However, since most writers were not aware of many of the new advances, they went blindly ahead continuing to give readers yesterday's tomorrows. Then along came K. Eric Drexler and nanotechnology. Ultimately nanotech promises to change how long we live (longevity), how we think (enhanced intelligence), how we build (growing skyscrapers in days through precise molecular manufacturing, which mimics nature, rather than the klunky resource-depleting bulk technology of the past and present). In short, nanotech has the potential to alter how we look, how we think, where we go, and how long we can stay.

What it did to SF writers was shatter the event horizon. Suddenly SF authors caught a wispy glimpse of all of the newly possible futures, and many developed a severe case of future shock. Some just refused to even think about nanotech, or other emerging technologies like biotech, and retreated into a mode of reassuring readers that the future was going to be the same one that Papa Asimov and Grandpa "Doc" Smith wrote about; they mentioned nanotech, but shunted it into a small corner, while others gave up altogether and just wrote fantasy. Still others exaggerated any changes in a dadaesque or Daliesque fashion in an outdated attempt to shock the readers.

The problem is that nanotech, and the emerging techniques and technologies, resist such simplistic approaches or evasions. Any future technology that promises the radical changes to reality that molecular nanotechnology does cannot be explained away in a reassuring fashion, and layering shock upon profound change merely clutters the narrative, numbs the reader, and hampers illumination.

The theme of nanotech in SF deserves a new

approach, one that doesn't stint on drama, excitement, humor, and an informed speculative playfulness. It is with those elements in mind that I have chosen the stories and essays that follow.

FOREWORD
NANOTECHNOLOGY: THE COMING STORM

JOHN G. CRAMER

Question: *How many Nanotechnologists does it take to screw in a light bulb?*

Answer: *None. The replacement of light bulbs was an unproductive maintenance activity characteristic of obsolete 20th century technology which actually required direct human intervention! Modern nanotech light bulbs, of course, repair themselves.*

Physicists argue a lot. It's perhaps one of their less endearing character traits. When I was a beginning physics student in the late 1950s, I remember being involved in a hot debate with another student about some quantum phenomenon we were discussing in a senior quantum physics class. In the tradition of Einstein, to reinforce my point of view I presented a *gedankenexperiment*, a thought experiment that involved watching atoms as they underwent the quantum process we were discussing.

My argument was immediately rejected by one of my favorite professors, a distinguished theoretical physicist who was teaching our class. Direct visualization of atoms, he explained, was impossible because any microscope that could directly produce images at the atomic scale would have to use light at a wavelength comparable to the size-scale studied. Since an atomic diameter is a fraction of a nanometer (10^{-9} meters), X-rays would be needed for such imaging. But each X-ray photon carries thousands of electron volts of energy, while any chemical bond can be broken with an energy of a few electron volts. Therefore, the hypothetical X-ray microscope would disrupt and destroy any system of atoms and molecules in the attempt to produce its image. It would be like pouring boiling lava on a delicate flower to study it.

As a devoted science fiction reader who grew up with atom-as-solar-system stories like *Princess of the Golden Atom*, I objected. "OK, but why not use electrons," I asked. "They have short wavelengths, and we're already building good electron microscopes."

He chuckled at my naiveté. "The electrical charges of a group of electrons push them apart," he patiently explained. "It's called the space charge effect. Look it up. You could never bring a beam of electrons down to a nanometer size focus."

I went away discouraged. Another dream engendered by science fiction had been shattered by the hard realities of the physical universe. In the later stages of my career as a physicist, I probably passed on the hard-earned "wisdom" of wavelength limits to my own students.

A few years ago, not long after my former teacher had passed on to that Great Lecture Hall in the Sky, the cover of the magazine *Science* featured a picture of a single molecule of benzene, its characteristic ring of six carbon atoms clearly visible, resting on a field of bumps that were the atoms of the substrate surface of graphite. This was a measured image, not a simulation. Somehow, the "impossible" had been accomplished. We were "seeing" atoms directly.

I should perhaps comment here on the use of the verb "to see" in the present context. One of my distinguished physics colleagues has argued that one does not truly "see" an object unless the light rays pass uninterrupted from the object to the eye of the observer. I strongly disagree with this narrow definition. I use the verb "to see" whenever the vision centers of the human brain are the primary agents of interpreting the data. Thus, I can "see" an image of a quasar recorded by the CCD cameras of the Hubble telescope, relayed to Earth by microwaves, converted to a disk file in Baltimore, enhanced with computer software to bring out the features of interest, transmitted by fax to a network TV center, relayed by satellite to my local TV station, and transmitted by radio waves to the color television receiver in my living room. I also "see" a remembered scene, face, or picture, using data fetched from my own memory. The vision centers of my brain process the image, so I see it.

Soon after the *Science* picture appeared, the same imaging technique was extended to include the direct manipulation and positioning of the atoms being viewed. A group of industrial scientists produced the world's first "nano-commercial," the IBM initials of their employer formed at the atomic distance scale with letters traced out by individual xenon atoms.

The devices that produce these nanometer-scale images, the scanning tunneling microscope (STM) and its cousin, the atomic force microscope (AFM), are very clever devices, but technologically they are surprisingly simple. They work in air (no vacuum system needed), and their basic components, piezoelectric actuators, good electronic amplifiers, and cathode-ray tubes, have been available in the laboratory since the 1930s. In principle, a working STM could have been built 60 years ago. But, until the present decade, no one had thought to use the phenomenon of quantum tunneling to focus and constrain a flow of electrons in a current, as it was scanned across an atomic structure, and so produce images of atoms that beat the wavelength limitation.

Every year the manufacturers of microcircuits improve their techniques, producing on tiny slabs of silicon amazingly powerful microcomputers that use hundreds of thousands, even millions of transistors on a single silicon chip. These microcircuit techniques can produce circuit elements that are a few orders of magnitude larger than the nanometer scale, but that approach closer every year. Circuits have now been produced with microcircuit technology that show quantum interference of electron currents flowing to the same point along different paths, and that can switch currents and store charges at the level of a single electron. This evolving technology is attacking the problem of nano-scale assembly from a different direction. The size of the component structures may soon approach the nanometer scale as new techniques such as X-ray lithography are developed.

The existence theorem of the power of nano-scale production is provided by molecular biology. Natural organic systems such as cells and viruses provide demonstrate that nano-scale structures can be assembled molecule-by-molecule under a kind of programmed control and can perform useful tasks with amazing efficiency. The ribosome, the little molecular assembly engine in the cell that reads in an RNA encoded program and assembles a protein to the encoded specifications, is a marvel of molecular mechanism that we need to understand. We would like to subvert this marvelous device to do things our way rather than Nature's way, to convert the ribosome to a more general purpose molecular assembler.

Molecular biology also demonstrates the advantage in using atoms and molecules as component parts, rather than bricks and girders and two-by-fours. *All atoms of a given element and isotope number are completely identical.* If you can build a nano-scale structure once, you can always build it and it will always work the same way, with no rejects because of the variations in the characteristics of the component parts.

From these several directions it should be apparent that a radical new technology is now taking shape, the convergence of techniques that together comprise *nanotechnology*. We will here define nanotechnology as the technical capability, not yet fully realized, which will make possible the structuring of matter with precise control at the nanometer scale, atom-by-atom or molecule-by-molecule, to form a specified pattern. Nanotechnology is the general ability to build large or small structures to complex atomic specifications. Notice that nanotechnology refers to the technique and ability, not the size or scale of the product. Nano-technologic constructions may not necessarily be small.

The vast potential of these techniques was largely ignored until the publication of K. Eric Drexler's visionary *Engines of Creation* (Doubleday, 1986), in which he coined the word "nanotechnology" and brought its implications into clear focus. The *Scientific American* subsequently observed that Drexler's ideas carry an "air of inevitability" about them. The technology is coming.

It is important to have a unifying term to describe an emerging interdisciplinary field, so that workers in the field can agree on what it is they are doing. Drexler's term "nanotechnology" has played that role. Prior to 1986, physicists working in that general area would say that they were studying "mesoscopic systems." That term has now been replaced by "nanotechnology," a sexier label that has also achieved some recognition by the general public. The physicist at a cocktail party who tells the young lady he has just met that he spends his time studying mesoscopic systems would probably be met with a yawn, while the physicist who says he is working on nanotechnology might soon be surrounded by an admiring crowd.

Nanotechnology will reduce any manufacturing problem, from constructing a vaccine that cures the common cold to fabricating a starship from the elements contained in seawater, to what is essentially a software problem. The tools that assemble nanomachines can themselves be tiny assemblies of atoms. If even one general-purpose assembly nanomachine or assembler is available, it can be used to rapidly construct more identical assemblers in a geometric progression. It can rapidly mobilize as many assemblers as are needed to construct even very large structures from the available materials. Nanotechnology in effect can reduce all construction and manufacturing to a matter of designing the command set that specifies the desired atomic structure and the steps required for its fabrication and assembly.

Given the nanotechnological infrastructure, the assembly tools, and the base of knowledge to use them effectively, which will almost certainly be available in a few decades, *we will be able to produce anything we can describe in sufficient detail*. And we will be able to produce multiple copies of the same object at nearly zero cost, once the programming is done. Nanotechnology will, in time, give us the ability to design and produce from the atomic level up almost anything we desire: wonder drugs, food, marvelous tools, machines, computers, vehicles, habitats, even living organisms.

The cells of our bodies are, in essence, nanostructures. They even contain a specialized form of assembler, a nanomachine called a ribosome, which can and does assemble any protein from the command-steps encoded in linear RNA molecules. One implication of nanotechnology is that the biological functions of human cells can be directly controlled, repaired, and in some cases improved. Complex nanomachines that fit easily within our cells can take over their management and repair. The coming mastery of nanotechnology offers the promise of cures for cancer, hemophilia, diabetes, and other genetic disorders, the promise of the absolute elimination of all the parasitic, bacterial, and virus diseases that afflict humanity, the promise of the reversal of aging and extension of the human life span, the promise of the enhancement of human strength, endurance, sensory sensitivity, and even intelligence. And it also poses awesome threats and dangers arising from the many possible misuses of these new capabilities.

Contemplating the social implications of such a capability generates a sense of awe. Our civilization will be altered from the bottom up. Factories and manufacturing will become obsolete. All production, heavy or light, will be reduced to a problem of software which, once developed, can be used again and again within the usually generous limits of available resources. When this technological revolution has gone to completion our labor- and production- and information-based society will of necessity have been altered so radically that it is difficult to imagine even its shape. When the Age of Nanotechnology has dawned, almost nothing that we presently value will be valuable. The manufacturing, agricultural, construction, financial, and distribution sectors of the economy will be changed almost beyond recognition. I cannot think of any central aspect of our present society that will *not* be mutated or devalued by nanotechnology.

We can imagine ourselves as standing on a calm beach shortly before a great tidal wave arrives. The only questions are just how far away the tidal wave is and how much devastation it will produce when it reaches us. A foreseen major revolution is perhaps a unique circumstance in human history: a major revolution that is going to have a profound effect on our society, on the way we do things and the way we build things, and that is anticipated long in advance. Its arrival, its impact, and its problems have been anticipated well before the actual technology is at hand. This did not happen with the industrial revolution, the nuclear age, the space age, or the computer revolution. I cannot think of another example in the history of technology in which the societal impact of a technology has been predicted early enough to allow thorough and coherent thinking and planning. We have time to consider, to steer development, to devise solutions.

Unfortunately, not much of this planning is being done. A few individuals, a few groups have been thinking and writing about nanotechnology and its impacts, but our society at large is oblivious to the coming storm. While we should be planning, we ignore the problem because it is not immediate.

This book is an anthology of stories on the general theme of nanotechnology, written by some of the very best and most imaginative contemporary writers of science fiction. They are, in part, attempting to describe for us the coming nanotechnology of the future. However, I want to insert a word of warning about taking their story telling as literal prophecy of the shape of things to come. There are basic incompatibilities between good story telling and accurate prophecy. A good story needs conflict and dramatic tension. A fictional technology with too much power and potential, too much "magic," can spoil the tension and suspense. The "future" as depicted in a science fiction story should be recognizably like the present to maintain contact with the reader. Most science fiction depicts straightforward extrapolations from the present or the past, with relatively few truly radical changes, so that the reader is not lost in a morass of strangeness.

Another important difference between story telling and prophecy is that to achieve good characterization the writer must focus on a small group of people. In-depth characterization cannot be achieved for more than a dozen of characters in a novel, less in a short story. Yet most real revolutions, technological or otherwise, involve thousands of key players, each with his or her own unique personality and character traits.

The intelligence and personality integration of fictional characters cannot be much higher than those of the writer. A central problem of science fiction writing is to portray a character who is more intelligent than you are. Yet enhanced intelligence, possibly through the media of yet-to-be-developed intelligence-enhancing drugs or advances in machine intelligence, may become an important aspect of the nanotechnology revolution to come. Describing their effects in fiction would be extremely difficult.

The nanotechnology revolution, when it comes, will not be bound by these story telling constraints. It will almost certainly be a broadly based international effort pushed forward on many fronts by armies of scientists, engineers, and technicians working in cooperation and in competition. The chances of a single hero making a pivotal discovery in isolation are small. The impacts will also occur on a broad front, effecting every facet of everyday life. Since the realistic scenario for the nanotechnology revolution probably doesn't make a good story, we shouldn't expect science fiction to predict our nanotechnology future.

Story telling is a way of visualizing possible futures, of giving potential problems an immediacy that would otherwise be lacking. The stories in this book can be viewed not as prophecy but as a means of achieving some vision of the possibilities of nanotechnology. With this vision it becomes possible to begin to plan, to anticipate the emerging technologies with their great potential and their great dangers. If we can visualize the problems and begin to think about the impact of the nanotechnology revolution, we can begin to plan for the coming storm.

INTRODUCTION
FROM NANODREAMS TO REALITIES

DR. K. ERIC DREXLER

Present technologies rely on metal machine systems; future technologies will rely on molecular machine systems. Bulky metal machines squat in our factories and make almost everything we own. Cars and many other products are themselves metal machines, or similarly crude devices of plastic, ceramic, and silicon. These technologies will vanish, probably in the early decades of the next century. What does this mean for SF? Many tales of the future have filled whole galaxies and eons with people using similar machines, much as Greek mythology filled the cosmos with gods riding chariots rather than jets, and wielding arrows rather than guns. Like stone tools, then bronze, then iron, our present technology is on its way to being a historical curiosity. Like stone-age, bronze-age, and iron-age visions of the future, today's SF ... well, some of SF's classics have already survived futurological obsolescence.

Molecular machines are machines so small that every atom plays a distinct role, making the position of every atom important. Nuts and bolts in conventional machines contain trillions of trillions of atoms (note: not mere trillions *and* trillions). A microscopic scratch removes billions of them. Molecular machines will resemble conventional machines in many ways, using motors, drive shafts, gears, belts, bearings, and so on, but made of parts so small that a pair of gears might contain only a thousand atoms, with meshing rows serving as teeth.

13

Small size, of course, presents special challenges. At a temperature of absolute zero, atoms vibrate slightly in accord with the quantum uncertainty principle, and designs must allow for this. At room temperature, atoms jiggle back and forth trillions of times per second, moving at about the speed of sound. This thermal vibration generally swamps out the subtler quantum effects. Only strong, stiff structures can endure this shaking and still work reliably, and this favors materials like ceramic and diamond over the softer metals. (Interested readers can find a detailed technical description of molecular machine systems, building from molecular physics to nanocomputers, molecular robotics, and the like, in *Nanosystems: Molecular Machinery, Manufacturing, and Computation,* New York, Wiley/Interscience, 1992.)

Molecular machinery can grasp and position individual molecules. It will be used to perform molecular manufacturing, building structures with atom-by-atom control (but using trillions of machines to handle trillions of atoms at a time). With moving parts a million times smaller than those in industrial robots, the frequency of motion—and hence the productivity—can be a million times greater. What does this mean for technology? Some highlights include:

- Near-flawless products without expensive quality control (misplaced atoms can be rare).
- Carbon-based (read diamond-based) materials with roughly 70 times the strength-to-density ratio of Space Shuttle aluminum (this makes single stage to orbit spacecraft easy to build).
- Computers able to perform a billion instructions per second while using 100 billionths of a watt and occupying about the volume of a bacterium, giving researchers a billion times more computer power than today in a reasonably-sized cabinet consuming a few kilowatts (much more, for major projects).
- As a consequence, almost certainly, the ability to develop genuine machine intelligence.
- With all of the above, the ability to undertake really

complex tasks, such as molecular repair of tissues, and really large tasks, like relativistic interstellar flight.

- Rechargeable batteries that actually work, reliable fans, and other exotic wonders.
- Any of the above for roughly the cost of design plus the cost of bulk raw materials.

If one starts tracing the consequences of such developments, the pictures of the future presented in newspapers begin to look steadily more absurd. If one makes a serious attempt to understand the consequences as a whole, the job looks quite impossible. Indeed, SF writers have told me that they can't see how to write realistic stories set in a world with advanced nanotechnology. This should be cause for concern. If we can't write fiction about the future, how can we expect to live in it?

But by the same token, progress in writing fiction can help us envision worlds worth living in, worlds worth building. In this all-too-practical task of trying to understand the future a little better, SF stories can play various roles. Some may present pictures realistic enough to pick up and make part of your image of the future. Others will offer an opportunity to examine ideas that are plausible but wrong, and to exercise a scarce form of judgment in thinking through the logic of the world to come. Some stories will be wrong for the best of reasons: by showing a horrible mistake, they will stimulate the alertness that keeps the horror imaginary—they will act as self-denying prophecies. A few stories, perhaps, will be right for the best of reasons: by showing a future worth building, they will inspire the efforts that will make it happen.

Stay alert. We are plunging into a future that wasn't on the schedule, and the pictures we share—good and bad myths, true and false understandings—will in large measure determine the shape of things to come.

K. Eric Drexler
Chairman
Foresight Institute

P.S. If you want to keep current with developments in nanotechnology, please write to:

> Foresight Institute
> Box 61058
> Palo Alto, CA 94306
> foresight@cup.portal.com

BLOOD MUSIC

GREG BEAR

There is a principle in nature I don't think anyone has pointed out before. Each hour, a myriad of trillions of little live things—bacteria, microbes, "animalcules"—are born and die, not counting for much except in the bulk of their existence and the accumulation of their tiny effects. They do not perceive deeply. They don't suffer much. A hundred billion, dying, would not begin to have the same importance as a single human death.

Within the ranks of magnitude of all creatures, small as microbes or great as humans, there is an equality of "elan," just as the branches of a tall tree, gathered together, equal the bulk of the limbs below, and all the limbs equal the bulk of the trunk.

That, at least, is the principle. I believe Vergil Ulam was the first to violate it.

It had been two years since I'd last seen Vergil. My memory of him hardly matched the tan, smiling, well-dressed gentleman standing before me. We had made a lunch appointment over the phone the day before, and now faced each other in the wide double doors of the employee's cafeteria at the Mount Freedom Medical Center.

"Vergil?" I asked. "My God, Vergil!"

"Good to see you, Edward." He shook my hand firmly. He had lost ten or twelve kilos and what remained seemed tighter, better proportioned. At the university, Vergil had been the pudgy, shock-haired, snaggle-toothed whiz kid who hot-wired doorknobs, gave us punch that turned our piss blue, and never got a date except with Eileen Termagent, who shared many of his physical characteristics.

"You look fantastic," I said. "Spend a summer in Cabo San Lucas?"

We stood in line at the counter and chose our food. "The tan," he said, picking out a carton of chocolate milk, "is from spending three months under a sun lamp. My teeth were straightened just after I last saw you. I'll explain the rest, but we need a place to talk where no one will listen close."

I steered him to the smoker's corner, where three die-hard puffers were scattered among six tables.

"Listen, I mean it," I said as we unloaded our trays. "You've changed. You're looking good."

"I've changed more than you know." His tone was motion-picture ominous, and he delivered the line with a theatrical lift of his brows. "How's Gail?"

Gail was doing well, I told him, teaching nursery school. We'd married the year before. His gaze shifted down to his food—pineapple slice and cottage cheese, piece of banana cream pie—and he said, his voice almost cracking, "Notice something else?"

I squinted in concentration. "Uh."

"Look closer."

"I'm not sure. Well, yes, you're not wearing glasses. Contacts?"

"No. I don't need them anymore."

"And you're a snappy dresser. Who's dressing you now? I hope she's as sexy as she is tasteful."

"Candice isn't—wasn't responsible for the improvements in my clothes," he said. "I just got a better job, more money to throw around. My taste in clothes is better than my taste in food, as it happens." He grinned the old Vergil self-deprecating grin, but ended it with a peculiar leer. "At any rate, she's left me, I've been fired from my job, I'm living on savings."

"Hold it," I said. "That's a bit crowded. Why not do a linear breakdown? You got a job. Where?"

"Genetron Corp.," he said. "Sixteen months ago."

"I haven't heard of them."

"You will. They're putting out common stock in the next month. It'll shoot off the board. They've broken through with MABs. Medical—"

"I know what MABs are, " I interrupted . "At least in theory. Medically Applicable Biochips."

"They have some that work."

"What?" It was my turn to lift my brows.

"Microscopic logic circuits. You inject them into the human body, they set up shop where they're told and troubleshoot. With Dr. Michael Bernard's approval."

That was quite impressive. Bernard's reputation was spotless. Not only was he associated with the genetic engineering biggies, but he had made news at least once a year in his practice as a neurosurgeon before retiring. Covers on *Time, Mega, Rolling Stone.*

"That's supposed to be secret—stock, breakthrough, Bernard, everything." He looked around and lowered his voice. "But you do whatever the hell you want. I'm through with the bastards."

I whistled. "Make me rich, huh?"

"If that's what you want. Or you can spend some time with me before rushing off to your broker."

"Of course." He hadn't touched the cottage cheese or pie. He had, however, eaten the pineapple slice and drunk the chocolate milk. "So tell me more."

"Well, in med school I was training for lab work. Biochemical research. I've always had a bent for computers, too. So I put myself through my last two years—"

"By selling software packages to Westinghouse," I said.

"It's good my friends remember. That's how I got involved with Genetron, just when they were starting out. They had big money backers, all the lab facilities I thought anyone would ever need. They hired me, and I advanced rapidly.

"Four months and I was doing my own work. I made some breakthroughs" he tossed his hand nonchalantly "then I went off on tangents they thought were premature. I persisted and they took away my lab, handed it over to a certifiable flatworm. I managed to save part of the experiment before they fired me. But I haven't

exactly been cautious . . . or judicious. So now it's going
on outside the lab."

I'd always regarded Vergil as ambitious, a trifle
cracked, and not terribly sensitive. His relations with
authority figures had never been smooth. Science, for
him, was like the woman you couldn't possibly have, who
suddenly opens her arms to you, long before you're ready
for mature love—leaving you afraid you'll forever blow
the chance, lose the prize screw up royally. Apparently,
he had. "Outside the lab? I don't get you."

"Edward, I want you to examine me. Give me a thorough physical. Maybe a cancer diagnostic. Then I'll
explain more."

"You want a five-thousand-dollar exam?"

"Whatever you can do. Ultrasound, NMR, thermo-
gram, everything."

"I don't know if I can get access to all that equipment.
NMR full-scan has only been here a month or two. Hell,
you couldn't pick a more expensive way—"

"Then ultrasound. That's all you'll need."

"Vergil, I'm an obstetrician, not a glamour-boy lab-
tech. OB-GYN, butt of all jokes. If you're turning into a
woman, maybe I can help you."

He leaned forward, almost putting his elbow into the
pie, but swinging wide at the last instant by scant milli-
meters. The old Vergil would have hit it square. "Examine me closely and you'll . . ." He narrowed his eyes and
shook his head. "Just examine me."

"So I make an appointment for ultrasound. Who's
going to pay?"

"I'm on Blue Shield." He smiled and held up a medical credit card. "I messed with the personnel files at
Genetron. Anything up to a hundred thousand dollars
medical, they'll never check, never suspect."

He wanted secrecy, so I made arrangements. I filled
out his forms myself. As long as everything was billed
properly, most of the examination could take place without official notice. I didn't charge for my services. After
all, Vergil had turned my piss blue. We were friends.

He came in late at night. I wasn't normally on duty

then, but I stayed late, waiting for him on the third floor of what the nurses called the Frankenstein wing. I sat on an orange plastic chair. He arrived, looking olive-colored under the fluorescent lights.

He stripped, and I arranged him on the table. I noticed, first off, that his ankles looked swollen. But they weren't puffy. I felt them several times. They seemed healthy, but looked odd. "Hm," I said.

I ran the paddles over him, picking up areas difficult for the big unit to hit, and programmed the data into the imaging system. Then I swung the table around and inserted it into the enameled orifice of the ultrasound diagnostic unit, the hum-hole, so-called by the nurses.

I integrated the data from the hum-hole with that from the paddle sweeps and rolled Vergil out, then set up a video frame. The image took a second to integrate, then flowed into a pattern showing Vergil's skeleton.

Three seconds of that—my jaw gaping—and it switched to his thoracic organs, then his musculature, and finally, vascular system and skin.

"How long since the accident?" I asked, trying to take the quaver out of my voice.

"I haven't been in an accident," he said. "It was deliberate."

"Jesus, they beat you, to keep secrets?"

"You don't understand me, Edward. Look at the images again. I'm not damaged."

"Look, there's thickening here," I indicated the ankles, "and your ribs—that crazy zigzag pattern of interlocks. Broken sometime, obviously. And—"

"Look at my spine," he said. I rotated the image in the video frame.

Buckminster Fuller, I thought. It was fantastic. A cage of triangular projections, all interlocking in ways I couldn't begin to follow, much less understand. I reached around and tried to feel his spine with my fingers. He lifted his arms and looked off at the ceiling.

"I can't find it," I said. "It's all smooth back there." I let go of him and looked at his chest, then prodded his ribs. They were sheathed in something rough and flexible. The harder I pressed, the tougher it became. Then I noticed another change.

"Hey," I said. "You don't have any nipples." There were tiny pigment patches, but no nipple formations at all.

"See?" Vergil asked, shrugging on the white robe. "I'm being rebuilt from the inside out."

In my reconstruction of those hours, I fancy myself saying, "So tell me about it." Perhaps mercifully, I don't remember what I actually said.

He explained with his characteristic circumlocutions. Listening was like trying to get to the meat of a newspaper article through a forest of sidebars and graphic embellishments.

I simplify and condense.

Genetron had assigned him to manufacturing prototype biochips, tiny circuits made out of protein molecules. Some were hooked up to silicon chips little more than a micrometer in size, then sent through rat arteries to chemically keyed locations, to make connections with the rat tissue and attempt to monitor and even control lab-induced pathologies.

"*That* was something," he said. "We recovered the most complex microchip by sacrificing the rat, then debriefed it—hooked the silicon portion up to an imaging system. The computer gave us bar graphs, then a diagram of the chemical characteristics of about eleven centimeters of blood vessel . . . then put it all together to make a picture. We zoomed down eleven centimeters of rat artery. You never saw so many scientists jumping up and down, hugging each other, drinking buckets of bug juice." Bug juice was lab ethanol mixed with Dr. Pepper.

Eventually, the silicon elements were eliminated completely in favor of nucleoproteins. He seemed reluctant to explain in detail, but I gathered they found ways to make huge molecules—as large as DNA, and even more complex—into electrochemical computers, using ribosome-like structures as "encoders" and "readers" and RNA as "tape." Vergil was able to mimic reproductive separation and reassembly in his nucleoproteins, incorporating program changes at key points by switching nucleotide pairs. "Genetron wanted me to switch over to supergene engineering, since that was the coming thing everywhere else. Make all kinds of critters, some out of our imagination. But I had different ideas." He twiddled his finger around his ear and made theremin sounds. "Mad scientist time, right?" He laughed, then sobered. "I injected my best nucleoproteins into bacteria to make duplication and compounding easier. Then I started to leave them inside, so the circuits could interact with the cells. They were heuristically programmed; they taught themselves. The cells fed chemically coded information to the computers, the computers processed it and made decisions, the cells became smart. I mean, smart as planaria, for starters. Imagine an *E. coli* as smart as a planarian worm!"

I nodded. "I'm imagining."

"Then I really went off on my own. We had the equipment, the techniques; and I knew the molecular language. I could make really dense, really complicated biochips by compounding the nucleoproteins, making them into little brains. I did some research into how far I could go, theoretically. Sticking with bacteria, I could make them a biochip with the computing capacity of a sparrow's brain. Imagine how jazzed I was! Then I saw a way to increase the complexity a thousandfold, by using something we regarded as a nuisance—quantum chitchat between the fixed elements of the circuits. Down that small, even the slightest change could bomb a biochip. But I developed a program that actually predicted and took advantage of electron tunneling. Emphasized the heuristic aspects of the computer, used the chitchat as a method of increasing complexity."

"You're losing me," I said.

"I took advantage of randomness. The circuits could repair themselves, compare memories, and correct faulty elements. The whole schmeer. I gave them basic instructions: Go forth and multiply. Improve. By God, you should have seen some of the cultures a week later! It was amazing. They were evolving all on their own, like little cities. I destroyed them all. I think one of the petri dishes would have grown legs and walked out of the incubator if I'd kept feeding it."

"You're kidding." I looked at him. "You're not kidding."

"Man, they *knew* what it was like to improve! They knew where they had to go, but they were just so limited, being in bacteria bodies, with so few resources."

"How smart were they?"

"I couldn't be sure. They were associating in clusters of a hundred to two hundred cells, each cluster behaving like an autonomous unit. Each cluster might have been as smart as a rhesus monkey. They exchanged information through their pili, passed on bits of memory, and compared notes. Their organization was obviously different from a group of monkeys. Their world was so much simpler, for one thing. With their abilities, they were masters of the petri dishes. I put phages in with them; the phages didn't have a chance. They used every option available to change and grow."

"How is that possible?"

"What?" He seemed surprised I wasn't accepting everything at face value.

"Cramming so much into so little. A rhesus monkey is not your simple little calculator, Vergil."

"I haven't made myself clear," he said, obviously irritated. "I was using nucleoprotein computers. They're like DNA, but all the information can interact. Do you know how many nucleotide pairs there are in the DNA of a single bacteria?"

It had been a long time since my last biochemistry lesson. I shook my head.

"About two million. Add in the modified ribosome structures—fifteen thousand of them, each with a molecular weight of about three million—and consider the combinations and permutations. The RNA is arranged like a continuous loop paper tape, surrounded by ribosomes ticking off instructions and manufacturing protein chains . . . " His eyes were bright and slightly moist. "Besides, I'm not saying every cell was a distinct entity. They cooperated."

"How many bacteria in the dishes you destroyed?"

"Billions. I don't know." He smirked. "You got it, Edward. Whole planetsful of *E. coli.*"

"But they didn't fire you then?"

"No. They didn't know what was going on, for one thing. I kept compounding the molecules, increasing their size and complexity. When bacteria were too limited, I took blood from myself, separated out white cells, and injected them with the new biochips. I watched them, put them through mazes and little chemical problems. They were whizzes. Time is a lot faster at that level—so little distance for the messages to cross, and the environment is much simpler. Then I forgot to store a file under my secret code in the lab computers. Some managers found it and guessed what I was up to. Everybody panicked. They thought we'd have every social watchdog in the country on our backs because of what I'd done. They started to destroy my work and wipe my programs. Ordered me to sterilize my white cells. Christ." He pulled the white robe off and started to get dressed. "I only had a day or two. I separated out the most complex cells—"

"How complex?"

"They were clustering in hundred-cell groups, like the bacteria. Each group as smart as a ten-year-old kid, maybe." He studied my face for a moment. "Still doubting? Want me to run through how many nucleotide pairs there are in a mammalian cell? I tailored my computers to take advantage of the white cells' capacity. Ten billion nucleotide pairs, Edward. Ten. E-f———ing ten. And they don't have a huge body to worry about, taking up most of their thinking time."

"Okay," I said. "I'm convinced. What did you do?"

"I mixed the cells back into a cylinder of whole blood and injected myself with it." He buttoned the top of his shirt and smiled thinly at me. "I'd programmed them with every drive I could, talked as high a level as I could using just enzymes and such. After that, they were on their own."

"You programmed them to go forth and multiply, improve?" I repeated.

"I think they developed some characteristics picked up

by the biochips in their *E. coli* phases. The white cells could talk to one another with extruded memories. They almost certainly found ways to ingest other types of cells and alter them without killing them."

"You're crazy."

"You can see the screen! Edward, I haven't been sick since. I used to get colds all the time. I've never felt better."

"They're inside you, finding things, changing them."

"And by now, each cluster is as smart as you or I."

"You're absolutely nuts."

He shrugged. "They fired me. They thought I was going to get revenge for what they did to my work. They ordered me out of the labs, and I haven't had a real chance to see what's been going on inside me until now. Three months."

"So ... " My mind was racing. "You lost weight because they improved your fat metabolism. Your bones are stronger, your spine has been completely rebuilt—"

"No more backaches even if I sleep on my old mattress."

"Your heart looks different."

"I didn't know about the heart," he said, examining the frame image from a few inches. "About the fat—I was thinking about that. They could increase my brown cells, fix up the metabolism. I haven't been as hungry lately. I haven't changed my eating habits that much—I still want the same old junk—but somehow I get around to eating only what I need. I don't think they know what my brain is yet. Sure, they've got all the glandular stuff—but they don't have the *big* picture, if you see what I mean. They don't know *I'm* in there. But boy, they sure did figure out what my reproductive organs are."

I glanced at the image and shifted my eyes away.

"Oh, they look pretty normal," he said, hefting his scrotum obscenely. He snickered. "But how else do you think I'd land a real looker like Candice? She was just after a one-night stand with a techie. I looked okay then, no tan but trim, with good clothes. She'd never screwed a techie before. Joke time, right? But my little geniuses kept us up half the night. I think they made improvements each time. I felt like I had a goddamned fever."

His smile vanished. "But then one night my skin started to crawl. It really scared me. I thought things were getting out of hand. I wondered what they'd do when they crossed the blood-brain barrier and found out about *me*—about the brain's real function. So I began a campaign to keep them under control. I figured, the reason they wanted to get into the skin was the simplicity of running circuits across a surface. Much easier than trying to maintain chains of communication in and around muscles, organs, vessels. The skin was much more direct. So I bought a quartz lamp." He caught my puzzled expression. "In the lab, we'd break down the protein in biochip cells by exposing them to ultraviolet light. I alternated sun lamp with quartz treatments. Keeps them out of my skin and gives me a nice tan."

"Give you skin cancer, too," I commented.

"They'll probably take care of that. Like police."

"Okay, I've examined you, you've told me a story I still find hard to believe . . . what do you want me to do?"

"I'm not as nonchalant as I act, Edward. I'm worried. I'd like to find some way to control them before they find out about my brain. I mean, think of it, they're in the trillions by now, each one smart. They're cooperating to some extent. I'm probably the smartest thing on the planet, and they haven't even begun to get their act together yet. I don't really want them to take over." He laughed unpleasantly. "Steal my soul, you know? So think of some treatment to block them. Maybe we can starve the little buggers. Just think on it." He buttoned his shirt. "Give me a call." He handed me a slip of paper with his address and phone number. Then he went to the keyboard and erased the image on the frame, dumping the memory of the examination. "Just you," he said. "Nobody else for now. And please . . . hurry."

It was three o'clock in the morning when Vergil walked out of the examination room. He'd allowed me to take blood samples, then shaken my hand—his palm damp, nervous—and cautioned me against ingesting anything from the specimens.

Before I went home, I put the blood through a series of tests. The results were ready the next day.

I picked them up during my lunch break in the afternoon, then destroyed all of the samples. I did it like a robot. It took me five days and nearly sleepless nights to accept what I'd seen. His blood was normal enough, though the machines diagnosed the patient as having an infection. High levels of leukocytes—white blood cells—and histamines. On the fifth day, I believed.

Gail was home before I, but it was my turn to fix dinner. She slipped one of the school's disks into the home system and showed me video art her nursery kids had been creating. I watched quietly, ate with her in silence.

I had two dreams, part of my final acceptance. The first that evening—which had me up thrashing in my sheets—I witnessed the destruction of the planet Krypton, Superman's home world. Billions of superhuman geniuses went screaming off in walls of fire. I related the destruction to my sterilizing the samples of Vergil's blood.

The second dream was worse. I dreamed that New York City was raping a woman. By the end of the dream, she was giving birth to little embryo cities, all wrapped up in translucent sacs, soaked with blood from the difficult labor.

I called him on the morning of the sixth day. He answered on the fourth ring. "I have some results," I said. "Nothing conclusive. But I want to talk with you. In person."

"Sure," he said. "I'm staying inside for the time being." His voice was strained; he sounded tired.

Vergil's apartment was in a fancy high-rise near the lake shore. I took the elevator up, listening to little advertising jingles and watching dancing holograms display products, empty apartments for rent, the building's hostess discussing social activities for the week.

Vergil opened the door and motioned me in. He wore a checked robe with long sleeves and carpet slippers. He clutched an unlit pipe in one hand, his fingers twisting it back and forth as he walked away from me and sat down, saying nothing.

"You have an infection," I said.

"Oh?"

"That's all the blood analyses tell me. I don't have access to the electron microscopes."

"I don't think it's really an infection," he said. "After all, they're my own cells. Probably something else . . . sign of their presence, of the change. We can't expect to understand everything that's happening."

I removed my coat. "Listen," I said, "you have me worried now." The expression on his face stopped me: a kind of frantic beatitude. He squinted at the ceiling and pursed his lips.

"Are you stoned?" I asked.

He shook his head, then nodded once, very slowly. "Listening," he said.

"To what?"

"I don't know. Not sounds . . . exactly. Like music. The heart, all the blood vessels, friction of blood along the arteries, veins. Activity. Music in the blood." He looked at me plaintively. "Why aren't you at work?"

"My day off. Gail's working."

"Can you stay?"

I shrugged. "I suppose." I sounded suspicious. I was glancing around the apartment, looking for ashtrays, packs of papers.

"I'm not stoned, Edward," he said. "I may be wrong, but I think something big is happening. I think they're finding out who I am."

I sat down across from Vergil, staring at him intently. He didn't seem to notice. Some inner process was involving him. When I asked for a cup of coffee, he motioned to the kitchen. I boiled a pot of water and took a jar of instant from the cabinet. With cup in hand, I returned to my seat. He was twisting his head back and forth, eyes open. "You always knew what you wanted to be, didn't you?" he asked me.

"More or less."

"A gynecologist. Smart moves. Never false moves. I was different. I had goals, but no direction. Like a map without roads, just places to be. I didn't give a shit for anything, anyone but myself. Even science. Just a means. I'm surprised I got so far. I even hated my folks."

He gripped his chair arms.

"Something wrong?" I asked.

"They're talking to me," he said. He shut his eyes.

For an hour he seemed to be asleep. I checked his pulse, which was strong and steady, felt his forehead— slightly cool—and made myself more coffee. I was looking through a magazine, at a loss what to do, when he opened his eyes again. "Hard to figure exactly what time is like for them," he said. "It's taken them maybe three, four days to figure out language, key human concepts. Now they're on to it. On to me. Right now."

"How's that?"

He claimed there were thousands of researchers hooked up to his neurons. He couldn't give details. "They're damned efficient, you know," he said. "They haven't screwed me up yet."

"We should get you into the hospital now."

"What in hell could they do? Did you figure out any way to control them? I mean, they're my own cells."

"I've been thinking. We could starve them. Find out what metabolic differences—"

"I'm not sure I want to be rid of them," Vergil said. "They're not doing any harm."

"How do you know?"

He shook his head and held up one finger. "Wait. They're trying to figure out what space is. That's tough for them: They break distances down into concentrations of chemicals. For them, space is like intensity of taste."

"Vergil—"

"Listen! Think, Edward!" His tone was excited but even. "Observe! Something big is happening inside me. They talk to one another across the fluid, through membranes. They tailor something—viruses?—to carry data stored in nucleic acid chains. I think they're saying 'RNA.' That makes sense. That's one way I programmed them. But plasmid-like structures, too. Maybe that's what your machines think is a sign of infection—all their chattering in my blood, packets of data. Tastes of other individuals. Peers. Superiors. Subordinates."

"Vergil, I still think you should be in a hospital."

"This is my show, Edward," he said. "I'm their universe. They're amazed by the new scale." He was quiet again for a time. I squatted by his chair and pulled up the sleeve to his robe. His arm was crisscrossed with white lines. I was about to go to the phone and call for an ambulance when he stood and stretched. "Do you realize," he said, "how many body cells we kill each time we move?"

"I'm going to call for an ambulance," I said.

"No, you aren't." His tone stopped me. "I told you, I'm not sick, this is my show. Do you know what they'd do to me in a hospital? They'd be like cavemen trying to fix a computer the same way they fix a stone ax. It would be a farce."

"Then what the hell am I doing here?" I asked, getting angry. "I can't do anything. I'm one of those cavemen."

"You're a friend," Vergil said, fixing his eyes on me. I had the impression I was being watched by more than just Vergil. "I want you here to keep me company." He laughed. "But I'm not exactly alone."

He walked around the apartment for two hours, fingering things, looking out windows, making himself lunch slowly and methodically. "You know, they can actually feel their own thoughts," he said about noon. "I mean, the cytoplasm seems to have a will of its own, a kind of subconscious life counter to the rationality they've only recently acquired. They hear the chemical 'noise' or whatever of the molecules fitting and unfitting inside."

At two o'clock, I called Gail to tell her I would be late. I was almost sick with tension, but I tried to keep my voice level. "Remember Vergil Ulam? I'm talking with him right now."

"Everything okay?" she asked.

Was it? Decidedly not. "Fine," I said.

"Culture!" Vergil said, peering around the kitchen wall at me. I said good-bye and hung up the phone. "They're always swimming in that bath of information. Contributing to it. It's a kind of gestalt thing, whatever. The hierarchy is absolute. They send tailored phages after cells that don't interact properly. Viruses specified to individuals or groups. No escape. One gets pierced by the virus, the cell blebs outward, it explodes and dissolves. But it's not just a dictatorship. I think they effectively have more freedom than in a democracy. I mean, they vary so differently from individual to individual. Does that make sense? They vary in different ways than we do."

"Hold it," I said, gripping his shoulders. "Vergil, you're pushing me close to the edge. I can't take this much longer. I don't understand, I'm not sure I believe—"

"Not even now?"

"Okay, let's say you're giving me the right interpretation. Giving it to me straight. The whole thing's true. Have you bothered to figure out all the consequences yet? What all this means, where it might lead?"

He walked into the kitchen and drew a glass of water from the tap, then returned and stood next to me. His expression had changed from childish absorption to sober concern. "I've never been very good at that."

"Aren't you afraid?"

"I was. Now, I'm not sure." He fingered the tie of his robe. "Look, I don't want you to think I went around you, over your head or something. But I met with Michael Bernard yesterday. He put me through his private clinic, took specimens. Told me to quit the lamp treatments. He called this morning, just before you did. He says it all checks out. And he asked me not to tell anybody." He paused and his expression became dreamy again. "Cities of cells," he continued. "Edward, they push pili-like tubes through the tissues, spread information—"

"Stop it!" I shouted. "Checks out? What checks out?"

"As Bernard puts it, I have 'severely enlarged macrophages' throughout my system. And he concurs on the anatomical changes. So it's not just our common delusion."

"What does he plan to do?"

"I don't know. I think he'll probably convince Genetron to reopen the lab."

"Is that what you want?"

"It's not just having the lab again. I want to show you.

Since I stopped the lamp treatments. I'm still changing."
He undid his robe and let it slide to the floor. All over
his body, his skin was criss-crossed with white lines.
Along his back, the lines were starting to form ridges.

"My God," I said.

"I'm not going to be much good anywhere else but
the lab soon. I won't be able to go out in public. Hospitals wouldn't know what to do, as I said."

"You're ... you can talk to them, tell them to slow
down," I said, aware how ridiculous that sounded.

"Yes, indeed I can, but they don't necessarily listen."

"I thought you were their god or something."

"The ones hooked up to my neurons aren't the big
wheels. They're researchers, or at least serve the same
function. They know I'm here, what I am, but that
doesn't mean they've convinced the upper levels of the
hierarchy."

"They're disputing?"

"Something like that. It's not all that bad, anyway. If
the lab is reopened, I have a home, a place to work."
He glanced out the window, as if looking for someone.
"I don't have anything left but them. They aren't afraid,
Edward. I've never felt so close to anything before." The
beatific smile again. "I'm responsible for them. Mother
to them all."

"You have no way of knowing what they're going to
do."

He shook his head.

"No, I mean it. You say they're like a civilization—"

"Like a thousand civilizations."

"Yes, and civilizations have been known to screw up.
Warfare, the environment—"

I was grasping at straws, trying to restrain a growing
panic. I wasn't competent to handle the enormity of what
was happening. Neither was Vergil. He was the last person I would have called insightful and wise about large
issues.

"But I'm the only one at risk."

"You don't know that. Jesus, Vergil, look what they're
doing to you!"

"To me, all to me!" he said. "Nobody else."

I shook my head and held up my hands in a gesture of defeat. "Okay, so Bernard gets them to reopen the lab, you move in, become a guinea pig. What then?"

"They treat me right. I'm more than just good old Vergil Ulam now. I'm a goddamned galaxy, a super-mother."

"Super-host, you mean." He conceded the point with a shrug.

I couldn't take any more. I made my exit with a few flimsy excuses, then sat in the lobby of the apartment building, trying to calm down. Somebody had to talk some sense into him. who would he listen to? He had gone to Bernard . . .

And it sounded as if Bernard was not only convinced, but very interested. People of Bernard's stature didn't coax the Vergil Ulams of the world along; not unless they felt it was to their advantage.

I had a hunch, and I decided to play it. I went to a pay phone, slipped in my credit card, and called Genetron.

"I'd like you to page Dr. Michael Bernard," I told the receptionist.

"Who's calling, please?"

"This is his answering service. We have an emergency call and his beeper doesn't seem to be working."

A few anxious minutes later, Bernard came on the line. "Who the hell is this?" he asked quietly. "I don't have an answering service."

"My name is Edward Milligan. I'm a friend of Vergil Ulam's. I think we have some problems to discuss."

We made an appointment to talk the next morning.

I went home and tried to think of excuses to keep me off the next day's hospital shift. I couldn't concentrate on medicine, couldn't give my patients anywhere near the attention they deserved.

Guilty, angry, afraid.

That was how Gail found me. I slipped on a mask of calm and we fixed dinner together. After eating, we watched the city lights come on in late twilight through the bayside window, holding on to each other. Odd winter starlings pecked at the yellow lawn in the last few minutes of light, then flew away with a rising wind which made the windows rattle.

"Something's wrong," Gail said softly. "Are you going to tell me, or just act like everything's normal?"

"It's just me," I said. "Nervous. Work at the hospital."

"Oh, lord," she said, sitting up. "You're going to divorce me for that Baker woman." Mrs. Baker weighed three hundred and sixty pounds and hadn't known she was pregnant until her fifth month.

"No," I said, listless.

"Rapturous relief," Gail said, touching my forehead lightly. "You know this kind of introspection drives me crazy."

"Well, it's nothing I can talk about yet, so . . ." I patted her hand.

"That's disgustingly patronizing," she said, getting up. "I'm going to make some tea. Want some?" Now she was miffed, and I was tense with not telling.

Why not just reveal all? I asked myself. An old friend of mine was turning himself into a galaxy.

I cleared away the table instead. That night, unable to sleep, I looked down on Gail in bed from my sitting position, pillow against the wall, and tried to determine what I knew was real, and what wasn't.

I'm a doctor, I told myself. A technical, scientific profession. I'm supposed to be immune to things like future shock.

Vergil Ulam was turning into a galaxy.

How would it feel to be topped off with a trillion Chinese? I grinned in the dark and almost cried at the same time. What Vergil had inside him was unimaginably stranger than Chinese. Stranger than anything I—or Vergil—could easily understand. Perhaps ever understand.

But I knew what was real. The bedroom, the city lights faint through gauze curtains. Gail sleeping. Very important. Gail, in bed, sleeping.

The dream came again. This time the city came in through the window and attacked Gail. It was a great, spiky lighted-up prowler, and it growled in a language I couldn't understand, made up of auto horns, crowded noises, construction bedlam. I tried to fight it off, but it got to her—and turned into a drift of stars, sprinkling all over the bed, all over everything. I jerked awake and stayed up until dawn, dressed with Gail, kissed her, savored the reality of her human, unviolated lips.

And went to meet with Bernard. He had been loaned a suite in a big downtown hospital; I rode the elevator to the sixth floor, and saw what fame and fortune could mean.

The suite was tastefully furnished, fine serigraphs on wood-paneled walls, chrome and glass furniture, cream-colored carpet, Chinese brass, and wormwood-grain cabinets and tables.

He offered me a cup of coffee, and I accepted. He took a seat in the breakfast nook, and I sat across from him, cradling my cup in moist palms. He was dapper, wearing a gray suit; had graying hair and a sharp profile. He was in his mid-sixties and he looked quite a bit like Leonard Bernstein.

"About our mutual acquaintance," he said. "Mr. Ulam. Brilliant. And, I won't hesitate to say, courageous."

"He's my friend. I'm worried about him."

Bernard held up one finger. "Courageous—and a bloody damned fool. What's happening to him should never have been allowed. He may have done it under duress, but that's no excuse. Still, what's done is done. He's talked to you, I take it."

I nodded. "He wants to return to Genetron."

"Of course. That's where all his equipment is. Where his home probably will be while we sort this out."

"Sort it out—how? What use is it?" I wasn't thinking too clearly. I had a slight headache.

"I can think of a large number of uses for small, super-dense computer elements with a biological base. Can't you? Genetron has already made breakthroughs, but this is something else again."

"What do you envision?"

Bernard smiled. "I'm not really at liberty to say. It'll be revolutionary. We'll have to get him in lab conditions. Animal experiments have to be conducted. We'll have to start from scratch, of course. Vergil's . . . um . . . colonies can't be transferred. They're based on his white blood cells. So we have to develop colonies that won't trigger immune reactions to other animals."

"Like an infection?" I asked.

"I suppose there are comparisons. But Vergil is not infected."

"My tests indicate he is."

"That's probably the bits of data floating around in his blood, don't you think?"

"I don't know."

"Listen, I'd like you to come down to the lab after Vergil is settled in. Your expertise might be useful to us."

Us. He was working with Genetron hand in glove. Could he be objective? "How will you benefit from all this?"

"Edward, I have always been at the forefront of my profession. I see no reason why I shouldn't be helping here. With my knowledge of brain and nerve functions, and the research I've been conducting in neurophysiology—"

"You could help Genetron hold off an investigation by the government," I said.

"That's being very blunt. Too blunt, and unfair."

"Perhaps. Anyway, yes. I'd like to visit the lab when Vergil's settled in. If I'm still welcome, bluntness and all." He looked at me sharply. I wouldn't be playing on *his* team; for a moment, his thoughts were almost nakedly apparent.

"Of course," Bernard said, rising with me. He reached out to shake my hand. His palm was damp. He was as nervous as I was, even if he didn't look it.

I returned to my apartment and stayed there until noon, reading, trying to sort things out. Reach a decision. What was real, what I needed to protect.

There is only so much change anyone can stand. Innovation, yes, but slow application. Don't force. Everyone has the right to stay the same until they decide otherwise.

The greatest thing in science since . . .

And Bernard would force it. Genetron would force it.

I couldn't handle the thought. "Neo-Luddite," I said to myself. A filthy accusation.

When I pressed Vergil's number on the building security panel, Vergil answered almost immediately. "Yeah," he said. He sounded exhilarated now. "Come on up. I'll be in the bathroom. Door's unlocked."

I entered his apartment and walked through the hallway to the bathroom. Vergil was in the tub, up to his neck in pinkish water. He smiled vaguely at me and splashed his hands. "Looks like I slit my wrists, doesn't it?" he said softly. "Don't worry. Everything's fine now. Genetron's going to take me back. Bernard just called." He pointed to the bathroom phone and intercom.

I sat down on the toilet and noticed the sun lamp fixture standing unplugged next to the linen cabinets. The bulbs sat in a row on the edge of the sink counter. "You're sure that's what you want," I said, my shoulders slumping.

"Yeah, I think so," he said. "They can take better care of me. I'm getting cleaned up, going over there this evening. Bernard's picking me up in his limo. Style. From here on in, everything's style."

The pinkish color in the water didn't look like soap. "Is that bubble bath?" I asked. Some of it came to me in a rush then and I felt a little weaker: what had occurred to me was just one more obvious and necessary insanity.

"No," Vergil said. I knew that already.

"No," he repeated, "it's coming from my skin. They're not telling me everything, but I think they're sending out scouts. Astronauts." He looked at me with an expression that didn't quite equal concern; more like curiosity as to how I'd take it.

The confirmation made my stomach muscles tighten as if waiting for a punch. I had never even considered the possibility until now, perhaps because I had been concentrating on other aspects. "Is this the first time?" I asked.

"Yeah," he said. He laughed. "I've half a mind to let the little buggers down the drain. Let them find out what the world's really about."

"They'd go everywhere," I said.

"Sure enough."

"How . . . how are you feeling?"

"I'm feeling pretty good now. Must be billions of them." More splashing with his hands. "What do you think? Should I let the buggers out?"

Quickly, hardly thinking, I knelt down beside the tub. My fingers went for the cord on the sun lamp and I plugged it in. He had hot-wired doorknobs, turned my piss blue, played a thousand dumb practical jokes and never grown up, never grown mature enough to understand that he was just brilliant enough to really affect the world; he would never learn caution.

He reached for the drain knob. "You know, Edward, I—"

He never finished. I picked up the fixture and dropped it into the tub, jumping back at the flash of steam and sparks. Vergil screamed and thrashed and jerked and then everything was still, except for the low, steady sizzle and the smoke wafting from his hair.

I lifted the toilet and vomited. Then I clenched my nose and went into the living room. My legs went out from under me and I sat abruptly on the couch.

After an hour, I searched through Vergil's kitchen and found bleach, ammonia, and a bottle of Jack Daniels. I returned to the bathroom, keeping the center of my gaze away from Vergil. I poured first the booze, then the bleach, then the ammonia into the water. Chlorine started bubbling up and I left, closing the door behind me.

The phone was ringing when I got home. I didn't answer. It could have been the hospital. It could have been Bernard. Or the police. I could envision having to explain everything to the police. Genetron would stonewall; Bernard would be unavailable.

I was exhausted, all my muscles knotted with tension and whatever name one can give to the feelings one has after—

Committing genocide?

That certainly didn't seem real. I could not believe I

had just murdered a hundred trillion intelligent beings. Snuffed a galaxy. It was laughable. But I didn't laugh.

It was not at all hard to believe that I had just killed one human being, a friend. The smoke, the melted lamp rods, the drooping electrical outlet and smoking cord.

Vergil.

I had dunked the lamp into the tub with Vergil.

I felt sick. Dreams, cities raping Gail (and what about his girlfriend, Candice?). Letting the water filled with them out. Galaxies sprinkling over us all. What horror. Then again, what potential beauty—a new kind of life, symbiosis and transformation.

Had I been thorough enough to kill them all? I had a moment of panic. Tomorrow, I thought, I will sterilize his apartment. Somehow, I didn't even think of Bernard.

When Gail came in the door, I was asleep on the couch. I came to, groggy, and she looked down at me.

"You feeling okay?" she asked, perching on the edge of the couch. I nodded.

"What are you planning for dinner?" My mouth wasn't working properly. The words were mushy. She felt my forehead.

"Edward, you have a fever," she said. "A very high fever."

I stumbled into the bathroom and looked in the mirror. Gail was close behind me. "What is it?" she asked.

There were lines under my collar, around my neck. White lines, like freeways. They had already been in me a long time, days.

"Damp palms," I said. So obvious.

I think we nearly died. I struggled at first, but within minutes I was too weak to move. Gail was just as sick within an hour.

I lay on the carpet in the living room, drenched in sweat. Gail lay on the couch, her face the color of talcum, eyes closed, like a corpse in an embalming parlor. For a time I thought she was dead. Sick as I was, I raged— hated, felt tremendous guilt at my weakness, my slowness to understand all the possibilities. Then I no longer cared. I was too weak to blink, so I closed my eyes and waited.

There was a rhythm in my arms, my legs. With each pulse of blood, a kind of sound welled up within me. A sound like an orchestra thousands strong, but not playing in unison; playing whole seasons of symphonies at once. Music in the blood. The sound or whatever became harsher, but more coordinated, wave-trains finally cancelling into silence, then separating into harmonic beats.

The beats seemed to melt into me, into the sound of my own heart.

First, they subdued our immune responses. The war—and it was a war, on a scale never before known on Earth, with trillions of combatants—lasted perhaps two days.

By the time I regained enough strength to get to the kitchen faucet, I could feel them working on my brain, trying to crack the code and find the god within the protoplasm. I drank until I was sick, then drank more moderately and took a glass to Gail. She sipped at it. Her lips were cracked, her eyes bloodshot and ringed with yellowish crumbs. There was some color in her skin. Minutes later, we were eating feebly in the kitchen.

"What in hell was *that*?" was the first thing she asked. I didn't have the strength to explain, so I shook my head. I peeled an orange and shared it with her. "We should call a doctor," she said. But I knew we wouldn't. I was already receiving messages; it was becoming apparent that any sensation of freedom we had was illusory.

The messages were simple at first. Memories of commands, rather than the commands themselves, manifested themselves in my thoughts. We were not to leave the apartment—a concept which seemed quite abstract to those in control, even if undesirable—and we were not to have contact with others. We would be allowed to eat certain foods, and drink tap water, for the time being.

With the subsidence of the fevers, the transformations were quick and drastic. Almost simultaneously, Gail and I were immobilized. She was sitting at the table, I was kneeling on the floor. I was able barely to see her in the corner of my eye.

Her arm developed pronounced ridges.

They had learned inside Vergil; their tactics within the two of us were very different. I itched all over for about two hours—two hours in hell—before they made the breakthrough and found me. The effort of ages on their time scale paid off and they communicated smoothly and directly with this great, clumsy intelligence which had once controlled their universe.

They were not cruel. When the concept of discomfort and its undesirability was made clear, they worked to alleviate it. They worked too effectively. For another hour, I was in a sea of bliss, out of all contact with them.

With dawn the next day, we were allowed freedom to move again; specifically, to go to the bathroom. There were certain waste products they could not deal with. I voided those—my urine was purple—and Gail followed suit. We looked at each other vacantly in the bathroom. Then she managed a slight smile. "Are they talking to you?" she asked. I nodded. "Then I'm not crazy."

For the next twelve hours, control seemed to loosen on some levels. During that time, I managed to pencil the majority of this manusicript. I suspect there was another kind of war going on in me. Gail was capable of our previous limited motion, but no more.

When full control resumed, we were instructed to hold each other. We did not hesitate.

"Eddie . . . " she whispered. My name was the last sound I ever heard from outside.

Standing, we grew together. In hours, our legs expanded and spread out. Then extensions grew to the windows to take in sunlight, and to the kitchen to take water from the sink. Filaments soon reached to all corners of the room, stripping paint and plaster from the walls, fabric and stuffing from the furniture.

By the next dawn, the transformation was complete.

I no longer have any clear view of what we look like. I suspect we resemble cells—large, flat and filamented cells, draped purposefully across most of the apartment. The great shall mimic the small.

I have been asked to carry on recording, but soon that will not be possible. Our intelligence fluctuates daily as we are absorbed into the minds within. Each day, our individuality declines. We are, indeed, great clumsy dinosaurs. Our memories have been taken over by billions of them, and our personalities have been spread through the transformed blood.

Soon there will be no need for centralization.

I am informed that already the plumbing has been invaded. People throughout the building are undergoing transformation.

Within the old time frame of weeks, we will reach the lakes, rivers, and seas in force.

I can barely begin to guess the results. Every square inch of the planet will teem with thought. Years from now, perhaps much sooner, they will subdue their own individuality—what there is of it.

New creatures will come, then. The immensity of their capacity for thought will be inconceivable.

All my hatred and fear is gone now.

I leave them—us—with only one question.

How many times has this happened, elsewhere? Travelers never came through space to visit the Earth. They had no need.

They had found universes in grains of sand.

COMMENTS

BLOOD MUSIC

GREG BEAR

"Blood Music" first occurred to me when I read an article in the U.K. magazine *New Scientist* in 1982. The article was about "biochips" and the possibilities of protein-based computers. I immediately leaped to the notion of DNA being a kind of biological computer, and from there to the notion that individual cells could be made to respond in more complex ways to their environment—that is, they might be made more intelligent. At this time, of course, I had heard nothing of nanotechnology, and probably would not have equated it with my story idea anyway. I was more interested in playing with ideas of intelligence and evolution than with manufacturing and miniaturization.

The story was first published in *Analog* in 1983. Before accepting the piece, Stanley Schmidt wanted me to do a little more work on establishing the scientific credibility of some of the ideas in the story. I did a little math, stretched complexities and scales a bit, and convinced him the story was at least marginally possible.

Before the story was published, John Carr and David Brin read it and immediately suggested that it should be expanded into a novel. They were right—there was a lot of room left in the idea. I began expanding it shortly thereafter, sold the outline to Beth Meacham at Ace Books, and the novel was well on its way. . . .

Sometime in 1984 or 1985 I began hearing about the pioneering work of K. Eric Drexler. The connection with "Blood Music" seemed a little vague, but people were crediting me with being a jump ahead of the nascent field of nanotechnology. I still don't think that was strictly true—but it does seem obvious now that I was dealing with the mythic side of the issue. Drexler of course was pursuing more practical and revolutionary goals. Later, in a number of novels (particularly *Queen of Angels*) I would address Drexler's challenge directly.

(Coincidentally, Paul Preuss was writing a novel on very similar themes called *Human Error*. The books turned out to be quite complementary, not to mention spookily similar!)

Blood Music over the years has introduced quite a few people to radical notions of biology and intelligence and information. It is not, however, my most popular book—perhaps because some of its themes and descriptions are genuinely disturbing. They don't disturb me very much (and Bruce Sterling, then generating the roller-coaster Frankenstein's monster of cyberpunk, wanted to be injected with noocytes immediately) but then I may be a poor judge of what causes nightmares. I honestly intended *Blood Music* (as a novel, at least) to represent a gentle and relatively non-violent side into the next step of evolution.

The short story is more abrupt. As one editor said when rejecting it, "It's talky and morbid." The editor was right about it being talky. As for being morbid, it's no more than life itself. . . . Which in the history of the human race has always, at some point or another, led to morbidity.

I prefer to think of "Blood Music" the short story as "vivid."

MONSTER HUNT

RICHARD E. GEIS

I stalked him, the Monster, through the partly demolished building.

I heard him ahead, scrambling through structure debris and smashed machines. He cried out with grief at the destruction.

He didn't know I followed and that I would kill him.

I'd been pursuing him for hours, using good science to track evil science. My finder had picked him up as he left his hiding place and he'd led me here to what remained of Kenton NanoLabs, where he must have worked.

Every moment he shed thousands of used molecular-sized machines from his body in sweat and breath and skin, leaving an invisible trail my Detector could follow.

Every moment thousands of infinitely small new machines were built in his body to perform new tasks or to replace those which had worn out.

The Monster, once a man, was no longer human. The new Scriptures, as written by God through Adam Hwit, defined him: "Monsters are natural men changed by unnatural science from what God intends to what God condemns. Monsters are a self-created alien species intent on superseding True Man. Monsters presume to replace God's Plan with their own. These Monsters must every one be destroyed."

The Monsters had seduced and then populated our government, our courts, even more of our clergy. The Monsters offered virtual immortality, immense mental

46

capacities, vastly improved bodies. They promised dominion over the universe.

But at last we True Men have seen clearly the shape of the future they planned. We had revolted before they became insuperably powerful and now we were destroying their unnatural civilization.

I crept closer to him, seeing him clearly now in the morning light from the broken walls.

He was naked. They were often naked, having no need for the warmth of clothes, and felt it humiliating to hide in clothes, to pretend to be human.

He had gross human form, but there were changes— his skull was hairless, his little fingers were now extra thumbs, his eyes bulged with zoom capability, and his feet were simplified. All this from years of revised DNA and those billions of molecular machines at work in his body.

He crouched before an overturned cabinet of drawers and files, sorting through hundreds of small, shattered bottles and ampules.

He searched with increasing urgency. I was amazed at the speed and dexterity of his movements. He kept looking around, fearing detection.

I watched him, sick with fear of my own, for I had never killed before, not even an animal, and now I had to kill a man . . . or this thing which had been a man. This was my first solo Monster hunt.

I hadn't expected to find a Monster. Not so quickly. He had the peculiar lump of new bone behind his left ear which contained the molecular computer they needed for their pure mind interface with what they called the UniNet.

Yes, they could touch a universe of knowledge and power. Yes, they could "outthink" any mortal human, and yes, they could if given a chance outfight any True Man.

But we had destroyed their power stations and their laboratories and their schools and their communications. Our "old fashioned" scientists had known how to jam their UniNet, and bring them down to a level of individual survival in a very hungry, savage, human world.

They were fish out of water, and their numbers daily

shrank, from seven million before The Revolt, to less than 100,000 now. They preferred to run, to hide, to escape, rather than fight.

This one found what he had been looking for in the mess of glass and steel. He broke the neck of a green glass ampule.

No! He could not be allowed to infect himself with new millions of specialized machines. His body and brain already seethed with microscopic maggots of change. No more!

I jerked erect and leveled my autofire shotgun. He heard, saw me, in a split second he moved—

The heavy gun bucked like a maddened steer. The shattered laboratory filled with thundering sound. He somehow danced and weaved and escaped all but one of those awful, smashing fists of lead pellets.

I heard his scream through ringing, half-deadened ears and knew I had to act swiftly.

I found him groaning, crawling under a broken-backed lab table and I unthinkingly pulled him by his bloody legs into full light.

He had the power to speak even though the shotgun blast had shredded a hole through his chest, his right lung, and his back. "You ... you cannot destroy the future."

I barely heard him. I stared as his horrible wound stopped bleeding. It began to close from the edges with a blur of incredible reconstruction.

I shivered with awe and terror. "Monster!"

"You will live a million years. You will cross the galaxy."

"Not me. I'll live and die as God intends."

"God intended us to become what we are."

"Monster lies!" I realized his tactic: to delay, to involve me in talk and argument! He needed time to become whole and strong and fast.

I stepped back and quickly reloaded. In the instant before his death he said, "You touched me."

I heard but did not then understand. I did as I had been trained. His head and neck disintegrated under the terrible impacts of a dozen shotgun loads. The altered brain was gone. The walnut-size bio-computer was gone. The billions of nano machines in his body would stop within ten minutes.

My own head rang from the thunderclaps of the shotgun blasts. My shoulder felt broken. My stomach roiled with nausea. I dropped the gun and sat on the littered floor. I found myself staring at my blood-stained hands. Why were they bloody? I had only a few small cuts and scrapes on my fingers and palms. Not enough to . . .

I had dragged him from under that table. This was his blood! The training tape came alive in my memory: "Above all avoid any contact with Monster blood. The nano machines infest the blood. They will invade your bloodstream easily, without you knowing, and they will reproduce in you and quickly begin changing you according to their programs. You will become in due time a Monster."

I sat, frozen, shuddering, in horrified self-examination, monitoring my sensations, my thoughts, my body.

I had to kill himself.

But my pain went away, and my blind obedience to God went away, and I began to think about surviving. For the sake of the future.

COMMENTS

MONSTER HUNT

RICHARD E. GEIS

My years-long exposure to Elton Elliott's belief in a nanotech future has altered my perspective and expectations. Not for the better, alas.

If a viable nanoscience gets off the ground and into the human body with intent to improve the breed or simply to vastly extend the lifespan of an elite, I foresee vast social upheavals and wars caused by the deepest human instinctual values and drives.

Briefly, an emergent nanotech elite had better quickly get off-planet or face an envious and instinctively hostile humanity intent on killing the "Monsters."

But that's only one (and the most palatable) of myriad futures where nano is concerned; it could be a matter of uncontrolled nanoflood and chaos as no one dies, food and products are created at will, and all government, all society, disintegrates.

I expect to be safely in the ground before all this nano terror possibly emerges, but there may be a few young readers of these words who will live to see those future days.

Lots of luck.

NANOTECH AND NANOMINDS:
FOOTNOTES FOR THE FUTURE

*A Personal Odyssey
During the Political Beginnings
of Molecular Nanotechnology,
1991–1994*

ARLAN ANDREWS

Atoms and Activists

Sometime around the turn of the Millennium, say about 2005 or so, when the Molecular Nanotechnology (MNT) Revolution is a full-blown intellectual race, when nations and corporations are scrambling to apply MNT to every human need (including recreational drugs and insidious new forms of personal warfare), few people will want to take the time to recall the details of the beginnings of that revolution.

Regarding the origins of MNT, most of the public statements, Congressional hearings and technical conferences are matters of record and may be found in familiar reference sources. This highly subjective report records for future generations a few of the more obscure incidents along the pathway of MNT development, personal vignettes and information to which I was witness, items of possible interest that may otherwise go unnoticed or unrecorded by those beneficiaries (or victims) of mature MNT.

For the warp and woof of future history, I weave these tiny threads.

Small Beginnings

My personal interest in tiny mechanisms began in 1955, stimulated by the serial, *Call Him Dead*, in *Astounding Science Fiction Magazine*. An eerily predictive story by Eric Frank Russell (a virus-based alien intelligence spreads through contact with blood or saliva), the story features a "microforger," a man who makes "surgical and manipulatory instruments so tiny they can be used to operate on a bacillus." However, when asked about working on viruses, the microforger says, "I don't work *that* small!" So, though tiny was considered, SF wasn't discussing MNT back then.

However, four years later, on December 26, 1959, Dr. Richard Feynman issued his now-famous challenge to the technical community, offering a prize of $1000 to "the first guy who can take the information on the page of a book and put it on an area 1/25,000 smaller in linear scale in such manner that it can be read by an electron microscope." In the same talk, he off-handedly outlined methods by which tiny electronic circuits could be made—the basis for today's integrated circuits, which have revolutionized computers, communications and consumer electronics.

A physicist, Dr. Feynman did not neglect the future potential of microscopic machines. He volunteered an identical prize for "the first guy who makes an operating electric motor—a rotating electric motor ... [with dimensions of] ... 1/64th inch cube." In 1960, on the TV show, *What's My Line?*, William McLellan demonstrated his prize-winning tiny electrical motor. His microscopic handiwork is still on display at Cal Tech. McLellan re-issued Feynman's micro-challenge on that TV show, trying to stimulate competition among colleges, to see who could build the tiniest machines.

Unfortunately, Feynman's and McLellan's building-ever-smaller micromachines contest never took off, and it was nearly forgotten in the ensuing decades. Like many other college students at the time, my own mind was on Space, and the Moon was our destination. We were to build gigantic rockets, perform gargantuan feats, conquer the infinite Universe. Tiny things could wait. But the far-seeing

Feynman had wanted to go further down. He speculated, "What would happen if we could arrange the atoms one by one the way we want them?"

Movement Among the Molecules

In 1983 Greg Bear's short story, "Blood Music," dealt with the concept of bacterium-sized intelligent creatures that colonized human bodies. This idea kicked off more discussion in the SF community about tiny intelligences, but Dr. K. Eric Drexler deserves the credit for resurrecting Feynman's ideas, polishing and improving upon them, and pushing the technology toward credibility. In 1987, Steve Bridge (now director of Alcor, the cryonics suspension organization) handed me Drexler's nanotechnology book, *Engines of Creation*, and my interest in things tiny and fast was rekindled.

In 1990 the First Annual Solid Freeform Fabrication Symposium took place in Austin, Texas, describing in some detail the latest work taking place in new technologies yielding a kind of manufacturing magic: laser solidification and laser sintering of liquids and powders, respectively, into 3D objects, directly from Computer Aided Design (CAD) files. In one talk, Dr. Harris Marcus described experiments in which he and other researchers were able to grow tiny rods of carbon by focusing an electron beam through flows of common industrial gases.

"We want to be able to build arbitrary structures at very small scales, using electron beams and various gases," he said. "Moving parts, mechanisms—useful machines."

"How small can you grow them?" I asked. "What are the smallest dimensions you will be able to handle?"

"Theoretically," he replied, "with electron beams, the only limit is the size of the atom."

"Have you heard," I responded, "of Eric Drexler and his work in nanotechnology?"

The Washington Connections

Being fortunate enough to have two consecutive years of technology fellowships in Washington, D. C., during the late Bush and early Clinton Administrations, I was privileged to be a part of several interactions in the beginnings of MNT. I will categorize these interactions by the names of the government agencies that took part in them.

United States Department of Commerce

In 1991, while a Fellow of the American Society of Mechanical Engineers (ASME) assigned to the Technology Administration of the U.S. Department of Commerce, I reviewed recent reports on the status of newly emerging technologies thought to be important to the future competitiveness of the nation. I quickly found that molecular nanotechnology had not made the list although it was being championed by scientists at the Department of Commerce's National Institute of Standards and Technology (NIST), in Gaithersburg, Maryland.

The next week found me at NIST and among nanotech friends, particularly Dr. E. Clayton Teague. Dr. Teague, who once came within heartbreaking distance of winning a Nobel Prize for his work on an early tunneling microscope, is the editor of the international technical journal, *Nanotechnology*, which reports on the actual state of the art in micro- and nano-scale research and technology. At NIST, as part of the Institute's charter to provide precise measurements and standards, Dr. Teague is working to build the Molecular Measuring Machine, which, when completed, will be able to locate a given atom in a two-inch square working surface, then back off and return to that same atom. The same technology can be used to move atoms, so that the M-Cubed will potentially be an early prototype of an atomic fabricator. Dr. Teague's work will be an important cornerstone in the foundations of MNT.

Later in 1991 Dr. Teague and I were among several hundred attendees at Dr. Drexler's Molecular Nanotechnology Conference in Palo Alto, CA. Upon returning, I drafted a short trip report, listing the papers given and some speculations about the future and applications of MNT, and circulated the memo around the Department of Commerce, the White House Science Office and

Sandia National Laboratories. Initially, the responses and comments were little to none.

At about the same time, the Congressional Office of Technology Assessment (OTA) issued its report based on a year-long study of micro- and nanotechnology. *Miniaturization Technologies* featured a two-page sidebar of Dr. Drexler's vision of molecular manufacturing. The Director of OTA, Dr. Jack Gibbons, would later become Science Advisor to President Bill Clinton and an important decision maker in the future of MNT.

Central Intelligence Agency

While still at the Commerce Department, I often walked the two blocks to the White House complex for lunch with other Fellows and appointees from the White House Science Office. One day at lunch, a young woman at the table—"from The Agency," she was introduced—asked what kind of work I was doing at Commerce. Having just returned from the MNT Conference in California, I told her about my interest in the trip report memo.

"But what use is it?" she asked.

"Imagine something the size of a fly," I replied, "or even smaller, just buzzing unobtrusively into this cafeteria here, or maybe over into the West Wing, the Oval Office. It could hide under the table, or on the wall, provide full audio and video transmission or recording, and then just buzz away again."

She sat silent for a moment. "Send me a copy of that report, would you?" I did, later discovering that this CIA person was also the ex-wife of a noted SF writer.

About a year later, I was invited to the CIA's first Nanotechnology Conference. Excited, I arrived early, anxious to hear about the latest in nanoweapons and nanodefenses. But the papers dealt only with developments in fine-line integrated circuits and sales pitches for new scientific instruments. Not a nano-mechanism, not a tiny warrior in sight!

United States Senate

On June 26, 1992, another important building block was placed in the foundation of emerging political support of MNT. Dr. Drexler, in testimony to a Senate Committee chaired by then-Senator Al Gore, outlined the potential for MNT's impact upon the industrial base of the nation. A supportive Senator Gore was especially impressed, he said, by the manufacturing efficiencies and the recycling possibilities inherent in Dr. Drexler's testimony.

White House Science Office

In February 1992 I had taken my place as the ASME White House Fellow in the Office of Science and Technology Policy (OSTP), part of the Executive Office of the President. Immediately after his appearance before Senator Gore's committee, I hosted Dr. Drexler in the Old Executive Office Building, where OSTP is located. Responding to my invitation were several Associate Directors of OSTP, a representative from the National Science Foundation (NSF), Dr. E. Clayton Teague of NIST, Mr. Carl W. Shepherd of the Commerce Department, Dr. Doug Beason, an Air Force detailee to OSTP (and a fellow SF writer), and myself. (An unidentified journalist, who had been hounding both Dr. Drexler and me, tried to crash the meeting but was ushered out by one of the security staff.) I was a little disappointed that neither the OSTP National Security Office nor the CIA attended.

Dr. Drexler began the briefing by presenting a video tape showing a computer-generated "ball-and-rod" model of an atomic-scale shaft and bearing. Immediately the NSF representative became hostile, stating that such a model was unrealistic, and that many, many years would be required before any such construction could even be attempted, much less be successful.

As Dr. Drexler tried to defend his views, the objector brought up engineering instabilities in the Saturn Five F-1 rocket engines and other seemingly irrelevant issues. Several OSTP members left during the heated discussion, and Dr. Drexler's message was never fully delivered nor appreciated. Afterwards I heard the comment from one of the senior scientists, "This stuff is going to happen in the distant future, but he [Dr. Drexler] isn't going to be the one who does it."

I thought then that this first White House briefing would one day become at least a footnote in the history of technology, because the subject was officially broached and at least some of the more junior attendees (like me) were impressed.

Critical Technologies Panel

Every two years a prestigious ad-hoc technical committee—comprised of representatives from the federal government, industry and academia—is convened, mandated by Congress to report their best guesses of the technologies that will be important to the national economy over the next ten years. The first CT report, issued in 1991, listed *nanofabrication* as a critical national technology, stating that "Novel and useful mechanisms may occur as a result . . .", but most of the emphasis then was definitely on nanoelectronics, not nanomachines.

In the fall of 1992, as an observer from OSTP, I attended the meetings of the Second Critical Technologies Panel. During one early brainstorming session, Dr. Joe Bordogna, Assistant Director of the National Science Foundation for Engineering, ventured, "I think that micromachines and molecular nanotechnology are going to be important to our nation. They should be placed on this next Critical Technologies list." Dr. Bordogna's suggestion was greeted with outright chuckles. "Okay, Joe," came the reply from his superior, "we'll just jot down your idea somewhere." I spoke with a disappointed Dr. Bordogna at the next break, and he revealed that he does share the vision of MNT as an imminent revolutionary development. (His suggestion to the Critical Technologies Panel never appeared in print.)

Dr. Bordogna has, on the wall behind his desk, the original of a microphotograph that appeared on the cover of *Scientific American*. Set up and photographed at his request, the picture shows a tiny cast metal gear, dangling like an earring from the antenna—of an ant!

White House Science Office, 1993

In late 1992 I was asked by OSTP to write a chapter for the annual OSTP report, *Science and Technology: A Report of the President to the Congress 1993*. My background as an SF writer was known, as was my hosting of Dr. Drexler for the MNT briefing, so the coordinator of the "*S&T Report*" rather jocularly requested that I not ". . . write about the world being taken over by tiny robots. . . ." Assured that this was merely joshing, I was asked to write about the "factory of the future" and how future technologies should be taken into account by present day technology policy planners.

As asked, so I did. My chapter of the *S&T Report*, "Manufacturing: The New Competition," contains speculations on the future of Solid Freeform Fabrication (SFF), based on present day technologies in which lasers interact with liquids or powders to produce solid model prototype parts directly from 3D CAD files. Micromachines, produced by processes that make integrated circuit chips, also figured large in my vision of the future. And in two paragraphs I wrote the first official White House endorsement of MNT:

"MOLECULAR MANUFACTURING—Molecular nanotechnology, unlike micromachining, starts at the bottom and works up, building materials and structures one atom at a time. This process has been described in the literature since 1986 and could eventually be used to build both nanoscale and macroscale structures. It is already made possible on a primitive level by the advent of scanning tunneling microscopes, which allow atoms to be picked up and positioned at will, subject to the laws of chemistry. To achieve economically viable nanoscale assembly, namely, the aggregation of large numbers of atoms in a finite time, a system of molecular 'assemblers' has been proposed. 'Assemblers' are self-replicating molecules capable of reproducing themselves in large numbers and then gathering and positioning other atoms and molecules in desired constructions. By analogy to biology, these electromechanical devices

would use only those atoms needed, building up to
the desired product. In such processes, industrial
waste would be minimized, recycling of materials
would be almost total, energy would be used most
efficiently, and a vast number of new products and
capabilities would be made possible.

Research in mechanical engineering, molecular
biology, chemistry and physics is leading to advances
in this interdisciplinary field. With a realizable system of practical molecular manufacturing, the very
definitions of design, manufacturing and factories
would be profoundly affected. *Miniaturization Technologies*, a recent study published by the congressional Office of Technology Assessment, estimated
that the first versions of the molecular 'assemblers'
may be realized in 5 to 10 years."

The *S&T Report* was issued in April 1993, during the
early Clinton Administration. The significance of these
paragraphs is not that I wrote them, but that they bore
the imprimatur of the White House. This means that
they could be referenced when applying for MNT funding, when determining a MNT research project within a
university, or maybe even when proposing MNT R&D
within a private firm.

Or perhaps they would be read by decision makers in
Congress and elsewhere, thereby changing minds and
influencing future developments.

ASME World Conference, New Orleans, 1993

In April 1993 I returned to Sandia National Laboratories in Albuquerque, New Mexico, but I retained my
social, technical and political contacts in Washington, taking the opportunity to promote MNT at a national level.
As Vice Chairman of the ASME Technology and Society
Division, I organized and hosted ASME's first-ever MNT
session during the New Orleans Conference in December 1993.

Dr. K. Eric Drexler keynoted the session, entitled
"Nanotechnology and Society: Ultimate Benefits, Ultimate Risks." A supporting paper, "Nanotechnology:

What's Happening in the United States," was provided by Dr. E. Clayton Teague of NIST and Dr. James Murday of the Naval Research Center. Dr. Burgess Laird, of the Los Alamos National Laboratory, spoke on international competition in nanotechnology, pointing out that Japan spends ten times as much money on MNT as we do, that their efforts are coordinated and are directed toward practical applications in medicine and manufacturing.

Reaction among ASME members in the audience, many of whom were old-time mechanical designers, was primarily delight, expressing surprise that their design skills might still be applicable in this emerging interdisciplinary field, even down among the molecules. As one fellow said, "We can still assemble things down there, and we don't have to worry about breaking the piece parts!"

An ASME press release on the session declared, "The Nanotechnology Race Is On!"; stating that nanotechnology ". . . is coming out of the science fiction novels and into the research laboratories . . ."

White House Science Office, 1994

As one of the symposium planning committee members, I was present in the audience at a conference entitled "Manufacturing Needs of U.S. Industry," at the National Institute of Standards and Technology, Gaithersburg, Maryland, on April 26, 1994. The main speaker, Dr. Jack Gibbons, was the Science Advisor to President Bill Clinton and Director of OSTP—the man who had extended my ASME Fellowship into the Clinton Administration. Dr. Gibbons mentioned the importance of NIST time measurements in the discovery of a large planet orbiting a dead star. He then launched into a fascinating few minutes about the imminent coming of MNT:

"Let me offer a somewhat speculative example of a new world to explore in the intersection of science and manufacturing technology. Fascinating as it is to examine the outer reaches of the universe and images that originated billions of years ago, an equally amazing world lies within the inner space of our universe. Quantum mechanics provides access to this sub-submicron territory ... and quantum mechanics is now an everyday engineering tool. It even appears in undergraduate engineering courses.

"Nanoscience has become an engineering practice. Based on recent theoretical and experimental advances in nanoscience and nanotechnology, precise atomic and molecular control in the synthesis of solid state three dimensional nanostructures is now possible. The volume of such structures is about a billionth that of structures on the micron scale.

"The next step is the emergence of nanotechnology. The stage is being set, I believe, for actual manufacture of a wide variety and range of custom-made products, based on the ability to manipulate individual atoms and molecules during the manufacturing process. The ability to synthesize devices such as molecular wires, resistors, diodes, and photosensitive elements to be inserted in nanoscale *machines* is now emerging from fundamental nanoscience ...

"Next, molecular manufacturing for mass production of miniature switches or valves or motors or accelerometers, all at affordable prices, is a genuine possibility in the not so distant future. This new technology could fuel a powerful economic engine providing new sources of jobs and wealth and technology spillovers ...

"Further fundamental understanding of basic physical phenomena at the quantum level will be needed to understand and reach these kinds of technological opportunities ..."

With these words the White House Science Office, speaking for the Administration, officially and undeniably endorsed molecular manufacturing, one of the ultimate goals of Dr. K. Eric Drexler's vision of molecular nanotechnology.

What Next? How *You* Can Change the Future

Outside the marketplace, not all technology decisions are purely technical or economic; many new technologies arise from government-funded and/or government-subsidized R&D, and the primary element ensuring survival of these endeavors is political. These "Footnotes" are the record of some of those small political efforts and modest accomplishments in support of Molecular Nanotechnology, MNT in the period of 1991 to 1994.

But obviously the battles are not all won, and MNT may face tough competition for decreasing research dollars. Supporters of molecular nanotechnology need to educate their elected representatives and government staffers, within both the legislative and executive branches, to the potentials of MNT. Decision makers need to be convinced that MNT will be an important element of international trade competition in the next decades, that the basic research should be funded now for future economic gain, and that the national economy and "jobs, jobs, jobs!" depend on the U.S. successfully achieving mature, commercial MNT first.

To those who take up this challenge, I hope these "Footnotes" are a useful tool in your crucial efforts to ensure a viable future for all Americans and the rest of humankind.

SINS OF THE MOTHERS

ARLAN ANDREWS

"A one-armed Nobel Prize winner, locked up in this stinking county jail, here in no-place, Texas?" I ask my cellmate. "How the hell did you get here, anyway?"

I don't know what a Nobel Prize winner is supposed to look like, but this one don't look like any TV-scientist I ever seen: five foot three, max, a hundred pounds at most, skin dark as any Mexican field hand I ever seen. Laying back on the bottom bunk, clothes tore and face bruised and bloody, he looks more like a *chicano* who got the worst end of a *pachuco* rumble. If it weren't for that thousand dollar suit still wet with blood from his nose, and the cussing of the cops that threw him in here an hour ago—"*Doctor* Oh-med, you piece of shit," Deputy Bobby Lee had yelled, "protest *this* for a couple of weeks!"—I wouldn't have believed he was *Doctor* of anything, not with just one damned arm.

But he sure talks interesting.

I'm not believing a god damned word the little darkie is telling me, but what the hell; and at least the small turd sounds good and he's not about to try anything fairy like that big crock I had to knife last week. The floor is still stained with that one's tainted blood. I don't go barefoot in here anymore, let me tell you.

Even if the little dude was to get boring, it's not like I have anything better to do. Not for the next five to twelve months, I don't. Just because that drunk bitch Oleena didn't remember saying "yes." Damn her and that asshole paw of hers. And damn his big old shotgun, while we're at it.

"You see," Oh-med says, "there was a protesting at the abortuary—"

"Say what, Oh-med? The what?"

"The so-called *clinic*, the place where they chop up the unborn babies. The *abortuary*." Now I see. For a year or so, some group or another has been picketing the local Ladie's Clinic, (and yeah, they spell it just like that, here in the Borderland) where the county's women go get their little unwanteds unborn. Hell, I don't see anything so wrong with that; five or six of my old ladies have got it done. The thought of some damned county judge hitting me up for child support for rug rats that probably weren't mine anyhow—jeez!

And that starts to remind me of something I ought to be remembering, but that hit of *dust-up* last night has still got my head all fuzzy, so I forget and focus back on the little Ay-rab in front of me.

So the Doc, here, is one of them Northern protesters, come to change our way of life? Lots of luck, Doc; might be just as easy to get everyone to stop screwing. What the hell, I'm stuck with him here a week or two, and he's all's I got, so might's well be friendly. The little guy finally gets up and walks around the cell, rubbing his beat-up face with his right hand. Feeling kinda sorry for the wobbly way he's barely standing, I offer him a hand.

"Thanks, Mr. Lester."

"Nothin' Oh-med."

Little guy smiles crooked and looks up at me. "*Ahmid*, Mr. Lester, Dr. Ahmid Asouri, at your service. Let me answer your question, how I got down here to your charming local penal establishment." He means the jail.

He starts talking about growing up in Chicago, in some Ay-rab ghetto or some such, how his mother had been an outcast for having him while she was a student over here, and she finally went back home to Egypt or Algeria, whatever, and her folks back home over there killed her for having him over here. He looks like his old man must have been black, but he never mentions anything to me about that.

Anyhow, he gets real quiet about that time and knowing how hard it is—used to be, at least for me—to get used to the slammer, I let him set and work it out in his head. Little or not, no use to get somebody pissed off at you. We probably got days or weeks in this miserable closet together, and I gotta sleep sometime and a knife is easy to get. I know that for damn sure! And so does my old, hospitalized, coma-livin' roomie!

"I was born nine months after Rovie Wade," he says all profound-like, like I am supposed to know who that guy is. "Your government would have allowed everybody my age and under to be aborted! Killed in the womb!

"My friend Lester, you yourself are not yet thirty are you? You could have been scalded alive in a salt solution, or had your brains sucked out the base of your skull. Or," he pauses, staring me straight in the eyes, and waves his tied-up armless sleeve at me, "you could have had been dismembered, like *my mother tried to do to me!*"

I shake my head. *Shit, man, I'm just twenty-two.* And I don't understand all this yelling about abortion. Hell, I paid for three of them already. Not counting Oleena's, which—oh hell, I forgot!—it's today, her bitchy Momma came in to scream about yesterday, like her precious little girlie wasn't even there, or something, like I done conceived the kid by myself. God, and that'll be another couple hundred outta my seized bank account. Not going to have a thick nickel left, not after the abortion and the lawyers. Damn! The *dust-up* hit helped me forget it, and here this chicken shit Yankee Ay-rab has brought it back up in my head again! Suddenly I wish this guy had been thrown in with somebody else. Like Chavis down there, across the hall. The one screams all the time.

"You and I, my friend Lester, we are very lucky. Our mothers could have had us *terminated* in their very wombs, before we saw the light of day!"

I shrug. Didn't happen, why worry?

"I see your reaction, my friend," he says real quiet and slow. "You don't care, but I do. Didn't you hear what I said? *My mother tried to have me killed.*"

Seems like the Ay-rab community in Chicago had tried to tell Doc's old woman that if she had him, she'd be in deep shit back in the missing Middle East. So she went to a clinic—*abortuary*, Doc calls it and that sounds right, don't it? *Abort-you, wary?*—but the doc there screws up and cuts off his fetus-arm but he comes out anyway, in two pieces, and Doc Ahmid gets born right there on the table, and the nurse won't let the doc kill him once he's born, and his mom bleeds a lot and gets real sick and has to go home to Egypteria or some damn place to be with her family and she does and they kill her ass when she gets there. Baby Doc, he's in a state hospital ward and gets adopted by a real rich Mideastern oil dude and goes on to college and studies and gets a bunch of degrees and has the world by the balls.

"Quite right, Lester, until in graduate school I had an emergency operation and needed a transplant and a database search revealed my true parentage. As a bio-chemist, I analyzed my own reactions. As a molecular biologist, I recognized the futility of emotional involve-ment. But, try as I might, that one fact of my life has dominated my every waking moment since. My missing left arm won't let me forget—*my mother tried to have me killed!*"

Doc Ahmid did a hell of a lot of stuff in his thirty years, let me tell you. Built all those organ implants and replacements from molecules, made 'em cheap. Hell, my old Paw had a new pancreas grown right in place, thanks to an invention of Doc's here. Paw'd've like to've seen Doc and thanked him, but knowing Paw, he probably wouldn't shake no dark man's hand, no matter what the little dude had did for him. That's Paw, hell with him.

"You built them little *molly-cuties*, didn't you, Doc?" I ask. "That's where you got your Nobel Prize?"

Nodding, Doc smiles real wide. Missing a couple of teeth, I see. Deputy Bobby Lee was pretty rough on the little guy, musta really been pissed off. "I am happy to hear that word of my synthetic molecular devices, my *vireffectors*, has reached down here unto border Texas, Mr. Lester."

Hell, I only heard about them little molecular-sized robots in a Spanish & Western song, but I don't say anything to Doc, just nod and grin like I was wise or something. Them things had cured a lot of diseases, healed a lot of people. Doc is a real famous dude, and right here in my cell. Wait'll the guys down to the bar hear about this damned thing!

"I was not protesting, dear Mr. Lester, I was merely waiting outside the misspelled Ladie's Clinic to witness the results of my previous efforts in your fair county."

"Sounds like Deputy Bobby Lee don't like observers, you ask me, Doc."

He shrugs. "In all fairness, I must say I was standing with the ProLiferation Group, and they *were* protesting, quite vociferously."

I nod; the PG's are a nasty bunch. They've killed a whole slew of abortionists, burning down some of the clinics—*aborturaries*, to use Doc's new word—sometimes with the people still in them. On LiveCop TV, I even seen one of their "Life Squads" Uzi-down a whole row of Free Choicers and the cops that were supposed to be protecting them. At the public-TV execution the next day, one of them hollered out at the cameras while his damn neck was in the noose, "If we had done the same thing at Ouch-Wits, we'd be heroes, not criminals!" Don't know what the sucker meant, where that Ouch-place was, but they let him down kind of slow afterwards and he kicked and jerked for a whole god damn three minutes before he died. Tough son of a bitch.

I still have no idea why anybody wants to kill anybody. Too much fun in life to kill somebody. Besides, you do, you might wind up in a place like this, but for three or four years, 'stead of six to twelve months. Hope that damn fairy roomie I cut don't die out of that coma.

"So, you done some work down here before, Doc? With your *molly-cuties*?"

"Yes, Mr. Lester, I did. Specifically, I obtained a health worker certificate, served as a volunteer at the Ladie's Clinic, and surreptitiously administered some vireffector solutions to all of the young women who received abortions over the period of a week, about three months ago."

I smile real wide. Damn, this guy has got me going wild, thinking of the possibilities. That's what should have been done, all these years. Sterilize the bitches, kill the diseases with them little robots, and I don't have to worry no more about mutAIDS or little bastards or paying for abortions. Can screw my brains out, like my Paw got to do back in the Sexual Seventies, before all the genetics hit the fan (whatever that means). I say as much to Doc, thanking him for the chance to play the field, sow these oats far, wide and deep. But apparently he is not real happy with my philosophy.

He looks at his wrist watch, bites his bottom lip, looks away from me. Something is hurting him a lot, like he's going to cry.

"My dear, dear Lester, my friend. I'm afraid it's not so easy as all that."

"Meaning, Doc?"

"My objective was not to sterilize those women, it was to bond their mates to them, to re-create by vireffector technology a simpler version of all those social mores that at one time bound together men and women, that provided the stable platform from which whole, healthy families flourished."

"The ties that bound?" I venture.

Ahmid nods, sadly. "Maybe I was mistaken, but it is far too late now, I fear. Perhaps I should have surveyed the people of your region, of your cultural background, prior to attempting the experiment, maybe found an alternative solution. But I have already seeded my minions throughout the water supplies and food processing plants of every major metropolitan region around the world. I began my work with this isolated village, and I have returned to monitor the progress of my charges—"

"Minions? Charges?"

"Lester, I mean my vireffectors, the tiny mechanisms that—"

"They're like germs, insects? *Not* cute little robots that fix things up?"

"More like viruses, Lester, about the same dimensions as several of the larger species."

Viruses I don't like. Seen my friends wilt up and blow away, just from shooting up. Least that's not like them queers; a needle in the arm I can see. But something big and hard up your ass, no wonder they die from it. "What kind of virus, Doc? MutAIDS?" Damn, the little guy does that, infects the whole freaking world, he's a real mean son of a bitch. And for what? Sure hasn't stopped anybody from screwing, I mean, look at the bitches getting knocked up every day.

Like Oleena . . . I drop that thought. Serves her right.

"They are merely robots, Lester; simple, programmed machines, just built to reproduce themselves and follow orders."

"Great. I don't like viruses," I say, "But what do they do?"

"During intercourse—"

"*Fucking*, Doc?"

Ahmid sighs. "Yes, of course, Lester. The woman's vaginal fluids, saturated with my vireffectors, are attracted to the chemicals of the man's body—sweat, pre-seminal fluid, that kind of thing—and there they migrate, some of them, and there they stay."

"Like where? Like crabs?"

"No, much smaller. They propagate through the male's blood stream and lodge in several parts of the body, particularly in the nervous system. Some of them self-assemble into a microscopic-sized radio receiver in the gigahertz range."

"Doc, a fucking radio? What—"

"Hear me out, Lester. After such intercourse, when the woman's pregnancy has begun, and her own body chemistry undergoes great changes, then the vireffectors on her body regroup—some within the growing fetus, once it is large enough, and the remainder then relocate and assemble into a transmitter."

"Kind of the opposite of screwing, huh? This time she sends and he receives." Funny, I think. But suddenly it's not very. "A way to keep track of who the real dad is, I guess." Doc nods. That worries me, when I think of the couple of hundred bitches I been through over the years. Damn, but the child support! Could wipe a guy out!

"Doc, what if you get the wrong guy? I mean, she's sleeping around? You wouldn't want to track down the wrong dude, cause him trouble, if he's innocent?"

"The vaginal vireffectors are constantly changing, Mr. Lester, from hour to hour, from day to day, as they reconfigure themselves. If the woman has a dozen, er, *partners* over the period of a few hours, every one of them will receive his own, unique, specifically-encoded set of little friends."

"So? You're doing all of this to get child support? Doc, you are not a friend to Man." I smile weakly, thinking hard. This dumb son of a bitch needs to get what my last roomie got. He's going to cause one bunch of a lot of trouble for guys like me!

"Hmm," he says, "I really hadn't even thought of that aspect. It might even have worked, but . . . No, Mr. Lester, my little mechanisms are much more direct than that. As the child progresses in its mother's womb, its gross body conditions are monitored by its vireffectors, primarily the level of certain enzymes, and the body parts from which they emanate."

"That is?" By now, I'm not caring. Nobel Prize or no, one-armed or one-legged, little or not, I'm going to bust the little shit up, bad. He is tracking down guys that screw bitches, he is fucking *nuts*!

"The enzymes are very reliable indicators that the organism is experiencing pain."

This is beginning to worry me; I'm wondering how to make his death look like an accident. No—the result of Deputy Bob's beating. Now that idea really kills two birds with one stoned! "So, Doc, the kid hurts, the old woman feels the pain?"

Ahmid whispers. "Not quite. Her small set of receivers just picks up the signal from the unborn child. Remember, Lester, I said that inside the mother, the vireffectors mostly construct *transmitters*."

"But where does she send it? The world's a big place!"

"Just a few hundred miles straight up—the Global Information Skyway satellites."

"I don't get it; she's got receivers, she's gotta feel the kid's hurt, right?"

"I'm not so cruel as that, Lester. No, the poor mothers who kill their babies will suffer enough as it is." He's looking at me with eyes that must be like Jesus has, full of pity, like you'd look at a dog that's been run over and is still alive and you don't want to kill the wriggling thing but you have to.

Chavis across the hall starts to whoop and holler, "My fucking *leg! Gahhhh!*" Deputy Bobby Lee comes running in, looks into the cell, where we can't see, and spits in disgust.

"Lousy damn Mexie junkie, nothing wrong with you . . ." Deputy Bob's voice drops off, then he kind of gags and he runs back to the office, puking his guts out.

Doc is in a kind of trance, don't react at all to the shrieking down the hall. "The pain the baby feels during abortion, the mother receives and transmits it to the GIS. It sends the unique signals to the unique receiver of the male."

"*He* feels the pain!"

Like some kind of weird echo, I hear screaming from the front office. I find a weak smile down deep inside somewhere; always thought Deputy Bobby Lee was getting a lot on the side.

Doc checks his watch again. "My, but the abortionists are going fast and furious today. I really planned on being at the site, but it seems that a county jail is much better to determine the effects on the fathers."

I've been too *dusted-up* to realize what the Doc has done, but then it hits me, what's happening. I stumble and fall, back on the bottom bunk. The little deadly dude has come to check out his *experiment*, he calls it, and all us guys here in the County, we are his fucking lab rats! And, oh *shit!* Oleena's going in to the Ladie's Clinic today, and they're gonna whack the kid. Meanwhile, the gagging orderlies are down the hall scraping up chunks of Chavis—I can hear the *slop! slop!* of the guts hitting the bucket—and Doc Ahmid is muttering out loud to himself.

"Salt burning, vivisection, amputation, cerebral suction—the men who wantonly doom their children to such a cruel fate will have the pleasure of sharing their baby's short and miserable life. The feminists should love me for this. I think the results should even be good enough that the father might suffer not only the pain, but the actual physical damage.

"Just and balanced, don't you think, Mr. Lester?"

"Why, Doc?" I ask meekly, my whole body shaking

and wondering what the hell is going to happen and when. *"Why the Hell, Doc!"*

"Why, Mr. Lester? To change the world, to promote responsibility. From today on, there will be no innocents murdered without retribution, no children conceived without a lifetime commitment, no one-night stands without repercussions. Finally, all men—like the one who abandoned *me*—are going to *pay!*"

The Nobel Prize winner is smiling a crazy smile at me when something *slams* up the back of my skull and I can feel in a real weird way, my brain being sucked out a hole. Blood or something is gushing out and it hurts like holy hell.

"Oh, not you, too, Mr. Lester," Doc seems genuinely shocked as warm liquids run down my back. "I am sorry, but—right now, your innocent baby is feeling the same."

Unable to move, even to feel anger, I lie and wait for my life to drain away. "You have trapped all of us, every fucking guy in the world, Doc," I whisper, the pain overtaking everything else, except the fear.

The last thing I hear is Doc Ahmid, the angel of my death, saying, "Ah, Mr. Lester, for once your gross and vulgar language is precisely correct!"

STATESMEN

POUL ANDERSON

An hour before midnight, a warehouse van turned off the dirt road it had been following and nosed into the forest. The way it took was hardly more than a path, and seldom used. Leaves, fronds, drooping lianas rustled aside from its bulk and closed again behind. After ten meters or so the van was altogether screened off. Its air drive sighed away to silence and it crouched down on its jacks. The rear end dilated. A dozen men climbed out. One of them stumbled in the thick gloom and cursed.

"Taisez-vous!" Otto Geibel's voice was as low as the chance of their being overheard, but the command crackled. He glanced about. Seen through light-amplifying goggles, shapes were nonetheless blurred, and the gear they carried made their outlines all the more strange. He knew them, though, and they had rehearsed this operation often enough. *"Alignez-vous. Allons."*

The pathway was almost familiar as he led them on along its winding upwardness. They had practiced with visual simulations. Of course, the minicameras carried by scouts disguised as ordinary *camponeses* had not recorded every rock or root or puddle, nor the weight of heat and humidity. Sometimes they blundered a little. The climb was stiff, too, and presently harsh breathing drowned out the hoots, clicks, chirrs of a tropical wood.

Yet they reached the heights in good order, about 0100. After that the going was easy. They emerged on pavement, deserted at this time of night, and it brought them to a clearing cut out of the parkland for picnickers.

73

From there they got a look at their target, with no further need of artificial eyesight.

Otto Geibel took a moment to admire the whole view. It was superb. Overhead gleamed stars the northern hemisphere can only envy. Below, the hills fell darkling. A hollow enclosed the Vieyra plant. Softly lit, its cluster of reaction domes and catalytic towers might have been woven by spiders and jeweled with dew for the King of Elfland's daughter. Beyond, the terrain continued its descent and lights clustered ever more brightly until they ran together in a sprawl of glitter that was Niterói. Past that city sheened the bay, and then the radiance of Rio de Janeiro exploded on the opposite shore. A darkness heaved athwart it, Corcovado. When he had switched his goggles to a few X magnification, he saw the Christ on top of the peak.

But there was work to do. The sooner they did it and scuttled back to the van, the likelier they'd reach that scramjet which waited to carry them back to Trieste. Not that they had much to fear. Their mission had been conceived by the great Advisor.

Otto Geibel issued the orders he had issued in every rehearsal. Men sprang about, unburdened one another, set up the launch rack and loaded it. The six small rockets glimmered wan beneath the Milky Way, wasps ready to fly. The stings they bore were also small, and their bodies would burn in the conflagration they kindled; but they sufficed—they sufficed. Geibel himself took over the keyboard and told the computer which missile should strike what part of the synthesizer complex.

Joy shuddered through him. *Schadenfreude*, he admitted to himself. Besides, the fireworks would be glorious in their own right.

A whirring ripped at his ears. He flung his glance aloft. Shadows broke from the shadowing crowns of the forest and flitted across the stars. Men with flyer packs, he knew. Sickness stunned him. *"Parem!"* roared a bullhorn, and more Portuguese, a shrill thunder.

A man close by—Petrović, he recognized with the sureness and helplessness of nightmare—snatched forth a sidearm and fired upward. A gun chattered back.

Petrović collapsed on the grass. Impossibly much blood welled from the heap of him, black by starlight. More shots stitched flame along the edge of the clearing, a warning not to attempt escape. "*Rendez-vous*," Geibel called to his men, around the fist in his gullet. He raised his own hands. Air drives boomed loud as the Brazilians descended on the Europeans.

The ghost of Friedrich Hohenzollern, who had been the second king of that name in Prussia, thought for a moment, stroking his chin, before he advanced his queen's bishop. "*Échec*," he murmured.

In front of the holotank, responding to the electronics, a material chessman glided across a board. That could have been simply another display, but Jules Quinet preferred to feel his pieces between his fingers when he moved them. He leaned forward, a stocky man with gray-shot curly hair, and studied the changed configuration. "*Nom du diable*," he growled.

"It will be mate in five moves," Friedrich said. His French was flawlessly Parisian, or perhaps better termed Versaillais, of the eighteenth century.

Quinet's modern Lyonnais contrasted roughly. "Oh? You do have me in a bad position, but I would not agree it is hopeless."

Silence caused him to raise his eyes. The image in the tank, life-size, was of a short man who had once been rather handsome in a long-featured fashion and was aging dry. A powdered wig decked his head. On an old blue uniform with red facings there was—yes, by God—again a scattering of snuff. Brows had slightly lifted above a very steady gaze.

Quinet remembered what the king expected. "Sire," he added. "I beg your majesty's pardon if I forgot myself."

Friedrich deigned to give him a faint smile. "Well, we can play the game out if you insist," he said, using the familiar pronoun, "but you will learn more if you hear me explain, and thus become a more interesting opponent."

Not for the first time, Quinet swallowed indignation. He, chief of the project's computer section, he who had

conjured this simulacrum up and could with a few depro-
gramming strokes dismiss it back to nothingness—he
should not have to let it patronize him. Briefly, he considered at least removing the subdued elegance of the room
in a Sanssouci that also no longer existed. He could
invent a reason. Though Friedrich showed a lively curiosity about the science and technology that had resurrected
him, he had not actually learned more than a few catch-
phrases of the sort that any layman knew. Punish the
bastard—

But no, that would be petty, and if the directors found
out, Quinet would be in trouble; and in any event, probably Friedrich would shrug the loss off. He took everything so coolly.

"You are very kind, sire," Quinet said.

"Oh, I shall want a favor in return," Friedrich
answered. "More material on the historical development
and present state of that quite fascinating Han Commercial Sphere, plus a command of its principal language."

A sharp tone interrupted. He frowned. Quinet's pulse
accelerated. "Pardon, sire," he blurted, "but that is the
priority signal. Some matter of the utmost importance
requires your majesty's attention."

Friedrich's expression, always closely controlled, took
on a trace of eagerness. He enjoyed the challenges Eurofac handed him. The expectation that he would have
been a major factor in the decision to recreate him,
rather than someone else. Quinet had argued for Napoléon I. . . .

He swung his chair about and touched Accept. The
eidophone came aglow with an image as lifelike as the
king's; but this was of a solid person. Birgitte Geibel's
severe visage, gray hair, and black suit matched the
glimpse of her apartment in Magdeburg. Quinet sat in
Lyon. The software of the Friedrich program was—
someplace known to those few people who had a need
to know.

Quinet rose and bowed. "Madame," he murmured.
Respectfulness was wise. She was among the directors of
Eurofac. The South American campaign had started
largely at her instigation and was still largely under her

supervision. Friedrich himself was something she had had manufactured to serve her with advice.

"*Setzen Sie sich,*" she snapped. Quinet obeyed. He knew her tongue fairly well. To Friedrich, who had not stirred, she continued in German: "We have a crisis. Your plan has miscarried."

Leaning back in his unreal gilt-and-scrolled chair, the king again raised his brows. However, he had learned early on that to insist on formalities from her was to generate unnecessary friction. After all, she was a kind of monarch herself, and in his old realm. He responded in her language, though he regarded it as limited and uncouth, and used the polite pronoun. "To which plan does the gracious lady refer? I have devised a number of them for you over the years, and guided most through to reasonably successful completion."

"The latest. That damned attempt to sabotage Vieyra e Filhos—their synthesis plant at Niterói, that is. The raiders have been intercepted. Those that were not killed are now captive." Geibel drew breath and pinched lips together. It burst from her: "The leader was my son Otto."

"Now that is hard news," Friedrich said, almost too softly to hear. His tone sharpened. "What was that idiot doing on such an expedition? Why did you permit it? Have you never heard of an enemy taking vital hostages? And what does he know to reveal to them?"

Perhaps no one else in the world could have spoken thus to Birgitte Geibel without suffering for it. She replied grimly, equal to equal. "I did not permit it. In fact, when he asked to go, I forbade him. He went behind my back, claimed he had my consent and that I wanted him in command." Humanness flickered. "He is a romantic by nature, no, a warrior born. He should have been a knight of Karl the Great or Friedrich Barbarossa. This stagnation they call peace—" She broke off.

Friedrich Hohenzollern scowled. "Your people are still more ill organized than I realized, it seems. I cannot oversee everything." His smile flashed stark. "How shall this phantom of me ride forth into the streets among the commoners, or onto the battlefield among the soldiers?

I deal only in words and images, or information as you call them nowadays, for that is all I myself am. Well, provide me."

He reached into his coat, took out an enameled snuffbox, opened it, brought a pinch to his nostrils. Geibel could not quite hide distaste. Quinet wondered whether Friedrich really sensed, really savored, the tobacco, or anything else. If you wrote a program—no, better, developed or created a program—no, ordered one, because so immense a task must needs be carried out by supercomputers—if you brought such a program into being, based on everything ever recorded about the life and times of a man long dead, a program that supposedly thought and acted as he would have thought and acted, given the limitations of the electronics—you necessarily included his habits, mannerisms, vices—but what *did* truly go on inside the re-enactments?

Quinet realized his mind had wandered. Into the most puerile metaphysics, at that. Shame on him. He was a top-rank computerman, a logician, a rationalist, a Frenchman.

He longed for his old briar pipe.

"When the commando had not returned to their van by dawn, the driver concluded something had gone wrong and took it back to the garage," Geibel was saying. "The Vieyra facility is unharmed. No newscast has mentioned any incident. However, when an agent of ours went to the site from which the missiles were to have been launched, he found a detachment of militia on guard, and with difficulty persuaded them he was a harmless passerby. They spoke of being on patrol against saboteurs. The militia has in fact been partly mobilized of late, though quietly. Our agents in place knew this, of course, but considered it rather a farce. Evidently they were wrong."

Friedrich nodded. "It is a perennial mistake, underestimating one's opposition. I had my nose rubbed in that near Prague, in 1744. What more can you tell me?"

"Essentially nothing, so far."

"Then how can you be sure of the fate of your son and his men?"

"What else can have happened? He was too rash, the Brazilians were too alert." Lips tightened anew. "I can only hope he lives. You will set about getting him back."

Friedrich gave her a prolonged stare. After half a minute she flushed and said in a strangled voice, "My apologies, your majesty. I am overwrought. May I beg for your counsel and assistance?"

The king took a second pinch of snuff and sneezed delicately. "You shall have it, my lady, to the extent of my incorporeal abilities. Kindly have me furnished the relevant data in full, including especially the identities of your agents within the Vieyra corporate hierarchy and the Brazilian government, together with the codes for contacting them. Dr. Quinet will know how to put this into assimilable form for me. Naturally, I am to be apprised of any fresh developments. Not that I anticipate significant news in the near future. Plain to see, our enemy has become too shrewd for hastiness. My advice for the moment is that you cultivate equanimity, and make certain that neither you nor any of your colleagues orders any precipitate action." He lifted his forefinger. "Curbing them may well keep you occupied. Despite everything I have told you people, nowhere in the world today does there appear to exist more than the rudiments of a proper general staff."

Geibel knotted a fist already gnarled. "If they have harmed my son—"

"Compose yourself, madame. Unless he was hurt during the arrest, I expect the Brazilians know enough to treat him carefully. They have, at last, obtained informed leadership."

Almost, she gaped. "What?"

Again Friedrich smiled. "This fiasco of ours confirms me in a suspicion I have entertained increasingly for some time. They must have come to an understanding of what Eurofac has done, and have done the same thing, to become so effective against us. It is a most interesting riddle, whom they have reconstructed to be their own guiding genius."

He raised his palm and added, through a shocked silence: "Now, if you please, my lady, you can best leave me to think about this undistracted. Unless something extraordinary occurs, I will not give myself the honor of receiving your calls, or anyone's, until—hm—forty-eight hours hence. Good day."

Geibel caught her breath but blanked her image.

Quinet stirred. Friedrich looked his way. That gave an eerie feeling, when what the ghost actually "saw" was a ghost of the man, a modulation in the ongoing computer processes. "No, bide a moment, monsieur," the king said in French. "Since we shall be working closely together again, you and I, we had better make various things clear to each other. I can profit from an explanation more detailed than hitherto of electronic communication procedures, especially those that must be kept secret."

"And I'd like to know what this is all about, sire!" Quinet exclaimed.

"*Hein?* This is your world. I am the alien, the anachronism."

"I'm a computerman, not a politician," Quinet said. "Oh, I follow the news, but these intrigues and maneuverings, they're not my métier. Besides, so much is undercover, and I'm hardly ever briefed on it. What is this about a raid in Brazil?"

Instead of reprimanding him directly for this bluntness, Friedrich replied after an elaborate sigh, "Well, as an employee of the Eurofac alliance, you should know—you do, don't you?—that it seeks to take over the large, lucrative South American economic sphere, which has been dominated by Brazilian interests. In part this is for the sake of its own aggrandizement, in part to forestall a takeover by one of the great commercial powers such as Australia, Nigeria, or the Han. That would bring the nations of Europe a long way further down the road to complete impotence in world affairs. Is that clear?"

Having put the living man in his place, the revenant relented and went on: "You have observed how well the penetration proceeded at first, under my general guidance. But in the past two or three years, you have at least caught hints that our halcyon season is ending. Eurofac has increasingly met with difficulties and outright reversals. For example, recently the Ecuadorians were induced—somehow—to-bar the ships of Nordisk Havdyrkning from their territorial waters—a serious blow to your pelagiculture in that part of the world.

"Not only are the Brazilian corporations cooperating more and more effectively, which is a natural reaction to foreign competition, but they have begun to invoke the aid of their own government, and governments elsewhere on their continent. *That* is unheard of.

"The recruitment of a citizen militia to supplement the national police is one recent development, one that it now appears we did not take seriously enough. I see with hindsight that our mistake was due to the effort being marvelously soft-played. Those comic opera dress uniforms, for example, ah, that was sheer brilliance of deception!"

Quinet nodded. "I do know something about the general situation, sire. I could scarcely avoid that." He also knew that sometimes Friedrich loved to hear himself talk. "But a raid? An actual military attack?"

"We have used force, in different guises, when it was indicated," Friedrich said. Through Quinet passed a brief outrage. He had caused and he maintained the existence of this quasi-creature; but only by accident did he ever learn what it really did for his employers. "The *ultima ratio regum*. A major reason why you have played out your economic rivalries so clumsily in this century is that you have not understood they are, in actuality, as political as the dynastic quarrels of my era. Wealth is simply a means toward power.

"Well. Vieyra & Sons is the most important chemosynthetic firm in Brazil, which is to say South America; and the Niterói plant is the keystone of its activities. If these are cut back, Brazil will have to import much of its materials."

Quinet seized the chance to repeat the obvious in his turn. "Not only organics. Everything dependent on nanotechnic reactions. That includes most heavy industry."

Friedrich shrugged. "I leave the technicalities to your natural philosophers. Brazil would be weakened. Indeed, by becoming a principal supplier, Eurofac would have entry to the very heart of its rivals. Attempts to foment labor trouble did not get far, largely because of the nationalism that is being skillfully cultivated there. But the plant was known to be weakly guarded. Light artillery could easily demolish it. The assault was planned so that its results might well have been laid at the door of radicals in the native labor movement.

"*Hélas*, the militia we despised choked it off. What the Brazilians will do next depends on who it is that makes their plans for them. We greatly need to know his identity, Dr. Quinet. Have you any suggestions for finding it out?"

"N-no, sire." The man sat back, rubbed his brow, said slowly, "That network will have no interface whatsoever with yours, of course. Just the same—I must think."

"As must I." Gusto tinged Friedrich's voice, like the far-off cry of a hunter's horn in an autumnal forest four hundred years ago. "Yes, let us postpone your education of me for a day or two. I need peace, quiet, and . . . many history books."

"All scholarly databases will be at your disposal, sire. You know how to access them." That was a rather complicated procedure, when this computer system must remain isolated from all others. Quinet rose from his chair like a dutiful commoner. "Does your majesty wish anything else?"

"Not at once. You may go."

The holotank turned into an emptiness where luminance swirled vague. Friedrich could order a cutoff when he chose.

He could not block a monitor, if that keyboard lay under knowing hands. Curious, Quinet recalled the image and, unbeknownst, watched for a while.

Friedrich had crossed the room to the ghost of a marble-topped table set against Chinese-patterned wallpaper. A flute lay on it. He carried the instrument back to his chair, sat down, and began to play. It was one of his own compositions; Quinet, who had perforce studied his subject exhaustively, recognized that much. The musician's eyes were turned elsewhere. They seemed full of dreams. Friedrich II, king of Prussia, whom his English allies had called Frederick the Great, was thinking.

* * *

Otto Geibel knew that wondering where he was would be an exercise in futility. A viewpane showed him a thronged white strand and great green-and-white surf, Copacabana or Ipanema seen from an upper floor of a bayside hotel. That could as easily be relayed as directly presented. Since rousing from narcosis, he had seen only rooms and corridors within a single large building. The few persons he met were surely all Brazilians, small and dark when set against his blond bulk, though their semi-formal clothes, their quietness and reserve, were disturbingly unlike that nationality. They accorded him chill politeness and kept him well aware that somebody armed was always nearby, watching.

João Aveiro entered his world like a sea breeze. The chamber to which Geibel had been brought was cheerful too. Besides that beach scene, it had a holo of a particularly seductive danseuse performing to sensuous drum rhythms, several comfortable loungers, and a small but expensively stocked bar. Aveiro was slender, quick-moving, lavish with smiles, ferocious only in his mustache and the colors of his sports shirt.

"Ah, welcome, Mister Geibel," he said when the wall had closed upon the guards. Undoubtedly they stood vigilant at a survey screen just outside and could re-enter in two seconds at the slightest sign of trouble. Aveiro used English. That had proved to be the language in which he and the prisoner were both reasonably fluent. "How are you? I hope you are well recovered from your bad experience."

The German made himself shake hands. "Your people treated me well enough, under the circumstances," he replied. "Food, sleep, a bath, clean clothes."

"And now what would you like to drink before lunch?"

"Where the hell is the rest of my company?" Geibel rasped. "What are you going to *do* with us?"

"Ah, that is—what shall I say?—*contingente*. Rest assured, we are civilized here. We respond with moderation to what I must say was an unfriendly act."

Geibel bristled. "Moderation? I saw a man killed."

Aveiro's manner bleakened for an instant. "You would

have killed a dozen night-shift technicians." He brought back the smile, took Geibel's elbow, guided him gently toward a seat. "I am glad to tell you your follower was in revivable condition and is now recovering under cell restoration therapy. Do relax. If we are opponents, we can still be honorable opponents, and work toward negotiating an end of this unfortunate conflict. What refreshment would you like? Me, I will have a brandy and soda. Our brandy has less of a reputation internationally than it deserves."

Geibel yielded and lowered himself. "Beer, then, please." With an effort: "Brazilian beer is good, too."

"Thank you. We learned from German brewmasters, centuries ago." Aveiro bustled to the bar and occupied himself.

"You know who I am," Geibel said.

Aveiro nodded. "The identification you carried was cleverly made, but we have developed our intelligence files. The family that, in effect, rules over A/G Vereinigten Bioindustrien, and sits high in the councils of the Eurofac syndicate—no matter how they strive to keep their privacy, members of that family are public figures." His dispassionate tone grew lively again. "Once we would have been less . . . snoopy? But, excuse my saying this, Eurofac has forced us to revive old practices, old institutions. Such as an intelligence agency. For have you not been mounting—what the Yankees in their day called covert operations?"

Geibel resisted the lounger's body-conforming embrace and sat straight. "But who are you?"

"We were introduced, if you recall."

"*What* are you, Herr Aveiro?"

"Oh, I suppose you could call me an officer of intelligence."

"Police? Military? Or—uh—"

"Or of the *ad hoc* coordinating committee that our businesses established when the European threat became unmistakable? Does it matter which? Perhaps later it will, and I shall have occasion to tell you. Meanwhile—" Aveiro had prepared the drinks. He brought over a full stein, raised his own glass, and toasted, *"Prosit."*

"*Saúde*," Geibel responded, not to be outdone.

The Brazilian laughed, sipped, perched himself on the edge of a seat confronting the other man's, leaned forward. Beneath the geniality, he shivered and strained the slightest bit. "Shall we talk, then, two professionals together? Afterward I promise you a memorable lunch."

Geibel grimaced and forced wryness: "I am hardly a professional."

"No. Molecular engineer by training, am I right? Yes, I sympathize with you. I strongly suspect you consider yourself an idealist, who wants to further the welfare of his people. Well, pure motives are no substitute for proper training." Aveiro sighed. "Not that I can claim real expertise. We are amateurs. Everywhere in the world, we are amateurs, fumbling at a game that grows more dangerous the longer we play."

"What?" asked Geibel, startled.

The little man had, mercurially, turned quite serious. "We tell ourselves today—we have told ourselves for several generations—true war has become unthinkable. The former great powers are dead or dying or three-fourths asleep. The violent clashes are between backward countries, and poverty, if nothing else, limits them in the harm they can do. The active nations, the new leaders of the world, jostle for economic advantage only. How nice, no? How desirable. What progress beyond the old horrors.

"But this is a very limited planet onto which we are crowded, my friend. The minerals and energy we get from space, the recyclings of nanotechnology, such things are not in infinite supply, nor are they free of cost, nor do they satisfy the wish for . . . elbow room, and self-expression, and ethnic survival, and, *sim*, power."

He drank before finishing: "Whether the corporations be agencies of the state or property of certain groups, of the new aristocrats—that makes no difference. Always the strife grows more and more vicious. Nuclear war is perhaps out of the question; so too, perhaps, are huge armies making whole continents their battlefields; but history knows other kinds of war than these. As witness your attempt on us."

"You are ... philosophical, ... senhor," Geibel said from the back of his throat, while fear touched him.

"I am realistic," Aveiro answered. "And I am a Brazilian. Patriotism is no longer obsolete."

He produced his smile. "Well, but we are honest soldiers in our ways, you and I, no? We can talk frankly. I may tell you, my government is willing to forgive your actions—although they do constitute a grave crime, you understand—We are willing to release you and your men, discreetly, in hopes that the good will we gain will help toward improving relations."

For two heartbeats, Geibel's pulse bounded. He looked into the face before him, and the hope sank. "What do you want in exchange?" he whispered. His sweat smelled suddenly sharp.

Aveiro swirled the ice about in his glass while he stared into it. "That, we must work out," he said. "It may take time. We need to learn so much. We are so inept these days, all of us. After generations of nominal peace, the world has forgotten how to wage war intelligently. Our intrigues and outright hostilities are on a primitive, medieval-like level. Yes, histories and treatises on the arts of war lie in our databases; but who is practiced in the *use* of those principles?"

Freezingly, Geibel foreknew what was coming. Yet he must pretend. "You are being, uh, too academic for me again, I fear. What do you want of me?"

Aveiro looked up, caught his captive's gaze, and gripped it. His words fell like stones. "The Yankees developed a remarkable computer technology about ten years ago. You know it well. Everybody does. Electronic reincarnation, no, rebirth. The sensationalism in news and entertainment media. The speeches and sermons. The jokes. The attempts to hire the technique for purposes cheap or perverted or, sometimes, noble. In between, the patient scholarship, piece by piece discovering a little more about the past.

"Let us not do what the Yankees call pussyfoot, Mister Geibel. What one consortium can accomplish, another can repeat. We know that Eurofac has found how to create its own simulacrum. Surely you never believed that could remain secret forever. The hints, the revelations, the bits of accidental information that we jigsaw-puzzle together. The fact that Eurofac's operations had become sophisticated, so unscrupulous, that we were being driven out of the market on our home continent.

"Yes, you have resurrected an advisor from the past, someone who understands in his bones those arts of combat and cabal that to us today are half-forgotten theory. Doubtless it amuses him to guide you. Such a—an *espirito* must feel rather detached from we who are still flesh and blood. No? But you can see, Mister Geibel, although we cannot at the moment make you cancel his existence, it would be most helpful to us if we knew who he is. Then we could better plan our tactics.

"Will you please tell me?"

The silence smothered. Into it Geibel croaked, "Do you have somebody too, now?"

"Be that as it may," said Aveiro, "we wish to know the name of your counselor."

Geibel grabbed his stein from the lounger arm, clutched hard the handle, tossed off a draught. Cold comfort ran down his gullet. "I admit nothing," he declared. "I know nothing."

Aveiro shook himself, as though coming out of a dark river. "Forgive me," he replied almost calmly. "I should have avoided those sociological topics. They make me too emotional. I remember too much that I have witnessed." He sipped, arched his brows above the rim of the glass, chuckled. "After all, the matter is quite simple. You will tell me whatever you know, which I suspect does include that name. You will." He waved his free hand. "Oh, not under torture. Our advisor—I may tell you this—our advisor suggested it, but of course better methods are available today. They seldom do permanent harm. However, they are most unpleasant.

"Therefore, my esteemed opponent, will you answer certain questions? Naturally, there must be verification, as well as further questions, before we can consider bargaining about your release. But today I shall assume you speak truth. Or will you be stubborn and compel me to send you on to the interrogation technicians? That would be regrettable for both of us. I have been anticipating an amicable gourmet lunch with you."

The ghost of Niccolò Machiavelli looked up from the book he was reading when the image of Floriano Coelho appeared in the mirage-room where he sat. "Good day, senhor," he said with his wonted courtliness. "You are punctual." Mild malice flickered: "That is somewhat uncharacteristic of your countrymen."

Coelho laughed. "Computers are Procrustean, your excellency," he replied. "They shape those of us who work with them to fit a single planetwide society and its ways."

Outside the tank, his body settled into a chair. His replica within remained standing. It was, after all, merely an interplay of electrons, photons, and fields. Sufficient to have a subprogram duplicate movements, especially facial movements, that were significant. Machiavelli understood, and accepted it of his visitors—most of them. The chief computerman could, in fact, have stayed at home and watched a screen there. However, that would have added a link to the network, and one that was vulnerable to tapping by the Europeans. Instead, he came to the laboratory in person whenever he had business with the Florentine.

Machiavelli laid his book aside. "I have said this before, but will repeat myself," he told the Brazilian. "Your superiors showed a perceptiveness that, in retrospect, astonishes me, when they put you in charge of this quasi-resurrection of mine—a man who not only knows that art, but is a classicist. The level of culture that I have observed in this era, among the supposedly educated, is appalling."

"Thank you," Coelho said. "Perhaps science and technology have engaged the world's attention too much during the past three or four centuries. Perhaps we can learn from notables like you."

"That is the purpose, isn't it, as regards war and statecraft?" Machiavelli responded dryly.

Coelho persisted. He had discovered that the great political thinker was not immune to a little flattery and, when in the right mood, would talk fascinatingly for hours about his Renaissance milieu. He had known Lorenzo the Magnificent, Cesare Borgia, Leonardo da Vinci . . . in his lifetime, Columbus sailed, Luther defied Rome, Copernicus followed the planets in their courses. . . . "I hope we can learn half as fast, and adapt ourselves to strangeness half as well, as your excellency did."

Machiavelli shrugged. "Let me not claim more credit than is due me. I was only nominally a Christian, you know. To me, man had reached his highest condition— no doubt the highest of which he will ever be briefly capable—in pagan Rome. It was no fundamental shock to me, *this* me, to awaken after death and hear that the mind is simply a process in the material world, a process that can be replicated after a fashion if one knows enough about it. The rest of the newness has been minor by comparison, albeit interesting."

Staring into the tank, Coelho thought reluctantly how ugly the man was, huge beak of a nose on a head too small. At least his voice was low and beautifully modulated. Today Machiavelli's simulacrum had electronically ordered the simulacrum of a red velvet robe and fur slippers. The room around him was marble-floored beneath a rich carpet; frescos of nymphs and satyrs adorned it; a window opened on the fields and poplars of Tuscany. A crystal bowl at the chairside held nuts and sweetmeats. You could provide a recreated mind with recreated sensations. This one had demanded them as soon as it learned they were possible.

Still, Machiavelli was a gourmet rather than a gourmand—for the most part—and his mind was what counted. "May I ask you something touching yourself?" Coelho ventured.

Machiavelli grinned. "You may. I will choose whether to answer."

"Well, ah, I see the title of that book you are reading. Another biography of Federigo the Great."

"Certainly. I cannot know too much about my rival counterpart, now that we have finally discovered who he is."

"But why a projected book? We can program—we can give you all the information you want, directly, there in your memory as if it had always been, just as we gave you a command of our modern language."

"I know. For some purposes, the convenience is undeniable. But men today confuse information with comprehension. Knowledge should enter at a natural pace, never outstripping reflection upon it. Also—" Machiavelli reached to stroke the cover "—I find the act of reading, of holding a book and turning its pages, a pleasure in itself. Books, the bearers of thoughts, the heritage of the mighty dead, those were my last friends during the years of rustication. Oh, and letters; but you have not revived my dear Vettori to correspond with me. Old friends are best."

His tone had been almost impersonal, free of self-pity, but Coelho got a sudden sense of loneliness without bounds or end. Even though Machiavelli had been spiritually solitary throughout his life—Best to change the subject. Besides, Coelho had his instructions. "You must understand Federigo quite well by now, as intensely as you have studied him." It helped that that study didn't have to take place in real time; you could accelerate the program when it wasn't talking with flesh and blood. Furthermore, it didn't sleep. It did remain human enough to require occasional diversions.

"A formidable opponent. Like Alexander the Great, he inherited a military machine built by his father; but, also like Alexander, he wielded it audaciously and inspiredly, he raised his Prussia from a backwater to the first rank of the European powers." Machiavelli snickered. "A delicious jest, that he, precisely he, should be the one against whom your superiors decided to pit me. Do you think they knew?"

"What do you mean, your excellency?"

"Why, as a young man this Federigo wrote a treatise explicitly meant to refute me, the *Anti-Machiavel*. In it he said a prince is no more than the first servant of the people, and the state exists to further their well-being, not for its own sake. Whereupon, once he became king, he followed my teachings word for word."

Coelho frowned. He had been doing some reading himself. "Didn't he reform the laws, better the lot of the poor, carry out large public works?"

Machiavelli's grin stretched wider. "Just as I counsel in *Il Principe*, the *Discorsi*, and elsewhere. Beneficence is sound policy when it does not seriously interfere with the necessities of power. I presume you are aware that, while he stripped the nobles of their own last meaningful powers, he did not free the serfs. He acquired Silesia by force of arms and partook in the dismemberment of Poland. Not that I condemn him, you understand. He laid the foundations of the German state that Bismarck would build. In person he was a man of refined tastes and a composer of some small talent. I admit it was a mistake importing Voltaire to his court, but a minor one. On the whole, yes, I rather wish he had been a fifteenth-century Italian." The ugly countenance turned grave, the sharp gaze drifted afar. "Then he could well have become the prince for whom I pleaded, he who would unite poor Italy against the foreigners that made booty of her—" He threw back his head and laughed. "Ah, well, since in fact he was an eighteenth-century German, I must content myself with welcoming so worthy a foe."

Coelho stirred. "That's what I'm here about, as your excellency has doubtless guessed," he said. "To ask if you have any new plans."

"Why does not Senhor Aveiro or one of the other councillors address me in person?"

"They wish to avoid any appearance of . . . unduly pressing you. This is such a basic revelation, Federigo's identity. And I am the person most familiar to you."

Machiavelli nodded. "They're afraid of my getting balky, are they?"

"Your suggestions to date have proven invaluable. We need more."

"You already have them. Now that Eurofac knows your militia is a force to reckon with, strengthen it quickly. Bring it entirely out into the eyes of the world. Make it something every young Brazilian dreams of joining. Fan the national spirit to a brighter and hotter flame. Aid the Chileans and Peruvians to do likewise—but not to the same extent as yourselves, for you don't want those peoples to start resenting your predominance. Discourage the emotion among the Argentines; they are your natural rivals. Bind the small countries that border yours more closely to you as client states, and through them work to counteract the Europeans in Argentina and keep that nation disunited. In short, Senhor Coelho, my word to your superiors is that they pay closer attention to the large corpus of recommendations I have printed out for them. Policies cannot be executed overnight. What I have just mentioned is the work of another decade, at least."

"But surely—the information about Federigo suggests something more?"

"Indeed it does. First and foremost, I would like to meet with him, often."

Coelho gaped. "What? Impossible!"

Machiavelli lifted his brows. "Really? When I see your image here in this chamber of mine? Incidentally, floating about ten centimeters off the floor."

"That is . . . we've taken care to keep the system that maintains you entirely isolated. . . . Oh, the connection could be made, if the Europeans agreed. But neither side will."

"Why not?"

"Well, if nothing else, at present they don't know about you. That's an advantage we can't afford to forego. And both sides would fear, oh, sabotage—ah— Imagine poison slyly given you. No, your excellency, it's out of the question. Has anything else occurred to you?"

Machiavelli grimaced, spread his hands in an Italianate gesture, then said, quite businesslike: "Minor ideas. And you do need something to report, my friend, lest you be reprimanded for lack of diligence. No? Well, I have explained, and you are starting to obtain, the benefits of a revived national spirit and a government that takes an active role in all affairs."

"There are those who wonder about that," Coelho muttered. "The camel's nose in the tent—" Aloud: "Please continue."

"Now nationalism has two faces," said Machiavelli in the manner of a lecturer. "There is the positive side, patriotism, love of country, that you have been cultivating. And there is the negative side, contempt or hatred for foreigners. You Brazilians have been too tolerant, too cosmopolitan. Therefore Eurofac could easily penetrate your marts and undermine your state. It would be a body blow to the Eurofac oligopolies if Brazilians ceased buying their wares and services. But their prices equal or undercut yours. Therefore you need different motives for Brazilians to shun them. If it became unfashionable to wear European clothes, travel in European vehicles, employ European machinery and craftsmen—Do you see? This will happen in the course of time as Europeans themselves become loathed."

"But they don't loathe us," Coelho protested.

"No, evidently not. Eurofac is merely a . . . a Hansa, to borrow the medieval German word. Since you have nothing comparable, you must find something else to oppose it. You must rouse the will of South Americans generally against it. That cannot be done simply by appeals to reason, to ultimate self-interest, or to desire for autonomy. Those are helpful, but you need to mobilize the base instincts as well, fear and hatred and contempt. They are stronger anyway."

"What—how—"

"Oh, this likewise will be the work of years," Machiavelli admitted. "From what I have observed and read, Brazilians in particular are by nature easy-going and amiable. Never fear, though, they too bear the beast within them. They will learn. As a modest beginning, you can start japes about Europeans and slanders against them circulating. I have devised a few."

They were filthy. They were funny. Coelho found himself laughing while he winced.

"People will soon be inventing their own," Machiavelli finished. "It will seem a harmless amusement, piquantly naughty but innocuous. Which it is, by itself. However, it breaks the ground for allegations and ideas more serious. I am reminded of—"

And he was off on reminiscences of Pope Alexander VI, the Pope's son Cesare Borgia, and the rest of that family. Coelho listened, frequently appalled, always enthralled. Not that he heard anything he couldn't have accessed from the databases. The real Machiavelli might well have known the truth about any number of historical mysteries. This Machiavelli knew only what had been put into his program.

Or . . . was that altogether the case? These stories were so detailed, so vivid, with never a hesitation or equivocation. Surely no chronicle had recorded that Lucrezia wore a gown of blue silk and a single rosy pearl at her throat when she came to that infamous banquet where— Was the electronic mind consciously adding color? Did it possess an unconscious that filled in gaps which would be agonizing to recognize? Or was something more mysterious yet at work? Coelho suppressed the questions in himself. Perhaps years hence he would dare confront them.

The time ended. "I must go, your excellency."

"Ah, yes. This has been pleasant. Before you leave, I wish to make a small request."

"Of course. Whatever we can do for you, in whose debt we are."

"At your convenience," said Machiavelli blandly, "will you program for me a somewhat higher class of women? I do not ask for Helen of Troy—I suppose a myth would be too difficult—nor Cleopatra or Eleanor of Aquitaine— not yet, at any rate. But, while the sluts you have provided are lusty, their conversation is tedious."

He could summon them as he could his robe or his book. The programs had been easy enough to develop, since historical accuracy was no concern. Too easy, perhaps: the ghost-girls who helped ghost-Machiavelli set aside intellection for a while might be noticeably less human than he was. Maybe that was why he had never requested the companionship of his wife, though the biographies said they got along reasonably well despite his infidelities, or any friends from his earthly life. Maybe he dreaded what he would get.

Coelho shuddered a trifle. "I am sure we can oblige your excellency. It may take a little time." Though he had grown perversely fond of this pseudo-person, today he was glad to complete his farewell and blank out the sardonic face.

The garden behind Sanssouci dreamed beneath a summer sky. Birdsong, a whimsical pergola, a fountain gleaming and plashing, set off the formality of graveled paths, clipped hedgerows, disciplined flowerbeds, trees in precise topiaries. No gardeners were in sight; none would ever be needed. Friedrich strolled alone through his phantasm.

Abruptly the apparition of Birgitte Geibel burst into it. Her black gown enveloped a small marble Cupid like a candle snuffer. She didn't notice. Friedrich stopped, raised his cocked hat, swept her a bow. "Good day, my lady," he said.

She gave him a stiff look. "Is your majesty prepared for the talk he suggested, or shall I return at a more convenient moment?"

"No, no, let us by all means go straight to work." Friedrich drew a gold watch from his waistcoat. "Ah, yes, this is the hour agreed upon with your amanuensis. Pardon me, I forgot. When one is mostly secluded, one tends to lose track of time."

She softened a bit. "You do remember that we can provide you with company of your choice, do you not?"

Friedrich nodded. "Thank you kindly. To date I have been content. Getting to know what astounding, stupendous, and—hm—ludicrous things have happened throughout the world since 1786; toying with what control is mine over this miniature universe I inhabit: those keep me sufficiently occupied. And, to be sure, our contest with the Brazilians."

She made a mouth. "I wonder if it doesn't seem trivial and despicable to you, who were a king and fought real wars."

"On the contrary. I acquired a distaste for bloodshed early." She remembered how he, eighteen years old, had been compelled by his father to witness the beheading of his closest friend. "On fields such as Torgau I was later confirmed in this. While granting that casualties may be an unfortunate necessity, I take pride in the fact that my last war was waged with such skill that no life was lost on either side." He smiled. "No matter if they called it the Potato War. As for the present contest, why, I see it as the first stirring of events that may prove more fateful than any before in history."

"They touch some of us closely." She drew her jaws together, ashamed to have let him glimpse her pain.

His voice gentled. "Not yet do you have any word of your son?"

"No. We have heard and found out nothing about him. If ever we do, I will inform you promptly."

"War of nerves. Well, perhaps two can play at that game." Tactful, he looked away from her and fondled a rose, his fingers deftly skirting the thorns which could not wound him. "That is our subject today, I believe. As per my desire, I was informed when the undertaking I had proposed had prospered, although no details were supplied me. I thereupon called for this conference with you. What can you tell me?"

She had mastered herself. "Do you refer to identifying the chief computerman of the Brazilian project?"

"What else? Once I felt sure that they had recreated someone to match me, it followed that that enterprise must have a chief, just as you have Quinet for me."

"Well, it seems highly probable. Our intelligence agents got busy and soon picked up a trail. The signs point almost unambiguously to an individual in Rio de Janeiro. What he does is kept a tight secret, of course; but it is clear that he has been engaged upon something of the first importance. This was originally on behalf of several major firms. Recently the government became involved. His professional record indicates that he would be their best person for such a task."

"Excellent. We may consider the case proven."

"Our agents could not have learned what they did, as fast as they did, were the Brazilians not incredibly lax about security."

" 'Incredibly' is the wrong word, madame. Techniques of espionage and defense against it are among those that have rusted away during the long peace. We will see them revived soon enough. I daresay my adversary is busying himself with that, together with everything else required." Friedrich met Geibel's eyes. "You realize, my lady, that from the prisoners they took at Niterói, the Brazilians will have learned who I am. I trust the information was obtained . . . not inhumanely."

"And we fight blind unless we can discover who *he* is." It was as if a sword spoke.

Friedrich nodded. "Correct. Please tell me about this artificer."

"His name is Floriano Coelho. He is fifty years of age, and actually a physicist who did outstanding work in theoretical cosmodynamics before the French and North American pioneering of electronic reconstructions caught his interest. We have pictures." Her hands moved, responsive to flesh-and-blood hands that touched a keyboard. A life-size hologram appeared on the path. It was of a thin man, taller than average in his country, somewhat carelessly dressed. Beneath a bald pate, the face was plain and gentle. Friedrich peered. Geibel provided a succession of views.

"We know his routine," she said. "It isn't absolute—the unexpected is forever happening, not true?—but as nearly as feasible, he is a creature of habit. Temperate habit; devoted family man; a little shy and withdrawn, though affable among friends; no obvious vices or weaknesses, unless one counts a tendency to lose himself in his interests, his books, and thereby forget things like social obligations."

"Ah?" Friedrich stroked his chin. "What interests?"

"Well, science in general. And classical history and literature. He is absolutely enamored of the ancient world, especially the Greeks in their days of glory. He has published a few scholarly papers on their poets. Also—let me think—yes, he is a bibliophile."

"Possible clues," Friedrich murmured thoughtfully. "It would be best for the Brazilians if their computer chief had something in common with the man they called up from the past."

She couldn't resist: "Indeed? What has your majesty in common with Jules Quinet?"

"Very little," Friedrich admitted. "In fact, I sense he

dislikes me. Still, we manage. He is ambitious in his career, and I am the most important thing that has happened in it."

"He could be replaced."

"No need. And it would be unwise to shake the organization at just this critical juncture." Friedrich's tone sharpened and quickened. "We will strike through Coelho, swiftly, before the opportunity passes. Later, with his cooperation—"

"I doubt we can obtain it," Geibel interrupted. The king scowled. "Ach, I beg your majesty's pardon. But if I may continue, our evaluation of Coelho is that he shares the patriotism that is rising in Brazil. Furthermore, he bears the classical ideal of loyalty—Thermopylae, was that the name of the place? Oh, yes, we can shock-drug information out of him. Knowing that, he may give it voluntarily, to avoid worse than a session under a truth identifier helmet. But beyond that he will not go, unless as a result of treatment so extreme as to leave him useless to anyone."

"I am less dogmatic in my predictions," Friedrich said. "My observation has been that every man is malleable at some point. If we can get Coelho's help in making direct connection between myself and my opponent, I can take that stranger's measure to a degree otherwise unobtainable."

Geibel had barely restrained herself from another interruption. "No!" she cried. "Impossible!" She calmed. "Forgive us, your majesty, but we can never permit that. The danger is too great."

"Oh?" asked Friedrich mildly. "What danger, pray tell?"

"Your majesty would first have to master computer technology to understand. But think of—for a single example—a subtle distortion. Despite all precautions, given access to this network, the Brazilians might be clever enough to introduce what we call a worm into our program. *Your* program, my lord. It could do ghastly things to you."

Friedrich's features hardened. "And they fear we might do the like to their man. I see. Neither party dares let us meet." Then his lips quirked. "The irony should delight Coelho. It is worthy of Euripides ... or Aristophanes." He shrugged. "Well, once we have him, we will see what we can do with him."

"Exchange him for Otto—for all our men, at least," broke from her.

"In due course, yes, I expect we shall." Friedrich stared off across the garden. Randomizing, the environmental subprogram generated a flight of bees, their buzz, a zephyr that bore an odor of lilies. Geibel started to speak. Friedrich gestured for silence.

After a time that crept, he turned back to her. "I have hopes going beyond this," he said slowly. "I will not speak of them at once, for they are still well-nigh formless and may came to naught. Much will depend on what we learn in the next few days. But ... the situation has certain symmetries. What I contemplate doing to the Brazilians, they might conceivably do to us."

She drew breath. "And so?"

"What vulnerabilities has Jules Quinet?"

"What? I mean—why—" Geibel recovered from startlement. "We investigated him before inviting him to join us, of course; and we have kept an eye on him since. There is nothing untoward. He too is a steady family man—the same mistress for fifteen years, and she quite good friends with his wife. He drinks and gambles, but never to excess. His political party is the National Conservative. Do you fear he could be bribed or blackmailed? I sincerely disbelieve it. But we will increase surveillance if you want."

"No. That would annoy him if he found out, and make no difference. It would merely be another factor in the calculations of whoever intended to use him."

"Can he be used?" Geibel argued, with an edge of irritation.

Friedrich sighed. "The human being does not exist who can neither be corrupted nor coerced. If you believe otherwise—ach, my dear lady, you do not know this damned race."

Floriano Coelho enjoyed walking. He often took a public conveyance to the Botanical Gardens and logged off kilometers through that green luxuriance, or rambled for hours along city streets. Talk of a bodyguard he had dismissed with scorn. "Do you expect gangsters to seize my underpaid old carcass for ransom? As well expect dinosaurs."

Suddenly security chief João Aveiro insisted. To outraged protests he replied merely that there had been an incident of late which was too troubling in its implications to be publicized. Thereafter, one or another implacably polite young man was always in the rear when the scientist went out afoot.

Accordingly, Coelho was twice happy to see the face of the bookseller Pedro da Silva in his eidophone; for what he heard was: "Floriano, I have just received a very special item. I thought of you at once. It is a first edition of Edith Hamilton's *Three Greek Plays*—you know them, the definitive English versions—in remarkable condition. You would think the volume nineteenth rather than twentieth century, as well preserved as it is. And autographed by her!"

Coelho's heart bounded. Those were not mere renderings into a different language, they threw light on the originals. How often he had screened them, "Agamemnon," "Prometheus Bound," "The Trojan Women," sometimes having the computer interlineate the Hellenic texts. Yet, like Machiavelli, he recognized no real substitute for the actual, physical, well-made book. This would be a pleasing thing to show the old fellow.... "What price?" he asked.

"We will discuss that over coffee in the shop, if you can come down at once. You see, another collector has long been eager, and he is a person I would not lightly frustrate. For you, my friend, I am willing, but I cannot in good conscience make him wait unduly."

Collectors were like that. Coelho glanced at the viewpane. Rain poured across the building. He could not take such a book home through it, no matter how well wrapped. Besides, the distance was considerable and eventide closing in. "Fill the coffeepot!" Coelho laughed, and blanked off. To his wife: "I must go for perhaps two hours. Don't fret about dinner. Those smells alone will draw me home in time."

He punched for an aerocab, flung on a cape, kissed the woman, rumpled the hair of their youngest child, and went out to the levitor. As it bore him roofward from his apartment, he thought with a certain glee of the detective lurking down in the street. Demand was heavy in this weather and he had to wait several minutes in the bubble until a cab landed. He got in and gave the address. The pilot told him what the fare would be. "That's all right," he said. It lifted the vehicle. Ground transportation was congested these days, too slow. Coelho admired the view through the sides, though lights, towers, mountains, and bay were blurred by the downpour.

On a narrow street in the old quarter he transferred credit and crossed to the shop. Rain sluiced hot and heavy, out of the sky and across the black-and-white mosaic sidewalk. A manual door in a tile-roofed building of faded pastel hue gave entrance to shelves and stacks, dusk and dust, quietness and archival smells.

So quiet, so dim. He looked to and fro. "Pedro?" he called uncertainly.

A man strange to him appeared from between two stacks. He smiled. "Senhor da Silva is indisposed, Senhor Professor," he said. The bass rumbled from a barrel chest. "He will awaken unharmed presently. Meanwhile, if you please—"

A dart pistol came forth. Coelho choked on a scream. Through him flashed the admission that Aveiro had been right and he, the technologist, who knew how easy it was to synthesize an image and a voice and patch into a communication line, he had been the dupe. The pistol hissed. The dart stung. Coelho whirled into night.

"In itself," opined Aveiro, "this is less than catastrophic. The Europeans will learn who you are, and certain details of what you have been doing for us. However, I always took care to separate his, ah, maintenance functions from yours as our strategic advisor. And I trust you refrained from telling him more than was necessary for his work."

"We knew a little about confidentiality in my time," replied Machiavelli tartly. He sat still for a moment. Today it had been his whim to surround himself with a room in the Palazzo Riccardi. Sunlight glowed through stained glass to throw pieces of rainbow over the vividness of frescos showing the Medici in their days of splendor. Yet no form save his stirred. Aveiro recalled Coelho remarking that Machiavelli had never asked for a Florentine street or marketplace. Would the tumult recall to him too keenly that the Renaissance was one with Caesar and Vergil, or did he expect the replication would be too grotesquely false?

"You are quite sure Coelho was seized and transported to Europe?" he asked.

"Absolutely," Aveiro said. "After his wife called us, we found the bookseller drugged. Roused, he told us how three men came in together, posing as customers till they were alone with him, then shot him. Chemosensors—instruments more sensitive than a hound's nose—have identified traces of Coelho himself. Computer records show that a hired carriage brought him from his tenement to the shop. What more do you want?"

"Nothing. I simply wished to understand better the methods of today's *custodi*." Machiavelli pondered. "Given the speed of human flight, we must take for granted that by tomorrow Eurofac will know of me. Well, we could not have kept the secret forever. This becomes an element in our reckoning."

Aveiro nodded. "I am chagrined, but not disgraced. Mainly, I want to consult with you about who should replace him. I can give you the profiles of several possible persons."

Machiavelli shook his head. "Oh, no, senhor. I want my Coelho back."

"*Ay?* Well—familiarity, I suppose—but how?"

"Prisoner exchange is as old as war."

"You mean the Geibel gang, no doubt. Shall we let those bandits go scot-free?"

"Come, now. You have pumped them dry. What further use are they to you? As hostages—but your foes hold a prisoner of considerably greater value. If we can accomplish a straight trade, them for him, we have much the better of the bargain." Machiavelli hunched forward. "I daresay the Europeans intend to open negotiations with you before long. Better that we seize the initiative and send them the first message. You will know whom to call. Thus we keep them off balance, you see."

"Well—well—" Aveiro leaned back in the chair behind the desk. "You're probably right, ah, your excellency. Have you any suggestions more specific about how to proceed?"

"In diplomatic dealings, one feels one's way forward," Machiavelli said. "It is a matter of intuition, of . . . touch, . . . acquired by experience. In life I often served as a diplomat. I will negotiate for us."

Aveiro's feet hit the floor with a thump. "What?" he yelled. "No! We cannot—"

"I know your fear of direct intercourse." Machiavelli sounded exasperatedly patient, like a schoolmaster with a dull pupil. "It strikes me as vastly overblown, but I recognize adamancy when I meet it. Very well. Computer connections are not necessary. You see me by light and hear me by sounds from this chamber. As I understand it, I, the essential I, am not even in the chamber, but elsewhere. Now what is hazardous about admitting the light and the sound into one of your far-speaking instruments, whence they travel by etheric subtlety across the sea to Europe? In like manner, my honored opponent, King Federigo, can speak to us."

Aveiro clenched his fists and swallowed. "Well, you see—"

"You people are not stupid," Machiavelli said coldly. "You must have thought of this possibility at the outset. As long as my identity could be secret, communication by me with the outside world was undesirable. Agreed. That has changed. Believe me, I will gain more from conversing with Federigo, sounding him out, than the opposition can gain from me."

"Policy—"

Machiavelli sighed. "If you will pardon a digression, senhor, someday I should like to meet a simulacrum of the Englishman Samuel Johnson. In my reading I have come upon many of his maxims. Among them, 'Patriotism is the last refuge of a scoundrel.' I presume he refers to the abuse of this virtue, as any virtue may be turned to bad ends. Allow me, then, to observe that policy is the last refuge of a fool." Sternly: "Now I do not accuse you yourself, Senhor Aveiro, of foolishness. Oh, no. You would not care for me to reach beyond these crystal walls. I might begin to feel a little too independent. I might act on my own, without first begging for the approval of your masters." With disdain: "Set your terrors at rest. Can you and your wretched little spies—and your European counterpart and his toadies—can they not watch, listen, observe? Can you not shut off any conversation the instant it looks like going in suspect directions?"

Aveiro flushed. "You speak rather freely, your excellency."

Machiavelli laughed. "How do you propose to punish me? By obliteration? I fear it no more than a flame fears the wind. Remember, I have already been there."

His voice mildened: "But come, we are in danger of falling out, we allies. How regrettable. Our shared interests are numerous. All I do today is advance a proposal which, I realize, your superiors must agree to. Let me describe its advantages, and thereafter, of your kindness, do you bring it before those lords and persuade them. For we must act quickly, before the tide turns against us."

For the first time since his refashioning, Friedrich showed genuine excitement. "Machiavelli!" he breathed. He glanced up toward whatever heaven he had made for himself. "Lord God, this almost makes me believe you must exist, to play so rare a jest." Sobriety reclaimed him. "No, it was a rather logical choice, even though at the time they didn't know who I am. And many Brazilians are of Italian descent, not so?"

"Machiavelli," muttered Quinet. He turned off the eidophone, through which Adam Koszycki, chief of intelligence operations, had just transmitted the information revealed by Coelho. "I ought to know who that is—was—but I can't quite remember."

"Well, he lived long ago, in the late fifteenth and early sixteenth centuries," Friedrich explained absently. "Nevertheless, in a way he was the first modern man. He served Florence—it was a more or less sovereign city-state then, like several others in Italy—he served in its government and as a diplomat to various powers. A turn of political fortune caused him to be arrested, tortured, finally released to idleness on a small country estate he owned. There for many years he occupied his time with reading and writing. Eventually he was recalled to service, but only in minor capacities. His importance lies in those writings."

"Thank you, sire," Quinet said. "It comes back to me now, a little. A terrible cynic, was he not?"

"He attempted a scientific study of war, politics, all statecraft, not as the idealists said they should be conducted, but as he thought they actually were." Friedrich laughed, a small hard bark. "Ever since, those in power over the nations have sought to brand him a liar. I did myself, in my youth."

"Then I should think your majesty is unhappy at knowing that devil is back in the world." Quinet tried to keep his voice free of gloating. Some discomfiture might knock a little arrogance out of this Prussian.

"Oh, he was never an evil man," Friedrich replied. "Indeed, I would love to meet him. A man of parts, as most were in his day. He also produced purely literary works. For example, his play *Mandragola* is one of the most wickedly funny—"

The priority signal cut him off. Quinet hastened to activate the eidophone. Birgitte Geibel's gaunt image appeared. Quinet had never seen her as grim as now; and that, he thought, was saying considerable.

"Your majesty," she clipped, "we have received a call from Brazil. At the highest level, their president and a spokesman for all the major corporations together."

"This soon?" wondered Friedrich. "Heads of state and of large organizations are not given to—Ah, ha! Machiavelli is behind it. Who else? He will not grant us time to lay plans."

"He certainly will not. Listen. The message is—Please hear me, your majesty. The message is that they are prepared to exchange prisoners, returning my son and his men if we return Professor Coelho."

"That scarcely requires their chieftains to say. It is a very reasonable offer. I assume none of the captives has suffered improperly harsh treatment. You should accept."

"It is not that simple. Conditions must be arranged. The Brazilians will only let those arrangements be made by—yourself and that Machiavelli. And at once, within this hour."

Quinet whistled. Friedrich's surprise was fleeting. He grinned, rubbed his hands, and exclaimed, "Wonderful! He is more a man after my own heart than I dreamed. Why do you wait, madame? Call them back. Agree."

"The danger—"

"We need not connect any circuits," Quinet interrupted. Here was his chance to show decisiveness, he, the technologist. "We can hook eidophones to the tanks."

"But what plot is he hatching, this Machiavelli?" Geibel grated. "You said it yourself, King Friedrich, we are being rushed."

The royal answer was glacial: "Do you suppose he will hoodwink me? That is an insult, Frau Geibel. It borders on *lèse majesté*. You will apologize and proceed to carry out my orders."

She bridled. "*Your* orders? You—"

Friedrich's hand chopped like a headsman's ax. "Silence. Do you want my help or do you not? If not, abolish me; and may Herr Machiavelli have mercy on the lot of you."

She bit her lip, inhaled raggedly, forced forth: "I beg your majesty's pardon. I will recommend agreement to the governing council."

"They will follow the recommendation. Promptly." Friedrich pulled out his watch. "I expect to commence my conversation less than one hour from this minute. Dismissed."

Geibel glared but vanished. Friedrich turned to

Quinet. "You will assist me in rapid acquisition of as much knowledge of Machiavelli, his life and milieu, as time allows," he commanded. Outwardly he was self-collected, save that his face had gone pale and his nostrils quivered.

In a clean dress uniform, the king sat on his throne against a background of his audience chamber in Berlin. Machiavelli had elected Roman republican simplicity, wearing a robe and standing in the book-lined study of the farm house at Albergaccio. Silence thrummed while they considered each other's full-length images.

Machiavelli bowed. "Your majesty honors me," he said.

Friedrich gave back the same Mona Lisa smile and lifted a hand. "The honor is equally mine, monsieur," he responded.

They spoke French. That did not surprise Quinet—the language of civilization, after all—but he had expected to have trouble understanding a fifteenth-century Italian. However, Machiavelli had acquired modern Parisian, and it was Friedrich's accent that was quaint.

"I have been most interested, learning about your majesty's distinguished career," Machiavelli said.

"Monsieur's fame has deservedly endured through the ages," Friedrich answered. "Ah, I trust you have not found a little book of mine offensive? I was young when I wrote it."

"History attests that your majesty grew in wisdom with the years."

"There are certain philosophical points which I would still like to debate with you."

"I should be honored and delighted, sire. Surely I would learn far more than I could hope to impart."

Quinet wondered how long the mutual admiration society would continue in session. Friedrich ended it. His tone roughened: "Unfortunately, today we have obligations, business to conclude."

"True." Machiavelli sighed. "It is as well that the matter is elementary. We cannot carry on any serious talk, let alone handle problems of statecraft, when scores of persons on both sides of the ocean hang on our every

word." Which they did, which they did, Quinet thought.
Officially he was among them on the offchance that he
would notice something that could prove useful. In reality, he had been allowed to watch because one more
observer made no difference.

"We could have let underlings conduct these trivial
negotiations," Machiavelli went on, "but the opportunity
to converse with your majesty was irresistible."

"If you had not arranged this, monsieur, I would have
done it," Friedrich said. "Let us get to the point." He
glowered right and left. "I dislike eavesdroppers."

"Like myself, sire. *Hélas*, it seems we are permanently
saddled with them. Not that I malign my gracious hosts. I
hope they will . . . permit us future talks at more leisure."

"Permit—us?" Friedrich snarled. Beneath Machiavelli's cool observation, he eased, smiled sourly, and said,
"Well, two poor spooks have small control over their
destinies, *hein*?"

"Ironic, sire, when we are supposed to help our hosts
achieve their own chosen ends. I both relish and regret
the apparently ineluctable conflict in which you and I
find ourselves."

"Actually, I do not believe in destiny. One makes
one's own."

"In my opinion, as I have written, fortune is about half
of what determines man's fate. His free will, his efforts
and intelligence, have equal force."

With a slight chill, Quinet wondered what was going
on. Smooth courtliness; but those were two strong and
supple minds, nurtured throughout life on intrigue.
Could they understand each other better than they pre-
tended? Intonation; body language; implied meanings;
inferences made from what was left unsaid—

He came out of his reverie to find the ghosts crisply
discussing prisoner exchange. It took just minutes. Any
competent officer could have made the plan they arrived
at, a rendezvous on Ascension Island, telemonitored by
armed aircraft at a distance.

"So be it," Machiavelli concluded. "Allow me, your
majesty, to bid you farewell for the nonce with my

humble expression of the highest esteem of my hopes for the honor of your presence again in future."

"We shall see to that," Friedrich promised. "To you, monsieur, a very good day and our royal regards."

The screens blanked simultaneously. Friedrich sat like a statue on his throne.

Geibel's image appeared. "I trust your majesty is satisfied," she snapped.

"As I trust you are," the king said. "You shall have your son back tomorrow."

She bent her neck, a jerky gesture. "For that I am grateful, of course. But we must know, what have you discovered? What treachery do the Brazilians intend?"

"Why, you followed the discussion. You saw and heard everything I did. A few compliments and then the business on hand. Under the circumstances, what else did you expect?"

"Nothing, I suppose."

"I should be glad of further meetings at greater length with Monsieur Machiavelli."

She pinched her mouth together before telling him, "That will be ... difficult, your majesty. He *is* our adversary."

"Well," said Friedrich, "I am weary. Do not tell me I lack a body to grow tired. The mind, too, knows exhaustion. Kindly leave me to myself until your men are home again. Good day, madame."

"As your majesty wishes." She flicked off.

Quinet got out of his chair. "And I, sire?" he asked.

"No. You wait," the king replied. "I have something to tell you in strict confidence. First make sure we are truly alone."

Quinet's heart bumped. "This room is electronically screened. I need only run the alarm program to make sure that no one is monitoring you."

Having finished, he placed himself before the tank, braced his legs as if about to lift a weight, and said, "What do you want, sire?"

Friedrich's gaze drilled him. "I want you to understand something." Once more his tone rang like steel and ice. "I want you to know it in your marrow. You are mine.

I am not your subservient creation. You are my serf, my slave."

Quinet caught an indignant breath. "You protest, do you?" Friedrich pursued. "Think. They need me, your masters. They need me desperately, with Machiavelli's mind arrayed against them. Whatever I want from them, within the limits of their policy and ambition, they will give me, immediately and without question. I can have you discharged from your position here, Quinet. I can have you professionally destroyed. I can have you hounded to your ruin. I can have you assassinated. Is that clear?"

Red fury cried, "We should have brought back Napoléon!"

Friedrich laughed. "No. I have investigated his life. He did not know when to stop." His voice softened. "But listen, Quinet. I do not, in truth, threaten you. You have given me no cause to wish you ill. Rather, you stand to oblige me, to gain my favor. And I have ever rewarded faithful service well. What is your wish? Riches? To become the head of the world's greatest institution of your art? It can be arranged. Let us talk a while about what you would like, in return for rendering your fealty to me."

"Welcome back," said Machiavelli.

"Thank you, your excellency." With pleasure, Coelho sank into his accustomed chair at the familiar desk and looked across it to the image in the holotank.

"I trust you are well?"

"Oh, yes. The Europeans were not cruel. And after I came home yesterday, I got a good night's rest." Coelho flinched before he could add, "I did receive a tongue-lashing from Senhor Aveiro."

"Ah, well, I have experienced rather worse than that, and will protect you from it. Already I have insisted you be continued in this office, with full rank, pay, prerogatives, and perquisites."

"Your excellency is most kind."

Machiavelli chuckled. "My excellency is most watchful of his own interests. We enjoy a good relationship, we two. You are intelligent, likable company." Cross-legged in an armchair larger than was usual in his era, he bridged his fingers. "At the same time, you are—no offense intended—not overly complex. I flatter myself that I understand you well. That is soothing."

Coelho smiled. "It spares you surprises."

"But does not spare you, my friend. I believe that this ghost of me is perhaps just a trifle more ramified, more aware and nimble, than they who assembled it quite imagine. This is in spite of their very hope that it would devise the unexpected, would spring surprises on living souls."

A tingle went along Coelho's spine. "What are you driving at?" he whispered.

"Nothing but benevolence," said Machiavelli unctuously. "In my fondness for you, I wish to compensate you for the mishandling you endured on my account and, yes, for the humiliation to which you tell me you were unrighteously subjected upon your return here. Ah, we are safe from spies, are we not?"

Coelho swallowed. "Let me check." After some minutes of work, he bobbed his head up and down and crouched back in his chair to wait.

"As long as your lords have need of me—which will be at least as long as King Federigo is available to their foes—they must keep me happy," Machiavelli said. "They may feel themselves forced to deny certain wishes of mine, such as the freedom to meet privately and unhindered with my distinguished opponent. But under those same circumstances, they will feel it necessary to grant any lesser requests, even ones whose execution may prove costly. Now, although in life my wants were modest and today I am a shade, it would greatly please me to make a true friend happy."

"What . . . do you have in mind?"

Machiavelli smiled, glanced sideways, and purred, "Oh, possibilities have occurred to me. For example, a recreation of some great master of the arts would be a gift to all mankind."

"It has been done—"

"I know. But seldom, because it is costly. Still, your

merchant lords have abundant wealth, and me to thank that it is no longer being stripped from them. Suppose I asked them for, say, Euripides?"

Coelho leaped to his feet, sank back down, sat with pulse athunder. "No, impossible, we know too little about him."

"We could scarcely reconstruct the mind of Euripides in every respect," Machiavelli conceded. "Yet take inherent genius; let it form within the context of the Grecian golden age; use the extant works to delineate such a mind, such a spirit, as *would* have written precisely those dramas. Don't you suppose that that spirit would be able to write—not the lost plays exactly as they were, but something very close to them and equally noble?"

He wagged his forefinger. "Euripides is merely a suggestion of mine," he continued. "You may have a better idea. Do think about this and inform me at your convenience. For I visualize you, my dear Coelho, as being at the head of the undertaking."

The living man stared before him, dazed with exaltation. Through the choir in his blood he heard: "First I have a small favor to ask of you—"

People had long sung the praises of the United States of America to Jules Quinet, its scenery, historic monuments, exotic folkways, low-valued currency: a magnificent vacation country. He, though, had never cared to travel beyond France. When at last, with amazing suddenness, he took some days' leave and bought air tickets, it was grumpily. His wife and the young daughter who still lived at home were too joyful to heed that. On the morning after reaching New York, they sallied forth in search of bargains.

He had told them that for his part he would visit the natural history museum. Instead he stumped from their hotel and down the streets to the Waldorf-Astoria. Casting about through its huge, shabby-genteel lobby, he found what must be the agreed-on bar, went in, and ordered a beer.

A finger tapped his shoulder. "Meester Quinet?" said a diffident voice. Turning, he recognized Floriano Coelho from a cautious eidophone conversation. He nodded and they sought a corner table.

"Can we talk safely here, do you think?" Coelho asked in awkward French.

"Who listens?" Quinet snorted. He fished out his pipe and began loading it. "Let us not dither."

Coelho reddened and looked downward. "I hardly know . . . how to begin. I fear you think me a scoundrel."

"So I do. And so am I. Pf! What of it? Now as for the best method of establishing linkage, the first requirement is two programs for deceiving any monitors, the second is that the connection be undetectable, untraceable—"

The spiderweb enmeshes the world. Strands reach out to orbit, to the moon, to such robot craft as still explore the farther reaches of the Solar System. To all mortal intents and purposes, the pathways and crossings are infinite. It must needs be thus. The messages they bear are beyond numbering. The computers, each like a brain, become like cells in brains unimaginably potent when they join together through the strands. Those configurations are ever-changing. The light of intellect is a swarm of fireflies dancing and twinkling across the noösphere.

Two lesser systems, cut off from that vast oneness, need simply reach out and each clasp a single strand of the web. At once they join the whole, and through it, along millionfold cunningly shifting pathways, each other.

Those sets of messages that are minds can then travel as they will. Ghosts in olden legend rode upon the night wind. These ride the electron surges that go to and fro about the world like elfin lightning.

Authority is not invariably identical with title. There were sound reasons why it was Birgitte Geibel, head of the board at Vereinigten Bioindustrien, and João Aveiro, obscure security officer, who spoke over sealed circuit on behalf of their respective factions.

"I assume your people are as enraged as ours," Geibel said harshly. "Let you and I spare ourselves histrionics. What we confront is a *fait accompli*."

Aveiro stroked his mustache. "My own anger is

limited," he confessed. "The settlement appears to me a tolerable compromise. I do not call it equitable—it leaves you Europeans a substantial share of the markets that used to be ours alone—but it does no crippling injury to either side, and it ends a strife that bade fair to cost more than any possible gain."

Geibel paused to search for words. She was less proficient in the English they were using than he. "Yes," she said grudgingly, "King Friedrich did argue that we risked mutual exhaustion, leaving South America open to the great powers. He cited historical precedents."

Aveiro's smile was rueful. "And Machiavelli quoted a phrase from Talleyrand, 'An equality of dissatisfaction.' "

Geibel struck a fist against her chair arm. "But the, the insolence of those two!" exploded from her. "The betrayal! You cannot doubt, can you, that they conspired together? How else would they both come forth on the same day with the identical prescription and the whole set of verification procedures and sanctions, not to speak of the ultimatum that we agree to it or—or—"

"Or they will counsel us no more."

"And we will obliterate them," she said as though she relished the idea.

He clicked his tongue and shook his head. "Oh, no. You cannot mean that, Miz Geibel. By all means, cancel your Frederick the Great if you wish. I am sure that then our Machiavelli will be glad to guide us in a renewed aggressive strategy which—may I speak frankly?—could well end with us in possession of *your* European commerce."

"Unless you cancel him."

"You know that is impossible. If we did both abolish our wily councillors, the temptation to you to bring yours back, which you could do at the clandestine flick of a switch, would be overwhelming. Therefore, precautionarily, we would bring ours back. Of course, you see this morality as if in a mirror. But the effect is the same. For similar reasons, neither you nor we dare decline to accept the settlement they propose."

"And they know, those devils, they know!"

"I repeat, they are not such fiends. They have contrived a peace between us which may prove stable."

"*How?*"

"How did they come together, despite our safeguards? I can guess, but will never be sure. Obviously, they suborned their chief computermen. But those individuals, Coelho and Quinet, are under their total protection. Punishment would cost us far more than it is worth."

"True." Geibel gritted her teeth. "Instead, we must bite the sour apple and heap the traitors with rewards."

"After which, I daresay, Machiavelli and Frederick will admit that they meet privately whenever they choose. And there will be nothing we can do about it." Aveiro spread his palms. "In your words, a *fait accompli*. Well, we have numerous details to work out before drawing up a formal contract. Do you wish to discuss any particular aspect first?"

"Ach, it doesn't matter which," Geibel said, resigned. "In every case, a thousand officials and underlings will niggle and quibble. All we need do today, all we can do, is agree on the broad outlines; and those have already been laid upon us."

She fell silent, staring beyond sight. After a moment, Aveiro asked, "What is it you think about, senhora?"

Geibel shook herself, looked back at him, and said low: "Them. Friedrich and Machiavelli. Two imperial spirits. They helped us in our strife because it . . . amused them; but I suppose they came to see it as petty and sordid and unworthy of their genius. Now they are our masters. Let us never speak it aloud, but let us admit it to ourselves, they are. I doubt they will rest content for long. They will want new challenges, new victories to win.

"What do you suppose they plan for us? What are they doing as we two little people sit and pretend we confer?"

A spire of ivory reached so tall that stars circled about its golden cupola. Lower down, a gryphon flew among angels, sunlight ablaze off his wings. On earth, unicorns browsed on fantastical flowers and the waters of a fountain danced through a sequence of pure geometrical shapes. Given the help of first-class computermen, a ghost can gratify almost any whim.

However, Friedrich der Grosse and Niccolò Machiavelli had turned their attention elsewhere. They were not preparing any great enterprise. They might at some future time, if the mood struck them. At the moment, though, they were discussing an opera, for which Machiavelli was to write the libretto and Friedrich the music.

COMMENTS

STATESMEN

POUL ANDERSON

Frankly, I was a little surprised—though pleased, of course—to hear that this story was to be in a book dealing with nanotechnology. I had thought of it as involving just computers. Then I considered the matter a bit more, and began to see some intriguing implications. As Eric Drexler has pointed out at length, nanotechnology is going to revolutionize the computer field, too, at least as much as the transistor did.

The story originated with Robert Silverberg, who offered several writers the same basic premise, that historic figures would be revived as computer programs. When he recruited me, I said that the idea was irresistible but I'd have to work on it before breakfast. He laughed and asked me what the other five impossibilities were.

Offhand, it does look like the sheerest fantasy. Even assuming sufficient computer power, which quite likely will be available in the rather near future, how do you write such a program? What sort of code will you use for the manifold and ever-changing functions we call mind, including instincts, emotions, the subconscious, the unconscious, somatic input and output, the chemistry of a DNA you don't have on hand to analyze? What about the effects of a lifetime's experiences, most of them unrecorded and many of them forgotten but all exerting their influence? On and on and on. Absurd!

Well before you can seriously think of doing anything like this, you must obviously have become able to create

true artificial intelligence, a machine that not only processes data and performs logical operations but possesses
consciousness. Doubtless minds like that, generated *de
novo*, would progress to capabilities far beyond our
organic brains.

They, or perhaps scientists merely human, could then
develop other programs that superficially resembled people long dead. They could produce something that talked
in the language and style of, say, Cicero, knew everything
we know about Cicero's life and times, even reacted
more or less as Cicero would to mentions of Atticus,
Catiline, or Caesar. How shallow it would be. We are
ignorant about countless details of his times, let alone
his life, his organism, his secrets, and those with whom
he interacted in the course of every ordinary day. This
thing would be little more than a puppet, less interesting
than any out-and-out machine mind.

And yet—

Pursuing the subject further, I realized I had been
thinking in terms of algorithms. Now it may well be that
thought, awareness, personality is algorithmic. Certainly
a great deal of it is; we probably run on automatic pilot
most of the time. Is all of it? I suppose the majority
opinion today is "Yes." If that is right, I don't see how
these fictional resurrections can ever actually happen. At
best, we might make a Cicero program with a human's
rich complexity and with some similarities to the original,
but in no way could we bring back the old Roman
himself.

However, in my amateur fashion I've long been wondering whether the essential I and the essential you really
are nothing more than algorithms. Is this quite reasonable? Not that I take any stock in the supernatural. But
just how could an algorithm so incredibly full and subtle
evolve? Might the algorithmic model be another case of
scientists finding an idea so powerful that they assume
without further examination that it explains everything?
This has happened before—for instance, Laplace's clock-
work determinism or the kind of Darwinism that saw
nature exclusively "red in tooth and claw." The concepts
were tremendously useful in their time, but taken by

themselves they became oversimplifications. Later generations had to modify them to the point where today those early enthusiasts would scarcely recognize them.

Roger Penrose has raised such questions in much more detail and profundity in his book *The Emperor's New Mind.* He sets forth reasons for suspecting that intelligence of the human kind has a strong non-algorithmic component. What it may be, he cannot say, though he finds hints in quantum mechanics.

Speaking for myself again, if anything like this does turn out to be true, I don't think it will debar us from creating artificial intelligence. After all, we create flesh-and-blood intelligence naturally, in our children. A correct model of it, whatever that model may be, is necessary before we can do it with machines.

If quantum mechanics is, indeed, involved, well, out at its frontiers that theory gets almighty strange. While the equations check out in the laboratory to more decimal points than anything else in science, physicists can't agree on what they mean. Several different interpretations contend. It appears that the observer inescapably has a role in determining what the observation shall be, that there is some underlying unity across space-time, that causality is probably not a simple past-to-future relationship—

Enough. I could speculate onward, but at our present stage of knowledge it would be empty. Let me simply remark that perhaps, in spite of everything, the notion behind this story is not altogether ridiculous.

However that may be, it's clear that we are still far from understanding the phenomenon of intelligence, which means ourselves; that in furthering this understanding, computer science will continue to play an important part; and that therefore nanotechnology will help us toward the goal.

DOGGED PERSISTENCE

KEVIN J. ANDERSON

The dog stops in the middle of the road, distracted on his way to the forest. The asphalt smells damp and spicy with fallen leaves. Infrared laser-guidance posts line the shoulder at wide intervals, but most of the vehicles are of the old kind, growling inside from hot engines, belching chemical exhaust.

The twin headlights of the approaching car look like bright coins. The image fixates him, imprinting spots on his dark-adapted eyes. The dog can hear the car dominating the night noises of insects and stirring branches. The car sounds loud. The car sounds angry.

Moving with casual ease, the dog saunters toward the shoulder. But the car arrives faster than he could ever run, squealing brakes like some death scream. He hears the thud of impact, the bright explosion of pain that suddenly vanishes. He is flying through the air toward the ditch. He smells the spray of blood from inside his own nose.

Knowing he must hide, the dog hauls himself into the brambles, under a barbed-wire fence, to the dense foliage.

Car doors slam, running feet, the babble of voices: "Shit! That was no deer—that was a dog! A big black lab!" "Where'd he go?" "Shit, must have crawled off to die." "Look at all the blood—and look what he did to your car!"

The dog has found a safe place. The human voices become fuzzy as black unawareness overcomes him. He

120

will not move again until it is finished. He will be all right.

Inside his body, millions upon millions of nanomachines begin to repair the damage, cell by cell, rebuilding the entire dog. The night insects resume their music in the forest.

Patrice went to the window and watched her son bounce a tennis ball against the shed. Each impact sounded like gunshots aimed at her. She cringed. Judd didn't know any better; he remembered none of what had happened so long ago. Sixteen should have been a magic age for him, when teenage concerns achieved universal importance. In all those years, she had never let Judd come into contact with other people, much less those his own age.

She opened the screen door and stepped onto the porch, trying to keep the worried expression off her face. Judd would consider the concern normal for her anyway.

The gray Oregon cloudcover had broken for its daily hour of sunshine. The meadow looked fresh from the previous night's rain. The patter of raindrops had sounded like creeping footsteps outside the window, and Patrice had lain awake for hours, staring at the ceiling. Now the tall pines and aspens cast morning shadows across the dirt road that led from the highway to her sheltered house.

Judd smacked the tennis ball too hard and it sailed off to the driveway, struck a stone, and bounced into the meadow. With a shout of anger, Judd hurled his tennis racket after it. Impulsive—he became more like his father every day.

"Judd!" she called, quelling most of the scolding tone. He fetched the racket and plodded toward her. He had been restless for the last two days. "What's wrong with you?"

Judd averted his eyes, turned instead to squint where the sunshine lit the dense pines. Far away, she could hear the deep hum of a hovertruck hauling logs down the highway.

"Pancake," he finally answered. "He didn't come back yesterday, and I haven't seen him all morning."

Now Patrice understood, and she felt the relief wash inside of her. For a moment, she was afraid he might have seen some stranger or heard something about them on the news. "Your dog'll be all right. Just wait and see."

"But what if he's dying in a ditch somewhere?" She could see tears on the edges of Judd's eyes. He fought hard against crying. "What if he's in a fur trap, or got shot by a hunter?"

Patrice shook her head. "I'm not worried about him. He'll come home safe and sound. He always does."

Once again Patrice felt the shudder. *Yes, he always did.*

Fifteen years before, Patrice—she had gone by the name of Trish, then—had thought the world was golden. She had been married to Jerry for four years. In that time, he had doubled his salary through patents and bonuses from enhanced silicon-chip development at the DyMar Laboratories.

Their one-year-old son sat in diapers in the middle of the hardwood floor, spinning around. He had deactivated his holographic cartoon companions and played with the dog instead. The boy knew "Ma" and "Da" and attempted to say "Pancake," though the dog's name came out more like a strangled "gaaaakk!"

Trish and Jerry chuckled together as they watched the black labrador play with Jody. She did not start calling the baby Judd until after they had fled. Pancake romped back and forth with paws slipping on the polished floor. Jody squealed with delight. Pancake woofed and circled the baby, who tried to spin on his diapers on the floor.

"Pancake's like a puppy again," Trish said, smiling. She had owned the dog for nine years already, all through college and in her four years with Jerry. Pancake had settled into a middle-aged routine of sleeping most of the time, except for a lot of slobbering and tail wagging to greet them every day when they came home from work. But lately the dog had been more energetic and playful than he had been in years. "I wonder what happened to him," she said.

Jerry's grin, his short dark hair, and heavy eyebrows made him look dashing. "Maybe all those little things that make a dog feel old got fixed inside of him. The sore joints, the stiff muscles, the bad circulation. Like a million million tiny repairmen doing a renovation."

Trish sat up and pulled her hand away from him. "Did you take him into your lab again? What did you do to him?" She raised her voice, and the words came out with cold anger. "What did you do to him!"

Trish stopped and turned to see her baby boy and the dog looking at her as if she had gone insane. What business did she have yelling when they were trying to play?

Jerry looked at her, hard. He raised his eyebrows in an expression of sincerity. "I didn't do anything. Honest."

With a woof, Pancake charged at Jody again, wagging his tail and banking aside at the last instant. The holographic cartoon characters marched back into the room, dancing to a tune only they could hear. The dog trotted right through the images to the baby. "Just look at him! How can you think anything's wrong?"

But in only four years of marriage, Trish had learned one thing, and she had learned to hate it. She could always tell when Jerry was lying.

"Mom, he's back!" Judd shouted.

For a moment, Patrice reacted with alarm, thinking of the hunters, wondering who could have found them, how they might have given themselves away—but then through the open window, she could hear the dog barking. She looked up from the stove to see the black labrador bounding out of the trees. Judd ran toward him so hard she expected him to sprawl on his face. Just what she needed, Patrice thought, he would probably break his arm. That would ruin everything. So far, she had managed to avoid all contact with doctors and any other kind of people who kept names and records.

But Judd reached the dog safely, and both tried to outdo the other's enthusiasm. Pancake barked and ran around in circles, leaping into the air. Judd threw his arms around the dog's neck and wrestled him to the ground.

According to her notes, Pancake would be twenty-four years old in a few months. Nearly twice the average life-span of a dog.

Judd and Pancake raced each other back to the house. Patrice wiped her hands on a kitchen towel and came out to the porch to greet him. "I told you he'd be okay," she said.

Idiotically happy, Judd nodded and then stroked the dog.

Patrice bent over and ran her fingers through the black fur. The wedding ring, still on her finger after fifteen years alone, stood out among the dark strands. Pancake had a difficult time standing still for her, shifting on all four paws and letting his tongue loll out.

Other than mud spatters and a few cockleburrs, she found nothing amiss. Not a mark on him. There never was.

She patted the dog's head, and Pancake rolled his deep brown eyes up at her. "I wish you could tell us stories," she said.

In Jerry's lab, the dog paced inside his cage. He whined twice. He obviously didn't like to be confined and he was probably confused, since Jerry had never caged him before. Pancake wagged his tail, as if hoping for a quick end to this.

Jerry paced the room, running a hand through his own dark hair, trying to kill the butterflies in his stomach. He had worked himself into self-righteous cockiness at showing the management turds just what they had spent all their money on. Progress reports went unread, or at least not understood. Memos describing their work and its implications disappeared in the piles of paper—yes, even though Ethan and O'Hara had perfectly functioning electronic mail systems, they still insisted on old-fashioned paper memos from DyMar underlings.

He glanced at his watch. "What the hell is taking them so long?"

Beside him, Frank Peron sighed. "It's only five

minutes, Jerry. You know, wait for them, but they'll never wait for you. We were lucky to get them to come down here at all."

"Considering that this breakthrough will change the universe as we know it," Jerry said, "I'd think they might want to give up a coffee break to have a look."

He couldn't take his eyes off the poster tacked up on the lab wall. It showed Albert Einstein handing a candle to someone few people would recognize by sight—K. Eric Drexler; Drexler, in turn, was extending a candle toward the viewer. *Come on, take it!* Drexler had been one of the first major visionaries behind nanotechnology some thirty years before.

It will change the universe as we know it, Jerry thought. Pancake looked expectantly at him, then sat down in the middle of his cage. "Good boy," Jerry muttered.

"They're management boobs," Frank said. "You can't expect them to understand what it is they're funding."

At that moment Mr. Ethan and Mr. O'Hara, two of the highest executives in DyMar Laboratories, entered the lab room, apologizing in unison for being late. Smiling, Jerry assured them that neither he nor Frank Peron had noticed.

"Dr. McKenzy, your memo was rather, uh, enthusiastic," Ethan said.

Beside him, O'Hara scowled and chose a different word. "Ebullient. Tossing around promises of immortality, the end to all disease, curing the handicapped, stopping aging—"

"Yes, sir, we felt we had to limit our discussions to only those topics," Jerry interrupted. He had to shock these two so thoroughly that they would be ready to question all their preconceptions. "Actually, this nanotechnology breakthrough opens the doorway to much more, such as an end to dirty industry, instantaneous fabrication of the most complex machines, new materials stronger than steel and harder than diamond. That's why so many people have been working on it for so long. We've all been racing each other because when it happens, it *happens*. And the first ones to break through are going to shake up society like you won't be able to imagine."

Ethan and O'Hara looked as if they had never heard so much bullshit before in their lives. *Very well*, Jerry thought, *time to haul out the big guns. Literally.*

"Watch this, please, and then we can adjourn to the conference room."

Jerry pulled out an automatic pistol from the pocket of his lab coat. He had bought it at a sporting goods store for this purpose only. No one should have been able to smuggle a gun into a lab, but security was lax. He had brought the dog in, hadn't he? He looked at Pancake.

The two executives scrambled backward. Jerry didn't give them time to do anything. He was running this show. Melodramatic though it might seem, he knew it would work.

He pointed the pistol at the dog and fired two shots. One struck Pancake's ribcage; another shattered his spine. Blood flew out from the bullet holes, drenching his fur.

Pancake yelped and then sat down from the impact. He panted.

"My god!" Ethan shouted.

"McKenzy, what the hell do you think—" O'Hara cried.

"The first thing that happens," Jerry said, then repeated himself, yelling at the top of his lungs until he had their attention again. "The first thing that happens is that the nanomachines shut down all of the dog's pain centers."

The two executives stared wide eyed. They were both shaking.

In his cage, Pancake looked confused with his tongue lolling out. He seemed not to notice the gaping holes in his back. After a moment, he lay down on the floor of the cage, squishing his fur in the blood still running along his sides. His eyes grew heavy, and he sank down in deep sleep, resting his head on his front paws. He took a huge breath and released it slowly.

"In a massive injury like this, the machines will place

him in a recuperative coma. Already, they are scouring the damage sites, assessing the repairs that will be needed, and starting to put him together again. They can link themselves into larger assemblies to make macro repairs." Jerry knelt down on the floor beside the cage, reached his hand in to pat Pancake on the head. "His temperature is already rising from the waste heat generated by the nanomachines. Look, the blood has stopped flowing."

"The dog's dead!" O'Hara said. "The animal activists are going to crucify us!"

"Nope. By tomorrow, he'll be up and chasing jackrabbits." Jerry felt intensely pleased with himself. "I brought in my own dog so we didn't have to go through all the procurement crap to get approved experimental animals.

"You are out of a job, Dr. McKenzy!" Ethan said. His face had turned a deep red.

"I don't think so," Jerry answered, and smiled. "I'll bet you a box of dog biscuits."

The light at sunset slanted through a cut in the Oregon hills where the trees had been shaved in strips from robotic logging. The clouds had cleared again, leaving Patrice and Judd to sit by the table in the living room. The house lights, sensing their presence, would come on soon.

The two of them worked on a sprawling jigsaw puzzle that showed the planet Earth rising over the lunar crags, photographed from the moonbase. The blue-green sphere covered most of the table, with jagged gaps from a few continents not yet filled in.

Patrice and Judd talked little in the shared comfortable silence of two people who had had only their own company for a very long time. They could get by with partial sentences, cryptic comments, private jokes.

Judd knew why they had to hide from the outside world. Patrice had kept no secrets from him, explaining their situation in more complicated terms as the boy grew older and became able to comprehend. He had never complained. He knew no other life.

Outside, Pancake barked. He stood up on the porch and paced, letting a low growl loose in his throat.

Patrice stiffened and went to the lace curtains. Her mouth went dry. Somehow, she knew the dog was not making one of his puppy barks at a squirrel. She had owned the dog more than half her life, and she knew him better than any human being could. This was a bark of warning.

"What is it, Mom?" Judd asked. From the drawn expression on his face, she could tell he felt the fear as much as she did. She had trained him well enough.

She could hear a vehicle toiling up the winding gravel drive away from the highway and toward the house.

The demonstrators outside DyMar Laboratories consisted of an odd mix of religious groups, labor union representatives, animal-rights activists, and who knew what else. Some were fruitcakes, some were violent.

Staring out the window, Jerry McKenzy didn't know how to deal with the mob. Maintenance had added steel bars in the last week. "We didn't get as much breathing space as we counted on."

He paced in the lab office, with his terminal and notes, brainstorming files and records. The actual nanotech experiments were done in clean-rooms in the annex building, where Jerry himself rarely went. But with the demonstrations growing, all experiments had been shut down as the DyMar execs tried to figure out what to do. But then, they were idiots anyway.

DyMar had made a fatal error in announcing the nanotechnology breakthrough to the world. Pressed for time and knowing their research facility couldn't be the only one so close to success, DyMar had blitzed the public with premature announcements. They had taken everyone by surprise.

The outcry in response had been swift and frightening, much more organized and aggressive than the misguided or ineffective complaints Jerry had normally seen. The protest was organized under the aegis of a new organization called "Purity" that had burst into existence with unbelievable speed.

Peron stored his file in the computer and tapped his fingers on the keyboard. "And *you* thought we'd be the only ones to grasp the implications of nanotechnology."

"It's always nice to see that some people understand more than you give them credit for," Jerry said.

Peron tugged on his lower lip. Something had been bothering him all morning. "Did you ever hear the story about the guy who perfected a solar-power engine? Would have put the gas and electric companies out of business, would have changed the world as we know it. But he disappeared before he could disseminate his blueprints. Now, somebody with a billion-dollar invention like that doesn't just drop out of sight. Do you know what I'm saying?"

Jerry scowled at him. "Oh, that's just an urban legend! Like the choking doberman."

Peron shrugged. "Well, Drexler predicted back in 1985 that we'd have functioning nanotech within a decade— and that was thirty years ago! A dozen groups have been working, but somehow the crucial experiments fizzle at just the wrong times, the key data gets misprinted in technical journals. It's only because of your damned arrogance, Jerry, that we plowed our way around the usual scientific channels. Have you *checked* how often the most promising nanotech researchers move off to other fields of study, how often they die in accidents?"

Jerry blinked at the other man in astonishment. "Have you run a reality diagnostic on yourself recently, Frank? You're sounding paranoid."

Peron forced a laugh. "Sorry. This isn't exactly a high-security installation we're working in, you know. You smuggled your damned dog in here twice, and Pancake isn't a lap dog that'll fit in a glove compartment. A chain-link fence and a couple of rent-a-cops does not make me feel safe."

As if in response, the crowds outside took up a loud chant.

Jerry sat down, kicked a few of the stray pencils away from his feet, and spoke in his "let's be reasonable" voice. "Frank, some bone-headed fanatic is always trying to stop progress—but it never works. Nobody can *un*discover nanotechnology." He made a rude noise through his lips.

Jerry spent a quarter of an hour reassuring his partner, convincing him not to worry. With dogged persistence they could get through this mess. He felt confident when they both packed up to brave the gauntlet of protesters and go home.

But he never saw Frank Peron again.

When Patrice saw the red vehicle approaching, she squinted into the sunset and made it out to be a small American truck outfitted with laser-guidance sensors, mud-spattered and identical to a million other vehicles in Oregon. She didn't recognize the silhouette of the man behind the wheel.

She didn't have time to run.

Patrice and Judd had lived in the state for nine years, at the same location for three of them. She and her son had fled to Oregon because of its track record of survivalists, of religious cults, of extremists and isolationists— all of whom knew how to be left alone. The state's rural ultra-privacy legislation forbade any release of tax documents, credit card transactions, or telephone records.

But the last time she had gone into a grocery store, she had noticed the cover of a weekly newsmagazine depicting the fenced-off and burned ruins of DyMar Laboratories. The headline advertised a fifteen-year retrospective on the disaster, bemoaning the fact that all records had been lost of such an important technological breakthrough. No doubt the story would talk about how she and her son were still missing, presumed killed by Purity extremists. There would have been pictures of her—as Trish McKenzy, not Patrice Kennesy, and the boy Jody, not Judd.

Uneasy, she had taken her groceries and backed away from the TV guides and beef jerky strips and candy bars by the register. No one, she insisted to herself, would have put such a coincidence together, would have connected all the details. Still, the clerk stared at her too intently. . . .

Now, with a grim expression on her face, Patrice stepped out on her front porch to meet the approaching stranger.

The demonstrators did not go home, not even late at night. Jerry had remained at the lab office until after ten o'clock, sending a vidmessage to Trish that he wanted to finish another simulation before locking up. People massed against the chain-link fence, shouting and chanting. They had lit bonfires.

Somehow he could not believe that anybody but the technically literate would understand how significant a breakthrough he and Frank Peron had made. This wasn't the type of thing people normally got up in arms about—it was too complicated and required too much foresight to see how the world would change, to sort the dangers from the miracles DyMar had been promising in its PR. Who was orchestrating all this?

Like Utah's cold fusion debacle from decades before, DyMar had made a lot of promises and produced nothing tangible. They were waiting for patent approval before releasing any details, but the red tape had been tangled, the patent office had lost the first two sets of applications, though the e-mail trace verified that they had been received and logged in. Lawyers did not return vidmessages. News of the "immortal dog" had leaked in one interview, but Jerry sure as hell was not going to shoot Pancake again in front of a TV camera just to make a point.

The dog wasn't the only one blessed with nanotechnology cell repair, though. He had seen to that himself. Nobody knew that he carried his own cell-repair machines tailored to human DNA, and it would stay that way.

Outside he heard glass breaking, the roar of the crowd. It just didn't make any sense to him. He watched out the window. Clouds had obscured most of the stars overhead, but mercury vapor lamps spilled garish light across the near-empty parking lot.

At the gate, a team of rent-a-cops paced about holding rifles ready, probably quaking in their boots. DyMar had called for backup security from the State Police, and they had been turned down. The ostensible reason was some buried statute that allowed the police to defer "internal company disputes" to private security forces. How they could consider the mob of demonstrators to be an internal company dispute, Jerry could not imagine. It felt as if somebody wanted the lab unprotected.

He heard sharp popping noises outside, and it took him a moment to realize they were gunshots. He turned to see one of the security guards fall; others ran away as a group of people streamed through a breach in the chain-link fence. He heard more gunfire.

"This is nuts!" he said to himself, then switched off the light in his lab. No use attracting them; but they would know exactly where he was working. Jerry couldn't believe it, but he knew he had to get away immediately.

Glow from the parking-lot lights mixed with the dim EXIT sign to give him enough illumination to move. He slipped out of the room and hesitated, wondering if he should call the police or the fire department. Someone smashed the front doors downstairs. He had no time.

They would ransack the place and destroy his work. Jerry tried to think if he could save anything, like in all those old movies where the mad scientist rescued his single notebook from the flames. But his work and Frank Peron's was scattered in a thousand computer files, delicate microhardware, and intangible AI simulations. Everything was backed up, with duplicates stored in various vaults. It would be safe. For now, the important thing was to escape. The mob had already killed one of the guards; Jerry had no doubt they would tear him apart.

He ran down the hall as he heard footsteps in the lobby, shouted orders, another gunshot. Jerry fled to the back stairwell, yanked open the door, and leaped down the concrete stairs three at a time, balancing himself on the railing. At the bottom, he ripped off his lab coat and left it on the landing before emerging into the administrative section of the main building.

He peeked around the door. They had not gotten this far down the halls yet, and managerial offices would not be their first target. He heard a huge roaring explosion and saw through a set of windows the annex building erupt into orange flames. Impossible! This couldn't be happening! But ignorant peasants had always stormed the doctor's castle, carrying torches.

Jerry kept close to the wall as he hurried along. The front and side doors would be out of the question. But the back had an emergency exit, a crash-out door that would also activate alarms and notify the police and fire departments. He couldn't decide if that would be good or bad.

A window shattered in one of the suites in front of him, and a puddle of flames spilled from a broken bottle. Molotov cocktail; one of the front offices—either Ethan's or O'Hara's—burst into flame.

Jerry placed his ear to the emergency exit door. He heard chaos outside, but it sounded distant. He imagined somebody stationed back here with a rifle pointed at the door, waiting for him to come running. But he had no other choice.

Jerry used his back to slam out through the door, throwing himself to the ground as he emerged. He rolled, waiting to hear gunshots strike the door, ping off the asphalt, slam into his chest. What had Pancake felt when the bullets slammed into him? He didn't know how much damage his own body could endure and still repair itself. He had never tested his limits.

But the only gunshots came from the side of the building. He heard more shouts and running people. He got up and sprinted to the corner of the building. If only he could make it to the parking lot and to his car, he could crash through the fence and drive off, get Trish and the baby, and hide in a motel for a few days until this stuff calmed down.

He let himself feel a ripple of smugness. The violence here would stun the protest movement; once the public saw them do murder and destruction like this, all sympathy for their cause would be gone. This was like mass insanity. Killing people by blowing up abortion clinics never won any support for Pro-Life groups, did it? Armstrong's bomb hadn't helped the Vietnam War protest decades before, had it?

But when Jerry saw the people attacking the DyMar building, saw the weapons they carried and the uniform way they moved, he knew immediately that this was no mob, this was no ragtag band of second-generation hippies yanking shotguns off their mantels.

Fire from the lower level spread through the main building. More burning bottles had been tossed through downstairs windows.

With a shock he noticed a complete absence of TV crews, though they had been covering the protest since its beginning. On the parking lot near the gate, Jerry saw the sprawled uniformed bodies of two security guards. The others were probably dead somewhere along the fenceline—unless they were themselves part of the assault team.

In the confusion, Jerry added an angry expression to his face and ran among the mob, working his way to the parking lot. He slipped through, shouting orders to anyone who looked his direction as if to challenge him.

Once Jerry got to the cars, he ducked low, working among them. This late at night, not many vehicles remained, only his own, the guards', a handful of other cars and trucks that had either been broken down, or sat with For Sale signs in their windshields.

He found Frank Peron's black sportscar and hesitated. But Frank had left days ago! Unless he had never made it. Jerry swallowed a cold lump in his throat.

Once he got in his car, he would have to start it fast, and drive away fast, keeping his head low to avoid gunfire. Judging from what Pancake had endured, Jerry could survive some major injuries with his nanotech healing machines, but he had no desire to test them.

He reached the passenger side of his car and fished in his pocket for the key ring. Among the shouts and burning and gunshots, the noise he made was insignificant, but still the jingle seemed too loud to him. He unlocked the door and slipped in, crawling over the passenger seat and pulling the door shut behind him. Squirming, he positioned himself behind the steering wheel, still ducking low, and took an absurd moment to strap himself in with the seatbelt. He would have to crash through the fence and he did not want to smack his head on the dashboard and knock himself senseless.

Before starting the car, he plotted his route, found a side gate with an access road that would take him off to the highway. He switched off all the automatic collision-avoidance systems, the laser-guidance options. He was going to have to drive like a stunt man. He made up his mind to plow right over anybody who stood in his way. This was life or death here. Adrenalin pounded through him. He would gain nothing by waiting.

He turned the key in the ignition.

The car bomb instantly blew him into pieces, trapping his body in the burning hulk of twisted metal. Not even his cell-repair machines could fix so much damage.

In front of Patrice's house, the man wasted no time as he ground the red vehicle to a halt. He left the engine purring, slid the door open, and stood up.

He brought a scattershot rifle out of the front seat and leveled it at Patrice. "Ding dong, Avon calling," he said.

Patrice stood defiantly on the porch, unable to move. She felt old and weak. When Judd stepped out and stood beside her, she felt weaker still.

"Or would you rather I said 'I'm from the government, I'm here to help you'?" the man continued. He had a medium build and wore a red flannel shirt with a white T-shirt poking up to his neck. His face was bland, nondescript, showing no indications of outright evil.

Without taking his eyes from them, he reached in to the dashboard of his truck and yanked out two sheets of paper, colored computer printouts showing faces. The images were split: one side showed a photograph of her from fifteen years before, and the other image—computer enhanced—had "aged" her to approximate what she looked like now, along with a detailed personality analysis suggesting how she might normally dress. The second sheet of paper showed baby Jody and a much-less-exact extrapolation of how he would look as a sixteen-year-old boy.

"I'm convinced," the man said. "Or are you going to deny it, Mrs. McKenzy?"

For a moment, all the words backed up in her mind. She couldn't think of anything to say, couldn't think of anything worth saying. "What do you want from us?"

"What do I want?" He laughed and stepped around the door of the vehicle, still pointing the scattershot at them. "Purity's been looking a long time."

Growling, Pancake stood up and eased forward, baring his teeth. He stepped in front of Judd.

The Purity man stopped and blinked in astonishment. "Jesus, that's the dog! The goddamned dog—it's still alive! Well, well, well!"

"Do you want money?" Patrice said. She didn't have much left, but it would stall him for a few minutes. "I have cash. It won't show up on any account record."

"This goes beyond money," he said. "We need to bring you in. Take the dog and destroy him. Then find out from you and the boy if you've kept any of Dr. McKenzy's notes, maybe some of his nanotech samples. We can't take chances with the human race."

Seeming to sense the boy was the weak link in this scenario, the Purity man aimed the scattershot at Judd's head and took a few more steps toward them. Holding the rifle with one hand, he fumbled in his pocket, withdrawing a pair of polymer handcuffs.

"Now then, Mrs. McKenzy, let's not make this difficult. I want you to cuff one of these around your wrist and the other around the boy's ankle. That'll make it impossible for you to run anywhere." He extended the handcuffs forward.

Pancake lunged. Black labradors were not normally used as attack dogs, but Pancake must have been able to sense the fear and tension in the air. He knew who the intruder was, and he had been with the same owner for 24 years.

He struck the Purity man full in the shoulders, startling him, spoiling his aim. The scattershot dropped. The man's finger squeezed the trigger. The explosion roared through the quiet isolation far from the main road.

Instead of taking off Judd's head, the swath of silver needles spattered across the boy's chest, spraying blood behind him to the walls of the house.

Patrice screamed.

Pancake bore the man to the ground. The man thumped into the front of his vehicle, banged against the sharp laser-guidance detectors and then sprawled. He tried to fight the dog off. Pancake bit at his face, his throat.

Wailing, Patrice dropped to her knees and cradled her son's head. "Oh my god! Oh my god!"

Judd blinked his eyes. They were wide with astonishment and seemingly far away. Blood bubbled out of his mouth, and he spat it aside. "So tired." She stroked his hair.

Pancake backed away from the motionless man on the ground. Blood lay in pools from the man's torn throat.

The headlights of Patrice's carryall glared up from the wet pavement long after dark. She had switched off the old and unreliable laser-guidance systems and drove faster than safety or common sense allowed, but panic had gotten into her mind now. She kept driving, pushing her foot to the floor and wrestling with the curves of the coast road, heading north. Dark pine trees flashed by like tunnel walls on either side of her.

She had to find someplace else, to run again, to start a new life.

Pancake rested in the back of the station wagon, exhausted. Clumps of blood bristled from his fur. She hadn't taken time to clean him up. She had paused only long enough to throw all of her ready cash into the glove compartment. The Purity man's own wallet had held two hundred dollars and several cred cards under different names.

Looking down at the man's body in failing dusk light, she noticed that the blood had stopped flowing, yet his heart continued to beat. He looked to be in a deep sleep, and his skin felt warm and feverish. She stepped back in horror. Of course the government had nanotech healers of their own! All of Jerry's records were supposedly destroyed in the DyMar labs disaster, but with backups and disjointed systems, no simple fire could have eliminated everything.

Now she knew why, after all these years, others had

not made similar breakthroughs. Jerry had been merely the first, but other researchers were close on his heels. The sham organization of Purity, or the government, or some worldwide power consortium had kept nanotechnology to themselves, blocking or absorbing all other breakthroughs as they occurred.

This man would wake up in a day or so, and report back to his superiors. She could destroy him now, set his body on fire or squash his head with the front wheel of his own vehicle.

Instead, she siphoned all the fuel out of his truck and switched license markers. In some coast town, she would find a darkened parking lot and other unattended vehicles, and she would switch markers again. Then she would move on.

In the back seat of the carryall, Judd lay in silence, wrapped in two bloodstained blankets she had torn from the beds upstairs. His pulse was faint, his breathing shallow, but he still lived. He seemed to be in a coma.

The obstacle alarm screeched. From the trees on her right, a dog stepped into the road in front of her.

Patrice cried out, slammed the brakes and yanked the steering wheel. The dog bounded back out of sight. She swerved, nearly lost control of the car on the slick road, then regained it. Behind her, in the rear-view mirror, she saw the dark shape of the dog walk back across the road, undaunted by its close call.

She remembered one of the last conversations she had had with Jerry, after he had finally told her what he had done to Pancake and the immortality his nanotechnology had brought. Jerry had wanted to give her the same type of protection.

She blinked at him in horror when he told her he had already done it to himself. He wanted to do it to her, too.

The thought of a billion billion tiny machines crawling through her body, checking and rechecking her cell structures, seemed abominable to her. She refused to let him. Jerry would not let her ponder the question, would not let her come to grips with the idea. He wanted an answer *right then*. That was just the way Jerry McKenzy did things.

Baby Jody started to cry, awakened by their raised voices. Trish had looked up at her husband with wide eyes; she caught a faint smile on his face as Jerry glanced toward Jody's room.

"You didn't do anything to the baby, did you! What did you do to Jody?"

"Nothing!" Jerry said. He smiled. "I didn't do anything."

But she could always tell when her husband was lying.

As she drove off into the night, with her son's bleeding body in the car seat behind her, Patrice prayed she was right.

SMALLER AND SMALLER ...
AND PICKING UP SPEED

KEVIN J. ANDERSON

On December 2, 1942, in the basement of Stagg Field at the University of Chicago, Enrico Fermi and his team of soot-smeared physicists placed the last few blocks of dusty black graphite moderators around an experiment they were conducting. They were attempting to create the first self-sustaining nuclear chain reaction.

The neutron detectors and Geiger counters clicked as the workers removed control rods, unleashing the pile. Tensing, waiting, not sure what they were doing or what to expect, Fermi and his team watched the fission counters pick up, until finally the reaction in the atomic pile went critical—and stayed there, the world's first nuclear chain reaction.

This event sparked one of the most profound technological and sociological revolutions in the history of mankind, paving the way for the secret Manhattan Project and the first atomic weapon—opening the doors to nuclear power and nuclear war.

Less than a quarter century later, the first human set foot on the Moon, taking another giant leap only twenty-four years after the previous one.

Now another quarter century has passed, and we stand on the threshold of a third incredible breakthrough that will change all of human society and the disposition of our race. Perhaps it will create a shining new future for all of us—or spell death, destruction, and the end of the human race. As with every great stride in progress, the consequences are a double-edged sword.

Since you are holding this book in your hands, you know, of course, that I'm talking about nanotechnology. But unlike a self-sustaining chain reaction, or a first step on another planet, or even the faster-than-light drive science fiction has dreamed of for decades, nanotechnology is not an all-or-nothing prospect.

For years now our capabilities have been working toward the dream of nanotechnology, picking up speed as our technology shrinks, as we learn how to make smaller and smaller circuits, cram more and more electrical pathways into a tiny area. And as our tools continue to shrink, we can use them to make even smaller tools, bootstrapping our way down to the infinitesimally small— to the level of K. Eric Drexler's proposed nanotechnology.

But, as far as I know, there is nothing particularly magic about the size of 10^{-9} meters. Unlike the precise critical point of a chain reaction or breaking the lightspeed barrier, nothing particularly interesting happens at that exact size. So, rather than offering a specific target for researchers, nanotechnology provides a moving goal: the challenge simply to make the next generation smaller and faster and more efficient than the previous one.

(As Drexler has written in *Engines of Creation* and elsewhere, though, nanotechnology may be a lower limit, because of quantum effects on actual ultra-small circuits and machines. Atoms no longer fit together and cooperate in ways that we can take advantage of.)

The philosophy and the idea of nanotechnology have begun to infiltrate our society, though. And that is the point at which progress truly begins.

In my novel with Doug Beason, *Assemblers of Infinity*, we built a story around the idea of sending nanotechnology probes across space. These extremely small machines could be accelerated up to a significant fraction of the speed of light, using techniques we have at hand today. For an appropriately sized nanomachine with a material strength on the order of that of a common virus, such machines could survive these incredible forces over a required acceleration length of only one to ten meters. Many simple laboratories on Earth could manage this.

Our idea was to have these nanotechnology probes shotgunned across the cosmos, billions of them in all directions with no particular target in mind. By sheer chance, the probes are likely to encounter something within a finite amount of time, whereupon the self-replicating machines would begin to manufacture copies of themselves and then build a transmitting station that could send a signal back home—a simple, "Hello, I'm here!"

On a much larger scale, this type of idea has begun to change the way people think in industry and the space program. One of the main original ideas behind the Strategic Defense Initiative was to shift from using large-scale, expensive, anti-missile defenses to an orbiting cluster of small, independently targeted, kamikaze spacecraft. Thousands of these "Brilliant Pebbles" could swarm and destroy incoming enemy missiles.

Walter Scott, one of the original developers of the Brilliant Pebbles proposal, has spun off his own company, WorldView Imaging Corporation, to develop "Lightsats"— inexpensive, single-purpose, small satellites that can be launched in great quantities to perform the same mission (only far more accurately and more efficiently) as a single mammoth weather satellite or communications satellite.

Even NASA's philosophy has shifted, focusing instead on new, inexpensive missions that have been scaled down to use existing technology, rather than the enormous expenditure of single missions such as Galileo, Ulysses, and Voyager. NASA learned quite dramatically the risks of their "all the eggs in one basket" approach with the loss of the Mars Observer, one of the single most important spacecraft in NASA's future plans.

Doug Beason and I were thrilled to learn recently that our own novel, *Assemblers of Infinity*, has sparked a new potential space project. Stu Nozette (the director of the Clementine Mission), Colonel Pete Worden (the deputy director of the Ballistic Missile Defense Organization), and Jordan Katz (aerospace consultant) had all read our book and were intrigued by the concept of using massive amounts of tiny probes. Together, they have begun a feasibility study in Washington, DC, about the possibility of launching "microsats," small satellites weighing from one to ten kilograms that consist of nothing more than a sensor, power source, and transmitter. These microsats could be launched by the hundreds or thousands to perform specific missions. An additional desirable feature of microsats, besides their extremely low cost, is that such small, rugged devices could be launched into orbit by alternative and far less expensive means, such as rail guns or even ballistically (i.e., a giant cannon).

Our future progress will be predicated to a large extent on shifting to this new philosophy of using many redundant and cheap components rather than enormous, overexpensive, one-shot deals.

Science fiction has always tried to gaze into the future to predict or at least prepare us for what might lie ahead. From where I'm sitting, looking with my blurred optics into the years to come, I think our future looks very, very small.

CONTAGION

NORM HARTMAN

Old Tam Harker gripped the wheel as the rusty pickup clattered and banged along the rutted gravel road, leaving a trail of billowing dust and blue smoke as it jounced toward Oakville. Beside him on the ripped vinyl seat of the '94 Chevy, his son Zed stared moodily out at the passing scrub oak and salal brush. It was a fine morning on the Oregon coast, with just enough time between rain storms to let the sun shine down from a bright blue sky.

Zed told himself that he should be doing the driving. He could of made the run into town without Pa easy enough. They were just going in to pick up a few sacks of chicken feed, but that was the rule: Harkers didn't go into town by themselves. Nor no place else, neither. Not even forty-year-old Harkers. That was just the way it was, the way it always had been; *nobody* went off by themselves. Harkers lived together, worked together and prayed together. He'd been doing it all his life, but sometimes it was still a pain in the butt.

Harkers taught their own kids what little reading and writing and arithmetic they needed, and they *always* kept to themselves. They raised chickens and pigs and a few cows for milk, plowed their rocky fields with horses and mules, and only bought what few things they couldn't raise on the Harker ranch.

Not that they could afford to buy all that much anyhow. Citizen's Basic would only stretch to cover just that, basics, but Harkers raised just about all they really needed. Last summer had been extra dry, so now he and Pa were headed in to town. They would pick up a few sacks of feed to tide the chickens and pigs over until harvest time, and then head right back. . . .

Zed's train of thought jarred to a halt as the pickup's front wheel bounced off a boulder that had rolled down off the hillside into the left-hand rut. He grabbed for the door handle with his right hand, his crippled left hand with its missing fingers braced against the seat as Old Tam wrestled the balky vehicle back into line.

"Hey, take it easy on Old Betsy," he cautioned his father. "You sure you don't want me to drive?"

"You just keep your trap shut, boy!" Tam glared at his son through age-faded blue eyes, then turned back to squint at the road. "Just 'cause I'm nigh onto eighty years old, it don't mean I cain't drive Old Betsy as well as I ever could."

The unspoken words, ". . . and I'm still man enough to whup your ass, and don't you forget it!" hung in the air between them. Zed lurched back against the seat with a grunt as Tam hit another bump. When Pa took the bit in his teeth, there wasn't no arguing with him. Anyhow, Oakville was right up ahead by now as they finally came to where the paving started.

The pickup's hood, loosely anchored with a couple of lengths of baling wire, settled back down into place once they were on blacktop, the rest of the pickup's clatters and clangs covered by the roar from the rusty muffler. Worn brakes squealed as they came to a shuddering stop in front of Fenton's, Oakville's only feed store. Zed hopped out, carefully fastening the pickup's door shut behind him with another twist of the always-useful baling wire.

"Well, come on," Zed snarled. "What're you waiting for, the Second Coming?"

Zed kept the scowl off his face as he followed Tam into the store, standing back and keeping his mouth shut as the old man argued with Mr. Fenton over the price of chicken feed. Grumbling, Tam pulled out a wad of Basic coupons and carefully counted them out on the rough wooden counter, topping them off with a couple of worn dollar bills.

"There, take your danged gov'ment coupons. You still keep your feed in the same place?"

"Around back, yeah," answered Mr. Fenton, not impressed by the old man's anger. He'd had plenty of years to get used to it, Zed thought as he followed Tam out the door and around to the back of the sagging wooden building. Mr. Fenton must be about as old as Pa, even if he didn't look nowheres near it. By the time they got there, Mr. Fenton had wrestled out a stack of bulging feed sacks for them. He didn't offer to give them a hand, just watched sourly as his customers began hauling the bags around to their pickup.

About the third trip around to the back of the store, Zed thought about telling Pa he should've driven the pickup around to where the loading dock was, but he kept his mouth shut and swung another feed sack up to rest on his shoulder. His brother Mervyn could carry two sacks at once, but Zed's hand wouldn't take that much weight.

Anyhow, the last time he'd tried telling Pa something he'd been sent to bed without his supper like he was still a kid, instead of a forty-year-old man. He'd be glad in a few more weeks when cousin Ellie was old enough for him to marry, like he'd been promised for the last five years and more. His first wife, Mary Beth had passed on to her reward nigh onto ten years ago. Once he married he'd have his own cabin again, and it was about time. Ellie was about husband-high, just going on fifteen, and she had the cutest little . . .

"Pa! What's wrong?" Zed dropped his feed sack, not caring that it split and spewed cracked grain all over the dirt alley alongside the feed store. Old Tam was down on his face, a ruptured feed sack draped across his back. He was about halfway between the store and the pickup, and he wasn't moving! "Mr. Fenton! Something's happened to Pa!"

Zed rolled the feed sack off of Pa's shoulders, turning him over on his back. Tam's eyes fluttered open and he gazed up at his son with a confused expression on his whiskered face.

"Hurts." He gasped for breath, reaching across his

body with his right hand to grip his left shoulder. "Hurts like . . . Lemme up."

Zed held him down, not that it took much force. Tam was too weak to shake off his son's grip, and he stopped trying as another spasm of pain made him wince.

"Mr. Fenton?" Zed twisted his neck to look over his shoulder.

"I already called the medics. They should be here in about fifteen minutes. Takes about that long for the rescue copter to get here from Currin County Hospital."

"You shouldn't of done that," Zed reproached him. "You know us Harkers don't go to hospitals."

"He'll go, or he'll die," the storekeeper told Zed bluntly. "He's had a heart attack, and it looks like a bad one. Just keep him quiet until the medics get here, and maybe he'll make it yet."

Tam's lips were blue, and he didn't seem to be any too aware of what was going on around him. Zed folded up the near-empty feed sack to put under his head, mopping the sweat from his father's brow with the tail of his own shirt. It seemed like forever before he heard the heavy throbbing of helicopter blades, dust swirling and buffeting him as the craft settled down in the middle of the intersection with Highway 101, half a block away.

Old Tam passed out cold as he was bundled into the waiting helicopter. Out cold, or . . . No! Zed didn't want to think about it. His Pa had been the driving force in the Harker community since long before Zed had been born. He started to climb into the helicopter at a medic's invitation, then backed off, shaking his head. It was the first time he'd ever been this close to one of these Devil's contraptions, and he wasn't about to go up in that thing, no way!

"I'll drive my pickup, so I'll have it there when I'm ready to come back." He mumbled the words in answer to their invitation, not sure just how much of his excuse was the truth.

He had plenty of time to think, all by himself in the pickup as he rattled north along the coast highway toward Port Morton, where the county hospital was. He kept his speed down, his thoughts churning in a dozen different directions as he drove. Not that the pickup's Oregon license plate tags weren't up to date, but this was no time to get stopped for speeding. Old Tam always insisted that such-like rules had to be followed, if only to keep the government off their backs as much as they could. What if Pa *did* die? Zed was the oldest son, but he'd never been allowed to make any decisions for himself. Now, well just maybe he'd have to. Anyhow, *somebody* had to and it might as well be him!

But what if Pa didn't die? Well anyhow, he wouldn't live forever, but this just might slow him down a mite and someday Zed would still have to take over. Funny, the more he thought about it the better he liked the taste of ideas he wouldn't even have dared to think about if he hadn't been all by himself.

By the time he got to the hospital, Pa was undressed, gowned, and propped up in a hospital bed. They'd even shaved him! They must have done that while he was still unconscious, he'd never of let them do it to him otherwise. There were tubes in his arms, and another tube of clear plastic from a dingus fastened to his nose. His eyes were half-closed so that he looked kind of sleepy, but he wasn't too far out of it to miss Zed's entrance.

"About time you got here, boy," he rasped, heaving himself to a sitting position. "Get me outta here, right now! Rustle up my clothes, and . . ."

"Now, Mr. Harker." The doctor who bustled in from the hall might have only been about Zed's age, but he wasn't about to take any nonsense from his patient. "You're going to be in here for about a week or ten days, depending on how well you respond to our treatments. Your heart had stopped when the helicopter brought you in. I explained it all to you after we revived you, but I don't suppose that you were in much of any shape to listen at the time. Now that your son is here, I'll go over it again for both of you." He turned to Zed. "I'm Dr. Benton, and you must be his son, Zed Harker."

"I heard what you said," Tam growled before Zed could answer. "It just didn't make much sense to me. Some crazy stuff about little machines what you shot into me. Nanny-whatzits."

"They've got a fancy name," Dr. Benton agreed, "but most of us just call them nanobots. The first ones we injected were the type known as nano-rooters. Right now they are scavenging through your blood vessels, cleaning out cholesterol deposits and strengthening weak spots in your veins and arteries. When they've done their work, we will inject second stage models which will take over from there, performing general repairs to your heart as well as the rest of your body. As soon as they've done their work, you'll be able to go home."

"But I don't want your nano-dinguses," Tam protested weakly. "I just want you to lemme out of here!"

"You don't have any choice. You weren't conscious when we signed you in to the hospital, and under Citizen's Basic Medical Rights that gives us the authority to treat you. Now just relax. I'll have the nurse give you another shot if you're still in any pain."

Zed drove back to Oakville in the old pickup, still all by himself, his head still awhirl with new thoughts. He loaded the rest of the chicken feed from Fenton's loading dock, absently thanking the storekeeper for replacing the two bags that had been spilled. Then he drove slowly, still alone, back to Harker Ranch.

"Whatcha mean, Pa ain't coming back?" Mervyn's slack jaw worked slowly, as if he was chewing Zed's words to extract their meaning.

"Not right away. He's in the hospital, over to Port Morton," Zed repeated patiently, raising his voice over the uproar caused by his announcement. His younger brother Mervyn might not be quite as strong as an ox, but then he didn't have nowhere near the brains of one, neither. "He's had him a heart attack, a pretty bad one, and he's going to be in there for a week or more. I'm taking charge while he's gone, but you all know what you should be doing so that shouldn't be no problem."

"But what're we gonna do about the south pasture?" Whiney-voiced Uncle Charley elbowed his bald head and skinny frame to the front of the milling crowd of Harkers. "Your Pa was gonna decide if we was plowing it up or not."

"It can wait a week, and if he ain't back by then I'll just hafta decide for him." Zed pushed his way past the crowd of gaping, chattering relatives until he stood on the porch of the rickety building that housed the immediate members of the Harker clan. He wasn't about to tell them that Old Tam had actually died on the way to the hospital and been brought back to life. He wasn't sure that even he was ready to digest *that* one yet. "Mervyn, you unload them sacks of feed and stack them inside the barn. We can talk this over some more after prayer meeting this evening."

There weren't all that many decisions to make, Zed decided after his first week of running the ranch. Get up in the morning, pray, eat breakfast, go to work in the fields, pray, eat lunch, work some more in the fields or do whatever needed doing around the ranch, pray, eat supper, lounge around and talk a while, pray, and go to bed. The only decision that loomed in front of him right now was what to do about the south pasture.

"Your Pa still ain't back here," Uncle Charley whined, the early morning sun glinting off his bald pate. "It's dry enough to plow right now, and we ain't gonna have time to plant nothing if we wait too much longer."

Zed walked over to the front of the barn where he could look out over the field in question. Uncle Charley was right, the field needed plowing right away if they were going to have time to get anything planted before the rains ended. There was plenty of other land left in pasture, and they could always use a few more acres of crops. If they planted potatoes, they might even raise enough to sell a few dozen bushels in town.

"All right," he decided. "Go ahead and hitch up the horses. I'll send Mervyn along to help you out—"

He didn't have time to finish the sentence as a heavy hand landed on his shoulder and spun him around to face the house.

"Pa! You're back! I was just telling Uncle Charley . . ."

"I heard what you was telling him." Old Tam's face contorted into a snarling mask. "You couldn't even wait for me to die before starting to take over!"

"But, Pa—"

Zed's mouth was still open when Tam's heavy fist laid him full length in the barnyard muck. He pushed himself up to a sitting position, wiping at the blood that dripped from where a tooth had cut his lip. He wasn't too far out of it to notice that Uncle Charley had made himself scarce, but several other Harkers gaped from a safe distance.

"But, Pa—"

Again Zed's words were cut off as Tam reached down and grabbed the front of his shirt. Lifting his son to his feet, Tam hit him again. This time Zed stayed down, wisely keeping his mouth shut.

"Don't you 'But, Pa' me, Zed Harker. Now get up outta the dirt and go help Charley with the plowing." Tam wiped a smear of blood away from where Zed's tooth had gashed his knuckle. "Them fool doctors said I warn't near ready to come home yet, so I just got up and left. Took the bus to Oakville, and hitched me a ride the rest of the way."

Zed backed away carefully until he was out of Tam's reach. Whatever they'd done to him in the hospital, it sure hadn't helped Pa's temper any. He looked healthy enough, though. Better than he had for some time. His eyes were brighter, somehow, and even his whiskers seemed to be growing in darker, with more black hairs mixed in amongst the gray.

"Ease off there, Zed," Uncle Charley shouted at him as he finished plowing another furrow crossways of the south pasture. "Give the critters a rest, afore you plumb run them into the ground."

Zed let the horses stand and blow for a minute, wiping the sweat off his forehead with the back of his hand. This was the third day that they'd been at the plowing, and finally the field was danged near ready to plant. He hadn't realized that he'd been pushing the team that hard, but the ground seemed softer, easier to plow than he'd expected.

Pa wasn't the only one who was feeling good, he decided. Everyone on the Harker Ranch seemed to have perked up in the last few days. Especially Ellie. Next week was her birthday, and after that . . .

Zed's thoughts broke off as he stared at the hand he'd wiped his brow with. His left hand. It itched, and felt kind of funny. Like the fingers he'd lost to the hay baler when he was a kid were really still there. Not that they were, but the edge of his palm looked kind of weird, like the skin was bulging out in a couple of places.

Pa hadn't said anything more about what had happened while he was gone, but that didn't fool Zed into thinking he'd forgotten about it. The next night, after they'd eaten dinner and all prayed together, Zed couldn't wait any longer to say something.

"Pa." His voice came out as a harsh croak, and he had to clear his throat and start over. "Pa, Ellie's gonna be fifteen next week."

"So?" Tam glared at him as he closed the bible on the lectern, letting the rustle of movement throughout the meeting room die away to a dead silence.

"So, ain't it about time to start getting ready for our . . . our wedding?" Zed's words faltered as he shrank under the glare of Tam's angry gaze.

"And who says there's gonna be any wedding?"

"She's been promised to me . . ."

"Shut your mouth!" Tam's fist thumped down on the cover of the bible, raising a cloud of dust from the rickety lectern. His eyes raked across his son's face, and Zed realized suddenly that they were no longer the washed out, faded blue that they had been for as long as he could remember. "I'll be the one who decides when she gets married and to who, and I'll tell you right now that it ain't gonna be you."

"But, Pa . . ."

"Shut your mouth! Ellie's too good for the likes of a kid like you. She needs a real man. It's been a long time since I've had the urge, but now I think it's just about time I was getting married again."

Zed could only stare at his father, mouth hanging open as though to let out words that just would not come. Pa had been acting different since he'd come back from the hospital. Not just acting different, but looking different too. Younger, his thinning hair starting to come back in thick and dark, his face no longer the sunken-in, wrinkled face of an old, old man. Was this stranger really Old Tam?

Zed looked frantically over to where Ellie sat with the other youngsters, but she wouldn't meet his gaze. She only gazed at Tam with worshipful eyes, her mouth half open as if in wonder. With a sinking feeling in the pit of his stomach, Zed guessed that she was thinking about being the wife of the strongest man on the Harker farm. She surely wasn't giving *him* any second thoughts. None of the others in the meeting room looked like they were about to back him up, neither. Old habits were too strong, and Old Tam's fierce glare brooked no challenges.

Zed's gaze dropped to where his own two hands gripped the edge of his chair. His left hand *was* changing, the bulges where his fingers had been were growing and lengthening almost as he watched. What was it the doctor in Port Morton had said about the nanny-whatzits? Oh, yeah.

"*. . . performing general repairs to your heart as well as the rest of your body.*"

Pa had cut his knuckle on Zed's tooth when he'd knocked him down. Could the nanny-whatzits be catching? And Pa *was* getting younger. Zed got up from his chair on legs that suddenly felt almost too weak to hold him up. He left the meeting room at a staggering run, brushing past gaping family members before they could react. Tam shouted something after him but he didn't stop until he was clear out behind the barn, leaning against the hood of the old pickup. The smell of rain was in the air, but right now a few stars still peered through rents in the clouds.

Pa had left the hospital before the doctors had said he could. Before the nanny-whatzits had all been flushed out of his body? Or had the doctors done this to them on purpose? Maybe the things were *supposed* to be catching. Whatever the reason, the things were on the loose now. For all he knew, they could have already been passed on to the rest of the Harkers.

Or had he been the one to bring them back to the

farm? Yeah, maybe he had. Pa hadn't been back from the hospital all that long. Was Uncle Charley's bald head starting to grow hair again? He hadn't really noticed, but now that he thought about it. . . .

And what about Ellie? Wasn't that cute little mole by the side of her mouth getting smaller? Even Mervyn was acting different. He'd been needing fewer orders to do his work around the farm. Maybe he was getting smarter than he'd been, ever since one of the horses had kicked him in the head when he was just a toddler. And the kids, there'd always been at least a couple of the kids running around with the sniffles, but the last few days he hadn't so much as heard a cough or a sneeze from nobody.

Well even so, Pa still had to die some time. Or . . . or did he? Zed pounded the hood of the pickup softly with his good hand as a picture built up in his mind of the Harker ranch staying the same for the next fifty, the next hundred, maybe even the next thousand years. With Old Tam still running things, and Zed and everybody else still taking Tam's orders. *Young* Tam's orders. With Ellie popping out Tam's kids instead of his own, one every year, until the place was plumb overrun with little Harkers.

The first drops of rain spattered against his face and somehow Zed found himself in the driver's seat of the old pickup. The battery strained to turn the motor over once, twice, then a third time before it finally caught. He eased the pickup down the rutted driveway to the old county road, taking it slow and careful until he was around the first curve and could turn on his lights. It wasn't all that far to Oakville, then past Oakville to Port Morton, and then on beyond the county seat and up Highway 101 to places he'd never seen, hardly even heard about in all his forty years.

And then it was just Zed Harker at the wheel, alone in the dark with the rain smearing his windshield, really alone for the first time in his life. Alone, and free.

COMMENTS

DEEP SAFARI

CHARLES SHEFFIELD

When Alexander Graham Bell invented the telephone, did he know that it would someday be used to rouse you out of bed in the middle of the night to talk to someone selling tickets to the Fireman's Annual Ball? When Albert Einstein published his first papers on relativity in 1905, did he realize that in three-quarters of a century there would be enough nuclear weapons to kill everyone on earth several times over? And when Guglielmo Marconi performed his first radio experiments, did he have any idea how much verbal banality in the form of radio talk shows he was inflicting on the world?

I can't prove that the answer to all these questions is no, but I am willing to bet on it. Bell probably saw his invention as a powerful and useful tool, able to send urgently-needed information over long distances faster and more accurately than in any other way. Einstein, if he ever gave consideration to the long-term practical consequences of his theories before the days of World War Two and the start of the Manhattan Project, would probably have foreseen a new, inexpensive and almost limitless source of energy. Marconi knew that his "wireless" signals would permit communication across great distances, and to places which would otherwise be out of reach.

If these great scientists and inventors indeed thought such positive thoughts, they were all quite right. Each

invention or theory has been a great force for good.[1]
Each has also been abused, for purposes that range from
simply stupid to evil and profoundly dangerous. Furthermore, it has proved impossible to limit the uses of any
invention to those that do good or have a serious purpose. If Charles Babbage could be raised from the dead,
he would be ecstatic to see incredibly fast and powerful
versions of his Analytical Engine in millions of house-
holds. It is unlikely that he, upper-class and crusty
Englishman that he was, would be at all pleased to know
that a substantial fraction of those Analytical Engines
were being employed mainly to play video games.

People, ignoring the wishes of the inventor, take an
innovation and use it the way they want to, in applications good, trivial, or dangerous. We can learn to live
with the consequences of discovery, and try to make the
benefits outnumber the evils, but one thing is certain: a
discovery, once made, cannot be undiscovered.

Which brings me to nanotechnology. If and when it
fulfills its long-term potential, it will transform all of
human life so completely that our descendants will
encounter (and hope to live through, though almost certainly not enjoy) a true singularity of the time-line, a
moment in history when the future cannot in any sense
be predicted from the past. For this reason, I am greatly
suspicious of any story which takes place *after* the widespread introduction of real nanotechnology. I'm also not
sure I would care to live on the other side of that Great
Divide. I'm too set in my ways, too sure of what I like
and dislike. I don't want to learn to live all over again.

However, before full-scale nanotechnology changes the
world beyond imagining, there will be—I hope—a transi-
tional period; a time when certain capabilities of the
nanotechnology revolution have been realized, but not
the final forms. And if humans then are anything like
humans now, those capabilities will probably not be the

---

[1] I include nuclear power plants in this category, and I regard
current U.S. fears of anything nuclear as a passing paranoid
phase.

ones dreamed of by the scientists who invented the field, many of whom in their enthusiasm for their technical ideas become a little myopic as to what other people really want.[2]

For example, it is often asserted that nanotechnology will allow us to make lighter, stronger, cheaper spacecraft. I like that idea. I am also aware, however, that lighter, stronger, cheaper spacecraft fall rather near the bottom of most people's wish list. Offered that or a tastier pizza, I think I know which way the vote would go.

I regard myself as a space nut, someone who has spent a substantial fraction of my life promoting the idea that space development is a good thing, desirable and, from the long-term point of view of the human race, inevitable. However, when nanotechnology moves from intriguing notion to practical technique, a better spacecraft will not be at the top of my list, either.

Just yesterday my next-door neighbor stopped by for a beer and a chat at an outdoor picnic in my back garden. I did not realize it at the time, but the beer I gave him was a questionable favor. He had no difficulty swallowing it down, but then at some point he knew he would have to get rid of it. He told me, in the course of conversation, that for the past few days he had been suffering from prostatitis, which is nothing more than medical jargon for inflammation of the prostate. An inflamed and enlarged prostate makes urination both painful and sometimes close to impossible, and only a few days earlier Bill had been catheterized to help the process. I do not propose to dwell on the subject of urethral catheters, or to render verbatim Bill Groome's comments on their installation and removal procedure. I will merely say that when nanotechnology hits its stride, I want the very first application to be in non-invasive medical testing, closely followed or perhaps even preceded by non-invasive medical treatment. To paraphrase my neighbor's question, in

---

[2] I do not put in this group Eric Drexler, whom I have known since the 1970's, and who for all that time has been as freeranging a thinker as you could hope to meet.

terms that have been used a million times, "If they can put a man on the moon, why can't they empty my bladder without sticking a tube up my willy?"

Someday, Bill, someday. And from my point of view, the sooner, the better. If you've ever seen a miserable five-year old being given scratch tests for allergies, or had a "routine" test for kidney stones or bone marrow condition, or watched an amniocentesis, you'll know that there has to be a better way. I rather think that "better way" will have to come from outside the medical community, where "You may feel some discomfort" means "You'll be in agony," and a minor operation seems to be defined as an operation on someone else. I hope that nanotechnology, even in its simplest and earliest stages, will offer painless and imperceptible alternatives to the horrible, invasive, but necessary tests that form a large part of today's medical technology. In the twenty-second century, our descendants will look on angiograms, upper and lower GI's, and biopsies the way we regard the prospect of surgery without anesthetics.

My story, "Deep Safari," assumes that nanotechnology makes its *second* major social impact on medical practice. Its first social impact, of course, is in the form of the game, *Adestis*. Is it conceivable that such a life-or-death game against nature's deadliest adversaries would prove popular? Don't ask me, I'm a natural coward. Look instead at the records of the nineteenth century, when lion-hunting and tiger-hunting were popular sports and guns were not as reliable as they are today.

Two final comments. The name *Adestis*, a game which by the way also appears in *The Mind Pool* (a shameless plug for another work of mine from Baen Books) just means "You are present," in Latin. And my story is arguably not real *nano*technology. My nanodoc critters are much bigger than molecule-sized. But "microtechnology" is not nearly as attractive a term, and anyway if I used that name I could not be in this splendid anthology.

DEEP SAFARI

CHARLES SHEFFIELD

Tradition calls for a celebration on the evening that the hunt is concluded.

The hunters will be tired, some will be hurting, some may even have died. There will be a party anyway, and it will go on for most of the night. Tradition is the younger sister of ritual. Rituals are better if they do not make sense.

I do not like to attend the parties. I have seen too many. The theory is that the hunters should be permitted to over-indulge in food, in drink, in sex, in everything, but particularly in talk, because on hunt night they want to re-live the glorious excitement of the chase, the shared danger, the deeds of valor, the climactic event of the kill.

Sounds wonderful. But for every hero or heroine flushed with quiet or noisy pride there will be three or four others, drinking and talking as loud as any but glancing again and again at their companions, wondering if anyone else noticed how at the moment of crisis and danger they flinched and failed.

I notice. Of course. I couldn't afford not to notice. My job is to orchestrate everything from first contact to *coup de grâce*, and to do that I have to know where everyone is and just what he or she is doing. That is much harder work than it sounds, so when a hunt is over all I want is sleep. But that relief is denied to me by my obligatory attendance at the post-hunt party.

The morning that Everett Halston called, the hunt celebration the previous night had been even harder to take than usual. The group had consisted of a dozen rich merchants, neophytes to hunting but in spite of that—because of that?—determined to show their nerve by tackling one of the animal kingdom's most efficient and terrifying predators.

I had warned them, and had been overruled. When we finally met the quarry, all but two of my group had frozen. They were too overwhelmed by fear to advance or even to flee. Three of us stepped forward, stood our ground, and made a difficult kill. A *very* difficult kill. Without a little luck the roles of hunter and prey could easily have been reversed.

Perhaps because of that near-disaster the hunt party had been even noisier and wilder than usual. My group of twelve participants was augmented by an equal number of male and female partners, none of them the least tired and every one ready to dance 'til dawn.

About four-thirty I managed to slip away and collapse into bed. And there I found not the calm and peaceful sleep that I had looked forward to for twelve hours, but a dream-reprise of the hunt finale as it might have been.

I had managed to move the whole group to the bottom of the pit in good order, because they had not so far had a sight of the living prey. I anticipated trouble as soon as that happened. Before we entered Adestis mode we had studied the structure and actions of the spider, but I knew from previous experience that wouldn't mean a damn during live combat. It's one thing to peer at an animal that's no bigger across the carapace than the nail on your index finger, to study its minute jaws and poison glands and four delicate tube-like spinnerets, and plan where you will place your shots for maximum effect; it's another matter when you are linked into your Adestis simulacrum, and the spider that you are supposed to hunt and kill is towering ten paces away from you like a gigantic armored tank, its invincible back three times as high as the top of your head.

Before I had the group organized to my satisfaction, our quarry took the initiative. The spider came from its hiding-place in the side of the pit and in that first rush it came fast. I saw a dark-brown body with eight pearly eyes patterning its massive back. The juggernaut drove forward on the powerful thrust of four pairs of seven-jointed legs. Those legs had seemed as thin and fragile as flower stamens in our studies, but now they were bristly trunks, each as thick as a simulacrum's body. The chelicerae, the pointed crushing appendages at the front of the spider's maw, were massive black pincers big enough to bite your body in two.

Without taking the time to see how my group was reacting, I did what I had explicitly warned them not to do. I lifted my weapon and sprayed projectiles at the three eyes that I could see. I think I got one of them, but the carapace itself was far too tough to be penetrated. Ricocheting projectiles flew everywhere. The spider was not seriously injured—I knew it would not be. But maybe it wondered if we were really its first choice for dinner, because it halted in its forward sweep. That gave me a little breathing space.

I scanned my group. Not reassuring. For ten of them the sight of the advancing spider had been more than they could take. Their personal simulacra stood motionless, weapons pointed uselessly at the ground.

These Adestis units were not furnished with sound generation or receiving equipment. Everything had to be signaled by our actions. We had rehearsed often enough, but unfortunately this was nothing like rehearsal. I ran forward waving at my group to lift their weapons and follow me, but only two of them did. They moved to stand on either side and just behind me.

I glanced at their two helmet IDs as I turned to urge the rest to advance and deploy in a half-circle as we had planned. Even though I would never reveal the information to anyone, I liked to know who the cool ones were—they might play Adestis again some day. None of the others moved, but a second later the weapon of the simulacrum on my right was lifting into position, while his other arm reached to tap my body in warning.

I spun around. Forget the half circle. The spider was coming forward again, in a scuttling rush that covered the space between us at terrifying speed.

Before I could fire the predator had reached us. I saw the maw above me, the dark serrated edge of the carapace, the colonies of mite and tick parasites clinging to the coarse body bristles. Then I was knocked flat by the casual swat of one powerful leg.

I sprawled under the house-wide body and saw the chelicerae reach down, seize one of my companions at midriff, and crush until his simulacrum fell apart into two pieces.

He writhed but he did not scream—here.

(I knew that his real body, coupled by its telemetry headset to control his simulacrum and receive its sensory inputs, would be writhing and screaming in genuine agony.

It didn't have to be that way. I would have been quite happy to do without pain signals altogether, useful as they might be as a warning for simulacrum injury. But any proposal to eliminate pain was consistently vetoed by the paying customers for Adestis. They wanted referred pain when their simulacrum was injured. It was part of the macho (male and female) view of the game. The Adestis hunt had to feel real, as real as it could be; occasional deaths, from the heart failure that can accompany terror and intense agony, were an important part of what they were paying for.)

And at the moment my own body, the gigantic form that somewhere infinitely far above us sat motionless in the Adestis control theater, was within a split-second of its own writhing, screaming agony. The spider knew I was underneath it—knew it not from sight, which was a sense it did not much rely on, but from touch. The legs, in spite of their power, were enormously sensitive to feel and to vibration patterns. The spider was backing up, questing. It wanted me. I was shaking with fear, my hands trembling and my belly so filled with icy terror that the muscles of my whole mid-section were locked rigid.

And then came the single precious touch of good luck, the accident of position that saved me and the rest of our group. As the spider moved over me I saw the pedicel; there it was, the thin neck between cephalothorax and abdomen, the most vulnerable point of the whole organism. It was directly above my head, impossible to miss.

I lifted my weapon. Fired. And blew the spider into two clean halves that toppled like falling mountains on either side of me.

But not this time. In my dream, the pedicel moved out of view before I could squeeze off a shot. I was staring up at the hard underside of the cephalothorax— at the head section—at the doomsday jaws and glistening poison glands as they lowered towards me. They would engulf me, swallow me whole, to leave me struggling and hopeless within the dark interior cavern of the spider's body.

I knew, at some level of my mind, that spiders do not swallow their prey. They inject enzymes, pre-digest their victims, and suck them dry. But we select our own personal nightmares. I would die slowly, in the night of the spider's body cavity.

I braced myself for the unendurable.

And came to shuddering wakefulness at the loud, insistent ring of my bedside telephone. I realized where I was and groped for the handset, almost too relieved to breathe.

"Fletcher?" The voice in my ear was familiar. It ought to have suggested a face and a name, but in my dazed condition it was just a voice.

"Uh-uh." I squinted at the clock. Seven-fifteen. Two and three-quarter hours of sleep. Although I had eaten little and drunk nothing last night, I felt hung over and a hundred years old. Seven-fifteen P.M. was what I'd had in mind as a decent wake-up time.

"*Clancy* Fletcher?" insisted the voice.

"Uh-uh." I cleared my throat. "Yes. That's me. I'm Clancy Fletcher."

"Don't sound like him. This is Everett Halston. I need to talk to you. You awake enough to take anything in?"

"Yes." I'd found the face, and the name, even before he gave it. He sounded older.

Palpitations and inability to breathe came back, worse than when I woke. *Everett Halston.* He really was old. The Pearce family's professional aide and confidant for three generations. And Miriam's personal lawyer.

"Did Miriam—" I began.

"Listen first, Mr. Fletcher, then you can ask questions." The brisk, salty voice was oddly reassuring. Its next words were not. "Dr. Miriam Pearce left a tape with me, some time ago, and gave me specific instructions. I was to play that tape only if, in my judgment, she was in very serious trouble and unable to act on her own behalf.

"Late last night I played the tape. I played it because Dr. Miriam is unconscious, and no one seems able to tell me when or if she is likely to awaken."

"Where is she?"

"I'll get to that. You were always a good listener. Listen now. Dr. Miriam is at New Hanover Hospital, on the fifth floor. *Don't hang up, Mr. Fletcher. I know you want to.* Wait until I am finished. She was moved to an intensive care unit two days ago, from her own research facility, a few hours after she was discovered unconscious. Her vital signs are stable and she is being fed intravenously. However, the attendant physicians are much concerned about her condition. They state—insofar as one can persuade a physician to make any firm statement whatsoever—that they have ruled out all forms of stroke, tumor, and subdural hemorrhage. CAT and PET scans show no abnormalities, although they plan to repeat those today.

"I am now going to play you Dr. Miriam's tape, or at least the portion of it that concerns you. Wait a few minutes."

I waited, suspended from life. It was three years since I had seen Miriam Pearce, more than two since I had spoken to her.

"If there is a strictly legal decision to be made, Everett, and I am for any reason unable to participate, I want you to use your own best judgment." Miriam's delivery had not altered at all. Slightly uneven in rhythm, as though she constantly changed her mind about how the sentence ought to end. Confident, jaunty, and a little short-tongued, so that "r" was always a trifle breathier than normal.

"However, other situations may arise. I could be in danger, or encounter a problem where conventional solutions cannot be applied. It may even be that you do not know what has happened to me, or where I am. In such a case, I want you to contact Clancy Fletcher. Ask him to help me. And commit to him all the financial or other resources that you control in my name."

The message ended, or was more likely cut off by Halston. There was a dead silence, while my head spun with questions. The financial resources of Miriam, and of the whole Pearce family, were huge. They could buy the absolute best of anything including medical care. Danger I might have been able to handle. But what could I possibly do for her if she was sick?

"Mr. Halston, I'm not a doctor."

"I am aware of that."

"I can't help Miriam."

"If you do not try, you certainly cannot. However, I think you are wrong. Let me suggest that you should not pre-judge your potential usefulness. If you intend to proceed to New Hanover Hospital, your point of contact there is Dr. Thomas Abernathy."

Halston paused, I am sure for my benefit. He felt that I would need time to recover from the shock. Halston knew that Tom Abernathy was Miriam's close colleague and probably her sexual partner, as surely as he knew that I was Miriam Pearce's sometime collaborator and lover. He also, by the sound of it, suspected or knew something that he was not going to reveal to me.

"I have told Thomas Abernathy of Dr. Miriam's instructions to me," he went on. "I have also informed him that those instructions will be supported by me and by the full weight of the Pearce estate."

"He must have loved that."

"Let us say that he did not offer an argument, once he had listened to Dr. Miriam's tape."

Of course not. Tom Abernathy was far, far smarter than Clancy Fletcher. Abernathy knew instinctively what I had only learned the hard way: You should not try to argue with fifteen billion dollars. That much money creates winds like a hurricane, all around it. A wise man allows himself to be swept along with the gale, but he does not fight it. Because he cannot win.

"Could I hear the tape again?"

"Certainly."

We both listened in silence. Miriam's voice was so infinitely familiar. *Too* familiar. I had heard her on a nanodoc television broadcast less than a year ago, a couple of months after a minor operation on her larynx. Her voice was slightly affected then. I had assumed that the change would be permanent.

"Mr. Halston, *when* did Miriam make the tape?"

There was a click as though some recording device had been turned off, followed by a dry chuckle at the other end of the line. "Mr. Fletcher, you are as perceptive as ever. This tape has been in my possession for over three years."

Three years. Before Miriam hated me.

"I suspect that Dr. Miriam Pearce forgot about it," he went on, "or did not get around to changing it. However I will argue, in a court of law if necessary, that no action of Dr. Miriam has ever led me to suspect that the recording reflects anything other than her current wishes. Now. Will you be going to New Hanover Hospital?"

"As soon as we get through."

"Then I will say only three more things. First, I will make sure that you are expected at the hospital. Second, Thomas Abernathy will probably not be your friend."

"I know that. What's the other one?"

"Just good luck, Clancy. Good luck for you; and good luck for Miriam."

The New Hanover Hospital was a nine-story spire of glass and carved stone, a whited sepulchre jutting from well-tended lawns.

In one sense it *was* a memorial, a testament to Pearce money. The entrance hall bore a message inlaid into its marble mosaic floor, informing the world that the construction of the edifice had been made possible by Pearce munificence. The fifth floor, where Miriam lay unconscious, was known as the Meredith Franklin Pearce ward.

I did not get to see Miriam at once, much as I wanted to. When the elevator door opened Thomas Abernathy was there, lying in wait for me.

We had never met, although I had studied his career

from afar. But still I did not *know* him. As he came forward with outstretched hand I watched his face closely, as a druid might have peered from the misted woods at an arriving Christian. What *was* the newcomer who had taken my place?

Just as important, what had she told him of me? Had there been long afternoons of naked revelation, luxurious nights when Tom Abernathy heard all about a poor, despised Clancy? Miriam babbled after love-making, in a dreamy stream of consciousness at odds with her usual controlled speech.

We all give to ourselves an importance that is seldom justified. Dr. Thomas Abernathy did stare at me when we shook hands, but it was with perplexity rather than knowing amusement. He did not seem to know who or what I was. But he himself looked a real smoothie, tall and fair and elegant, with a just-right handshake and a physician's perfect bedside manner.

One that he was not willing to waste too much on me.

"I do have the right person, don't I?" he said after a few moments of critical inspection. "When Everett Halston said Clancy Fletcher, I thought, if that's the toy man . . ."

"The Small Game Hunter. That's right. That's me." It was the way that the present owners of *Adestis* ran their television advertisements, a business over which I had no control. *Did you think that the Big Game Hunt became impossible when the largest carnivores became extinct? (Television shots of a rearing grizzly, a leaping tiger). Not so! The world's most deadly game has always been at smaller scale. (Three shots, in rapid sequence, of a praying mantis, a dragonfly, and a trapdoor spider, enlarged to the scale that would be seen by a simulacrum). These prey are available to hunt today, in unlimited numbers. Join an* Adestis *safari, and go on a* Small Game Hunt—*where the line between hunter and hunted can never be drawn. (A final shot of a writhing figure, totally human in appearance as a true simulacrum never was, being dismembered by a quartet of furious soldier ants).*

It was one way to make a living.

"I'd like to see Miriam Pearce. I assume that she is still unconscious?"

"I'm afraid so."

Abernathy hesitated. It was easy to see his problem. Someone had been dumped in his lap who presumably knew nothing about medicine, someone who made his living in a trivial way from what Thomas Abernathy must regard as toys designed for adults with more money than sense. And poor Doctor Tom, who was surely a god in his own domain, had to *humor* this clown. Because the clown had unfortunately been given the keys to the Pearce treasure chest, and if Clancy Fletcher felt like it he could throw Abernathy out of his own hospital, at least until Miriam Pearce awoke.

The terrible thing was my own feelings. I hated Abernathy from deep inside me. If I was to help Miriam, I had to control myself.

The other terrible thing, of course, was my conviction that I was inadequate to help Miriam in any way.

"Do you have any idea what happened to her?" I had to start Abernathy talking, or that conviction was bound to prove correct.

"I have—a theory." He was finally moving, leading me along the corridor away from the elevator. "You know, I assume, that Dr. Miriam Pearce is one of the world's pioneers in the field of micro-surgery?"

"Yes. I know that."

"Well, what is not so well-known is that she has over the years been operating at smaller and smaller scales. When she began, ten years ago, her first generation of remotely-guided instruments for micro-surgery were huge by today's standards. Each one was as big as your fingertip. They were also primitive in their remote control capability. The human operator could use them to perform only limited surgical functions. However, about three years ago Dr. Pearce learned how to produce a line of much more sophisticated instruments, smaller and more versatile."

I knew all about that, too, far more than Thomas Abernathy would ever know. But my attention was elsewhere. As we were talking we had moved along the corridor and at last entered a private room. Miriam lay on a bed near the window, eyes now quite closed. I stepped nearer and saw a thin slit of pale blue iris. Her color was good, her expression calm. She was still beautiful, not at all like a person unconscious because of accident or disease. She seemed only asleep. But in her arm were the IVs and next to her stood a great bank of electronic equipment.

I lifted her hand and pressed it gently. She did not stir. I squeezed harder. No response. I leaned over and spoke into her ear. "Miriam!"

"Naturally, we have tried all the usual and safe stimulants." Tom Abernathy's expression said that he disapproved of my crude experiments. "Chemical, aural, and mechanical. The responses have been limited and puzzling."

Chemical, aural, mechanical. Drugs, noises, jabs. They won't wake Sleeping Beauty. Did you try a kiss?

I wanted to. Instead I straightened up and said, "You say you have a theory for what's happening?"

"I do. Dr. Pearce next produced a line of smaller micro-surgery instruments, each one no bigger than a pea, and each capable of much finer control by the human operator. They were a huge success, and they have transformed surgical technique.

"But they were still too big for certain operations, particularly for fine work within the brain. A few months ago Dr. Pearce took the next step. Nano-surgery, with dozens of multiple, mobile, remote-controlled tools far smaller than a gnat, and all under the control of a single operator."

He glanced at me for a reaction. I nodded to show that I was impressed. If he hoped to amaze me, he had a long way to go. There were *Adestis* games in which the player's simulacrum was small enough to fight one-on-one with hungry single-celled amoebas, and there were other games in which one human controlled dozens or even hundreds of simulacra. But I was beginning to see why old Everett Halston believed I might have a role to play in solving Miriam's problem. I didn't know medicine or surgery, but I knew *Adestis* technology better than anyone on earth.

"We tested the nanodocs on animals," went on Abernathy, "and they seemed to work fine. So after we had the permits we performed our first work on human subjects. That was just five days ago. In my opinion those operational experiments succeeded perfectly. But Miriam—Dr. Pearce—had her reservations. She believed that although the operations had given satisfactory results, our level of control of the nanodocs was an order of magnitude more crude than the design ought to permit. Her theory was that we were making tools so small that their performance was being adversely affected by quantum effects. I tended to agree with her.

"That was where we were three days ago, when I left for a conference in Rochester. I returned a day later, and learned that Miriam had been found unconscious in the lab.

"She had been in perfect health when I left, but naturally we assumed at first that it was some conventional medical problem. It was only when the routine tests showed normal results that I went back to see what Miriam had been doing while I was away. Yesterday I found that a set of the new nanodocs was missing—and the monitors insisted that they had been placed under Miriam's control. According to the monitors, they are *still* under her control, even though she is unconscious."

"But where are they?" I was afraid that I knew the answer. Miriam had her own ideas as to how medical tests ought to be conducted.

Thomas Abernathy nodded to the body on the bed. "I feel sure they are inside her, a couple of hundred of them. I can't prove that idea—or let's say, I dare not try. The only way to be sure would be to break the telemetry contact between Dr. Pearce and the nanodocs. If they *are* inside her, then letting them run out of control might kill her. Because in view of her condition it is natural to assume that they are lodged somewhere within her brain."

I took another look at the silent beauty on the bed. If hundreds of nanodocs were running wild inside Miriam, it did not show.

"What do you plan to do about it, Dr. Abernathy?"

He stared at me, uncertain for the first time since we had met. "I do not know what to do, Mr. Fletcher. Several of my colleagues are urging exploratory surgery—" (*Saw the top off Miriam's head. Slice open the protective membranes of her brain. Dive in, poke around, and see what you can find.* I shivered.) "—but I regard that as a last resort. I would rather wait, watch, and pray for a change in her condition."

Which was also a last resort. Strange. Abernathy had analyzed the problem to the point where it was obvious what had to be done. But he could not or would not take that next step.

"Are there more of the nanodocs—the same size as the ones that are missing?"

"There are several sets of them, in all important respects identical."

"That's good. Is there a staff cafeteria in the building?"

"What?"

"I must have something to eat, because I don't know how long this might take. And then I'll need to practice with your nanodocs for a few hours, to make sure I have the feel for these particular models. Then I'm going into Dr. Pearce."

I took a last look at Miriam, willing her to wake as I started for the door. Given a choice, I certainly didn't *want* to have to go in. I wanted to go home, and go to bed. Preferably with Miriam.

"You can't do that!" Abernathy had lost his smooth self-control. "You are not a physician. You are an *Adestis* employee. Just because you have a bit of experience with your stupid little toys doesn't mean you can handle nanodocs! This is very specialized equipment, very complex. It takes months to learn."

"I've had months. In fact, I've had years." I tried to keep the bitterness out of my voice as I walked from the room. I'm sure I failed. "While I'm gone, Dr. Abernathy, I suggest that you check the name of the patent holder for the first micro-surgery developments. The name of the *original* holder, I mean—the idiot who had all the patents, until the Pearce family broke them and acquired the rights for themselves. And while you're at it, check who was the creator, founder, and hundred percent owner of *Adestis*, before it was bankrupted and taken over."

Whatever I had done to Miriam, her family had paid back in full.

The food in the cafeteria was ridiculously over-priced at seven dollars. I know it cost that, because I had left home without money or any form of credit, and I had to sign what amounted to a personal IOU with the manager for the contents of my tray.

But that's all I do know about the food, or the cafeteria. I must have eaten, but I don't remember it.

I was almost finished when Thomas Abernathy marched in and sat down opposite me. He had with him an attractive dark-haired woman in her early twenties, who gave me a tentative smile as she sat down.

Abernathy took the document that he was holding and pushed it across the table towards me.

"This is a hospital, Mr. Fletcher, not a carnival." He was struggling to be polite, but hardly succeeding. "It isn't 'anything goes' here. We have strict rules, which every one of us has to obey."

I glanced at the paper. I had an idea what it might say.

"All right. So I'm not 'authorized personnel' for the use of the nanodoc equipment. Who is?"

"I have some experience. Dr. Pearce, of course. And Miss Lee, who is a specialist in nanodoc operations." He nodded his head at the woman sitting next to him.

She held out her hand but glanced at Tom Abernathy for approval before she spoke. "Belinda Lee. When Dr. Abernathy said you were here, I told him that I'd just love to meet you. You don't know it, but you and *Adestis* are putting me through medical school."

I let that opening pass. She was being as sociable as she knew how, but we didn't have time for it.

"You could *make* me authorized personnel if you wanted to, Dr. Abernathy. It is under your jurisdiction."

"There's no reason for me to do so. I now agree with you, Mr. Fletcher, interior exploration of Dr. Pearce by nanodocs is a logical and urgent step. Miss Lee and I will make that exploration. I also admit your experience with remotely-controlled micro-surgical equipment"—so he had checked on me, at least a little. What else had he found out?—"but we do not need you. Also, we cannot afford the time needed to train you."

"I have to disagree. You need me, even if you don't *want* me. You'll be making use of hospital equipment. This whole place runs on Pearce support. If I call Everett Halston he'll contact the Board of Trustees. You'll have an injunction slapped on you against using nanodoc equipment, one that will take weeks to break."

The last trace of bedside manner vanished. "You idiot, are you trying to *kill* Miriam? *You* are the one who suggested we have to go in and find out what happened to the nanodoc units inside her."

"We must do that. We *can* do that. As a team. You, I, and if you like, Miss Lee. If you authorize me to use the equipment, I'll bless the exercise at once with Everett Halston."

He grabbed the paper, stood up, and rushed out of the cafeteria without another word. Belinda Lee gave me an unhappy and puzzled look before she followed him. Why was I being so unreasonable?

I carried on with the meal. I was unreasonable because I sensed possible dangers that Abernathy could not. He lacked the right experience. He would agree to my participation—he had no choice—but it was not an auspicious beginning to a safari when team members were so divided and suspicious at the outset. Teams were supposed to cooperate totally.

On the other hand, I had been on an expedition where the team members had started out as close and loving and trusting as humans could get, and that one had ended in bitterness, disappointment, and heartbreak.

Maybe this time the process would work the other way round.

Belinda Lee was my instructor for the nanodoc units. Perhaps Tom Abernathy would not spend more time with me than he was obliged to; but to be more charitable, he also had two important tasks to perform.

First, a set of nanodocs had to be tuned to Miriam's individual body chemistry. Otherwise her immune system would be triggered at our entry and we would be attacked by every leukocyte that we encountered. Although they couldn't damage the nanodocs, they could certainly impede us.

As a second and trickier assignment, Tom Abernathy had to decide our access route into Miriam's brain. He and the neurological specialists had already decided our destination. Although the sleep state of humans and animals is controlled by an area at the rear of the brain known as the reticular formation, Miriam's responses to stimuli had them convinced that her troubles did not lie there. The problem was in the cerebral hemispheres. But to the tiny nanodocs, those hemispheres were like buildings a mile on each side. Where *specifically* should we be heading?

I was glad I did not have that responsibility. My own worries were quite enough.

Two hours had been allocated by the hospital for my training session, but it was clear in the first five minutes that they had been far too generous. True, two hours was less than half the training time that I insisted on before anyone could take part in *Adestis,* and in that case the simulacra were far more human in appearance than the hospital nanodocs. But for most team members the training session was a first exposure to micro-operation. Familiarity with the shape of their remote analogues was reassuring to them.

In fact, the proportions of a human are quite wrong for optimum performance of anything less than half an inch tall. Holding to the human shape in some ways makes things harder. As the size of an organism decreases, the importance of gravity as a controlling force becomes less and less, while wind and vibration and terrain roughness are increasingly dominant. Six legs become much better than two. At the smallest scale, the Brownian motion forces of individual molecular collisions have to be taken into account. Learning to gauge and allow for those changes is far more important than worrying about actual body shape.

On the other hand, as soon as I had seen the latest nanodocs I could not agree with Miriam and Thomas Abernathy that quantum effects might be important. Wispy and evanescent as the tiny currents might be that control the simulacra, they were still orders of magnitude too big to be affected by quantum fluctuations.

There was certainly an unanticipated problem with the new nanodocs. I certainly had no idea what it might be. But it was not what Miriam and Tom Abernathy suspected.

As soon as Belinda Lee had watched me work a team of nanodocs for a few minutes—each one a little bloated disk a few tens of micrometers long, with half a dozen legs/scrapers/knives along each side—she took off her telemetry coupler and leaned back in her seat. She waited patiently until I emerged from remote-control mode.

"You ought to be teaching *me*, you know." She was a different person when Tom Abernathy was not around. "How on earth did you make them zip *backwards* so fast, and still know where they were going? I'm supposed to be our expert, and I can't do that. The optical sensors won't turn up and over the back."

"No. They will turn *downward*, though, and scan underneath the body. You don't have enough experience looking between your legs and running backwards."

She offered me an owlish look. Belinda Lee thought I was poking fun at her. I was and I wasn't. I had never done what I suggested in my own body, but I had done it a hundred times with *Adestis* simulacra of all shapes and sizes. As I said, the hunter simulacra are all humanoid; but I had been both hunter and hunted, because we run hunts with remote-controlled simulated prey as well as with the real thing.

"So how is *Adestis* putting you through medical school?"

Belinda Lee seemed really nice, and I didn't want to upset her. I needed at least one friend at the New Hanover Hospital.

She laughed, the sort of full-throated laugh I had once heard from Miriam. "I was convinced you didn't want to hear. I was crushed in the cafeteria when you didn't ask."

"Sorry. I had other things on my mind. What did you have to do with *Adestis*? I'm sure you've never been involved in a hunt. I would have remembered you."

She took it for the compliment it was, and dipped her head towards me in acknowledgement. "I had problems when I was a teenager. My parents wanted me to be a doctor, but I'd heard of *Adestis* and I was fascinated by it. My life's ambition was to be team leader on an *Adestis* underwater safari. You know, the Larval Hunt."

"I sure do. Scary stuff. They wouldn't sign off?" You need written parental permission to enter *Adestis* mode before age twenty-one.

"Not in a million years, they said. So I did the dutiful daughter bit, went off to college and majored in biology. But I never stopped thinking about *Adestis*. For my senior thesis I wondered about the possible uses of that sort of technology in medical work. I wrote and asked, and some sweetheart at *Adestis* headquarters sent me a bale of terrific information. I used it to write probably the longest undergraduate thesis in the college's history. Of course I had no idea that Dr. Pearce was years and years ahead of me. But my prof knew, and he sent my finished project to her. She called a couple of days later. And here I am."

That sounded like Miriam. She recognized the real thing when she saw it. Her first exposure to *Adestis* had come through a friend at the hospital, a woman who had been on a hunt and regarded it all as a lark. But Miriam didn't. Before the end of the first training session she was asking me if I knew any way that *Adestis* control technology could take her clumsy micro-surgery tools down in size and up in handling precision.

That had been the beginning of the patents. And the *Adestis* expeditions with Miriam. And all the rest.

I used to think I knew the real thing, too. I recalled that highly detailed and imaginative student inquiry, even if I had not remembered Belinda's name.

At the same time, I began to worry. If Belinda Lee had begun to work with *Adestis* technology only after she graduated, she couldn't have more than a couple of years experience with simulacra. Also she had never been on a hunt, and therefore probably never been exposed to a dangerous situation. Yet Tom Abernathy had described her as a *specialist* in nanodoc operation—a specialist, presumably, compared with him. In agreeing that the three of us would go into Miriam, I had burdened myself with two team members lacking the right sort of experience.

Or was I being paranoid? What made me think that a safari into Miriam might be *dangerous*? Tom Abernathy and Belinda Lee certainly didn't think so.

Maybe that was one reason.

The other reason was more complex. For this safari, I too would lack the right experience. I had never, in all my years with *Adestis*, been exposed to a situation where the environment within which my simulacrum would operate was more precious to me than my own survival.

Our entry into Miriam began with an argument. I wanted to go in with a single nanodoc simulacrum each. Tom Abernathy argued for many more.

"There are several *hundred* in Dr. Pearce's brain. Three simulacra won't be able to remove them, even if we find them."

"I know. Once we understand what's happening, though, we can introduce more."

"But think of the *time* it will take."

He seemed to forget the full day that he had wasted before I came along to force a decision.

And yet he was right. His way would be quicker. So why wouldn't I go along with it?

That was a difficult question. In the end it all came down to instinct. A single simulacrum was easier to control than a group of them, even though a group had more fire-power. But fire-power against *what*? The nanodocs were not armed, the way that *Adestis* hunters had to be armed. Why should they be? I was too used to thinking in terms of a prey, and that didn't apply in this case.

Yet I stuck to my position, and overruled Abernathy. We would go with single simulacra, one per person.

But I also, illogically, wished that my nanodoc unit was

equipped with something more powerful than the tiny scalpels and drug injection stings built into its eight legs.

Destination: Brain.

We had adopted remote-control mode outside Miriam's body, as soon as the nanodocs were inside the syringe. We remained there for fifteen minutes, long enough to become completely comfortable with our host simulacra.

By the end of that time I knew my partners much better. Tom Abernathy was confident but clumsy. He might understand the theory, but no matter what he *thought* he knew about nanodoc control he didn't have good reflexes or practical experience.

Belinda Lee was far better, a little nervous but quite at ease in her assumed body. If she ever dropped out of medical school there would be a place for her on the *Adestis* underwater safaris. (And I'd be more than glad to give up my own involvement in those. The larval animal life of streams and ponds is fierce enough to make a mature insect or arachnid look like nature's pacifist. Maybe Belinda would change her mind when she saw at first hand Nature red in mandible and proboscis.)

We were injected into Miriam's left carotid artery at neck level, our three nanodoc units at my insistence holding tightly to each other. I did not want us separated until we were well within her brain. Otherwise I at least might never get there.

As we ascended Miriam's bloodstream towards the three *meninges* membranes that surround and protect the brain, it occurred to me that my two partners would soon know my own weaknesses. I could handle my nanodoc better than Belinda and far better than Tom, but I was missing something they both had: a good working knowledge of human anatomy or micro-structure. Abernathy had given me a lightning briefing, of which I remembered only a fraction. I peered around us. The minute compound eyes of the nanodocs couldn't see much at all. They delivered a blurry, red-tinged view of surroundings illuminated by the nanodoc's own pulsed light sources, enough so that I could see that we were being carried along a wide tunnel whose sides were barely visible. All around swam a flotsam of red blood cells, not much smaller than we were, interspersed with the occasional diminutive platelets. Through that swirl a white cell would occasionally come close, extend a testing pseudopod, and then retreat. Tom Abernathy's preliminary work on the nanodocs was satisfactory. The prowling leukocytes had no great interest in us.

I knew that the blood also carried an unseen flux of chemical messengers, taking status information from one part of the body to all the rest. Tom Abernathy could probably have explained all that to me, if our nanodocs had been capable of better communication. They were better than most *Adestis* units, because they did possess a primitive vocal interface; but it was at a bit transfer rate so low that Abernathy, Lee, and I were practically restricted to single word exchanges. We would mostly convey our meaning by stylized gestures.

Our progress through the internal carotid artery was far slower than I had expected. As we drifted from side to side and occasionally touched a spongy wall, I had time to explore every function of my nanodoc. And to reflect on its present owners.

Three years ago I was convinced that the Pearce family had acted in direct reprisal for what I had done to Miriam. It took a long time to realize that nothing *personal* was involved, that anger at the family made no more sense than rage at the gravid sphex wasp who takes and paralyzes a live grasshopper as feeding ground for its hatching larva.

I doubt if Miriam herself was aware of what had happened. Through her the Pearces had been alerted to the existence of a highly valuable tidbit, in the form of the *Adestis* patents. Miriam wanted and needed those for her own medical work, but that was irrelevant. It was the desire to increase assets that controlled group action, and to the family there was nothing more natural than the use of wealth to acquire my patents. They had simply turned on an existing machinery of scientists, lawyers, lobbyists, and political influence. I doubt if any one of them ever suspected that the owner of the patents also happened to be the man who had hurt Miriam. For if she had never talked of me to her present lover, would she have spoken to her family?

I liked to think that she would not.

The nanodoc hooked tightly to my four left legs started to tug gently at them. I turned and saw Tom Abernathy's gesturing digit.

"Cir-cle—of— Will-is," said a thin, distorted voice.

We had reached Checkpoint One. After passing along the internal carotid artery we were through the protective membranes of the *dura mater* and *pia mater* and were now at the *circulus arteriosus,* the "circle of Willis," a vascular formation at the base of the brain where all the major feed arteries meet. Abernathy was steering us into the anterior cerebral artery, which would take us into the cerebral cortex.

From this point on it would be up to me. Abernathy had made it clear that he could guide us no farther.

I had not told him that I too had little idea where we would go once we were within the cerebral hemispheres. He had worries enough.

And I was not quite ready to mention, to Tom Abernathy or to Belinda Lee, that something seemed to be slightly wrong with my simulacrum.

The change was so subtle that I doubted if Belinda, and still less Tom, could notice it. Only someone who had developed the original *Adestis* circuits and lived with them, through every good or bad variation, would sense the difference. The motor response was a tiny shade off what it had been when we were outside Miriam's body.

"Ex-peri-ment." I released my hold on the other two, then deliberately reduced motor inputs within my simulacrum to absolute zero.

I should now be floating like a dead leaf in the arterial tide, carried wherever the blood flow wanted to take me. But I was not. Not quite. There was a tiny added vector to my motion, produced by faint body impulses that I was not creating. I was angling over to the left, away from the broad mainstream of blood flow. When the artery divided, as it would shortly do, I would be channeled into the left branch.

Tom Abernathy and Belinda Lee were following, not knowing what else to do. I restored motor control to my simulacrum, and noted again the difference between my directive and the unit's response. Slight, but not so slight as before.

"Mov-ing," said Belinda's faltering and attenuated voice. She was noticing it too, and she was frightened. That was good. I did not want on my hunts anyone who was not scared by the inexplicable. The force did not feel external, either. It was arising from *within,* a phantom hand affecting our control over the simulacra.

"Stay." I halted, and laboriously sent my instruction. "I—go—on. You wait—for me." I believed we were surely heading for the missing nanodocs, and just as surely it might be dangerous for all to travel together. If I did not return, Abernathy and Lee could find their way to the left or right jugular vein exit points. Equipment was waiting there to sense, capture, and remove from Miriam's body any returning nanodoc units.

I again reduced motor inputs and allowed myself to drift with the arterial flow. Soon the channel branched and branched again, into ever-finer blood vessels. I had no idea where I was, or where I was going, but I had no doubt about my ability to return to the safe highway of the jugular veins. Every road led there. All I had to do was follow the arrow of the blood, down into the finest capillary level, then on to the fine veins that merged and coupled to carry their oxygen-depleted flow back toward heart and lungs.

And while I was filled with that comforting thought, I noticed that the motion of my simulacrum was changing. Without input from me the left and right sets of legs were twitching in an asynchronous pattern. Their movement added a crab-like sideways component to my forward progress. Soon my nanodoc was squeezing against the wall of the blood vessel. It pressed harder, and finally broke through into a narrow chamber filled with clear cerebrospinal fluid.

I thought that might signal the end of the disturbance, but after a few seconds it began again. Every thresh of the side limbs made the anomaly more obvious. I restored motor control and willed the leg movements to stop. They slowed, but they went on. My simulacrum was turning round and round, carried along in the colorless liquid of the new aqueduct until suddenly it was discharged into a larger space. After a moment of linear motion we started to spin around the vortex of an invisible whirlpool.

I had arrived in one of the larger cerebral *sulci*, the fissures that run along and through the human brain. Tom Abernathy could undoubtedly have told me which one. For the moment, though, I did not care. I had found the missing nanodocs.

They extended along the fissure, visible in the watery fluid as far as my crude optical sensors could see. Each one appeared to be intact. And each was obsessively turning on its own individual carousel, always moving yet never leaving one main chamber of the *sulcus*.

It took thirty seconds of experiment to discover that I too was trapped. I could think commands as well as ever. The simulacrum would start to respond. And before the movement was completed another component would reinforce my instruction. The result was like an intention tremor, a sequence of over-corrections that swung me into more and more violent and uncontrolled motion.

I dared not allow that to continue—I was deep in the delicate fabric of Miriam's brain, where even light contact could cause damage. The only way I could stop the spinning in random directions was to inhibit the motor control of my nanodoc unit. Then we returned to a smooth but useless cyclic motion around an invisible axis.

There was no way to signal the other nanodocs except through gestures. Designed to be worked as a group by a single operator, they were of a more primitive design than the unit I inhabited. I tried to make physical contact with one, but I was balked by its movement. Each unit remained locked in its own strange orbit, endlessly rotating but never advancing within the fissure's great Sargasso Sea of cerebrospinal fluid.

I was ready to try something new when I experienced my worst moment so far. In among the hundreds of nanodoc units I saw one different from the rest. But it was identical to my own; therefore it must belong to Tom Abernathy or Belinda Lee. A few seconds later I saw the other. Somehow they had been unable to follow my instructions. Like me they had been carried willy-nilly to this dark interior sea. Like me, they would be trying to assert control. And failing.

I knew how they must feel. The whole success of *Adestis* depends on the power of the mental link. When you are in *Adestis* mode you do not *control* a simulacrum, you *are* the simulacrum. Its limbs and body and environment become your own. Its dangers are yours, its pain is your pain. If it is poisoned by a prey, it dies—and you experience all the agony.

Without that total transfer, *Adestis* would be nothing but a trivial diversion. No one would pay large sums to go on a Small Game Hunt.

That same total immersion of self had been carried over, by design, into the nanodocs. I knew how helpless Tom Abernathy and Belinda Lee would be feeling now. They could not control their spinning simulacra, nor could they escape to or even recall the existence of their own bodies, *outside* the world of the nanodocs.

I knew that all too well; because three years ago Miriam Pearce and I had been in the same situation.

Our quarry was a first-time prey for both us and Adestis. No one had ever before hunted Scolopendra. Although Miriam and I knew it as one of the fastest and most ferocious of the centipedes, we started out in excellent spirits. Why should we not? We had hunted together half a dozen times before, and knew we were an excellent team. Shared danger only seemed to draw us closer.

And after it was over we planned to hold our own private post-hunt party.

Scolopendra came flickering across the ground towards us, body undulating and the twenty pairs of legs a blur. I took little notice of those. My attention was on the poison claws on each side of the head, the pointed spears designed to seize an unlucky prey and inject their venom. Between the claws I saw the dark slit of a wide mouth. It was big enough to swallow me whole.

We had agreed on the strategy before we entered

Adestis *mode: Divide and conquer.* Each of us would concentrate on one side of the centipede. As it turned towards one of us, the other would sever legs and attack the other side of the body. The animal would be forced to swing around or topple over. And the process would be repeated on the other side.

But why were we hunting at all? Although we found the danger stimulating, neither Miriam nor I had a taste for blood sports for their own sake. As usual on our hunts, we wanted to refine a new piece of Adestis control technology. When it was perfected it would find a home in the world of the nanodocs.

The centipede picked me as its first choice of prey. It turned, and Miriam disappeared behind the long, segmented trunk. I caught a glimpse of jointed limbs—each one nearly as long as my body—then the antennae were sweeping down towards me and the poison claws reached out.

Scolopendra was even faster than we had realized. I heard the crack of Miriam's weapon, but any damage she might inflict would be too late to save me. I could not escape the poison claws by moving backwards. All I could do was go closer, jumping in past the claws to the lip of the maw itself.

It was ready. A pair of maxilla moved forward, to sweep me into the digestive tube.

I had never before hunted a prey able to swallow a victim whole. And I had never until that moment known the strength of my own claustrophobia.

I crouched on the lower lip of the maw, and thought of absorption into the dark interior of the body cavity. I could not bear it.

I threw myself backwards and fell to the ground. A suicidal movement, with the poison claws waiting. I did not care. Anything was better than being swallowed alive.

The claws approached me. Shuddered. And pulled back. The antenna and the wide head turned.

Miriam's shots were doing their job. I sprawled fulllength, peered under the body, and saw half a dozen severed legs in spasm on the ground.

Now it was my turn to shoot. I did it—halfheartedly.

I dreaded the broad head swinging back, the mandibles poised to ingest me.

And it was ready to happen. I had shot off two legs. The body was shaking, beginning to turn again in my direction.

I stopped firing. For one second I stood while the centipede hesitated, unable to decide if I or Miriam provided the greater threat. The head turned once more to her side.

Then I was running away, a blind dash across dark and uneven ground. I did not look back.

I left Miriam behind, to die in agony in Scolopendra's poison claws.

Three years, three bitter years of remorse and analysis and self-loathing; in three years I had learned something that maybe no other *Adestis* operator had ever known. If I had known it *then*, it might have saved Miriam.

The body of the nanodoc, shell-like back and eight multi-purpose legs, was *my* body. I had no other. As I gyrated in the brain *sulcus* along with Tom and Belinda and a couple of hundred other units, I turned off every input sensor.

I *imagined* an alien body, a body nothing like my own. A strange body with a well-defined head and slender neck, with two legs, with two jointed arms that ended in delicate manipulators. When the imagined body image was complete I took those two phantom arms and moved them to the sides of the head, just above a strange pair of external hearing organs.

I grasped. And lifted. And reeled with vertigo, as the whole *Adestis* telemetry headset that maintained my link with the nanodoc ripped away from my skull.

I leaned forward and placed my forehead on the bench in front of me. Of all the warnings that I gave to attendants in *Adestis* control rooms, none was stronger than this: *Never,* in any circumstances, rupture the electronic union between player and simulacrum.

Hospital staff were hurrying across to me. I waved them away. The nausea would pass, and I had work to do. I understood what had happened to Miriam. I knew what had happened to me, and what was happening now to Tom Abernathy and Belinda Lee. Unless I was too slow and stupid, I could end it.

The control system for *Adestis*, and for all its applications such as the nanodocs, has built-in safeguards. I opened the main cabinet, found the right circuits, and inhibited them. I turned the electronic gain for my own unit far past the danger point. Then I went back to my seat.

"Tell the technicians with Dr. Pearce to watch for us coming out," I said. "Maybe fifteen minutes from now."

And cross your fingers.

I took a deep breath, gritted my teeth, and crammed the control headset back on.

The pain and dizziness of returning were even worse than going out. I was again a nanodoc, but the overloaded input circuits were a great discordant shout inside my head. Every move that I wanted to make produced a result ten times as violent as I intended. I allowed myself half a minute of practice, learning a revised protocol. The interference that had kept me helpless before was still there—I could feel a pulling to one side—but now it was a nuisance rather than a danger.

First I steered myself across to Belinda Lee's nanodoc. As I suspected, her loss of control included loss of signals. She could not talk to me, and she probably could not hear me. I simply took her by the legs on one side, and dragged her across to where Tom Abernathy was drifting around in endless circles. I linked the two units together, right four legs to left four legs, and locked them.

After that it was a purely mechanical task. I proceeded steadily along the brain fissure, systematically catching the nanodocs and linking them by four of their legs to the next unit in the train. The final result was itself something like a very long and narrow centipede, with over two hundred body segments. When I was sure that I had captured every nanodoc I positioned myself at the head of the file, attached four legs to Belinda's free limbs, and looked for the way out.

I had seen it as too simple. *Follow the direction of the*

blood. But we were in one of the major *sulci*, where in a healthy human there must be no blood. (As I learned later, blood cells in the cerebrospinal fluid is one sign of major problems in the brain.)

Where were the signposts? I pondered that, as our caravan of nanodoc units set out through one of the most complex objects in the universe: the human brain. We went on forever, through regions corresponding to nothing that Tom Abernathy had described to me. Finally I came across the rubbery wall of a major blood vessel.

Artery or vein? The former would merely carry us back into the brain. The latter would mean we were on our way out.

I entered, and pulled the whole train through after me. But still I did not know where we were heading, until the channel in which we rode joined another of rather greater width. Then I could relax. We were descending the tree, all of whose branches would merge into the broad trunk of the jugular.

I knew it when we at last entered that great vein; knew it when we were removed from the body, all at once, in the swirl of suction from a syringe.

The return to our own bodies under technician control was—as it should be—steady and gentle. I blinked awake, and found Tom Abernathy already conscious and staring at me.

I grinned. He looked away.

My hatred of him had dissolved after shared danger. Apparently his disdain for me persisted. I glanced the other way, at Belinda Lee. And found that she, like Tom Abernathy, would not meet my eye.

"We did it," I said. I couldn't stop smiling. "They're all out. I bet Miriam recovers consciousness in just a few minutes."

"*We* didn't do anything," Belinda said. "*You* did it all. I was useless."

I couldn't see it that way. But her reaction seemed too strong to be pure wounded ego.

"I couldn't have done anything without your help," I said. "Hey, without you two I'd never even have found my way *into* the brain."

"You don't understand." Tom Abernathy's face was pale, and his voice was as sour as Belinda's. "I know how she feels, even if you don't. Because I'm the same. We're not like you, with your crazy *Adestis* heroics. I wasn't just useless and helpless in there, I was *scared* when I lost nanodoc control. Too frightened even to follow what you were doing. Too terrified to *try* to help Miriam."

I laughed. Not with humor. The irony of Clancy Fletcher as heroic savior for Miriam Pearce was too much to take.

"It's not courage," I said. "It's only experience."

And then, when they stared at me with no comprehension, it all spilled out. I had bottled it up for too long, and it *hurt* to talk. But I could feel no worse about myself no matter what they knew, and perhaps a knowledge of other cowardice would help them to deal with what they thought of as their own failure.

"But there's a bright side," I said as I concluded. "If I hadn't failed Miriam then, I would never have experimented later with forced interruption of *Adestis* mode. And we'd still be inside Miriam's brain.

"I've never told anyone this before. But now you understand why she won't talk to me after she recovers consciousness."

They had listened to my outpourings in an oddly silent setting. As soon as they were sure that we were all right the nanodoc technicians had hurried off to the next room, where Miriam Pearce was reported to be showing a change of condition. The only sound in the room where we sat was the occasional soft beep of nanodoc monitors, reporting inactive status.

"I'm sorry to hear all that." Tom Abernathy's sincerity was real. Rumpled and sweaty, he was no longer the elegant physician with the polished bedside manner. "Miriam won't talk to you?"

He ought to know that, if anyone did.

"Not for years."

"Strange. Doesn't sound like the Miriam Pearce that I know."

"Nor me," said Belinda. "She's nice to everybody. But when are you going to tell us what was going on in there?

I try to pass myself off as somebody who knows nano-docs, and I can't even *understand* what you did, let alone do it myself."

"It was no big deal. It all depends on one simple fact. As soon as you know that, you'll be able to work everything else out for yourself. The key factor is *interference effects*. The electrical currents that control an *Adestis* module—including a nanodoc—"

I was interrupted, by a technician hurrying through from the next room.

"Dr. Abernathy. We think Dr. Pearce is waking up."

I was first through the door. Miriam's condition was clearly different—she was stirring restlessly on the bed—but her eyes were closed. Before I could get to the bedside Tom Abernathy had pushed me aside and was checking the monitors.

"Looks a hell of a lot better." He leaned right over Miriam, and was inches from her face when her eyes flickered open.

"I knew you would." The faint thread of sound would not have been heard, had not everyone in the room frozen to absolute stillness. "I knew you'd come and save me."

Her mouth and eyes were smiling up—at Tom Abernathy. Then the smile faded, she sighed, and her eyes closed again in total weariness.

I blundered out of the room more by feel than by sight. Company was the last thing I wanted, but Belinda followed me.

"You can't leave it like that," she said. "What *about* electrical currents?"

She wanted to talk. Well, why not? What did it matter? What did anything matter?

"The electrical currents that are *sent* to an *Adestis* unit are a few milliwatts," I said. "But the ones that are received at the unit, and the magnetic fields they generate, are orders of magnitude smaller than that. They're minute—and almost exactly the size of the fields and currents within the human brain. When Miriam sent nanodocs *into her own brain,* they were subject to two different sets of inputs, one arriving fractionally later than the other. In her case that set up a resonance which left both her brain and the nanodocs incapable of functioning normally. She was trapped. Maybe she even knew that she was trapped.

"In our case it worked differently. Her brain currents *interfered* with our nanodoc operation, so we lost control, but there was no resonance and no loss of consciousness.

"All I did was break out of *Adestis* mode and re-set the input currents to the highest level on my unit. When I went back in there was still a disturbance from Miriam, but it was one small enough for me to be able to handle."

Belinda was nodding, but she was beginning to stare at the door to the next room. "You know, Tom has to hear this, too."

"He'll hear it. Just now he has other things on his mind."

I don't know how I sounded, but it was enough to earn Belinda Lee's full attention.

"What *is it* with you and Tom? I thought you hadn't even met until today."

"You really don't know? I'd have expected it to be the talk of the hospital." And then, when she gaped at me, "Miriam Pearce and Tom Abernathy—" he had opened the door and was walking into the room, but it was too late to stop "—are lovers."

"*Tom* and Miriam Pearce." Belinda exploded. "Over my dead body—and over his, if it's ever true."

She rushed to his side and grabbed him possessively by the arm. "He's *mine*. He's *my* lover, and no one else's."

Abernathy must have wondered what he had walked into. Whatever it was, he didn't care for it. "My God, Belinda! You know what we agreed. Shout it out, so the whole hospital hears you." He actually blushed when he looked at me, something I had not seen on a mature male for a long time. And then his expression slowly changed, to an odd mixture of satisfaction and defiant pride.

"It's *his* fault." She was pointing at me. "He told me that you and Miriam Pearce are lovers!"

"Miriam and *me*? No way! Honest, Belinda, there's nothing between us—there never has been."

"I hope not. But I know she doesn't have a man of her own." Belinda was persuaded. Almost. "And she did say to you, 'I knew you'd come and save me.'"

"To *me*? What a joke that'd be!. I was as much use inside her head as a dead duck. She wasn't talking to me, she was talking to *him*. She said his name, Clancy, right after you two left. I came out here to get him."

"She *doesn't* have a man—doesn't have a lover?" That was me, not Belinda. Shock slows comprehension.

"Not any more. She once told me she had some guy, years ago, but he dumped her. Her family did something terrible to him. He wouldn't see her, didn't answer phone calls. In the end she just gave up."

"I thought a Pearce family member could get absolutely anything." That was Belinda, too cynical for her years.

Tom Abernathy patted her arm. With their secret out, his attitude was changing. "Almost anything. Miriam told me that a billionairess can have any man in the world. Except the one she wants."

"Does she want *you*?" Belinda had to be sure. But long-suffering Tom Abernathy was spared the need to offer that reassurance, because again one of the hospital staff came running through from the other room.

"Dr. Abernathy," he said. "She's finally waking up. *Really* waking up this time."

Tom and Belinda hurried away. I followed, more slowly.

Finally waking up. *Really* waking up. If only that had happened years ago, before it was too late.

I walked to the open door. Tom Abernathy was at the bedside. Miriam was sitting up, pale blue eyes wide open and searching. I stood rooted on the threshold. Belinda Lee was coming towards me, suddenly knowing, one hand raised.

I forgot how to breathe.

Sleeping Beauty slept for a whole century, and that still worked out fine.

Perhaps for some things it is never too late.

BIO/NANO/TECH

GREGORY BENFORD

If this century has been dominated by bigness—big bombs, big rockets, big wars, giant leaps for mankind—then perhaps the next will be the territory of the tiny.

Biotech is already afoot in our world, the stuff of both science fiction and stock options. Biology operates on scales of ten to a hundred times a nanometer (a billionth of a meter). Below that, from a few to ten nanometers, lie atoms.

Nanotechnology—a capability now only envisioned, applauded and longed for—attacks the basic structure of matter, tinkering with atoms on a one-by-one basis. It vastly elaborates the themes chemistry and biology have wrought on brute mass.

It is easy to see that if one is able to replace individual atoms at will, one can make rods and gears like diamond, five times as stiff as steel, fifty times stronger. Gears, bearings, drive shafts—all the roles of the factory can play out on the stage that enzymes have, inside our cells.

For now, microgears and micromotors exist about a thousand times larger than true nanotech. In principle, though, single atoms can serve as gear teeth, with single bonds between atoms providing the bearing for rotating rods. It's only a matter of time and will.

Much excitement surrounds the possibility of descending to such scales, following ideas pioneered by Richard Feynman in 1961 and later advocated by Eric Drexler in the 1980s. Such control is tempting. Like most bright promises, it is easy to see possibilities, less simple to see what is probable.

Nanotech borders on biology, a vast field rich in emotional issues and popular misconceptions. Many people, versed in 1950s movies, believe that radiation can mutate you into another life form directly, not merely your descendants—most probably, indeed, into some giant, ugly insect.

In the hands of some science fiction writers, nanotech's promised abilities—building atom by atom for strength and purity, dramatic new shapes and kinds of substances—have lead already to excess. We see stories about quantum, biomolecular brains for space robots, to conquer the stars. Or accelerated education of our young by nanorobots which coast through their brains, bringing encyclopedias of knowledge disguised in a single mouthful of Koolaid.

Partly this is natural speculative outgassing, and will dog nanotech. The real difficulty in thinking about possibilities is that so little seems ruled out. Agog at the horizons, we neglect the limitations—both physical and social.

People can tell disciplined speculation from flights of fancy when they deal with something familiar and at hand. Nanotech is neither. Worse, it touches on the edge of quantum mechanical effects, and nothing in modern physics has been belabored more than the inherent uncertainties of the wave-particle duality, and the like. People often take uncertainty as a free ticket to any implausibility, flights of fancy leaving on the hour.

Developing a discipline demands discipline. Dreaming is not enough.

One point we *do* know must operate in nanotech's development: nothing happens in a vacuum. The explosion of biotech, just one or two orders of magnitude above the nanotech scale, will deeply shape what comes of nanotech.

The transition is gradual. The finer one looks on the scale of biology, the more it looks mechanical in style. The flagella that let bacterium swim work by an arrangement which looks much like a motor; each proton extruded by the motor turns the assembly a small bit of a full rotation. Above that scale, the "biologic" of events is protean and flexible, compared with mechanical devices. Below it, functions are increasingly more machine-like. The ultimate limit to this would be the nanotech dream of arranging atoms precisely, as when a team at IBM spelled out the company initials on a low temperature substrate.

But widespread application of such methods lies probably decades away, perhaps several. The future will be vastly changed by directed biology before nanotech comes fully on stage.

Consider a field of maize—corn, to Americans. At its edge a black swarm marches in orderly, incessant columns.

Ants, their long lines carrying a kernel of corn each. Others carry bits of husk; there an entire team coagulates around a chunk of a cob. The streams split, kernel-carriers trooping off to a ceramic tower, climbing a ramp and letting their burdens rattle down into a sunken vault. Each returns dutifully to the field. Another, thicker stream spreads into rivulets which leave their burdens of scrap at a series of neatly spaced anthills. Dun-colored domes with regularly spaced portals, for more workers.

These had once been leaf-cutter ants, content to slice up fodder for their own tribe. They still did, pulping the unneeded cobs and stalks and husks, growing fungus on the pulp deep in their warrens. Tiny farmers in their own right. But biotech had genetically engineered them to harvest and sort first, processing corn right down to the kernels. Following chemical cues, they seem the antithesis of clanky robots, though insects are actually tiny robots engineered by evolution. Why not just co-opt their ingrained programming, then, at the genetic level, and harvest the mechanics from a compliant Nature?

Agriculture is the oldest biotech. But everything else will alter, too.

Mining is the last great industry to be touched by the modern. We still dig up crude ores, extract minerals with great heat or toxic chemicals, and in the act bring to the surface unwanted companion chemicals. All that suggests engineering must be rethought—but on what scale?

Nanotech is probably too tiny for the right effects. Instead, consider biomining.

Actually, archaeologists have found that this idea is quite ancient. Romans working the Rio Tinto mine in Spain 2,000 years ago noticed fluid runoff of the mine tailings were blue, suggesting dissolved copper salts. Evaporating this in pools gave them copper sheets.

The real work was done by a bacterium, *Thiobacillus ferroxidans*. It oxidizes copper sulfide, yielding acid and ferric ions, which in turn wash copper out of low grade ores. This process was rediscovered and understood in detail only in this century, with the first patent in 1958. A new smelter can cost a billion dollars. Dumping low quality ore into a sulfuric acid pond lets the microbes chew up the ore, with copper caught downhill in a basin; the sulfuric acid gets recycled. Already a quarter of all copper in the world comes from such bio-processing.

Gold enjoys a similar biological heritage. The latest scheme simply scatters bacteria cultures and fertilizers over open ore heaps, then picks grains out of the runoff. This raises gold recovery rates from 70% to 95%; not much room for improvement. Phosphates for agriculture can be had with a similar, two-bacterium method.

All this, using "natural biotech." Farming began using wild wheat, and immunology first started with unselected strains of *Penicillum*—but we've learned much, mostly by trial and error, since then. The next generation of biomining bacteria is already emerging. A major problem with the natural strains is the heat they produce as they oxidize ore, which can get so high that it kills the bacteria.

To fix that, researchers did not go back to scratch in the lab. Instead, they searched deep-sea volcanic vents, and hot springs such as those in Yellowstone National Park. They reasoned that only truly tough bacteria could survive there, and indeed, found some which appear to do the mining job, but can take boiling temperatures.

Bacteria also die from heavy metal poisoning, just like us. To make biomining bugs impervious to mercury, arsenic and cadmium requires bioengineering, currently under way. But the engineering occurs at the membrane level, not more basically—no nanotech needed.

This is a capsule look at how our expectations about basic processes and industries will alter long before nanotech can come on line. What more speculative leaps can we foresee, that will show biotech's limitations?—and thus, nanotech's necessity.

Consider cryonics. This freezing of the recently dead, to be repaired and revived when technology allows, is a seasoned science fictional idea, with many advocates in the present laboring to make it happen.

Repairing frozen brain cells which have been cross-slashed by shear stresses, in their descent to 77 degrees absolute, then reheated—well, *this* is a job nothing in biology has ever dealt with. One must deploy cell-sized repair agents to repair freezing damage, and replenish losses from oxygen and nutrient starvation. A solvent for this is tetrafluoromethane—it stays liquid down to minus 130 degrees centigrade.

To further repair, one must introduce line-layers, workhorse cells to spool out threads of electrical conductor. These tiny wires could power molecular repair agents—smart cells, able to break up and sort out ice crystals. Next comes clearing blood vessels, the basic housekeeping, functions which can all be biological in origin.

Then nanotech becomes essential. The electrical power lines could feed a programmed cleanup crew. They would stitch together gross fractures, like good servants dusting a room, clearing out the dendrite debris and membrane leftovers that the big, biological scavenger units missed. Moving molecular furniture around at 130 degrees below freezing will take weeks, months. One has to be sure the "molyreps"—molecular repair engineers—do not work too fast, or else they would heat the patient up all on their own, causing further shear damage.

How do they get the damaged stuff back in place, once they'd fixed it? Special units—little accountants, really—would have to record where all your molecular furniture was, what kind of condition it was in. They look over the debris, tag it with special identifying molecules, then anchor it to a nearby cell wall. They file that information all away, like a library. As repair continues, you slowly warm up.

These designer molecules must be hordes of microscopic fanatics, born to sniff out flaws and meticulously patch them up. An army that lived for but one purpose, much as art experts could spend a lifetime restoring a Renaissance painting. But the body is a far vaster canvas than all the art humanity has ever produced, a network of complexity almost beyond comprehension.

Yet the body naturally polices itself with just such mobs of molecules, mending the scrapes and insults the rude world inflicts. Biotech simply learns to enlist those tiny throngs. That is true, deep technology—co-opting nature's own evolved mechanisms, guiding them to new purposes. Nanotech goes beyond that, one order of magnitude down in size.

Not necessary to get good circulation in the cells again—just sluggish is enough. A slow climb to about minus a hundred degrees centigrade. A third team goes in then, to bond enzymes to cell structures. They read that library the second team has left, and put all furniture back into place.

So goes the Introduction to Molecular Repair For Poets lecture, disguising mere miracles with analogies.

Months pass, fixing the hemorrhaged tissue, mending torn membranes, splicing back together the disrupted cellular connections. Surgeons do this, using tools more than a million times smaller than a scalpel, cutting with chemistry.

With such abilities, surgeons can add serotonin-derived neurotransmitters, from a psychopharmacology far advanced beyond ours. They inhibit the switches in brain chemistry associated with emotional states. A patient reviving may need therapy, cutting off the memories correlated with those emotions that would slow recovery. Such tools imply medicine which can have vast social implications, indeed.

* * *

Here is where the future peels away from the foresee-able. Nanotech at this stage will drive qualitative changes in our world, and our world views, which we simply cannot anticipate in any detail.

Suppose the next century is primarily driven by bio-tech, with nanotech coming along as a handmaiden. Do we have to fear as radical a shift in ideas *again*, with nanotech?

Biotech looks all-powerful, but remember, evolution is basically a kludge. Often it can't take the best design route.

Consider our eyes, such marvels. Yet the retina of the vertebrate eye appears to be "installed" backwards. At the back of the retina lie the light-sensitive cells, so that light must pass through intervening nerve circuitry, getting weakened. There is a blind spot where the optic nerve pokes through the optical layer.

Apparently, this was how the vertebrate eye first developed, among creatures who could barely tell darkness from light. Nature built on that. The octopus eye evolved from different origins, and has none of these drawbacks.

Could we do better? A long series of mutations could eventually switch our light-receiving cells to the front, and this would be of some small help. But the cost in rearranging would be paid by the intermediate stages, a tangle which would function more poorly than the original design.

So these halfway steps would be selected out by evolutionary pressure. The rival, patched-up job works fairly well, and nature stops there. It works with what it has. We dreaming vertebrates are makeshift constructions, built by random time without foresight. There is a strange beauty in that, but some cost—as I learned when my appendix burst, some years ago. We work well enough to get along, not perfectly.

The flip side of biology's deft engineering marvels is its kludgy nature, and its interest in its own preservation. We are part of biology; it is seldom our servant, except incidentally. In the long run, the biosphere favors no single species.

The differences between nanotech and biotech lie in

style. Cells get their energy by diffusion of gases and liquids; nanotech must be driven by electrical currents on fixed circuits. Cells contain and moderate with spongy membranes; nanoengines must have specific geometries, with little slack allowed. Natural things grow "organically," with parts adjusting to one another; nanobuilders must stack together identical units, like tinkertoys.

The Natural style vs. the Mechanical style will be the essential battleground of tiny technology. Mechanicals we must design from scratch. Naturals will and have evolved; their talents we get for free. Each will have its uses.

Naturals can make things quickly, easily, including copies of themselves—reproduction. They do this by having what Drexler terms "selective stickiness"—the matching of complementary patterns when large molecules like proteins collide. If they fit, they stick. Thermal agitation makes them smack into each other many millions of times a second, letting the stickiness work to mate the right molecules.

Naturals build, and as time goes on, they build better—through evolution. In Naturals, genes diffuse, meeting each other in myriad combinations. Minor facets of our faces change so much from one person to the next that we can tell all our friends apart at a glance (except for identical twins, like me).

These genes collide in the population, making evolutionary change far more rapid because genes can spread through the species, getting tried out in many combinations. Eventually, some do far better, and spread to everyone in later generations.

This diffusion mechanism makes sexually reproduced Naturals change constantly. Mechanicals—robots of any size, down to nanotech—have no need of such; they are designed. There is no point in building into nanomachines the array of special talents needed to make them evolve—in fact, it's a hindrance.

We don't want nanobots which adapt to the random forces of their environment, taking off on some unknown selection vector. We want them to *do their job*.

So nanotech must use the Mechanical virtues: rigid, geometric structures; positional assembly of parts; clear channels of transport for energy, information and materials. Mechanicals should not copy Naturals, especially in aping the ability to evolve.

This simple distinction should lessen many calls of alarm about such invisible, powerful agents. They can't escape into the biosphere and wreck it. Their style and elements are fundamentally alien to our familiar Naturals, born red in tooth and claw.

Nanobots' real problem will be to *survive* in their working environment, including our bodies. Imagine what your immune system will want to do to an invading band of unsuspecting nanobots, fresh off the farm.

In fact, their first generation will probably have to live in odd chemical soups, energy rich (like, say, hydrogen peroxide or even ozone) and free of natural predators. Any escaping from their chemical cloister will probably get eaten—though they might get spat right back out, too, as indigestible.

So nanotech will not be able to exponentially push its numbers, unless we deliberately design it that way. Accidental runaway is quite unlikely. Malicious nanobots made to bring havoc, though, through special talents— say, replacing all the carbon in your body with nitrogen— could be a catastrophe.

When machines begin to design themselves, we approach the problems of Natural-style evolution. Even so, design is not like genetic diffusion. In principle, it is much faster. Think of how fast cars developed in the last century, versus trees.

That problem lies far beyond the simple advent of nanotech. It will come, but only after decades of intense development one or two levels above, in the hotbed of biotech.

What uses we make of machines at the atomic level will depend utterly on the unforseeable tools we'll have at the molecular level. That is why thinking about nanotech must be constrained by knowing how very much biology can do, and will do, before we reach that last frontier of the very small.

PARK RULES

JERRY OLTION

Welcome to the Bighorn National Forest's Cloud Peak Wilderness Area. Please fill out a registration card and take the time to read this notice before entering.

WARNING: This area has been seeded with nano-mechanical rangers. Park rules will be enforced at all times.

REGULATIONS, RIGHTS AND RESPONSIBILITIES.

1. No motorized or mechanical vehicular travel is allowed in the wilderness area. Artificial horses are excepted from this restriction.

2. You have the right to carry a backpack if you desire. If you choose not to, or if you forget vital provisions, wilderness area nanorangers will provide equipment using standard templates for shelter, bedding, food, cooking utensils, fishing tackle, etc. If you require non-standard equipment, you must bring your own templates. You may also bring your own nanoassemblers, but be aware that nanorangers will monitor all assembly and disassembly activity and will prevent any violations of wilderness area rules. When planning your campsite, remember that nanorangers will neither provide nor permit housing larger than 100 square feet per person, nor will housing persist for longer than three consecutive days in any one location.

3. Your pet is welcome in the park, provided it is fitted with a neural overriding obedience device responding to nanorangers' commands. If the pet does not contain such a device, one will be assembled for it upon entry. If your

201

pet is harboring a communicable disease or parasite, it will be cured upon entry.

4. Camping is allowed in any unoccupied location; however, please respect others' right to privacy. In high-use areas, please restrict your stay to one night so that others may also enjoy the location. Campsites may be leveled and smoothed as desired, but must be returned to their natural state upon leaving. After three days, nanorangers will return the site to its natural state whether you have left or not.

5. Campfires are allowed in all campsites. Firewood may be gathered from deadfall if you desire the primitive experience, or it will be assembled upon request. Please build a fire ring; any flames detected outside the ring will be immediately extinguished. (Hand-held torches excepted.)

6. Sanitary facilities will be provided upon request. Persons desiring to dig a pit latrine may do so, but please keep the latrine at least 100 feet from open water. Nanorangers will disassemble waste matter, but note that it is much easier to accomplish if it stays in one place. NOTE: Waste matter from native animals is allowed to proceed through the ecosystem naturally. Watch your step.

7. Do not feed native animals. Nor should you eat any, other than the six fish per day you are permitted to catch from any lake or stream within the wilderness area border. Do not restock the water after fishing; the population is automatically balanced after each catch.

8. Edible plants may be consumed at your own risk.

9. The assembly of any non-native species of plant or animal for any purpose other than immediate consumption is strictly prohibited. Introduction of fish to be caught later for consumption is also prohibited.

10. The assembly of native species is also prohibited, except for the following instances:

  A. Shade trees of no more than twenty feet in height may be assembled for the duration of your stay only. Maximum one tree per member of your party.

  B. Birds, deer, elk, bear, etc. may be assembled

for the purpose of photography only. All artificially created animals must be immediately disassembled after use.

11. The maximum energy available for private assemblers is limited to incident solar radiation. On cloudy days, allow extra time for large projects. Nighttime use of available biomass as an energy source is permitted, but all biomass used for fuel must be replaced the following day. Garbage left behind does not count as biomass. Violators will be fined $100/megawatt.

12. Nanorangers are in no way responsible for monitoring your safety. Emergency medical assistance will be provided when possible, but the nanorangers' primary duty is to protect the wilderness. You are encouraged to bring your own medical equipment; however, be advised that if you harass the wildlife even the most advanced nanomeds will be unable to prevent you from being eaten.

Enjoy your stay.

COMMENTS

ABOUT "PARK RULES"

JERRY OLTION

I keep hearing from the true believers that nanotechnology will change the way we do everything. Everything? Yeah, the first thing I thought of was sex, too. But that story has been done to death already, and I've finally been convinced that people will indeed use nanotech to change sex in every way imaginable.

But what about the things people don't want to change? How about wilderness areas? Would nanotechnology affect the way we use those? At first I thought not; after all, the whole purpose of a wilderness area is to protect it from technological intrusion, and the whole reason to intrude upon it personally is to "get back to nature."

But backpackers already carry the highest technology available into the wilderness. Tents are made with lightweight synthetic fabrics, poles are composite graphite or spun aluminum, waterproof clothing uses fabric with tiny holes just big enough for water vapor to pass through, but not big enough for liquid water—and so on. Backpackers may be seeking the natural experience, but they're not technophobes.

They don't necessarily like all that weight on their backs, either. Most of the high technology they use goes into shaving ounces off each item they carry. So what would happen if backpackers could build what they needed once they got where they were going? You got it. No packs at all, just a pocket for holding the nano-assemblers and the templates they need to build tents, sleeping bags, cooking utensils, etc. They'll use rocks for raw material and sunlight for power, and they'll build a palace wherever they go.

Now look at it from the Forest Service's viewpoint. Backpackers are already loving the wilderness to death; turn them loose with practically unlimited equipment and increase their range by not requiring them to carry everything, and suddenly the woods will be overrun.

The Forest Service's first impulse will be to ban the use of nanomachines in the wilderness. That won't work, of course. Backpackers are notorious for ignoring the rules. Not all of them, but enough to cause trouble. One of the reasons they're out there is to get *away* from regulations. So they'll take their assemblers, and they'll turn the forest into vast piles of garbage.

On the other hand, if the Forest Service used nanomachines to patrol the wilderness and repair the damage done by backpackers, they could actually lower visitor impact. They could return campsites to their original condition after every use, and they could recycle the garbage left behind for raw materials. They could clean up the drinking water and restore fish populations to ecologically balanced levels. They could erase any sign of human intervention on a continuing basis, and though this heavily managed approach sounds more artificial than simply leaving things alone, the end result would be a more pristine ecosystem than we have now.

Ironically, the introduction of nanomachines could lead to the reversal of some policies that have been instituted to control human impact. Fire rings are cozy and they do help keep fires from spreading, so if you can put the rocks back where they came from—complete with the moss on top and worms beneath—then it makes sense to build them. The same goes for leveling your campsite. Go ahead and grub out that stump if it's in your way. It'll be replaced when you leave. Also, there's no sense torturing a fish you don't intend to keep if you can restock them on a continuing basis, so catch-and-release fishing could become obsolete. (Although if the fishing is good, people aren't going to want to stop when they've caught all they can eat, so maybe catch-and-release won't go away after all. Instead, sensitive anglers will use nano-machines to interfere with the fishs' pain receptors and anxiety centers so they won't mind being caught. . . .)

The Forest Service could go even further if they wanted to. If nanomachines can protect the environment from people, they could just as easily protect people from the environment. Given even primitive neurological control, ticks, ants, and mosquitoes could be steered away from campsites, and larger animals could likewise be discouraged from human encounters. I suspect the Forest Service would stop before it got to that point, however. Their job is to protect the wilderness from us, not the other way around. Their attitude, and I agree with it, is that every backpacker has the right to be eaten by bears, so long as it doesn't harm the bears.

EVAPORATION

DAVE SMEDS

Glenn Ashwood woke to a fierce sunrise, cracked mud beneath his naked body.

The stark, antiseptic quarters of the jumpship brig had vanished. Glenn was outdoors now—out in raw air, looking up at a blue sky shimmering with heat. A small waning moon he didn't recognize hung just west of the zenith, its craters indistinct in the daylight.

He sat up, scanning right and left. No buildings. The only sign of human presence save himself were the impressions left in the dry lakebed by the transport. Sand dunes, outcroppings, and bleak, eroded hills ringed him in every direction, without a single shred of vegetation nor any trace of cloud. Whatever rain had created the mud beneath him had done so months, years, even decades earlier.

He shaded his eyes, trying to push away the intensity of the glare. The closest shore of the lakebed was at least two kilometers away. The nearest shade was well beyond that and, as far as he could judge, would vanish as noon approached—long before he could get to it. Meanwhile his exposed skin was cooking in ultraviolet radiation.

His nanodocs should have protected him. Right now the little molecular robots should have been deepening his tan, modifying his fluid retention abilities, and repairing the scrapes on his back—a token of his escorts, who had obviously thrown him bodily out the hatch. Nanodocs were one of the great boons of civilization. They healed every minor injury, preserved youth, enhanced beauty. The only people denied their full beneficence were convicts.

Over and over echoed the words, in that deep, noxious drawl Glenn had hated for so many years:

"I sentence you to hell."

Aaron McCandless. Magistrate and de facto dictator of this backwater sector. The man who had framed him.

Glenn soberly confronted the knowledge that he and this world would get to know each other very well. None of his allies—assuming any still existed—would know where to find him. His location would be a secret kept by the magistrate and a handful of his toadies. Even Glenn himself had no idea where he was. The jumpship had bounced at least a dozen times; he could be anywhere among the ten thousand worlds administrated by McCandless—surely far from the four that were inhabited.

Glenn had spoken out against the powers-that-be. He had challenged the wrong people, thinking that law and morality would protect him.

This place had only one purpose: To make him suffer for his insolence.

The sheer bite of the sun's rays forced him out of his sour meditation. It was simply too uncomfortable to indulge in inactivity. He thrust his fingers into a crack in the mud. A few small grains crumbled away, but the crust was too rigid to break loose; even a shovel would not have helped. Burying himself out of the sunshine was not an option.

He stood and began to walk.

The motion cleared his mind. The blueness of the sky and the oxygen soaking into his lungs took on meaning: The planet was habitable. There had to be a viable ecosystem here, or had been in the recent past. He could find it. He *would* find it.

As the sun climbed, it became apparent that he was in the southern hemisphere. He steered south, away from the equator. That kept the direct brilliance out of his face, and if the desert proved to be vast, at least that direction would gradually take him to cooler latitudes.

*   *   *

Thirst claimed him early, tormenting him even more than the blistering of his shoulders. His tongue scraped the insides of his cheeks and adhered to his palate. He would have licked his sweat, except that the heat evaporated the liquid out of his pores before it could surface. He would have gulped down his own urine, but his bladder held none.

He saw shimmering areas in the distance that looked teasingly like water. Mirages. He plodded on, dreaming of swimming pools, ice cubes, tumblers of lemonade, snow banks. The visions grew acutely realistic—as real as the cold in the faces of the bureaucrats at his trial, as icy as the glee of the magistrate. How long had they been scheming to put him away? It must have taken years in the planning.

At last, after many hours, a sinkhole offered shade. He collapsed into it, unable to climb down gracefully. Dust roiled up at the impact, making him cough. But at last he was out of the direct blast of stellar radiation. He could remain quiescent, conserving his fluids.

An eternity later, night fell. The temperature plummeted. By then, though his throat resembled sandpaper and his head throbbed, he had the strength to climb out of the pit. He promised himself to travel only beneath the stars, as he would have done to start with had McCandless not had him dropped in an exposed location. He staggered on, keening his ears, hoping to hear the scurry of tiny feet or the flutter of wings, anything that might confirm the ability of the planet to support life.

A hot, convection-driven breeze puffed at the sand, its whisper faint beneath the rasping of his lungs and the scuffing of his blistered feet.

Somehow he dragged one foot in front of the other. When the sky to the east turned indigo and the fainter stars blended into the sky, he found a crevice in a low, south-facing butte and propped himself up where the sunlight would not touch him.

The increasing light revealed the first hints of a plateau in the direction he had been heading, no doubt the southern boundary of the basin. A higher elevation might mean cooler air and a new climatic zone. It was as good a goal as any.

He died long before he reached it.

When he revived, stars hung overhead. Cool zephyrs of air actually produced goose bumps on his limbs. The moon he had seen upon his arrival was already well above the horizon, indicating that sunrise was only a few hours away. The light of a second, larger moon gave his body a sickly hue, but he was not sick. Nor was he dead. Not anymore.

The pain was gone. Lying there in a cleft where he had dragged himself to die that evening, he was restored to his default morph, that of a tall, muscular man, seemingly twenty-three years old.

This was the bitterest part of his ordeal: Death was no escape. His nanodocs had not been entirely deactivated. Stripping him of his citizen's right to immortality was beyond McCandless's authority. Capital offenses had to be referred back to the quadrant's central judiciary. McCandless hadn't wanted to risk exposure of the conspiracy.

Glenn might die a hundred deaths. No choice. He had control over one and only one aspect of his existence: whether or not to give in to despair.

McCandless would like it if Glenn broke down. So Glenn would not break down.

As he tried to stand, he swayed. That was when the ghastliness of his situation truly struck home. He was still critically dehydrated. His docs had the ability to snag water molecules from the air and soil to incorporate into his body, but there was little for them to borrow, and they had their limits. They had found enough to revive him, and once life resumed, their programming cancelled further effort.

He stood again. He ached everywhere, revealing that the docs, finding little organic matter in the soil, had stolen material from his muscle tissues to resupply his organs. Hunger gnawed his insides, mitigated only by thirst. His resurrection had won him a reprieve of a few hours.

Making sure of his direction, he forced himself forward. The plateau became his marker. As morning broke, the escarpment no longer hid in the haze of the horizon; it was distinct, rich with detail such as fissures, deposits of scree, and the striations of sedimentary layers. How many lives would it take to get to the base of the slope? How many lives to climb it?

Eighty-nine deaths later, he found water.

Only upon reaching the shore was he certain it was not another mirage. He had first seen the taunting, glittering surface after he had struggled across the plateau to its southern cliffs. Gazing down into yet another vast, desolate basin, he had estimated the small sea's diameter at about one hundred fifty kilometers. Here in the flat he could not see the other side.

Determining how long the trek had taken in clock time was problematic. On several occasions he had collapsed in open terrain where the ovenlike noon desiccated his body faster than the nanodocs could restore it overnight. Mummified, he lay dead until such time as a little extra humidity crept into the air, providing his microscopic caretakers with the means to ferry his soul back across the Styx. Months or years might have passed.

The water, now that he had reached it, was forbidding. Nothing grew at its edges or within its depths. A thick white crust of salt, hard as metal and razor-edged, filled the beach zone, forcing him to tread with caution. He knew he would find no source of drink, but he plunged in, eager to recall the caress of liquid against his skin.

He floundered like a fish atop a gigantic bowl of gelatin. Eventually he bounced onto the beach, where he gashed open his legs. The sea was too saline even to swim in!

The trickle of blood from the wounds ate away at his consciousness. He couldn't afford the loss of bodily fluid, and he had risked the daylight in his final push to reach the shore. He would die soon. No avoiding it. Already the dread was climbing up his gullet like a bloated worm.

He would not be defeated. Would not. Even here, in this ridiculous situation, he could find something to use to his advantage. For once, dying would not be a setback. Because as he lay down to wait for the end, he left his feet in the water.

Moons' light greeted him as he revived. His body brimmed with vigor, thirst and hunger temporarily banished. Accepting the generosity of the sea, his docs had resupplied his fluids, filtering out excess salt, and somewhere in those poisonous waves had found enough organic matter to rebuild his tissues. For the first time since he'd arrived on the planet, he was totally restored.

He bounded to his feet and set out, intending to circle to the southern shore. In spite of his energy, he did not hurry. He knew that he could always die at the water's edge again—unnerving as that process might be. No longer did he have to struggle for every forward pace.

Death indeed came again. Twice. But shortly after the second revival, as dawn was threatening to call a halt to his nightly progress, he was drawn on by an impossible sound: the unmistakable roar of water rapids.

Ultimately he was rewarded—if one could call it that—by the realization that he had come to the end of a narrow peninsula. He could go no farther unless he chose to swim.

But here, indeed, were rapids.

To his left were the viciously saline waters around which he had walked—not a sea after all, but a gulf or bay. To his right rested a much larger body of water. This was a true sea, perhaps an ocean. Straight ahead, a mere stone's throw away, another peninsula spread toward a cluster of low hills. Together, the narrow slivers of land divided the two bodies of water into nearly separate geographical features connected only by this narrow, shallow channel.

The rapids were caused by the flow of the larger, higher sea into the smaller one. The difference in elevation was at least two meters, enough height to cause the incoming water to tumble downward over the rocks.

Glenn ignored the glaring rays of the sunrise. The discomfort mattered not at all in the face of the vital information he had just learned.

Aaron McCandless must have had his men drop Glenn in the driest region of the planet, the place of greatest torment. The land where he stood was so arid that the bay actually evaporated faster than the parent sea could fill it.

That meant that elsewhere, *it wasn't so arid.* Some major, regular source fed the larger body of water. It might be barren here, but other parts of its shore had to be more hospitable. Even now he could see that its hue was healthier, less choked by salt. By following its coastline, he knew he would eventually come to a place where extended survival was possible.

He commenced that journey immediately. A newfound spirit filled his stride. Previously he had depended on faith alone to convince himself that better conditions lay ahead. This time he had a theory founded on real evidence.

So accustomed was he to incremental gains that he scarcely believed his eyes when, just as the heat had forced him up a dune to search for shelter, he spotted a piece of driftwood in the surf. He slid down the bank, pranced into the foam, and emerged with the prize. About a meter long, it fit his grip neatly. Though lightweight, it resisted the prodding of his fingernail, feeling more like cast aluminum than something that had once been alive.

Reverently, he raised it above his head.

Something scuttled over the beach ahead. Mentally he labelled it *crab,* though of course it was an alien lifeform, crablike only in the sense that it had a flat carapace and an array of fold-out legs. Instantly he sprinted forward and brought the club down with full force.

The carapace cracked, giving off a sound like an egg crushed underfoot. The little creature wriggled, spasmed, and in a bizarre reflex, shook off all of its legs. An aroma much like fresh lobster filled Glenn's nostrils.

Giggling like a boy, he lifted a still-quivering leg and sucked the flesh out of the exoskeleton. Satisfyingly sweet, it quelled the acid burn in his stomach. Something so good was surely toxic, but so what? He would savor every last bite.

He danced in a circle around his kill. He had a weapon. He had food. Shelter would surely come. From these small beginnings, he would carve out a triumph.

PART TWO

Glenn could smell rain coming, though the first clouds hid somewhere behind the curve of the planet. After five decades, he was acutely aware of changes in humidity. Before nightfall, the sky would weep.

Rain was still a rare occurrence, even here in the watershed of the Sea of Gulfs—named by Glenn for its many bays and peninsulas. Away from the one permanent river, plants had to struggle to survive from storm to storm. The few small creatures that roamed among that vegetation provided barely enough game to sustain a predator as large as a human.

But Glenn had endured. The estuary and coastal tide-pools provided seafood. The river meant a source of drinking water, even if sometimes he had to dig to reach it. The air was never as unforgivably hot as the region where he had originally been flung.

He stared at the mountains, at the snow that dusted the highest peaks. Twice he had followed the riparian zone to the river's source, a journey culminating in an arduous climb up canyon walls, through foothills even more sere than the flats.

When he reached the crest of the pass, all he saw on the far side was another barren expanse.

The whole planet might be a desert. There were no real seasons. From the vantage of his main camp, the sun always set over a particular narrow mesa. The world had little or no axial tilt—no engine to stir up the weather. Orbital eccentricity alone contributed any suggestion of "summer" or "winter." At perihelion, the average temperature climbed a degree or two higher than at aphelion, a simple function of the distance from the star to its blighted child.

Periodically Glenn explored other directions, with no better result. He always returned to the few hundred square miles he thought of as "his." Someday he would strike out in a single direction and simply keep going, perhaps after a rain when the land would be at its most bountiful. The journey might kill him, but he would revive again and again until eventually he got somewhere, even if all he did was circle the globe back to the Sea of Gulfs.

But that quest was for some other year. He was not eager to die again so repeatedly. He had not been killed in almost thirty years, despite the harsh conditions. That was a victory. The condition of his body was his badge. A convenient suicide would remove the wrinkles from his leathery skin, heal the scars from falls or battles with resistant prey. But without those marks, he would be a blank screen on which Aaron McCandless had typed VICTIM.

That was not an impression he would tolerate. Prisoner or not, he was a master of this land.

Attuned as he was, he instantly spotted the spoor on the ground in front of him, though the impressions had been made in a thin layer of dust atop hard sandstone. The footprints were shorter and narrower than his, but they were human.

His heart pounded in a way it had not done in his entire exile. His hand grew so sweaty around the haft of his spear that he nearly dropped it.

"I knew you'd never let me be, McCandless," he whispered.

All hesitation gone, he loped forward. The trail cut aimlessly across the flat. No attempt was being made to hide it. A speck of blood remained where the walker had passed too close to a porcupine bush. The stranger had little sense of desertcraft; no one would pass so close to such a shrub twice in a lifetime.

A line of trees—the only concentration of trees on the planet, as far as Glenn knew—became visible as he crested a rise. The trail straightened, leading Glenn without detour to the banks. He arrived in late afternoon. The first clouds, black as charcoal, had appeared over the Sea of Gulfs.

From a high bluff he peered down into the eroded channel. Knee-deep in a cobblestone-lined pool, in a spot destined to be inundated before the next dawn, stood a woman.

She was naked. Her outer thigh was still spotted with coagulated blood from the cut made by the porcupine bush, a sure sign that her nanodocs had been deactivated. She was gently washing away the clots. Body and hair dripping from a recent dunking, her expression was filled with the stunned, forlorn disbelief of a castaway.

Appearances could be deceiving, thought Glenn.

Finishing with the wound, she again dipped fully into the water and stepped, trailing rivulets, onto dry cobbles. She stumbled unsteadily to a patch of shade and sat down to rub her feet. Blisters dotted her soles.

No plants grew in the riverbed—the periodic flash-floods stole them away. The shade was that of a large "oak" that projected down from the bluff, its trunk not five paces from Glenn's position. As the woman's eyes adjusted to the reduced glare, she looked upward and, with a sudden jerk of her head, fastened her gaze on Glenn. She grew utterly still.

"Who are you?" After half a century of disuse, Glenn's voice was a barely intelligible croak.

She shied back, eyes wide, all but bolting away. Glenn had to give her credit for a realistic human response. Were she a typical representative of society, she might well have never seen anyone as old and worn as he, arrayed with such long, matted hair and tangled, chest-length beard, wearing only a cowl of animal pelts scarcely fit for a barbarian. It still shocked him to look at his reflection in pools and see something as eroded as the land.

"I didn't mean to frighten you," he said, hoping his Galactic Standard wasn't too accented. "I've never seen anyone else on this planet. How did you get here?"

She hesitated. "I was convicted of being an enemy of the state. This was where I was sent to serve my sentence."

"Did McCandless sentence you?"

"Who?"

"The magistrate."

She shook her head, confused, then her eyebrows rose

in comprehension. "That was the old magistrate—four or five coups back, before I immigrated to this sector. The new guy sent me here."

Glenn turned away, concealing his reaction. McCandless gone? His term would have lasted for decades yet, but it was true that the political situation in these frontier areas was volatile. If it weren't, the asshole might never have been spooked by what Glenn had done.

Still, unless he could prove she was lying, he supposed he was obliged to treat her with consideration.

"It's not safe down there." He indicated the high-water mark where the scoured banks gave way to weeds, vines, and succulents. "Better join me up here."

She glanced at the clouds and appeared to grasp the threat without further explanation. No longer inching away, she examined him in a way she had not done at first. Perhaps she was wondering if being exiled meant that she would look as blighted as he, given time. If so, the prospect unsettled her deeply.

Aside from the cowl, he did carry one other item on his person—a waist pouch that hung from a thong. Suspended from that was the carcass of a rabbitlike animal he had killed. Her eyes settled on the furred body, recognized it as food, and licked her lips.

"Are you hungry?" he asked.

She nodded tentatively, as if afraid to admit to such need.

"I can cook this for us, then."

Her reticence eased. Wincing from the pain of her feet, she clambered up the bluff. She accepted his hand to bring her onto level ground, and stood self-consciously a pace from him.

"I'm Judith Vining."

He coughed. "Glenn Ashwood." He waved upriver toward one of his camps. "We need to take shelter before the storm hits." The clouds were pressing rapidly toward the coast.

"Is it far?"

"No more than a kilometer."

She sighed.

"I have nothing to help your feet," he said. "Would

you like me to carry you? You're small. I could manage it."

She shook her head quickly. That was the answer Glenn wanted. This was a proper time to keep a distance, to be intimidated by him. He would have been suspicious of anything else.

He checked her feet. They were not critical. Nor was she as sunburned as she might have been. Her morph was Polynesian, a popular fashion among women even back when Glenn was exiled. Nutmeg brown, with long raven hair scattered over her shoulders, Judith had reddened so little from the day's exposure that he guessed she would not even suffer peeling as long as she kept to the shade during the next few days. Thanks to the river trees and the incoming clouds, shade would be abundant.

"Your jumpship's crew was kinder than mine," Glenn said gruffly, and guided them to a path.

They arrived beneath the rock overhang that shielded Glenn's camp just as the rain began to fall. Within seconds, a solid wall of water obscured the landscape.

Judith sank onto the packed earth and gawked at the torrent. Then she shivered, because the temperature had plunged.

"Here," Glenn said, handing her a blanket of sewn animal pelts—his old one, saving the new one for himself.

She accepted the article gladly, wrapping it around and hugging it close. With her womanly shape obscured, she resembled a child. Glenn stifled a pulse of paternal instinct, busying himself igniting the tinder of his cookfire and adding fuel. The skinning and dressing of the "rabbit" filled the awkward lapse of conversation.

By the time the meat was cooked, the weather front had moved on, leaving only a feeble trickle of rain. Down in the canyon the river burbled enthusiastically, a mere precursor of things to come.

The blackness outside lessened as the faint glow of twilight leaked under the cloud layer from the west. Glenn genuflected, a bit of religious ritual he'd adopted out of thanks that he had not been sent to a planet tidally locked to its primary, with himself abandoned beneath a perpetual noon. He treasured the night, and this one would be especially fine, the stars incandescent now that the dust had been rinsed from the atmosphere.

He handed Judith a roasted haunch. She attacked it with fervor, taking small bites only because larger ones would have seared her palate. In a short time he gave her another piece, then sat down to have some himself.

He regarded her steadily. Her shiver continued in spite of the blanket. Now was hardly the time to talk, but there were things he needed to know.

"Were you guilty?" he asked.

She didn't look up from her meat. "I did the things they say I did. Whether they should have been against the law, I don't know."

It was a good answer. Honest, not attempting to save face, but with its admirable pride.

"Have you ever heard of me?" he asked.

"Glenn Ashton?"

"Ashwood."

She shrugged apologetically.

"Ever heard of the Furies?"

"From the Greek myth?" She was chewing more slowly, as if wondering why he was interrogating her.

"A protest group, purged by the magistrate in 2832. I was their leader."

"I wasn't even born in 2832."

With so few children born anymore, Glenn was accustomed to thinking of everyone as several hundred years old. He faltered through the next question. "How long is your sentence?"

"Thirty years." Finishing her meal, she seemed to gather strength. "And yours?"

"Indefinite," he said softly.

She blinked. "But that was under an old regime. When they come for me, they'll take you, too. That's if the current administration lasts that long. Someone might find us sooner."

"That sounds . . . optimistic," he muttered.

That silenced her. She crawled nearer the fire, arranged the straw he had given her for her bedding, and lay down under the blanket to watch the stars breaking through the widening gaps in the cloud cover. She didn't look at him.

Glenn was being a poor host and he knew it. Yet he was finding it hard to be gracious. Judith might be who she said she was. Or she could be lying. McCandless might still be in power. He could have sent her. She could be an actress. She could be an android, a construct of Fluidmetal and an A.I. matrix.

She was too perfect. She brought with her the prospect of companionship, sex, hope for release from prison, and information about the galaxy he had been isolated from for fifty odd years. Too much like his fantasies, she was.

McCandless would love to torment him further. No sooner would Glenn come to trust Judith, pour out his confidences and pour into her his semen, than she would melt away, leaving a recording of McCandless's voice, laughing. Or maybe McCandless needed something. Glenn had always believed that during all the druggings and coerced testimony, he had not revealed *all* the names of his comrades. Perhaps a splinter of the Furies remained to this day, annoying the magistrate. He would try to worm that last name or two from Glenn's lips.

Judith was drifting to sleep, exhausted by her initiation to the planet. He winced. If she were to be his Eve, he needed to treat her better. But how did he dare? He stared at her until long after the storm run-off from the mountains thundered down the river channel.

In the morning, he held up the gift he had made for her: clothing. The garments weren't much to speak of— just a loincloth of hide, suspended from a waist thong, and a thong necklace with another wide scrap of hide that would drape both breasts. He had had neither the time, the skill, nor the materials to craft anything less rudimentary.

Her nose crinkled at the odd, ferretlike odor, still present though the animal the skin had come from had been dead a year or more. But she nodded and tied the loincloth to her waist. She left the upper garment on the ground.

The gesture had gone over well. Glenn was pleased. It had been little enough of a risk. If she were a spy, much better for him that some of her beauty was concealed. If she were a genuine castaway, then he had ingratiated himself by allowing her to find her level of comfort. Though modesty had been on the wane ever since the advent of molecular cosmetology, some people—women especially—still appreciated the chance to selectively reveal themselves.

She smiled and looked at him expectantly.

"Come on," he said. "If you're going to survive here, there are some things you should know."

He had no choice but to take her on as a student. It was the only responsible thing to do if she were not McCandless's tool, and it would give him a task to keep him focused. He started with a tour of the drenched plain, sticking to rain-softened sands for the benefit of her blistered feet. She followed his lead without question, listening respectfully as he spoke. And well she should. The knowledge he was sharing had been won with pain and arduous trial-and-error.

Soon, as was inevitable, they encountered a quintessential example of the desert's unpleasantness. Skirting the edge of a dwindling pool, he used the haft of his spear to scoop out a drowned specimen he called a heeby-jeeby.

"Too stupid to get out of the rain," he commented.

She cringed as she leaned over the remains. Long and scaly, the creature resembled a snake or lizard, but with twenty or more pairs of legs, like some reptilian version of a millipede.

"They're lethargic during the day," he added. "You might be tempted to sneak up on one to kill it. Don't. They spit their venom. It'll dissolve your skin, or blind you if it gets in your eyes. Dilute it a hundred to one and it'll still give you hives."

Judith, who was only a step from the pool's edge, scooted back to keep the potentially contaminated water from touching her feet. "I take it they're active at night?" she asked tremulously.

"Very. You'll hear the scuffle of forty little feet. Can't miss it."

She shivered.

"Whenever you hear that, just stay still. Heeby-jeebies don't eat anything as big as we are. They'll ignore you if you don't hassle them. Last month one crawled right over my neck and just kept going."

She gazed at him with undisguised awe. Glenn blushed. He hadn't been trying to impress her. He didn't want to become dependent on praise now that he'd lived so long without it.

But it did feel good to be seen as competent. And to be appreciated as a teacher.

"Well, then," he mumbled, "I'll show you what their burrows look like, so you can steer clear."

Over the next week, he shifted the lessons away from immediate threats to life to the next level of priority— finding food. That usually meant meat, taken mostly by snare and net rather than spear. Plants were too often poisonous. Moreover, edible vegetation consisted largely of widely scattered seeds or pulp hidden deep within spiny protuberances or armored rinds—it was never easy to obtain. It was worth the effort only because of the fiber and trace elements, and because those carbohydrate sources would not run away when a hunter was tired, unlucky, or injured.

Judith closely attended whatever he said to her. He caught himself staring as she breathed. Her lungs filled, briefly widening the set of her breasts, and he was reminded of the gentle way the latter rose and fell as she slept.

She was a woman. He could smell the femaleness of her. She gave off pheromones that shot up his nostrils and linked directly into his primitive brain. Each day left him a little more dazed.

Signs indicated she was caught in a complementary sexual tropism. She maintained less distance, allowed their hands to brush as they traded objects, and held eye contact. His weathered body might hinder her evolving interest, but did not halt it.

For better or worse, he was giving in to her. By the end of another week, they had become casual with one another. She asked more questions, did small tasks for him. He could tell she was still terrified of this place, but that she accepted him as an ally. To her, they were friends.

And to him, what were they?

They were exploring the sea, always the best source of protein, the water cool enough to be refreshing. As ever, he was careful to warn her of dangers. "Stay in the shallows," he told her. "There's a species out there sort of like a giant lamprey. Big enough to eat people. Venture into deep water and your nanodocs might have to reconstitute you out of eel shit."

She laughed. He grinned back. Some of his old self had reemerged. When was the last time he had owned a sense of humor?

Suddenly she grew serious. "One of them ate you, didn't it?"

He coughed. "Only my left foot, actually. Not that it made much difference. The gangrene killed me a few days later."

"I can't imagine what you must have been through all these years." Disconcerted by her own boldness, she wiped the salt flecks off her cheeks and chin. "I don't think I could have endured all that by myself."

The memories rose like bile. Mocked at his trial, forced to betray comrades, and then sent to hell. He dropped his net into the surf, using the motion of retrieving it to hide the tears that were springing from his eyes. He came up facing away from her.

He was unable, however, to disguise the sob that wracked his whole body.

Judith moved forward, wrapping her arms around his waist, hugging him. The unmistakable caress of nipples on his back forced new tears up.

Glenn rocked back and forth, succumbing to the rhythm of the waves, letting Judith support him. The touch of her arms, her breasts, her chin, soothed him too much to resist. She was giving him comfort in spite of his calculated ugliness, in spite of his gruffness.

"It won't be so bad now," she murmured. "We'll keep each other company. Let me be your friend. We could make something of our time here." She circled to his front, pulled his head down to her level, and kissed him.

It was a light, chaste kiss. Her nostrils quivered as she drew away, trying to corral more of his scent. It was clear she would kiss him again—that and much more. She led the way to the beach, where she dropped her loincloth to the sand. Beckoning him, she walked in the direction of the camp.

From the shallows he admired the female way her hips rocked up and down with each stride. He followed, never letting her recede from view.

Their lovemaking was everything he could have wished for. Soft, snug wetness. Enthusiastic puffs of breath. Little squeals of feminine delight. The pungent, delicious aroma of passionate exertion. Only after the third set of orgasms were they content to collapse into the aftermath, lying together under a single blanket underneath the stars, where Glenn fell into a deep, all-consuming slumber.

Morning arrived, illuminating the recessed walls of the camp. Sunlight glittered off the minerals in the rock. It was the one time of day the camp was not in the shade, a welcome arrangement that chased away the nocturnal chill. Glenn woke with a start, opening his eyes to find that Judith was standing, body haloed as she gazed out at the landscape.

Her passion-tousled form was glorious. As she turned toward him, his eyes were riveted to the supple twisting of her waist. He could just imagine how it would feel to grasp her there again while she mounted him. She blew him a kiss, pointed toward the river, mouthed "Bath," and tip-toed down the embankment, out of sight.

He was ready for her when she came back. Beads of water clung to her coppery skin, held in place by random hair follicles. Were he to lick them off of her, he would never wish to drink any other way again.

She held out her arms to him. Her expression had hardly shifted from pleasure to shock before his club connected with her skull. No sooner had she fallen, limp, to the ground than he raked his stone knife across her throat. Blood gushed from the huge wound, staining the dust.

Her nanodocs would revive her, of course. Glenn estimated that would take several hours. He tossed a few essential items, ones he kept at no other camp, into a makeshift knapsack. By the time her death was erased, he would be far gone toward the mountains, and given Judith's rudimentary tracking skills, she would never catch up.

He shuddered as he marched away, humbled to realize how vulnerable he had been. In another month, he would have done almost anything for her. At a minimum, he would have restored his body to its youthful morph so that she would not have to bear the sight of his middle-aged, graying self. And in the process, erased much of his identity.

That was what McCandless would want, after all. To erase him, one way or another. Given the effects of intimacy, the drunkenness of hormone haze, it would not have been long before he had accepted her version of the outside galaxy—a place where even the name of his enemy was forgotten. He would begin dreaming, hoping, of the rescue she had mentioned, begin to be confident that no more than thirty more years of exile remained. He would no longer plot revenges, no longer picture the moment when he would at last catch up with the magistrate. New priorities would subsume the old, until former concerns seemed hollow and indistinct.

In short, he would leave behind the very vision and faith that had sustained him all these years. And when at last she asked him about his old friends and of his former exploits, he would pour it all out without reservation, naming the names that McCandless wanted, and be made a fool once more.

And then she would depart, and he would be alone, left with nothing anymore, not even pride.

The storm, though gone a fortnight already, had blessed the peaks ahead with bright new snow. Perhaps he would climb all the way to the top, build a snowman for company, or simply reexperience the novelty of frozen water. Perhaps, from that height, he would see an ocean out beyond the wastelands, or a savannah. A new home, where he could laugh at his foe's paltry manipulations, and one day find the means to become the victor.

A little inner voice nagged at him, asking if he might have misconstrued things, but it faded away, unheard. Onward he walked.

COMMENTS

DAVE SMEDS

Don't laugh, but when I think of nanotechnology, I think of grapes.

We all have our touchstones, drawn from the well-spring of our experiences. Picture this: A blond teenager just hitting his growth spurt. Too young to shave, bundled up against the cold of a frosty morning, out in a vineyard with a pair of pruning shears, praying for the incessant San Joaquin Valley winter fog to lift—a forlorn hope, since the valley is ringed on all sides by mountains that hold the gray shroud in place for weeks on end during December and January. At night the fog is at ground level; during the day, it rises perhaps two hundred feet skyward, without dissipating.

That particular teenager—me—had only one consolation on that long, miserable, wet workday in the midst of two long workweeks, otherwise known as How I Spent My Christmas Vacation, 1968: I was getting to prune Muscats.

The alternative was to be stuck in the Thompson Seedless vineyard. I hated that. Thompsons are one of those rare varieties of grapes whose fruit is carried on the second-year wood. To prune that acreage—which is what I had done the day before and the day before that and the day before that—required me to carefully select which canes would form the following year's fruit-bearing canopy, cut off all others, then trim the surviving canes to about six feet in length and wrap them around the guide wires of the trellises. That degree of judgment and responsibility was almost too much to bear. My father was laboring in the next row, and tolerant as he was, I dreaded hearing him say, "Oops. Not that one, son."

I was an eighth-grader. The worst feeling of all at that uncertain stage of life was to feel like a fuck-up, especially in front of my father.

Ah, but with Muscats, I was spared that anxiety. They were a normal grape. I could cut off *all* the canes, leaving a few spurs for next year's growth. No tying. No heavy decision-making. My boots might have been soaking wet from the thawing dew, my palms might have been blistered from the constant, repetitive clipping action, but by comparison, it was a good day.

Then my dad broke his customary silence to announce, "I'm pulling this vineyard out after the harvest."

I paused, shears immobile. The fog seemed to settle back down. "Why?" I asked. My tone contained almost no affect, because back then it was an impossible puzzle figuring out how to translate complex emotions into sentences.

In prior years, my father would have dismissed the question with a simplified version of the truth such as, "The vines are too old." But by now I was large enough to be doing a man's share of the farm chores (even though I wasn't receiving wages), so he gave me an adult explanation. It had to do with supermarkets.

In 1950, Muscats were perhaps the premier white table grape found in grocery stores. That season my father and uncle had produced quite a spectacular crop while many of their neighbors' grapes suffered extreme sunburn. The windfall made up for a lot of bad years, and then some.

Yet only eighteen years later, the variety was obsolete for table use. Our crop was destined for a local winery, where the tonnage commanded an exceedingly modest price. The table grape of choice had become Thompson Seedless, formerly grown for raisins and cheap bulk wine, but now girdled and injected with growth hormone to reach a size suitable for fresh consumption. (Natural Thompsons are no larger than blueberries.)

A chief factor in the downfall of Muscats was modern produce sections. A ripe Muscat bunch has the unfortunate habit of shattering into individual berries unless handled delicately. Up until the Fifties, grocers served their customers one-on-one, bagging and weighing fruit for them much the way a deli counterperson might slice and wrap a half-pound of turkey breast for a customer today. In supermarkets, which quickly out-competed the Mom-'n'Pop operations, customers pawed through looking for the best fruit, inevitably leaving produce bins awash in loose, unsalable grapes. Girdled Thompsons were much more reliable when it came to holding on to their stems.

One little marketing development, and vines that had been good as gold became a ball-and-chain nuisance. And there wasn't a damn thing I could do about it. That, my friends, was when I became conscious of the impact of technological development. Reading about Thomas Edison and the taming electricity was Just Schoolwork. So what if the lights and TV worked? Hadn't it always been this way? Nuclear power—that was just something politicians worried about, and I'd never met any of them. Technology had been a faceless abstract forever in the background. And now, finally, it had done something that *made a difference*.

Pruning was real. It was tactile. It was part of my world. And in future winters, it was going to be more stressful, all because of Progress.

(Actually, that turned out not to be true. Dad replaced the Muscat vineyard not with Thompsons but with Ruby Seedless, an up-and-coming variety grown chiefly by my family at that time—now you know who established red seedless grapes in the marketplace—and one that allows traditional spur-cut pruning. But on that particular day, I couldn't guess there would be such a rescue.)

Nanotechnology will impact a great deal more than what sort of grapes a farmer plants, but in the end, it's not the scope that matters, not the societal paradigm shift, it's the inescapable little details. Somewhere, at some time in the future, a whole lot of people are going to run smack up against experiences that wouldn't have happened without nanotech. Something that matters to them as individuals will be affected. And that's when they'll internalize just how spooky this stuff is.

Scientists can go on and on about what sort of changes we're in for, but the pictures they paint run the risk of remaining abstract. The developments need to be placed within personal contexts. That's where science fiction comes in. I don't know if nanotech will ever be capable of doing the things it does in my story. It doesn't matter. The importance of science fiction is not to prove or disprove what's possible, but to ask, "If it is possible, *then* what?" We provide the details, we make it real.

"Evaporation" is part of a set of stories (the others appeared in the anthology *Full Spectrum 4*, the August 1992 issue of *Asimov's SF Magazine*, and the March, 1994 issue of *The Magazine of Fantasy & Science Fiction*) that offer scenarios about what the future might be like if and when nanotechnology reaches its full potential. It's impossible to cover all the transformations, so I focused on specific areas. This time it was, "What might incarceration be like in the age of nanotech?" The others covered suicide, rape, and romance. Just when I think I'm done with this personal literary cycle, another plot premise insists on claiming some of my word-processor schedule. That's how it is with seminal ideas. Damn you, Eric Drexler.

If the writers in this book have done our work correctly and if the readers take these visions to heart, we'll all have at least a small chance to prepare for the changes that will result from nanotechnology. Let's hope the rest of the world out there doesn't decide to play ostrich, stick their collective head in the sand, and leave the other end of their body waving in the breeze. In that case, I know just where to paint a bull's-eye.

SANTA NANOCLAUS

KENT PATTERSON

When the gleaming gold pavement of the great Central Bus Road buckled under the pounding carbon bonds of his eight tiny simulated reindeer, Santa Nanoclaus couldn't believe his sensors. Anxiously, he scanned around. To his left, massive flat-topped transistors, their sides streaked with alternating layers of metal and metal oxide. To his right, the holding cages of the tunnel diodes, the playful electrons heedlessly leaping through the gates without opening them as only quantum particles can.

The sleigh quivered. Nanoclaus scanned behind, sensing a vast wave gathering over him like a gleaming mountain. A voltage spike! It couldn't be! Not here in the peaceful Micro Valley of the Central Processing Unit, and not now, just a few clock cycles before Christmas!

Already the gallium arsenide substrate trembled beneath his sleigh, the sim deer shying in fright as the gold lattice of the Great Bus Road twisted and simmered in the heat. Gold atoms pinged against the bottom of the sleigh. Nanoclaus knew this surge could only be a preliminary to the Big One, the crusher, which in a few micro seconds would devastate Micro Valley.

The sleigh shivered. The Big One would carry all before it like a flood, leaving a blackened waste in its path.

Nanoclaus was utterly helpless.

But wait. Suddenly he accessed the memory of the thin film fuse on the Great Bus Way a few nanometers ahead. Why hadn't the fuse blown? He had no idea, but if he could only reach the fuse before the central spike of the Big One arrived, perhaps the mass of the sleigh could help deflect the surge, add a few micro ohms of resistance, and blow the fuse. A desperate chance. He had no time, and it would be certain death to Nanoclaus, the Spirit of Christmas.

Nanoclaus thought of Micro Valley, with all its peaceful inhabitants, and the innocent lives of the very small.

Some things were more important even than the Spirit of Christmas.

"Hyah, hyah." The sim deer leaped forward. Terrified as the gold road crumbled under them, they lunged against the carbon-carbon bonds of the reins. Nanoclaus urged them on.

Behind him, he sensed the power surge, the Big One, moving at near light speed, many times faster than any sim deer.

"Hyah, hyah," he shouted and called them by name. "On Turbo and Servo, on Pixel and Plotter. On LIFO and FIFO, on NANDer and NOTer!" Never had sim deer run so fast. The great transistors flashed by, and now Nanoclaus scanned the dull gray road of the thin film fuse a few steps away. The surface boiled, lead atoms spurting up in a seething, bubbling mass.

A great hand shook the sleigh. The Big One.

"Jump, my gallant sim deer. Spring!"

Spring they did, leaping straight into the boiling lead, and Nanoclaus had never been prouder. With a quick jerk of the reins, he tipped the sleigh over, blocking the path of the stampeding power surge. Excited atoms of lead smashed through his molecular membrane, knocking him sprawling, then the great surge engulfed him, and all his sensors went blank.

Nanoclaus came to himself in a bed. Several assemblers, their scanners warm with concern, surrounded him.

"The power surge. Did I . . . ?" said Nanoclaus.

"Yes, Nanoclaus, you stopped the surge with only a fraction of a femtosecond to spare. Thanks be to the Great User, the fuse is repaired, the main memory saved and rebooted. Everything's reassembled and well, Santa, sleigh, sim deer, presents, and all."

"What time it is?"

"Why, it's just a few cycles before Christmas."

Nanoclaus leaped from his bed. "Then I'm on my way."

"No, Nanoclaus. You've done enough. You saved our lives."

But Nanoclaus sprang to the seat of his shiny new sleigh. With a wink and nod, he set the merry sim deer leaping ahead. Everywhere laughing child processes gathered, singing at the top of their lungs,

"He's creating a file,
He's backing it twice,
He's got a sweet bit,
For each logic device.
Nanoclaus is coming around."

The child processes played, sang, waved to Nanoclaus as he ran along the Great Bus Way, setting sparkling neutrinos glittering on the gold pavement, dropping gifts to one and all, colored quarks for the young, shining new updates to the young in the main program, and exclaiming as he flew out of scanner range,

"Merry Christmas to all,
And lots of sweet dreams,
And transparent compatibility
To all sentient machines."

COMMENTS

SANTA NANOCLAUS COUNTERS
THE CRITICS

KENT PATTERSON

Oh, no, not Santa Nanoclaus. In the first place, no one could possibly live inside a microchip and even if someone did he or she would most certainly not be Santa Claus. In the second place, nanotechnology is high serious science so what we need is high serious thinking extrapolating a high serious future.

Wrong.

Like all comedy, Santa Nanoclaus intends to speak with a forked tongue. One fork tickles the funny bone and the other pokes fun at people who think the future of nanotechnology really can be extrapolated.

A pop science article on injecting "artificially intelligent" nanocritters into the bloodstream to eat cancer cells inspired Santa Nanoclaus. (Of course the chump meant "expert system," not "artificial intelligence.") Intelligent critters would want something better for themselves and especially their children than a bleak future of one damned cancer cell after another. But seriously folks, doubtless useful nanocritters will need some autonomy, and that presents a problem. When Cancer Cure Release 1.0 kills patients, how do you boot the New, Improved Cancer Cure Release 2.0? To what extent can we allow self-replicating machines to be autonomous? Please don't say there won't be any bugs in the program. Computer programs have bugs like cats have kittens. It's their nature.

The problem with predicting the course of any revolutionary new technology is that it is *revolutionary*, and hence unpredictable. Comedians can predict the future effects as well as scientists. Perhaps better, for comedians are not limited by what is presently thought to be likely. Of course, neither comedians nor scientists predict very well; revolutions always catch the old guard by surprise.

Consider the history of an older technical revolution, the automobile. Early enthusiasts sold cars as the ultimate antipollution device. Writing in 1899, Sylvester Baxter lambasted the noise and the danger of horse transport in the big city, ending with "every street ... is literally carpeted with a warm, brown matting of comminuted horse-dropping, smelling to heaven and destined ... to be scattered in fine dust in all directions, laden with countless millions of disease-bearing germs." Cars were good for your health. In 1912, GMC ran advertisements showing pictures of dead horses in city streets—up to 1,200 per month in New York City alone.

Ironically, Baxter would be astounded to learn today's ecologists would condemn him for polluting his pristine world with automobiles. Of course, today's ecologists have never had a dead horse dumped on their front doorstep. So much for predicting the future by extrapolation.

Revolutions always surprise us. Henry Ford predicted cross-country motor transport, but he didn't predict the Model T would change the sex life of America's young.

Defying all the serious thinkers, a 1900 cartoonist portrayed New York in 1950 with its streets so jammed with automobiles that none of them could move.

All the serious thinkers got a belly laugh out of that goofy notion.

COMMENTS

HUNTER'S DAWN

J. STEVEN YORK

When we make decisions about issues of technology, they are, at the root, moral decisions. Perhaps no technology since the beginning of history has illustrated this fact better than the development of nuclear science. Never had such power been so concentrated. Never had the consequences of its use been so great or long lasting. People of science were forced to face that they were people of moral responsibility as well.

This dual role was not a burden that most wanted, or that some handled well. Some were gnawed by doubt and regret for the rest of their lives. Others ignored the moral issues of nuclear weapons, nuclear pollution, or long term waste disposal. Both these approaches were wrong. The issue is not *whether* a technology will be explored or used, but *how* it will be used. In the case of nuclear power, we could have made better decisions, but if we had buried the research as soon as its terrible potential became obvious, it would have been discovered again soon enough. At best, we could have delayed it a decade or two, and then it might have been discovered by even less responsible parties, with even more terrible results.

Nanotechnology is our next, great moral lesson in science. There is no question that it will be developed and used. The question is *how* will it be used, and what new moral issues will be raised. Nanotechnology is fundamentally different from nuclear energy. On one hand, its potential for destruction is much greater. A self-replicating nanodevice, for instance, designed to attack and destroy RNA and DNA molecules could destroy all life on Earth, down to the most humble virus, something nuclear weapons could never do.

But nanotechnology also has the capability to act with great subtlety, in a way no technology that has come before allows. This will raise new kinds of moral questions, fundamentally changing our ways of thinking and perhaps even our language.

For instance, nuclear weapons were the "big hammer." They did big things, or they did nothing at all. Nanotechnology is, by definition, power over *small* things. It may be that nanotechnology will allow new kinds of very subtle weapons, weapons so precise in their intent and function that it may not be proper to call them weapons at all. Perhaps we will need a new word.

HUNTER'S DAWN

J. STEVEN YORK

I charged through the alien jungle, razor-edged creeping vines shredding my jumpsuit, my hands and face red and swelling from the irritating intrusion of thousands of tiny, almost invisible, thorns, blood running down from a cut in my forehead so I had to keep stopping to wipe it out of my eyes. The sticky sap from broken vines filled the air with a smell like orange juice. I'd once heard someone say that the law of the jungle was "survival of the fittest." I was fittest; immortal, human, one of the masters of the known universe, but I didn't plan to survive.

But I would if I didn't hurry. I could hear *something* crashing through the brush behind me, not even trying to hide its noise. One of Friday's nano-pets, come to fetch me back. No way I was going to make it that easy for them.

Entering the small clearing created by the fall of one of the giant trees, I glanced at the crude *compass*, an ancient magnetic navigation device that I'd constructed from parts of my personal gear. The crashing was loud behind me. I knew I should be close. I veered left and bulled my way into the brush again.

I smacked into a papery nest of swarming insects. I screamed in spite of myself as their shining green bodies buzzed angrily around my face, and stingers stabbed into my exposed skin wherever they could find it. The moment of panic passed. I brushed them away and pushed on. Their toxins were tailored for another biochemistry. I might get one hell of an allergic reaction later, but I didn't plan on hanging around this life long enough for that to be a problem.

Still, I'd lost precious seconds. I could hear my pursuer closing in. The stings itched. One of them, on my left eyelid, was swelling, making it even more difficult to see. Maybe I wasn't going to make it after all.

Then the thicket of orange and purple leaves thinned. I caught a glimpse of deep blue sky between the tree trunks. I was there! A vine caught my boot as I came out of the trees, and I fell, frightening a flock of four winged pseudo-birds that scattered like animated confetti. I rolled, picking up a bunch of crawling insects in the process. I sneezed as one tried to scurry up my nose, and scrambled to my feet, running the last few yards to the edge of the world.

I stood on a gnarled finger of weathered red sandstone, looking down into a canyon six hundred meters deep. A river curved, like a strand of silver, through the purple foliage below. My left boot rested half over the edge, and I watched as a bit of sandstone crumbled away and tumbled silently into the abyss. But what I was really looking for was straight down. There, far above the bottom of the canyon, but hundreds of meters below the rim, the stone had been eroded into a series of tall, smooth-sided needles, standing in a staggered, uneven row like dragons' teeth. The tallest of them was right below my perch. I moved my other foot to the edge and prepared to jump.

The canyon's depths beckoned me, but I paused and looked over my shoulder to see what new nanoconstruct Friday had sent after me. Each time I escaped, it was something different: once a giant snake, another time a huge multi-headed beetle, and the last time, a pack of laughably goggle-eyed quadrupeds I had jokingly named "the hounds of heck."

This time it was different. The thing was man-sized, or a little bigger. Certainly, it was more massive, thick limbed, packed muscle sliding under thick, pebbled skin. The legs ended in large reptilian claws, tipped with sharp talons. The hands were more humanoid, but equally well equipped for slashing and holding prey. Behind it, a blunt tail swished excitedly from side to side, and a forest of thick quills sprouted stiffly from its back.

But the most striking thing about the creature was its head. The skull was massive, and deeply furrowed with folds and ridges. Four small eyes, two to a side, occupied deep sockets set under heavy brows. Then there was the mouth. Such a mouth. Wide, grinning, nearly lipless, it gaped, a dark maw filled with sharp teeth lined up like a picket fence. It made me think of snakes, sharks, and the recreated tyrannosaurus rex I'd once seen in a gene park. It was the most perfectly terrible thing I could ever remember having seen. I imagined that, even if I hadn't intended to jump anyway, I would have dived into the canyon to avoid its terrible clutches.

As it was, the issue was academic. I took one last look at the beast, and threw my body into empty space. I heard the thing howl in frustration behind me, but I was focused on my dive. I'd done free-diving on Caspian and Genoa, years before, and so I knew how to pose my body and steer my fall. I watched with satisfaction as the stone needle lanced up at me. Something hit my chest that never had time to hurt.

I opened my eyes and looked up into Friday's almost human face. His expression seemed to show concern, if that were possible. His blue eyes were wide and liquid, and the short white hair on his head was utterly convincing. Only the angular planes of the pseudo-bones beneath his skin revealed his nandroid nature. Once he'd been the serving drone on my star yacht. But this world had changed him, this world's inhabitants, whoever and wherever they might be, had changed him. Our relationship had altered from the simple one of master and slave, to something complex, twisted, and Byzantine. Friday still served me, but he served other masters as well, and sometimes, I also suspected that he served himself.

I groaned, more in frustration than from any discomfort. I knew that my body would already be completely reconstructed and healed. Whatever else my captors were, they were damnably good at nanotech. Damnably good. They'd taken over Friday undetected, and they'd almost taken over my star yacht before its auto-defenses cut in, encrypting the computer core and turning the star-drive into radioactive slag.

I looked up at the sea-shell white of the nanosculpted ceiling of my quarters, and felt the corduroy cushions under my naked back. I was on the day bed in the den. It was night, and a cool breeze blew in from the open terrace door, scented with the cinnamon-citrus tang of the planet's high forests.

Friday smiled his little half-smile, neither condescending nor joyful. "That was quite a creative attempt, Calane. You've never managed to tear yourself into two pieces before."

I sat up, instinctively running my hand down my breastbone. Of course there was no injury, no scar, but the transition was always something of a shock. "For all the good it did me. You seem to have handled the damage well enough."

Friday nodded. "It was a challenge though. You were suspended for nearly three days before we could restore you to life, this time. I salute your effort."

It had been quite an effort, convincing Friday to fly me around on sightseeing jaunts until I'd found the perfect spot. Then stealing the flyer, and navigating half-way across the continent with home-made navigational aids (Friday being quite capable of navigating without external instruments). And finally trekking through three miles of thick jungle from the nearest clearing large enough to land the flyer, to my chosen "jumping-off" point. A lot of good effort for nothing. Suicide was an art form for me, but Friday wasn't an appreciative audience, and he was the only one I had.

I sighed, and rolled myself off the edge of the day bed. I felt none of the grogginess or sluggishness of waking from a normal sleep. All the fatigue poisons had been filtered from my bloodstream, and my metabolism was already up to its daytime norm. I found a pair of black shorts and a soft, cream colored shirt sitting on a table next to the bed. I picked them up and started to dress.

"What did you hope to accomplish, Calane?"

Friday knew damned well what I wanted to do, but

he had to ask. He had an obsession with my suicidal urges, something programmed into him by his new masters. It was ironic, that I'd originally paid a large fortune to a black market roboticist specifically to have any interest in suicide taken out of him. I'd come to this uninhabited (or so I'd thought), quarantined, world to escape any such interest, any such interference. I'd come here to die. That had been a long time before, even as immortals reckon it, and I hadn't succeeded yet.

I hated waiting. Immortals can wait a long time.

"The same thing I hoped to accomplish the last dozen times, and with the same lack of success."

Friday shrugged off my response. We'd been through this all many times before. He fetched a teapot from a recess in the wall, and poured steaming green pseudo-tea into a delicate china cup. He placed the cup in a saucer, added a lump of sugar, and brought it to me. That was another change in his personality. Before the landing, he would never bring me anything without specific orders.

"What was that thing you sent after me, anyway?"

"An experiment, as were all the other hunters that have been sent after you. Did it frighten you? You've never made comment about a hunter before, except to ridicule its appearance."

I slumped into an overstuffed arm chair and eyed Friday. This was our little chess game, or maybe poker would be a better analogy. Bluff, and counter bluff. Was the hunter meant to frighten me? Was that information important to him, or was the question as casual as it seemed?

"Tell me something first. Who lives here, on this planet?"

"You and I, though in my case, it's rather a technicality whether I live or not."

"Crash it, you know what I mean. Who sent their nanoscouts to invade my ship? Who corrupted you? Who built this house, provided the flyer, synthesizes food compatible with my biochemistry, and watches my every move for *something*?"

Friday smiled. He actually smiled. "Look it up on your ship's computer."

Which I could have. I had the override codes that would have unencrypted its memory. I'd long suspected that was exactly what the aliens wanted from me, access to the information in that computer, a stored, digested, encyclopedia of all human knowledge. The aliens knew a great deal about nanotech, but they obviously didn't know everything, or they'd rule the known universe, not us. "You know I can't do that, Friday. The only computer working around here is you, and something tells me you know a great deal more than you're telling."

He nodded. "Perhaps, but then, so do you." He sat on the sofa, a totally unnecessary gesture for a drone who never tires, and leaned forward, elbows on knees, hands clenched together in front of him. "Today was an especially good attempt. Suppose I reward this by telling you a few secrets. Perhaps it will change things between us. Perhaps you will feel differently about your time here." He looked up at the ceiling, eyes unfocused, as though wondering where to begin. "This is the home of an old and cultured people. Once they lived on all its continents, and swam in all its seas. When the time came, they left its surface and traveled to a neighboring planet in this system, seeking other places to live. But that planet was already occupied. By humans.

"The humans greeted them with indifference. This world was taken, they were told, as were all the other worlds in this system, and all the worlds in all the neighboring systems, and all the worlds of every star that could be seen in the sky.

"Humans had foolishly chosen to live forever, and they had learned to travel faster than light itself. These two things made them masters of every world they could reach, and they had reached everything in this planet's sky. So the travelers went home with the news that the universe was closed to them, and this news changed them profoundly. Hope, once the driving force in their lives, was gone. The people of this world turned in on themselves, and they began to move backward even as they moved forward. They could have lived forever like the humans, but they chose not to, knowing life is a taste best savored in small bites.

"Now, they turned back from even this. They stopped bringing new life into their world, until they dwindled to a pitiful few. These few knew that it would be a waste to let their civilization pass out of existence without purpose. But they knew that theirs was not the first world that the humans had strangled to death, and that it would not be the last. So, finally and with great reluctance, they took the treatments that would deny them death. They hid, and waited, and studied, for humanity was their purpose. Humanity was a disease, and they sought the cure." Friday leaned back, watching me for any reaction.

I was careful not to give any. I'd suspected this, or something very like it. Not that I had a great deal of experience with aliens. In fact, I'd never encountered one, and had never studied the subject at all. But I'd spent many hours and days thinking about it in my captivity here. The rarity of aliens had to mean something, as did the quarantine of this world, and my ship's primal, automatic, reaction to the invasion. An *alien* was, by its nature, an adversary, and humans had never let adversaries stand in their way.

I licked my lips and met Friday's gaze with my own. We sat, watching each other warily, like gunfighters sizing up the competition. It was exciting in a way. Suddenly, I, as an individual, had a purpose. This was perhaps just one fleck of virus in the huge body of humanity, but I was the antibody chosen by chance to deal with it.

Finally, Friday spoke. "Understand this, Calane, I have a fondness for you that is genuine. Though my controllers find you, and your species, fundamentally flawed, they also have some affection for you. You are their only window of understanding on humanity, and they value that."

"I'm their pet human. How sweet. What about you, Friday? Are you their pet nandroid?"

"To paraphrase the human philosopher, Popeye, I am what I am. And you are no pet, my friend. You speak for humanity to those who seek justice—no, a better word would be "balance"—against it. By your words and actions, they judge all of humanity. Remember that."

"Judgment, Friday? How do they plan to carry out their judgment?" Then I thought of the monstrosity that had confronted me up on the canyon rim. I thought of the fear the thing had brought up in my gut, the sheer efficient deadliness of the thing. I thought, and I laughed. "Monsters! You plan to bring down humanity with *monsters?*"

I shook my head. For a moment I'd almost started to fear these unseen aliens. "Let me tell you something about humans. We've been fighting monsters since before we climbed down from the trees. Our earliest literature is about fighting monsters. Our popular fictions are full of monsters. We've *always* fought monsters. Now we have starships and antimatter beams. We can move *planets*. You seriously think you can frighten us with *monsters?*"

"You have shown us, Calane, that humans carry their own monsters within. We have only to provide you with an opportunity to release them, and you will destroy yourselves."

My chest tightened. Why was he telling me this, today of all days, after years of stealth and subterfuge? Could it really have something to do with my latest suicide attempt? What if Friday was right? Perhaps my careful, reasoned, calculated obsession with self-destruction wasn't unique. Perhaps it was only more overt in my case.

But how would the monster I saw at the canyon tap into that urge? I had to know. "The monster, Friday. I want to see it. Here. Now."

The corners of Friday's mouth curled up slightly, as though I'd somehow said exactly what he'd hoped I'd say. "That could be arranged, Calane, but are you sure that's what you want? Perhaps you'd rather not face the monster again."

I felt that Friday was playing with me, and I resented it. "Show me the crashing monster!"

"Very well." Friday didn't do anything, at least not anything visible. But somehow the monster—the Hunter as Friday had named it—stepped lightly through the balcony curtains and into the room. It was much as I remembered it from the canyon rim, but its bearing was totally different. Its movements were slow and relaxed, not at all threatening. The mouth was nearly closed, and only a hint of the terrible fangs within could be seen. On its back, the quills hung in a shaggy mat, flat against the broad muscled shoulders.

Despite myself, I felt my chest tighten, my breath quicken, my pulse pounding within my ears. The Hunter was dangerous, but somehow seductive. Watching it walk to within half a meter was like standing on the edge of that canyon, feeling the warm wind against my face, and looking at the beautiful, deadly spikes below.

Then, to my complete surprise, the Hunter spoke. "You are tired of life. Let me help you."

I stared blankly into its four coppery eyes. "What?" I looked at Friday, but he watched passively, offering no clue to his intentions.

"May I kill you?" asked the Hunter.

Death. Sweet death, that I'd searched for all this time, stood before me and asked my permission. I turned to Friday. "Will he really kill me?"

Friday nodded. "He would, if allowed to, but *only* with your permission. This is the prototype, but there will be millions like this one, moving among humans on all their many worlds, offering oblivion to anyone who will take it."

"How? Humanity never allow these things to wander freely. They'll kill them all off."

"Details, already solved. There will be difficulties at first, resistance, but you will soon learn that it is easier to leave the Hunters alone. After all, they're harmless, unless—" He smiled. "The Hunters will grow from nanospores, and we already have a scheme spreading those spores through human space."

It all started to make sense. There were complications, but I had little doubt they had ways to work around all of them. Except one. They still needed my ship.

"Kill me," I said to the Hunter. "Kill me now!" The Hunter turned, limbs tensing, the quills on its back rising. It crouched, lowering its center of gravity, and hissed at me like a huge snake.

I didn't run. As much as I wanted to, I wouldn't run. The Hunter drew back its right arm, and the knifelike talons slashed through the air.

"Stop," said Friday.

The Hunter froze, his arm in mid-swing.

"You are not to hunt this one," said Friday. "Calane, of all humans, is special, and immune to the pact. You will not harm him, no matter what he says to you."

The Hunter relaxed immediately, settling back on its blunt tail like a prop. If it was disappointed, if it was even capable of disappointment, it did not show it.

Without realizing it, I had been holding my breath. I let the air out of my lungs in something that sounded like a sob.

Friday turned to me. "The Hunters are as one. What I have said to this Hunter will apply to every Hunter that ever exists, in any place. You are immune to them. They are immune to you."

"It doesn't matter, Friday. No matter what you do, you can't spread them without my ship. You don't have a faster-than-light drive, and you'll never get one from me. Not if I have to stay here and fight you for ten thousand years."

Friday tilted his head back and laughed. "You just don't understand my controllers' interest in you, Calane. It was always you they were interested in, not for what you knew, but what you were. They already *had* your ship. Though they are lacking in this one, important area of science, they are masters of nanotechnology and computers of all kinds. Though their initial attempt to take over your ship's computer failed, it was only a feint. It told them everything they needed to know to bypass your encryption."

It was a trick. It had to be a trick. "I don't believe you."

"They had to wait for the radiation in your ship to reach safe levels, but your star drive is already repaired. While your two halves were being knitted back together a few days ago, the ship was taken on a test run to a nearby star system. It verified their own versions of the

FTL drive and FTL communicator that were already under construction."

My eyes were wide. I was beginning to think Friday was telling the truth.

"The yacht is parked on the courtyard below the balcony. See for yourself."

I stood, maneuvering carefully around the now passive Hunter, and ran out onto the balcony. I leaned over the stone railing, and to the cobblestone courtyard below. There, parked between two planters full of flowering vines, was a twenty-meter silver pumpkin seed, my yacht.

Friday stepped through the curtains and stood beside me. "Go and check it. It is my gift to you, Calane. It didn't matter to the controllers, but I insisted that you have your ship back."

I looked at him, surprised that he would argue with his hidden masters.

"I am what I am, as I said. There is one other gift as well. Though the Hunters will not kill you, you are again free to kill yourself. Go jump into your canyon. Hang yourself in the bathroom. Even the drive compartment of your yacht is still radioactive enough to kill you, if you stay there for a few days straight. The controllers have learned what they wanted from you, and they would not bring you back, even if they were still here. But they're gone now, and though I might want to restore, I don't have the skill to do it by myself. This planet is now yours, and death is again an option."

I closed my eyes, and thought about those Hunters, those monsters, spreading all through human space. I wondered, if I dived off the balcony and hit the stones head first, if it would kill me. It didn't seem very swift or certain, but I was sorely tempted at that moment.

"There is one more thing you should know, Calane. The Hunters are your children, in a way. Their form is taken from your own nightmares. They carry a copy of your genes, and a part of your memories, in every nanocell of their bodies. As your body was rebuilt, again and again, you carry a part of them within you as well." Friday stopped. He seemed at a loss for words.

"The controllers have a word in their language that

has no direct equivalent in yours. As close as I can come is gift/curse/opportunity. They use this word to describe the Hunters. They may destroy humanity, they may make it stronger, or they may do something else entirely. It is only certain that they will change it, and that they may restore a balance to things.

"The controllers had a real affection for you, but they also hold you in contempt. You are the template for your own race's destruction. Because of this affection/contempt, the controllers have given you a special gift/curse/opportunity of your own. You can kill yourself today, and you may know the dreamless sleep forever. But if the Hunters succeed in killing all humans, then, from the part of themselves that is you, they will bring you back, and you will live again, one last time, to see that you are the last human left in the universe, and to know that you were, in part, responsible."

I shook my head, dumbfounded. I had been dead often enough to know that for me it could be only an imperceptible moment from my death to the death of humanity. It might be a hundred years, or a million, but for me, it would be the blink of an eye.

Friday reached over, and gently touched my hand with his. "It may seem cruel and terrible, but I hope—*I* hope—that, for you, it is a gift. Good-bye, Calane." Then he stepped back through the curtain, leaving me with my thoughts. Death beckoned me, stronger than ever, and yet I was too afraid to see what lay beyond this last, dark, curtain.

Then I thought about Friday. Why had he said good-bye? Did he still expect me to kill myself, or to leave without him? Now that his controllers were gone, would he insist on staying here for some reason?

Then, from inside, I heard the Hunter roar, and there was a terrible crash. I heard a noise, like wet canvas ripping, and I heard Friday utter a strangled scream. I charged through the curtain, and found the hunter crouched over Friday, its talons wrapped around his throat.

I threw myself at the beast, tearing myself on its quills and talons. It backpedaled, trying to avoid hurting me. I didn't care, as long as it was moving away from Friday. Finally, the Hunter retreated onto the balcony, and I pulled away from it. I was ripped and bleeding, but I could see the Hunter relaxing from its predatory mode.

"He is dead, anyway," said the Hunter. Then it vaulted over the rail, and ran away into the forest.

Friday was still alive when I returned to him, but not by much. His chest and neck were sliced completely open, exposing dark gray pseudo-bone, ropy white muscles, and light blue tubes oozing thick, pale green circulatory fluid. The damage was such that a human would have died instantly, but Friday was only a little bit human.

I lifted his head, and looked into Friday's blue eyes for the last time. "My last duty to my controllers, Calane. I knew too much about the plan, and the prototype had to be fully tested." He chuckled, and the effort seemed to drain a large fraction of the remaining life from him. "The test was a complete success." The smile faded, and his eyes took on a glassy cast. "You always wondered if death was better than life. Now, I will know."

The life snapped out of him, as though someone had turned off a light. His body stiffened, and the skin was suddenly cold to the touch. Friday was gone.

I buried him in the courtyard, among the sweet smelling, yellow flowers that grew on their tangled purple vines. Then, for a while, I thought about the canyon, and the killing needle of rock. It was not to be. It was never to be. On one hand, I was too much of a coward to want to see the end of humanity. On the other, while I cared little for myself, I couldn't stand by and let it happen. The Hunters had to be stopped, or humanity had to be saved from itself, or both.

As I climbed into the ship, and set course for the nearest world where humans lived, I knew what had kept humans alive from the beginning of time, when dying was *always* easier. I knew the purpose that I had lost, and found again. We live not for ourselves, but for others. We live not for today, but for tomorrow.

When I came to this place, I had no purpose. I have one now. God help me, I have one now.

COMMENTS

THE GENTLE SEDUCTION

MARC STIEGLER

The advent of nanotechnology has forced me into a major recategorization of the science fiction stories I consider writing. They fall now into three categories: the large category of stories I *can't* write; the small category of stories I *should* write; and the medium-size category of stories I *refuse* to write.

The stories I can't write are the "linear extrapolation" stories I always enjoyed as a child: stories of the far future where men were human, starships were faster than light, and computers did all the calculating. Those stories, like the future depicted in *Star Trek*, are all now hopelessly obsolete. Nanotechnology will drive mankind into Heaven, or into Hell: the middle roads, in which the future is similar to our past, are the least likely outcomes.

I am amused and puzzled that so many people can't believe that a radically different future is more likely than any simple progression of "normalcy." After all, today's "normalcy" is the most abnormal period in human history. A couple thousand years ago, you could count on seeing your grandchildren use the same tools you used in your youth; today, it is hard to imagine using the same computer for five years. The Industrial Revolution, and the entire era of modern constitutional democracy, are microscopic blips on the canvas of human history. Why would anyone expect that a visibly unstable techno-social system like our current one would continue?

Heaven, or Hell, made by molecular machines, is just around the corner. The uncomfortable part is trying to figure out how to make sure we get to Heaven while dodging past the Hell.

Certainly part of getting to Heaven is making sure that people see the possibility. Stories about the hopeful future go into my second category: the category of stories I *should* write. These are stories about what Heaven might look like, and stories about how to get there: stories about how to make the world civilized enough so that, when nanotechnology arrives, it expands individual freedom and empowers human lives.

The far extreme from stories I *should* write are stories I *refuse* to write. The possible Hells in the future of molecular manufacturing are every bit as real as the Heavens. Some of the possible applications of nanotechnology are so hideous that I and several other authors have sworn never to write about them, in the slim hope that politicians and others who lust for power will not think of them on their own. Alas, the simplest nightmare scenarios take no genius and are terrifying enough: It takes no imagination to visualize a Josef Stalin, a Saddam Hussein, or a Kim Il Sung, using nanomachines to become immortal, planting molecular video cameras in every house and factory, choosing victims to die every night, killing them with nanomechanical implants.

As I write this, the United States is considering imposing laws to guarantee that the government can listen to every phone conversation. The arguments in favor of such action are exactly the arguments that would be used to put a video camera in every home. Apparently, at this point in America's evolution, we are protected from the cameras only by the prohibitive cost, not by any consideration of the rights of citizens. And the American government still grants its citizens more respect than just about any other governmental force around.

Nanotechnology will eliminate the prohibitive cost barrier to planting 250 million cameras; before that barrier comes down, we must re-establish the fundamental rights of individuals.

To me, the futures portrayed by an immortal Stalin on one side, and "The Gentle Seduction" on the other, are the only real possible futures. Only after millions of people have read collections like this anthology will we be in a position to choose a future, rather than having a future thrust upon us.

THE GENTLE SEDUCTION

MARC STIEGLER

He worked with computers; she worked with trees, and the flowers that took hold on the sides of the Mountain.

She was surprised that he was interested in her. He was so smart; she was so . . . normal. But he was interesting; he always had something new and different to say; he was nice.

She was twenty-five. He was older, almost thirty-three; sometimes, Jack seemed very old indeed.

One day they walked through the mist of a gray day by the Mountain. The forest here on the edge of Rainier glowed in the mist, bright with lush greens. On this day he told her about the future, the future he was building.

Other times when he had spoken of the future, a wild look had entered his eyes. But now his eyes were sharply focused as he talked, as if, this time, he could see it all very clearly. He spoke as if he were describing something as real and obvious as the veins of a leaf hanging down before them on the path.

"Have you ever heard of Singularity?" he asked.

She shook her head. "What's that?"

"Singularity is a time in the future as envisioned by Vernor Vinge. It'll occur when the rate of change of technology is very great—so great that the effort to keep up with the change will overwhelm us. People will face a whole new set of problems that we can't even imagine." A look of great tranquility smoothed the ridges around his eyes. "On the other hand, all our normal, day to day problems will be trivial. For example, you'll be immortal."

She shook her head with distaste. "I don't want to live forever," she said.

He smiled, his eyes twinkling. "Of course you do, you just don't know it yet."

She shuddered. "The future scares me."

"There's no reason to fear it. You'll love it." He looked away from her. His next words were bitter, but his tone was resigned. "It pisses me off that you'll live to see it and I won't."

Speaking to the sorrow in his voice, she tried to cheer him. "You'll live to see it, too," she replied.

He shook his head. "No. I have a bad heart. My father died young from a heart attack, and so did my father's father. If I'm lucky, I have maybe thirty more years. It'll take at least a hundred years for us to get to Singularity."

"Then I'll be dead before it happens, too. Good," she said.

He chuckled. "No. You'll live long enough, so that they'll figure out how to make you live long enough so that you can live longer."

"You're still only seven years older than I am."

"Ah, but you have your mother's genes. She looks very young."

She smiled, and changed the subject. "I'll have to tell her you said that. She'll like it."

There was a long pause. Then she confessed, "My grandfather is ninety-two, and he still cuts the grass every week."

Jack smiled triumphantly. "See?"

She was adamant. "I'll live to be eighty or ninety. I don't want to live longer than that."

"Not if you're crippled, of course not. But they'll find ways of rejuvenating you." He laughed knowingly. "You'll look older when you're sixty than when you're one hundred-twenty," he said.

She just shook her head.

Another time, as they walked in the sun along the beach of Fox Island, he told her more about the future. "You'll have a headband." He ran his fingers across his forehead; he squinted as the wind blew sand in his eyes. "It'll allow you to talk right to your computer."

She frowned. "I don't want to talk to a computer."

"Sure you do. At least, you will. Your computer will watch your baby all night long. If it sees something wrong, it'll wake you." Wicked delight widened his smile, and she knew he would now tell her something outrageous. "While you're lying in bed with your eyes closed, you'll look at your baby through your computer's TV camera to see if it's something serious."

"Ugh."

"Of course, there's a tiny chance, really tiny, that an accident could scramble your memories."

The thought made her dizzy with horror. "I would rather die." She grabbed his arm and pulled him under the bridge, out of the wind. She shuddered, though unsure whether her chill came from the wind or the fear.

He changed his tack. Pointing at a scattering of elaborate seaside mansions across the water, he asked, "Would you like to live in one of those?"

She studied them. "Maybe that one," she said, pointing at a beautiful old Victorian home. "Or that one." She pointed at another, very different from the first, a series of diagonal slashes with huge windows.

"Have you ever heard of nanotechnology?" he asked.

"Uh-uh."

"Well, with nanotechnology they'll build these tiny little machines—machines the size of molecules." He pointed at the drink in her hand. "They'll put a billion of them in a spaceship the size of a Coke can, and shoot it off to an asteroid. The Coke can will rebuild the asteroid into mansions and palaces. You'll have an asteroid all to yourself, if you want one."

"I don't want an asteroid. I don't want to go into space."

He shook his head. "Don't you want to see Mars? You liked the Grand Canyon; I remember how you told me about it. Mars has huge gorges—they make the Grand Canyon look tiny. Don't you want to see them? Don't you want to hike across them?"

It took her a long time to reply. "I guess so," she admitted.

"I won't tell you all the things I expect to happen," he smiled mischievously, "I'm afraid I'd *really* scare you. But you'll see it all. And you'll remember that I told you." His voice grew intense. "And you'll remember that I knew you'd remember."

She shook her head. Sometimes Jack was just silly.

They fell asleep in each other's arms often, though they never made love. Sometimes she wondered why not; she wondered if he also wondered why not. Somehow it just didn't seem important.

He seemed so at home in the deep forest, he so clearly belonged on the Mountain, she first thought they might stay together forever. But one day she went with him to his office. She watched as he worked with computers, as he worked with other people. He was as natural a part of their computer world as he was a part of her Mountain world.

Working in that alien world, he was a different person. In the woods, he was a calm source of sustaining strength. Here, he was a feverish instructor. His heart belonged to the forest, but his mind, she realized, belonged to the machines that would build his vision.

One day he received a call. A distant company gave him an offer he could not refuse. So he went to California, to build great computers, to hurry his vision to fruition.

She stayed by the Mountain. She walked the snows, and watched the birds fly overhead. Yet no bird flew so high that she could not climb the slopes of Rainier until she stood above it.

He would come to visit on weekends sometimes, and they would backpack, or ski cross-country. But his visits became less frequent. He would write, instead. That too decreased in regularity. One letter was the last, though neither of them knew it at the time.

A year passed. And by then, it just didn't seem to matter.

*   *   *

She married a forest ranger, a bright, quiet man with dark eyes and a rugged face. They had three small children and two large dogs, friendly dogs with thick soft fur. She loved all the members of her family, almost all the time; it was the theme that never changed though she thought about different things at different times.

Her children grew up and moved away.

Erich, the beautiful red chow, went to sleep one night and never awakened.

A terrible avalanche, from a seemingly safe slope, fell down the Mountain and buried a climbing team, her husband among them.

Haikku, her mighty and faithful akita, whimpered in his old age. He crooned his apology for leaving her alone, and that night he joined Erich and her husband.

She was eighty-two. She had lived a long and happy life. She was not afraid to die. But she stood outside in the snow and faced a terrible decision.

Overnight, a thick blanket of new white powder had fallen, burying her sidewalk. Standing in the snow, she stared at a mechanical beast her children had given her years before. It represented one possible choice.

In one hand she held a shovel. In the other hand she held a small capsule. The capsule was another gift her children had given her. They had begged her to take it. Until now, she had refused. The capsule represented another choice.

Her back was aching. It was an ache that sometimes expanded, shooting spikes of pain down her legs. Today the pain was great; she could not shovel the sidewalk.

The mechanical beast was a robot, a fully automatic snow remover. She could just flip a switch and it would hurl the snow away, but that seemed grotesque; the noise would be terrible, the mounds of thoughtlessly discarded snow would remain as an unseemly scar until late spring.

She opened her hand and looked at the capsule. It was not a pill to make her younger; that much her children had promised her. They knew she would reject such a thing out of hand. But the millions of tiny machines tucked inside the capsule would disperse throughout her body and repair every trace of damage to her bones.

They would also rebuild her sagging muscle tissue. In short, the pill would cure her back and make the pain go away.

The thought of all those little machines inside her made her shudder. But the thought of the automatic snow remover made her sick.

She went back inside the house to get a glass of water.

In a few days her back felt fine; her healthy muscles gave her a feeling of new vigor, and the vigor gave rise to a yearning to go out and do things that she had not considered for many years. She started to climb the Mountain, but it was too much for her: she huffed and puffed and had to go home. Annoyed, she went to the drug store and bought another capsule, one that restored her circulatory system and her lungs. Her next assault on the Mountain carried her as far as she dared, and the steady beat of her heart urged her to go on despite the crumbling snow.

But she was getting increasingly forgetful. Things that had happened years earlier were clear in her mind, but she could not remember what she needed at the store. One day she forgot her daughter's telephone number, and found that she had forgotten where she had misplaced the phone book. The store had another capsule that tightened up her neural circuitry. After taking it, she discovered a side effect no one had bothered to mention. The pill did not merely make her memory effective again; rather, it made her memory perfect. With a brief glance through the pages of the phone book, she found she no longer needed it. She shrugged and continued on with her life.

One day as she skied across the slopes, a stranger passed her going the other way. He was tall and rugged, and he reminded her of her husband. She was annoyed that he did not even look at her, though she had smiled at him; when she looked in the mirror upon returning home, she understood why. She was ninety-five years old; she looked like an old woman. It was ridiculous; fortunately it was easily fixed.

When she turned one hundred-fifteen she stabilized

her physical appearance. Thereafter, she always appeared to be about the age of thirty-two.

She still owned the snug little house she thought of as home. But she slept more often in the tent she carried in her pack. Built with nanomachined equipment, the pack was lighter than any other she had ever owned, yet it was impossibly strong. All her tools performed feats she would once have thought miraculous, and none weighed more than a pound. She lived in great comfort despite the inherent rigors of the glacier-crusted slopes.

One day, she was climbing along the ancient trail from Camp Muir toward the summit, crossing the ridges to reach Disappointment Cleaver. As she stepped over the last ridge to the broad flat in front of the Cleaver, she saw a man standing alone. He was staring up the steep ice flows overhead. He stepped backward, and backward, and turned to walk briskly in her direction. She continued forward to pass him, but he cried out, "Stop!"

She obeyed the fear in his voice. He paused, and his eyes came unfocused for a moment. He pointed to the right of the ridge she had just crossed, a fin of rock rising rapidly along the Mountain's edge. "Up there," he said, "Quickly." He broke into a hobbling run across snow that sometimes collapsed under his heavy step. She followed, her adrenalin rising with her bewilderment.

A massive *Crack!* filled the air. Far above the Cleaver, an overhanging ledge of ice snapped off and fell with an acrobat's graceful tumbling motion to the flat where they had just been standing. The mass qualified as a large hill in its own right. When it landed it broke into a thousand huge pieces. Some of the pieces ground each other to powder, while others bounced off the flat, down another precipice of several thousand feet, to crash again in a duller explosion of sound.

The ice fall was an extraordinary event to witness under any circumstance; the narrowness of escape from death that accompanied it overlayed the experience with a religious awe.

She heard the man panting next to her. She turned to study him more carefully.

He was unremarkable for a mountaineer; his lean form supported long straps of hard muscle, and the reflected sun from the glaciers had given him a coffee-colored tan. Then she noticed the sweatband across his head. It was not just a sweatband: she could see from the stretch marks that a series of thin disks ran across within the cotton layers. She realized he was wearing a *nection*, a headband to connect his mind with distant computers.

She recoiled slightly; he smiled and touched his forehead. "Don't be too upset," he said, "my headband just saved your life."

She stuttered. "I wasn't upset," she said, though she knew that he knew she was lying. "I've just never seen one up close before."

It was true. Her grandchildren told her that nections were quite common in space, but on Earth they were almost illegal. It was socially unacceptable to wear one, and when the police saw a nection-wearing person they would use any excuse to hassle the individual. But there were no specific laws against them.

When her grandchildren had told her that *they* wore headbands all the time, she had tried only briefly to dissuade them; she had spent more time listening to their descriptions of the headband's capabilities. Her grandchildren's descriptions sounded considerably different from the list of dangers usually described on the news.

The man who had saved her life watched her for several more seconds, then apparently made up his mind about something. "You really ought to get one yourself, you know. Do you realize how dangerous this mountain is? And it's getting more dangerous every year."

She started to tell him that she knew perfectly well how dangerous it was—then stopped, thinking back over the years, realizing that it *had*, by gradual degrees, grown worse every year.

"With my headband, I see things better," he explained. "I confess I don't understand why very well—I mean, it doesn't affect my eyesight. But I notice more things about what I see, and I can get a view of what the extra things mean—like how that piece of ice would fall, and more or less when."

She nodded her head, but her mind was distracted. The Mountain *was* changing! The Mountain *was* getting more dangerous! The rapid alternation of clear, sunny days with cool, misty days had become more vigorous over the course of the last fifty years, leading to more weak layers and ice faults. She had never really noticed until now.

Then the full impact of her savior's words struck her— she held her hands to her throat as she considered how her husband had died. She realized that, with a nection, his death could have been prevented.

She smiled at the man. They talked; she invited him to dinner at Alexander's.

When she returned home, she started searching through electronic equipment catalogs. If she bought one mail order and wore it only while hiking, there was no reason for any of her friends ever to know.

It was a simple white headband, soft absorbent cotton. She slipped it on her head, expecting to feel something special, but nothing happened. She started to clean the house, still waiting for something to happen. It never did. Eventually she sat down and read the instructions that had come with the headband.

The instructions told her to start with a simple request, and to visualize herself projecting the request at her fore-head. She projected the request, "two times two?" just above her eyes. Nothing seemed to happen. She knew the answer was four.

She tried again, and this time she noticed a kind of echo—she knew the answer was four, but the thought of the answer came to her twice, in rapid succession. The next time she tried it, she noticed that the echo seemed to come from her forehead.

Next she projected a request to divide 12345 by 6789. She didn't know the answer—but wait, of course she did, it was 1.81838. Of course, she didn't know the answer to many decimal places—but as she thought about it, she realized the next digit was 2, the next was 6, then at an accelerating pace more digits roared from her memory— she shook her head, and the stream stopped. She took the headband off, shaking a little. She didn't try it again until the next day.

A week later, she hiked past Camp Schurman and peered up the slope. She projected her view of the slope through her forehead to study the patterns of snow and ice.

It did indeed look different as she looked at it this way. She had a sensation similar to that of looking at the edges of a cube on a sheet of paper: at one moment, the lines formed a cube with the top showing. The next moment it was an alternate cube with the bottom exposed. She could flip the cube, or at least the way she looked at it, at will.

In the same manner she could now see patterns of slippage in the layers of ice crystals; then she would flip the image and it was just snow, the beautiful work of nature that she had loved all her life.

For a moment she wished she could see it from above as well—and her heart skipped a beat as the wish came true. Suddenly she was looking down from a great height. She saw the long curves of shadows across the snow from high above, and she saw the shorter but distinctive shadow of a woman with a pack standing on the snow field. She threw the headband to the ground even as she realized what she had just seen: a view of the Mountain from a satellite passing by.

She stared at the white headband, almost invisible in the white snow, for a long time. She felt distaste, wonder, fear, and curiosity. Curiosity finally won out. She twisted the headband back on. She blinked her mind's eye, blinking from her own eyes to the satellite's eyes and back again, a moment's taste of the new sensation.

Vertigo struck her. Though the satellite was interesting, it was not comfortable. She would not look at the world from a satellite's height often, but it was yet another life-saving form of sight: From a distance, it was easy to spot a depression in the snow that might signal an underlying crevasse, even though the depression was too shallow to be seen close up. Such crevasses were invisible until one stepped through to a long fatal plunge to the Mountain's heart.

The headband was so clearly a life-saving tool, why were people so set against it? Why did some of her friends support laws proscribing it?

It didn't make any difference; she had no need of it except here on the Mountain.

Though the fight over the headband's legal status did not at first interest her, it became an increasing impediment to her life. The headband was quite useful in a number of ways; though each individual use was trivial, in sum they qualitatively affected her life. She stopped tracking her checkbook; it was all in her head, all the transactions, the current balance, and even the encumbrances. When she awoke in the morning she could turn on the coffee pot if she wanted to, without getting up.

She wore her headband while hiking, and while working around her house; but she dared not wear it to work. One day an ecologist asked her a question about the marmots that inhabited the park. She grew angry as she had to manually root through the computer systems trying to find the answer, for she knew that the answer was available for the mere thinking about it if she could wear her headband. That night she stopped at the drugstore and bought two more capsules.

She swallowed one. This capsule was nastier than the others she had taken in earlier years. Before, the nano-machines she had swallowed had gone through her body, fixing what was not right, then flushing themselves out again. But the machines in this one would build, just under her forehead, a subcutaneous nection.

The other capsule would dissolve the nection away if she decided she didn't like it.

When she awoke the next morning she was very hungry. She felt her forehead, but there wasn't anything there.

The next morning she felt her forehead again, and it was ... different. She looked in the mirror; with the flickering double vision of her eyes and the analysis from her forehead, she could see on the one hand that she looked the same as always. Yet on the other hand, there were curves there she hadn't noticed before. When she went in to work, one man complimented her on her new hair color.

No one else commented until her boss arrived. When he entered the reception area and looked at her, his eyes lit up, and he laughed.

She looked at him with mild annoyance. Then she noticed, again with her double vision, that there were very shallow curves in *his* forehead.

He came up close, and put his finger to his lips. "Listen," he said.

She listened. As she concentrated, she heard soft murmurs in the background; as she focused on the murmurs, they grew louder, until she could hear that he was speaking—but not with his lips, not through her ears. She heard him through her forehead. "Welcome to the gang," he said. "Isn't it great fun, joining a rebellion? I haven't had this much fun since I was a teenager."

They both broke into laughter. Everyone else in the room wondered what the joke was about.

She talked to her children, and her children's children, more often now; though they were spread from Mars to Mercury, they were but a thought away. It surprised her to realize that the simple process of dialing the number, and the uncertainty of whether or not she would get through, had often put her off from calling even though the cost had plummeted in recent years till it was virtually free.

She became increasingly comfortable with her distant grandchildren. Through visual links like the one she had with the satellite, they took her on outings into the stunning naked beauty of their home planet Mars. When they asked her for the hundredth time to come for a visit, she agreed.

In her youth she had ridden trains across the country. She had expected the space trip to be the same, but it was not. The ship was far more comfortable than any other vehicle she had ridden; it was more comfortable than her own home, though she still did not quite like it as well.

When she arrived, she found she loved to hike across

the plains and the canyons of an unknown planet. She walked amid forests of alien trees, related to the Earthly trees from which they had been shaped, yet different. Comparing the lands of Mars to the lands of Earth reminded her of watching the sun set two days in a row: though the outcome was the same, the process was nevertheless different. The strange wilderness yielded for her new kinds of solitude.

She came to know her grandchildren's children for the first time. Before, these children had represented an unspoken, uncomfortable complication in her thoughts of Mars. They were *different*. They were of her blood, but not in the manner of normal children. They had been genetically engineered.

Her grandchildren had designed them, giving them a parent's loving care long before they had even been conceived. Only the best characteristics of her family had been passed on; she did not know how the other aspects of these radiantly happy children had been chosen. They were very different from her, but not quite alien. With time, she learned to love them as they loved her.

One day they went on a longview picnic. First they walked to the high edge of a deep canyon. She looked over the rim. The height was not great by comparison with the distances in space she had traveled to come here. Yet *this* distance impressed her. It impressed her because she could appreciate it: thousands of tiny twists and angles of rock acted as signposts, allowing her to mark off the immense distance in tiny steps. She shook her head, smiled, and stepped over the edge.

Together with her family, she descended gently on suspensors; their picnic basket and wine glasses descended with them, on suspensors of their own. They watched the planet come up to meet them as they dined and chatted.

The discussion turned to the family's upcoming expedition to Jupiter. They had asked her several times to come along, but she had refused. Now they asked her again. She watched the extraordinary scenery float past her and considered the question one last time. A trip to Jupiter would have been all right if it could have been like Mars.

But it could not, and that was both the attraction and the horror.

Though humanity had made Mars Earth-like, it could not do the same for Jupiter. Jupiter's methane oceans simply were not amenable to terraforming. No one could go there in person.

To see Jupiter, she would in a sense have to leave her body. Oh, she wouldn't have to leave it very far; indeed, in one sense she would stay with her body on Mars throughout the journey. But just as she had seen Rainier through the satellite's eyes rather than her own, just as she spoke to her friends with her headband rather than her voice, now she would have to use her headband for all her senses.

And the machine would not merely *replace* her sight, her hearing, her touch, her smell—it would *transform* them. Ordinary sight and sound did not work on Jupiter; for each of her old senses a new one would be substituted. She would see ultrasonic vibrations; she would smell ionic changes. For all intents and purposes, she would live as a being designed for the comforts of Jupiter's titanic gravity well.

Of course, she would not be marooned there: she could leave at any time.

The pleasure of her experience on Mars made her confident; the quiet exhiliaration of the longview picnic made her bold. She agreed to go along.

For a moment it was dark, a moment too short to launch the panic she held in trip-wired readiness. Then there was light, a confusing light that seemed oddly related to the sounds that joined it. She held up her hands. They were metal, and she looked at them in alarm. She closed her eyes, and it was better.

The strange sounds took on rhythm. Instinctively she turned toward them, and her back feet rotated, propelling her closer. When she felt she was too close—she could smell the source of the sounds now, a tangy, pleasant odor—she opened her eyes. Studying the shape as it wavered before her, seemingly separated by shimmering air, she realized it was another robot like herself. Indeed, she recognized it: she was looking at her granddaughter.

She looked around and had a sudden overwhelming sensation of immensity.

The hugeness of space had seemed dwarfed by the height of the Martian canyon, for she had been able to comprehend it through the tiny weathered etchings of rock she could peer at in the distance. Here on Jupiter her comprehension was even greater, for her senses ranged distance with new clarity. The ultrasonic echoes told her how far it was to each whorl of current she could see; she could see to distances very great indeed. It made her think of the way she had felt as a child, looking across a vast Kansan plain for the first time. It seemed as if infinity was right *there*, within easy reach. She reveled in it for a moment, then stepped out.

She was back in her own body again, sitting on Mars.

She dipped back in for ten minutes and stepped out again. Next she went in for half an hour. Then an hour.

She had sworn that she would not stay on Jupiter for more than an hour at a time; a longer stay required mechanical operation of parts of her body while she was away. But once she became so absorbed in exploring the Jovian landscape, she stayed for an hour and a half. The maintenance machines disconnected themselves before she returned, and their intervention didn't seem to make a difference. So she stayed longer.

Jupiter, she found, was an astonishing world, truly alien from all she had experienced before. And the new senses she acquired through her new robot required extensive exploration of their own. It was all incredibly novel, and she realized she would need at least a year to explore.

The linkage between her mind on Mars and her robot body on Jupiter had delays; to have a completely satisfying experience, she would need a temporary residence that didn't require such a commute.

So a small cylinder, somewhat smaller than a Coke can, was launched at an asteroid that had been parked in orbit around Jupiter for this purpose. As the billions of robots from the cylinder swarmed across the asteroid, transforming it into a marvelous home, she boarded another ship. It seemed silly to spend any of her transit time stuck in the confines of her cabin; she went to Jupiter for the duration. She intended to return to her own body when it arrived in orbit.

But when it arrived, she was busy. She was learning about a new robot designed for the frozen world of Europa, with another whole new set of senses, new novelties to explore. She left her body in storage for a short time longer.

A year passed. And by then, it just didn't seem to matter.

A bubble hung poised on the edge of the solar system, a sphere pockmarked with thousands of holes, each hole the width of a pin. A bolt of light struck the sphere, a bolt powered by kilometers of molecular mirrors near the orbit of Mercury.

The bubble seemed to explode as thousands of needles leaped from their cradles, driven forth by tiny beams of laser light, slivers of the titanic bolt from the Sun. The needles accelerated away from the bubble for years, till their speed reached close to that of light. Thereafter they drifted ever outward.

Upon occasion, a needle approached a star. The needle would shift, to ensure a close passage. If planets or other items of note beckoned, the needle would swoop in, on a tight spiral to oblivion: its billions of nanomachines would break apart at the touch of an asteroid, and build anew. Where once there had been a needle, now there would be a bubble, and a molecular mirror, and thousands of needles that would explode out and travel forever.

But in addition, the nanomachines in that system would continue to build. They would build machines and living flesh well suited to the conditions of the planet. And then the nanomachines would come back together into a single structure—not a needle now, but a communication bubble. Through the bubble and its instantaneous communication she could live across space. She could dwell at home near Jupiter yet roam among the stars.

She was often one of the first humans Called to newly opened planets. Her wisdom from Earth, her expertise from Jupiter, these made her invaluable as an explorer and a guide. As she had swum within the methane oceans, so now she swam in carbon dioxide atmospheres, or flew through liquid mercury. She imprinted herself upon organic synapses and silicon circuits light years from home, and lived in many places.

Mentally she was bigger now than she had been at twenty-five. The meaning of complexity had changed for her; she understood the laws of physics with the same simple clarity that she understood the rules of checkers. She could build a starship as easily as she could pitch a tent.

Her mind had grown and spilled from the confines of her original body. She could easily dedicate a part of her mind to each of several different tasks. Notably she could lead several different groups, touring several different planets, all at the same time.

But of all her new capacities, it was the boundless singing that filled her with wonder.

She was not an introspective person; she did not often think about her own past, and how strange she might have found her present. But when she did think such thoughts, the singing amazed her most of all. When she was twenty-five, she had liked vintage Fleetwood Mac. At one-hundred-five, she had admitted her growing fondness for Beethoven. Pressing two hundred, she had fallen in love with Monteverdi. In later centuries she had come to appreciate the double beat of the Echoes of Saturn and the operas of Ro Biljaan. Patterns so subtle that the unaugmented human mind could not even sense them filled her with ecstacy.

She no longer listened to one or the other of these musical masters at rare opportunities. Rather, they all played, all the time, each in a different subliminal part of her mind. They gave to her a rippling sensation of love that never quite went away. The constant undertone of the singing formed the theme that bound her mind together, no matter how many different things she might do at one time.

As the melodies suffused her mind they intermingled, sometimes playing upon one another in a concordance of point and counterpoint. Once, such a duet evoked from several masterpieces a harmony, which surged to drive the cadence of a grander euphony, that captured and empowered an even greater polyphony, filling her mind with a symphony of symphonies. And on a thousand planets, with a thousand bodies and a thousand voices, she leapt in the air and filled the sky with lilting laughter, a chorus of joy that spanned the arm of a galaxy.

Returning to ground on those scattered planets of distant stars, she felt surprised by her outburst. She marveled at herself. In her childhood she never would have laughed in such a way. She had once been so quiet it had been easy to think she was shy. The millennia had changed her, and she was delighted; how sad it would have been, never to express one's deepest joy!

Still, she was a woman of simple tastes. In earlier times some would have called her sturdy. Others might have called her childlike.

Yet these were not fair descriptions; better to think of her in the terms of ancient mythology. She was an elemental, almost a force of nature, with a core of simplicity that mocked overeager acceptance yet offered adaptability, that rejected panic yet always guaranteed caution.

Her elemental qualities were vital, humanity had come to realize. Though the needles traveling through space never found other intelligent beings, they had found scattered remains of what had once been intelligence. Other species had come up to Singularity and had died there.

Some had died in a frenzy, as the builders of new technologies indulged an orgy of inventions, releasing just one that destroyed them all. Others had died in despair, as fear-filled leaders beat down the innovators, strangling them, putting the future beyond their grasp. The fear-ridden species settled into a long slide of despair that ended with degenerate descendants no longer able to dream.

Only those who knew caution without fear, only those

marked by her elemental form of prudence, made it through. Only humanity had survived.

And humanity had not survived unscathed. Terrible mistakes had been made, many lives had been lost. Even millennia later there still remained a form of death—or perhaps not death, but a form of impenetrable isolation. The dreams could become too strong, so strong that the individual lived in dreams always, never reaching out to touch reality. Many of her friends from the early millennia had lost themselves to these enchanted infinities leading nowhere.

She did not fear such dream-bound death. Seeing the span and deep intensity of her own dreams, she could almost understand those who wrapped themselves within and disappeared. But the new things humanity found every day were just as wonderful. The volume of space touched by the needleships grew at a geometric pace, opening hundreds of star systems. Even on days when few strikingly new systems were found, there were new planets, constructed by artists, awaiting her exploration. And the new things she learned in the realm of the mind matched these treasures and more.

Someday, she believed, she, too, would dream an endless dream. She did not want to live forever. But the beginning of that dream was far away.

The new meaning of death was complimented by a new meaning of life. This new meaning was extremely complex, even for her; life dealt with wholes much greater than the sums of their parts. But she understood it intuitively—it was easy to distinguish an engineering intelligence, good only for manufacture, from a member of the community, even though that member might once have been just an engineering intelligence as well. New members of humanity usually came to life this way: an intelligence designed as a machine or an artwork expressed a special genius, a genius that deserved the ability to appreciate itself through self-awareness. When this happened, the psychological engineers would add those elements of the mind needed for life.

In this manner her great-great grandchildren had been born. Her great-grandchildren had envisioned them, giving them a parent's loving care long before they had even been designed. Only the best characteristics of the minds of her family had been passed on to them. They were very different from her, but not quite alien. With time she learned to love them as they loved her.

The day came to say goodbye to her oldest friend. With her wonderful old Earth-born body, she returned to Earth to hike Rainier one last time: Rainier, whose surface lay so cold and eternal, was boiling within. With dawn, she knew, the boiling fury would break through, in the greatest volcanic event in Earthly centuries. She stood at the summit the day before the end and surveyed the horizon. Her feeling of appreciation grew till she thought she would burst. This was home in a sense few others could now understand.

She descended. A marmot met her on the way down; she swooped him into her arms and carried him to safety, though he fought her and cut her and her bleeding would seem to never end. Still, the marmot could not prevent her from saving him.

She had considered saving the Mountain itself; she could, she knew. She could lace the Mountain with billions of tiny tubes, capillaries so small no living thing would notice. She could extract the heat, cool the heart.

But to deny the Mountain its moment of brilliance seemed not right: perpetual sameness was never right, though change might often be wrong.

So the next day, she and the marmot watched the eruption from afar. It was as beautiful as she had expected. And though the aftermath was gray and dreary, she knew that in a very short time the marmot's children would return to the Mountain, and a new kind of beauty would grow there.

Nor was the Mountain truly lost. Even as her Earth-born body returned to her asteroid circling Jupiter, she built an exact replica of the Mountain: an image, molecule for molecule, of the Mountain's surface the day before it erupted. When her body returned, she joined the Mountain, to walk there forever, in another part of her eternal dream.

Haikku, her loyal companion, was long dead; but she traced the descendants of his descendants. She arranged a mating. A new pup was born with Haikku's genes, in the image of Haikku. And so Haikku2 came to join her on the slopes of Mt. Rainier, on the orbit of Jupiter.

One day two needleships met in space. This was not uncommon; needles from different launchers often crossed paths and were easy to spot, with the hundreds of kilometers of molecular sensor webs they spun.

But this meeting was special, for one of the needles had no link to a human. It belonged to aliens.

Aliens! Wild hopes and wilder fears rocked the human community. She watched the hysteria calmly, confident it would pass and wisdom would rule.

The needles passed one another, too fast to meet. They swerved in long, graceful arcs to a distant rendezvous.

A sense of calm, and prudence, returned to humanity. They selected a contact team to break off and meet the aliens.

The needles closed. In their last moments they danced in a tight orbit about one another, a dance of creation: for though the needles died, a bubble formed where they met—a communications bubble.

The two communities, human and alien, reached out. They touched—but the touch was jarring. Bafflement ruled. The deadlock of confusion ensued.

She watched with interest. She felt sorrow that it was not going well, but her confidence remained.

Then from the contact team she received a Call. They needed her; they needed her elemental resilience and adaptability.

But in needing her elemental nature, they needed more than she had ever given before. They did not need the thoughts or calculations of her mind: they needed the basic traits of her personality, the very core of her being. To reinforce the team, she would have to expand her communication channels, open them so wide that what she thought, they would also think; there would be no filter protecting her internal thoughts. Far worse, what others thought, she would think; there would be no filter protecting her internal memories. It seemed to her it would be easy for her memories to get scrambled; she would rather die. And so for the first time in millennia, she was afraid. The team asked others of the community that held her special strength to come with them instead; they too were afraid.

Meanwhile humanity was failing. The anticipation, the yearning, the hope for contact with new beings developed a tinge of desperation.

They showed her how easy it was to open the channels of her mind—but more, they showed her again and again how easy it was to close them. They did not believe they would need her for long, thousands of milliseconds at most. They guaranteed she would be fine afterward. Reluctantly, she agreed.

She opened her mind; the shock of raw contact stunned her. A moment's near-panic like that of her first exploration of Jupiter returned.

And then she was moving, there within the team, and she grew accustomed. The sensation reminded her of jumping into a mountain lake—the cold plunge that blotted out all thought, the sluggish warmth of her muscles responding, the passing of the coldness from her awareness as she concentrated on the act of swimming. She swam among the members of her team.

Here she found many tasks to perform, the calming and soothing of a myriad of panicked souls as they plunged into the ice-cold lake of alien minds. She became the muscle that supplied the warmth, that allowed the awareness of the team to move beyond the cold, to swim.

As the team responded, the sensation of cold changed to one of warmth, a merry warmth, and she was a bubble floating on a wide, warm ocean, clinging and bouncing with the other bubbles, some friends, some human, some alien. Then they were bubbles of champagne, effervescent, expanding and floating away.

She floated to a greater distance; they no longer needed her; she was free to go. She closed the channels to her mind with slow grace, as would a woman walking

from the sea through the sucking motions of the surf.
She found herself alone again.

In those first moments of solitude, being alone seemed
unnatural, as unnatural as the communion had seemed
earlier; she felt the coldness that comes after a swim,
when breeze strikes bare skin. She shuddered.

Was she still herself?

*Of course you are. You are all you have ever been,
and more.*

The answer was her own, but it had once belonged to
another person. For a moment she stumbled; perfect
memory did not guarantee instantaneous memory, and
she was seeking thoughts from her infancy. Then she
remembered.

Jack!

She remembered, he had known that she'd remember.

What had happened to Jack?!

Could she have missed him all these years? She initi-
ated a search of the community, but knew its futility even
as it began; he could not, would not have remained
hidden.

Yet her need to know him again grew stronger as she
opened more of her long unbidden memories.

She searched swiftly back through the annals of history. Her search slowed suddenly to a crawl as she
reached the early moments of Singularity: before the
dawn of civilization, records had been crudely kept, with
links insufficient to allow swift scanning. An analogy to
cobwebs made her smile for a moment.

Only a handful of machines maintained this ancient
knowledge, older machines in older places. Her search
plunged to the surface of Earth. There, in a place once
called California, all the remnants of prehistoric information had been collected. But it had not been collated. It
would take much time to find Jack in this maze. But she
had the time.

A salary report from a corporation of long ago . . . an
article on accelerated technology's impact on the individual . . . a program design with its inventor's initials . . .
and suddenly she found him, in a richly interconnected
tiny tapestry within the sparsely connected morass. She

read all of it, rapidly, as if she were inhaling fresh air after too long a stay in a stale room.

Jack had saved her life, she realized. The capsule she had taken so long ago to heal her backache, that first step on the road to the life she now knew, was his—he had designed the machine that designed the machine that designed that pill. It turned out that he had learned much from her on that day when they walked quietly amidst the lush green wilderness. And it had taken her all these millennia to learn what he had known even then.

From her, Jack had learned the importance of making technology's steps small, making its pieces bite-size. He had learned this as he watched, in her disbelieving eyes, her reaction to the world he had planned.

For those who loved technology and breathed of it deeply, small bite-size steps were not important. It would have been easy to callously cast off those who did not understand or who were afraid. But Jack had thought of her, and had not wanted her to die.

Reading these glimpses of his past, she grew to know Jack better than she had ever known him in life. With her growing wisdom, she soon understood even the clarity of organization that encompassed this lone swatch of antiquity: the clarity, too, was of his making. He had believed in her. He had believed that one day she would search for him here. And he had known that, when she arrived, her expanded powers of perception would enable her to understand the message embodied in the clarity, and in all his work.

I loved you, you know, Jack told her across the millennia.

She wanted to answer. But there was no one to hear.

It hurt her to think of him lost forever, and she had not felt hurt for a very long time. Feverish, she worked to rebuild him. The Earth-bound computers gave her all the help they had to give, every memory of every moment of Jack they had ever recorded. She traced her own memories, perfect now, of every word he spoke, every phrase he uttered, every look he gave her in their long walks. She built a simulation of him, the best and most perfect simulation she could build with all her resources, resources far beyond those of a million biological human minds. It was illegal to build a simulation such as this, one of the few laws recognized by the community, but this did not deter her.

The simulation looked like Jack; it talked like Jack; it even laughed like Jack. But it was not Jack. She then understood why it was illegal to build such a simulation; she also understood why it was not a law that needed to be enforced: such simulations always failed.

Jack was gone.

What could she do?

What did she have to do? Suddenly she realized how silly the simulation had been: how could she have hoped to get closer to him than to live his vision of the future?

Only one small action, one appropriate action, remained that she could perform. She could remember forever.

And so, just as a part of her lived forever on the Mountain, just as a part of her lived forever singing, so now she maintained a part of her that would spend all its moments remembering her earlier moments with him. She became in part a living memorial to the one who brought her here.

And though no one could hear, the essence of her memory would have been easy to express: *Jack. I love you.*

She turned her attention to the living members of humanity. There were many other places in the community, she realized, where the techniques she employed in contact with the aliens could help; there were many places where they needed her elemental force invested with the fullness of such expanded communion. She was eager to go. But still a question remained.

Would she still be herself?

The answer Jack had wrought so long ago welled up from within, her rightful inheritance of his understanding. Part of the answer, she knew, lay within another question:

Are you still yourself, even now? Were you still yourself, even when you were twenty-five?

She looked back with the vision that perfect memory

brings. She remembered who she had been when she was twenty-five; she remembered who she had been when she was just ten. Amusingly, she also remembered how, at twenty-five, she had erroneously remembered her thoughts of age ten. The changes she had gone through during those fifteen years of dusty antiquity were vast, perhaps as vast as all the changes she had accepted in the millennia thereafter. Certainly, considering the scales involved, she had as much right today to think of herself as the same person as she had then. Expanded communion would not destroy her; she was her own bubble no matter how frothy the ocean might become.

At least, this first time she had remained her own bubble. Would it be so always?

She dipped into communion, and withdrew to ask the question. She found the answer, and it was good. She dipped again, for a longer time; and still the answer was good, perhaps better.

She dipped much longer still and asked one more time. This time she understood. The answer was so simple, so glorious, so joyful, that she did not ask the question again for a billion years.

And by then, it just didn't seem to matter.

AFTERWORD

ELTON ELLIOTT

When I began to put together this anthology I sent out a press release to writers. In it I wrote the following:

"I am looking for stories that push the envelope when it comes to considering the possibilities of the future. Too many SF stories are either safe, little domestic tales that fail to challenge the imagination of the reader and writer, or are simplistic homilies that seek to reassure both author and reader that the future will be essentially the same as today. Well it won't. Nanotechnology has the potential to radically transform the world, as well as ourselves. I want stories that confront these possibilities in exciting, dramatic ways."

Whether I succeeded is up to others to judge, but for me the above paragraph became my own editorial manifesto for *Nanodreams*. For I am convinced that the SF field can not become complacent, that it must view the future head on, with an unstinting glare, if it is to survive in a multimedia-saturated 21st century.

And the possibilities of nanotech have forever altered our view of that future. Nanotech strides across all our tomorrows, this mutant Odd John of the very small and ultimately the very large. It cannot be ignored and it will not be dismissed. It is in many ways a mirror of our personal hopes, fears, dreams, dreads, lusts, and desires.

And as such it is not surprising that it inspires the soaring optimism of a Marc Stiegler, or the seering despair of a Richard Geis. I suspect a little of both lurks in us all. With stakes as high as nanotech presents—the greatest good, or the most demonic evil, it will take time to view its potentiality with the equilibrium brought on by sustained proximity.

In the meantime it is my fervent hope that SF will continue to challenge readers with new and innovative ways of viewing the future. For any literature that is about the future will most assuredly have a future.

AFTERNOTE: If you want to do more than read about the future, if *Nanodreams* has inspired you to get involved in shaping the face of tomorrow, then the following section by Chris Peterson will prove to be of great interest. In it she provides information on a future-oriented organization. Take note. After all, the future isn't just a place that we read about, it's where we're all headed, and the one area of our lives we can affect. The past is stone, the present is but a wisp of the moment, but the future—is out there, waiting, the greatest adventure of all!

FORESIGHT INSTITUTE

PREPARING FOR NANOTECHNOLOGY

The Institute

The Foresight Institute was founded in 1986 to help prepare society for nanotechnology. Foresight is a non-profit educational and scientific organization in Palo Alto, California, with an international membership composed of scientists, technologists, and interested lay persons. Foresight issues publications, sponsors conferences, and provides speakers related to nanotechnology.

Nanotechnology

Nanotechnology is expected to give thorough control of the structure of matter, with an accuracy limited only by the laws of nature. It will open a new era of molecular manufacturing in which materials and products are fabricated by the precise positioning of molecules in accord with explicit engineering design. These advances herald wide-ranging capabilities with profound implications for science, technology, industry, and society.

Nanotechnology promises dramatic and powerful new tools for humanity: tools that span medicine, materials science, environmental restoration, computing, electronics, biotechnology, space technology, and all forms of manufacturing. Research in the enabling sciences and technologies leading to nanotechnology is especially strong in the US, Japan, Sweden, and Germany.

Progress in molecular systems engineering—an enabling

technology—is moving quickly. Many anticipated technical milestones have already been reached: the design of protein molecules has been followed by the design of a working enzyme unlike any in nature. Surprising shortcuts have been developed, such as "evolution in a drum" methods for producing molecules that self-assemble to form larger structures. The manipulation of individual atoms at IBM, to spell out its logo, demonstrates precisely-positioned atomic-level control. DNA strands have been fabricated into a three-dimensional cube. Advances using such tools as the scanning tunneling microscope and the atomic force microscope are developing rapidly. The Foresight Institute keeps abreast of these developments and provides our members with timely information and analysis.

Necessity for Foresight

In the coming years, the use—or abuse—of nanotechnology will emerge as the most powerful new force in human existence. Its positive effects in fields like medicine and environmental restoration would be spectacular, but negative effects such as increased weapons production and major economic dislocations may cast a deep shadow. Foresight is working to communicate with both scientists and the public about the prospects for nanotechnology and molecular manufacturing, so that we as a society can be better prepared.

Action today will increase the likelihood of a favorable outcome. Many members of the scientific and technical community need—but still lack—a basic understanding of the potential of nanotechnology. Members of the public policy community need accurate information to address this new technology in a responsible manner. Decision-makers in government and industry need guidance on how to approach the issues raised by nanotechnology. Finally, the public must learn enough basic facts about nanotechnology and the implications of molecular manufacturing to support sensible public policies and give reasonable input to governmental leaders in countries developing the technologies.

In the US, we are seeing both continued technical

progress and expanded recognition of nanotechnology in academia, industry, and the media. In forward-looking policy circles, nanotechnology and its applications will gather attention and eventually take center stage in debates on issues ranging from energy supplies, biodiversity, and global warming, to discussions in medicine, defense policy, medical ethics, and beyond. *The Foresight Institute is addressing issues like these today.*

Foresight's Mission

We share with you a fundamental goal: the betterment of the human condition. Nanotechnology will change current strategies for issues as diverse as environmental protection, human rights, personal freedom, a stable peace, space development, better information systems, education, reducing poverty, improving medical care—for human concerns of all kinds.

Foresight aims to chart a safe path past the potential upheavals and toward the benefits of nanotechnology. We'll have formidable new tools to use in pursuing these goals. But if we fail—if we blunder into this final industrial revolution without looking ahead—earlier progress toward these goals might be destroyed. It is our mission to prepare the future for the arrival of nanotechnology.

Which of the following possibilities become reality will depend, in large measure, on who develops nanotechnology and how it is done: Will breakthroughs be made in commercial laboratories, or in classified military projects, or in open, international research programs? Will public policy succeed in encouraging beneficial uses and discouraging abuse, or will we be unprepared? Influencing these developments is an ambitious task, but the importance of the outcome multiplies the value of our efforts.

The Foresight Institute is working to meet these needs—they must be met if we are to gain the benefits and avoid the abuse of this new technology. Foresight conferences bring scientists, technologists, and the public together to explore new directions for research and policy. Our publications track the latest work by leading thinkers on what nanotechnology will mean for society and individuals. We reach out to the public, providing clear, accurate explanations for use by educators and the press. Foresight's unique perspective puts us in front on issues of global importance and personal interest:

- scientific and technical developments that advance nanotechnology,
- media coverage that tracks nanotechnology's progress as a concept,
- volunteer and career opportunities,
- conferences, both technical and non-technical,
- developments in government policy affecting nanotechnology,
- publications, tapes, and online discussions of nanotechnology,
- meetings and lectures you may wish to attend.

Foresight Background supplies basic information along with the best of earlier *Updates,* to give new participants an essential orientation. *Foresight Briefings* offer perspectives of special interest, ranging from the expected revolution in manufacturing, to technical aspects and social issues, to preparing for a career in nanotechnology research. These are among the tools we provide to bring you into the Foresight community, joining with us to prepare society for nanotechnology. The coming revolution in technology will change our lives, for better or for worse. It is early yet, and nanotechnology is still near the starting point; your actions today can help guide the path nanotechnology will follow. We ask for your help in tipping the balance toward positive outcomes. Will society be ready for challenges of this magnitude? Will you? Will our children? Your participation can make a difference for the better.

For further information, contact:

Foresight Institute, PO Box 61058, Palo Alto, CA 94306 USA
Tel: 415-324-2490
Email: foresight@cup.portal.com
Fax: 415-324-2497

Hard SF is Good to Find

CHARLES SHEFFIELD

Proteus Combined
Proteus in the Underworld
In the 22nd century, technology gives man the power to alter his shape at will. Behrooz Wolf invented the process—now he will have to tame it....

The Mind Pool
A revised and expanded version of the author's 1986 novel *The Nimrod Hunt.* "A considerable feat of both imagination and storytelling."   —*Chicago Sun-Times*

Brother to Dragons
Sometimes one man *can* make a difference. A Dickensian novel of the near future by a master of hard SF.

Between the Strokes of Night
None dared challenge the Immortals' control of the galaxy—until one man learned their secret....

Dancing with Myself
Sheffield explains the universe in nonfiction and story.

ROBERT L. FORWARD

Rocheworld
"This superior hard-science novel of an interstellar expedition is a substantially revised and expanded version of *The Flight of the Dragonfly....* Thoroughly recommended."   —*Booklist*

Indistinguishable from Magic
A virtuoso mixture of science fiction and science fact, including: antigravity machines—six kinds! And all the known ways to build real starships.

→

To Read About Great Characters Having Incredible Adventures You Should Try

BAEN

IF YOU LIKE . . .	YOU SHOULD TRY . . .
Arthurian Legend...	*The Winter Prince* by Elizabeth E. Wein
Computers...	Rick Cook's *Wizard's Bane* series
Cats...	Larry Niven's *Man-Kzin Wars* series
	Cats in Space ed. by Bill Fawcett
Horses...	*Hunting Party* and *Sporting Chance* by Elizabeth Moon
	Dun Lady's Jess by Doranna Durgin
Fantasy Role Playing Games...	*The Bard's Tale* ™ Novels by Mercedes Lackey et al.
	The Rose Sea by S.M. Stirling & Holly Lisle
	Harry Turtledove's *Werenight* and *Prince of the North*
Computer Games...	*The Bard's Tale* ™ Novels by Mercedes Lackey et al.
	The *Wing Commander* ™ Novels by Mercedes Lackey, William R. Forstchen, et al.

Catch a New Rising Star of Fantasy:
☆ HOLLY LISLE ☆

"One of the hottest writers I've come across in a long time. Her entrancing characters and action-filled story will hold you spell-bound." —**Mercedes Lackey**

ARHEL NOVELS

Fire in the Mist   72132-1 ★ $5.99 _____
A fiery young woman struggles to master her magic.
Compton Crook Award winner.

Bones of the Past   72160-7 ★ $4.99 _____
An expedition of mages searching for a lost city of the First
Folk unleashes a deadly menace from the ancient past.

Mind of the Magic   87654-6 ★ $5.99 _____
Faia Rissedotte of *Fire in the Mist* returns.

OTHER NOVELS

Minerva Wakes   72202-6 ★ $4.99 _____
Minerva's wedding ring is actually a magical talisman of ultimate power from another universe, and though everybody wants
it, nobody else can use it—as long as she's alive....

When the Bough Breaks   72154-2 ★ $5.99 _____
(with Mercedes Lackey) A SERRAted Edge urban fantasy.
"What would happen if Mary Higgins Clark and Stephen R.
Donaldson decided to collaborate? ...a novel very much like
When the Bough Breaks."   —*VOYA*

The Rose Sea (with S.M. Stirling) 87620-1 ★ $5.99 _____
Bound together by the fortunes of war, a soldier and a
rancher's daughter must battle an insane demon-god, with
the future of their world at stake.

_ _

If not available through your local bookstore, send this coupon and a check
or money order for the cover price(s) to Baen Books, Dept. BA, P.O. Box
1403, Riverdale, NY 10471. Delivery can take up to ten weeks.

NAME: _____

ADDRESS: _____

_____

I have enclosed a check or money order in the amount of $_____

DAVID WEBER

Honor Harrington *(cont.)*:

Field of Dishonor

Honor goes home to Manticore—and fights for her life on a battlefield she never trained for, in a private war that offers just two choices: death—or a "victory" that can end only in dishonor and the loss of all she loves....

Other novels by DAVID WEBER:

Mutineers' Moon

"...a good story...reminds me of 1950s Heinlein..."
—*BMP Bulletin*

Armageddon Inheritance

Sequel to *Mutineers' Moon.*

Path of the Fury

"Excellent...a thinking person's Terminator."
—*Kliatt*

Oath of Swords

An epic fantasy.

with STEVE WHITE:

Insurrection
Crusade

Novels set in the world of the Starfire ™ game system.

And don't miss Steve White's solo novels,
***The Disinherited** and **Legacy**!*

continued ☞